Flying Time

By the same author:

Non-fiction

SIMPLE SIMON

LOST AND FOUND

Flying Time

ANN LOVELL

LONDON
VICTOR GOLLANCZ LTD
1988

First published in Great Britain 1988
by Victor Gollancz Ltd,
14 Henrietta Street, London WC2E 8QJ

British Library Cataloguing in Publication Data
Lovell, Ann
  Flying time.
  I. Title
  823′.914[F]   PR6062.085/

ISBN 0-575-04154-4

Photoset in Great Britain by
Rowland Phototypesetting Ltd, Bury St Edmunds, Suffolk
and printed by St Edmundsbury Press Ltd
Bury St Edmunds, Suffolk

To my dear friend
Joy Simmons

Chapter 1

Creaking ominously, the great plane slid away from the passenger terminal and began trundling its unwieldy length towards the runway.

The passengers sat quietly, their poses betraying the heightened awareness that precedes take-off. Some read books or magazines with self-conscious concentration. Others sat with their eyes closed, only the rigidity of their jawline revealing the effort they were putting into their relaxation techniques. Yet others turned to their neighbours in a febrile attempt to establish a contact that might distract their attention from the alarm signals flooding from a million nerve endings.

There were too, of course, a number of veterans for whom the experience held no apprehension, for whom flight had become as routine as driving a fast car down a motorway, and whose metabolisms seemed unaffected by this defiance of the laws of gravity, this tinkering with the rules of time and space. These were the true children of the twentieth century, who regarded as their unthinking right what had once been the prerogative of the gods, and who now sought only to alleviate their boredom during a period of physical inactivity, oblivious to any wisps of divine status that might have clung to them from the past.

As usual, Jeffrey Wren wished he were of their number. He was himself a veteran—but somehow his nervous system had failed over the years to provide itself with a shell. A near-miss over Heathrow the previous year had not helped. Perhaps, he reflected now, as he felt the familiar tension at the back of his neck, and the sweat breaking out on the palms of his hands, it was because he was a writer. Imagination was his stock-in-trade, and it was not a tap that could be turned off at will. There was no way he could ever come to regard flying as a normal human activity, a mere convenient means of moving rapidly around the planet. Nothing, he felt sure, could ever numb his sense of the miraculous.

A glance at his next-door neighbour confirmed this conclusion. He had long accepted as inevitable that the airline's computer should sit him beside middle-aged businessmen who drank their way steadily across the oceans, or elderly ladies with a compulsion to tell their life stories. Of the two, he preferred the elderly ladies—their tales were often remarkable, and he enjoyed the protective feelings roused in him by their frailty and indomitableness in the pursuit of new experience. He hoped they would prove an inspiration to him when brittle bones and arthritic joints reduced his own horizons.

On this occasion, however, it seemed that someone young and thoughtful had programmed the computer. The neighbour on his left was neither bibulous nor elderly. Dark silky hair, beautifully cut so that it curved shining from crown to nape, fair skin, and rather full, chiselled lips, set now in concentration as she intently studied the pages of a magazine, completely focused the whole of his attention so that for the first time he forgot all about the hazards of leaving the ground. The next six hours took on an attraction they had completely lacked before. There was not even any danger of competition, for he was in the middle seat of a row of three, and she was next to the aisle. Six hours—it was not long enough . . .

She looked up, as if aware of his thought processes, and their eyes met. She smiled. Those eyes—the plane could have been heading for the moon now, for all he cared—they were like wreckers' lamps luring the unwary navigator on to the rocks. They were a deep, soft grey, luminous with intelligence and humour, fringed with long, dark lashes—the sort of eyes no man should look into without warning, as he just had, for fear of losing his sense of direction.

He gave her an idiotic grin, then looked away in panic at the unexpected pounding of his pulses. Trying to steady himself, he turned to the occupant of the window seat on his right, only to behold a small, rosy-cheeked man sitting bent over a large bible, his lips moving soundlessly, as if in prayer. Embarrassed, he turned again to the glossy hair, and mind-disintegrating lips, to find that he was himself the subject of an interested scrutiny. The words that rarely failed him on paper turned tail and fled now. He could only give her a friendly nod, and pluck desperately at the newspaper provided by the airline to distract its customers from their many discomforts.

Verity Wells bit her lip. She had noticed his reaction, and recognized it as the prelude to the usual approach. She was not in the mood for it. She was tired, and had been hoping for an uneventful journey, followed by two weeks of respite from normal routines, from the demands of other people, and from the small daily trivia which prevented her from seeing clearly any more. The expensive hairstyle and carefully chosen clothes were the armour she had put on to protect herself from the curiosity of her wealthy relatives in Toronto, who knew only what she had chosen to tell them of the disasters of the last eleven years. She had wanted to greet them with all flags flying, that was all. She had not intended to run up signals for anyone else.

Someone was answering them, however, and now she was not sure how to deal with the situation—the more so as she took in the appearance of the young man sitting beside her. His thickly springing sandy hair, high cheekbones, and general air of angularity seemed to indicate Scots descent, but when he had spoken to the stewardess it had been with a Canadian accent. He had a warm, open grin, but there was a wariness about his eyes that intrigued her, despite herself. She was beginning to wonder about his background, when she gave herself a mental shake. She was being absurd. It wasn't as if anything real could come into existence during these hours spent thousands of feet up in the air—hours which did not exist on a Canadian clock. She, and the man beside her, had stepped into a time pocket when they boarded the plane. Ordinary rhythms lurched out of sequence, normal activity was suspended. There was no point whatsoever in becoming interested in a fellow traveller in this temporary, wholly artificial environment—especially not for someone like herself who had come through such a bitter struggle in order to accept realities.

The roar of the engines interrupted her thoughts, and she shut her eyes as the huge machine, no longer unwieldy, sped down the runway and thrust up into the air. The sensation both exhilarated and scared her. She felt as if they were making a great bolt for freedom, piercing the clinging layers of stratus clouds like an arrow through cobwebs in a surge of power that took them up and up until they broke free into the clear brilliance of the wide blue sky. She opened her eyes to see sunlight and space outside the tiny window, and involuntarily glanced at the little man in the seat beside it as if to share her pleasure with him, only to perceive that his eyes were fixed on the book in his lap, and that he was oblivious to all around.

Jeffrey observed her look, and interpreted her expression.

"I guess he misses a lot."

She coloured guiltily, then smiled.

"I expect he finds a lot, too."

The general level of tension in the passenger cabin was dropping perceptibly as the plane gained altitude, and people realized that airport buildings, trees, houses and pylons were all safely far below. A buzz of conversation broke out as seat belts were unbuckled, and air hostesses began taking orders for drinks. The fearful were anxious to regain face, while the rest were happy to exhibit their complete poise.

Verity, when her turn came, ordered a sherry. Jeffrey asked for a Scotch. The little man by the window apologetically requested a fruit juice. Jeffrey managed to catch her eye again, as the drink was passed along, and lifted an eyebrow significantly. She smiled a little distantly as she sipped her drink. She was still hoping the inevitable conversation would not happen.

"You going to Toronto on holiday?"

She gave a little shrug of exasperation, and gave up.

"Yes, I am. My sister and brother-in-law live there. I'm going to stay with them. It's my first visit."

"Do they live in the city?"

"No—in the country outside. You're Canadian, aren't you?" She preferred to be the one asking questions.

"First generation. My parents are both Brits. I've been in London on business."

"What do you do?"

"I'm a writer. I write crime novels. The business was the publication of the English edition of my latest book. How about you? Do you have a job?" He eyed the wedding ring on her left hand uneasily.

"I help run an art gallery—just a small one. And I paint a little myself."

His interest increased with every word she spoke. Her voice was warm and unusually low pitched. Nothing about her was ordinary.

between the faded gilding of the leaves. It was obviously the object of continuous, minute study.

Jeffrey smiled bitterly to himself, remembering the compulsory gatherings for family prayers and long readings from pious works that were the milestones of his days in the rectory. Even food could not be enjoyed without the preliminary of a lengthy grace, recited at speed in an emotionless monotone. It had never occurred to him to rebel until a year or so after Julie's death, when he had suddenly understood that all those words—however moving and beautifully couched, however earnestly invoked by his father's resonant baritone—only made the pain worse. It crouched deep inside him like a savage dog, and refused to go away. And he had begun to resent what he saw as specious promises and false claims, and to criticize his authoritarian father and meek mother. Because they never spoke of Julie, they sentenced him to silence also, and he hated them for it. He felt they were deliberately killing her memory.

He surveyed the small, mild-faced man beside him and wondered what terrors had driven him, too, to seek safety in this world of make-believe. Bible, Koran, Vedas—so many fortresses had been constructed to protect shivering humanity from that desolation of space he could see through the window of the plane. They shut it out—a hostile reality no-one could bear to face. They were powerful fortresses, all but impregnable. The trouble was that they shut in as well as shutting out.

He experienced a sudden, strong urge to change his seat. He did not want to talk about death, even to an incredibly beautiful girl, and that open bible beside him reminded him too sharply of things he would have preferred to forget. Even the humility and meekness of the little man's features offended him. He looked hopefully round the passenger deck, but the big plane was full and there were no empty places. He sighed, tilted his seat back, and determinedly closed his eyes.

Verity had sensed that he was disturbed, and was reproaching herself. It was not the first time she had scuppered a promising conversation by too direct an approach. Now she was recovered she frequently felt like someone who had regained their sight after years of blindness, and who as a result had little or no perception of depth. She had become so used to exploring her feelings with the therapist in the psychiatric unit where she had been sent after the loss of the baby, that she was apt to forget that such explorations could be foreign and frightening to others. It was difficult to remember all the elaborate conversational rules that enabled one to skate gracefully along on the surface uninhibited by the strange shapes that swam in the depths below. She had just broken them again, and regretted it. There was something very appealing about this young man with his sandy hair and sensitive mouth. She no longer wanted to avoid conversation with him. He interested her. She decided to try and make amends.

"Do your books sell well—or is that an indelicate question?"

It was a fresh start. She saw the relief in his eyes as he responded to the teasing note in her voice.

"Highly indelicate. But since they do, I'll forgive you." They both laughed.

"Do you begin with finding the body?"

"Almost invariably. Then every so often you drop another one in just to keep the tension going. And there is always, always a twist at the end."

"Why is that?"

"It makes the reader feel good if he's spotted the outcome, and if he hasn't he's full of admiration for the ingenuity of the author. Either way, I win."

"So all you need is a good formula. I see what you mean about thrillers being mathematical. But don't they all come out the same?"

"Do you cook?"

"Yes, but . . ."

"Do your recipes all turn out the same?"

Verity smiled. This was more like it.

"Touchée. It sounds a very pleasant way of earning a living."

"Don't you believe it. You live in constant fear . . ."

"You mean you're afraid one of your murderers might actually exist and be out to get you?"

"Well, I have seen guys suspiciously like some of them lurking round airports, but that wasn't what I meant. The fear is of not getting another idea. The well might run dry."

"Has that ever happened?" She looked at him wide-eyed, and his pulses began to throb again. He was in love with her eyes.

"Not so far. Though right now I must declare there isn't an idea in my head—not of that sort, I mean."

"You don't know what you're going to write next?"

"Nope."

"Perhaps you need a holiday—something to jolt you out of routine."

He made a face.

"The trip to England was supposed to do that. It didn't work. Everything looked the same as it always does. I guess I'm not good at visiting places on my own. Now if I'd only met you on the plane going over it might have been a different story."

She smiled again. He felt they were safely back on the rails.

"Do you live in London?"

"No, I live in the country—in Wales. The gallery where I work is in a small town in Pembrokeshire, and I live in a village nearby. I like small, quiet places—though I used to live in London when I was younger."

He thought she looked absurdly young as she said it.

"Do your paintings sell? Or would that be another indelicate question?"

"They sell quite well. They're not particularly good, but the tourists like them. I make a living—and I enjoy my work. The countryside's very special in that part of Wales."

"I thought it always rained in Wales," he teased her.

"It rains a lot," she took him seriously, "but I think that when the clouds lift it's one of the most beautiful places on earth. The rain makes the colours more vivid—yellow laburnum, red fuchsias, pink blossom, all against a background of slate grey and misty blue. No creative artist could live there and *not* have ideas . . ."

"Sounds like I've missed something. I'd better make sure I go there some day." He was looking at her now in open admiration. Her enthusiasm had brought the colour to her cheeks, and her eyes were shining. She was the most wonderful creature he had ever seen. Something about her—the carriage of the head, the courageous set of those full lips, or the warmth of the grey eyes—filled him with an almost irresistible desire to put his arm round her and bury his face in that silky hair.

Her words had trailed off, and she sat there looking at him

strangely. The air between them suddenly seemed to be charged with static. If he touched her there would be a burst of sparks. God, how he wanted to touch her . . .

"Pardon me," he said suddenly, in a voice that sounded more like a croak, "I guess I've got to disturb you."

In the small flurry that followed, he contrived to stumble against her. For a couple of seconds he felt her warmth, and received the full impact of her perfume. He apologized incoherently, and made his way unsteadily down the aisle. The momentary contact had only made matters worse. He wondered if he was quite sane.

After his return and another stumble, they sat in awkward silence. For some reason, there no longer seemed to be anything to say. Words seemed extraordinarily futile. He glanced at his watch, then out of the window. Craning his neck, he could see snowy expanses of cloud, far below, but that was all. He judged they must be well out over the Atlantic. Time was slipping away, and he had so little. He felt trapped, hemmed in by cramped seats and absurd conventions. The pious little man with the bible irritated him by his remoteness and lack of concern, and the air hostess irritated him still more by handing him his hygienic plastic tray of lunch so that he was forced, in lowering the back of the seat in front, to trap himself still further. He was in fact slightly dizzy with hunger, having missed breakfast. Perhaps, he hoped, food would calm him down. Something had to.

Verity was willing the air hostess to hurry. She needed a distraction. Every nerve had become tight strung. She wished she could change her seat, but there was no sign of an empty one. She felt she could not cope with this new acquaintance. He made her feel too ill at ease. One moment they were talking enjoyably, and the next everything had swung out of joint. He attracted her, but his boyishness, the vulnerability in his eyes worried her. She wanted to comfort him, but was not sure she would be able to do so. For all her painfully acquired insight, her scars of battle, she felt inadequate. She had had several lovers since her recovery, but none of them had disturbed her as deeply as this stranger, in so short a time. The whole thing was absurd. They had only just met. They would only be together for a few hours, and here she was longing to run away. Something inside her, some sixth sense, instinct, intuition—something deeply female, had scented danger.

16

She picked up the polythene-wrapped packet of cutlery and was struggling vainly to open it, when the captain's voice was heard on the intercom. She looked up, expecting to hear the usual explanation of the plane's whereabouts, height and speed. Then she froze.

The captain was, in fact, apologizing. It appeared that an electrical fault had developed among the controls. There was absolutely no danger, but, as the plane had not yet reached what the air authorities termed the "point of no return", he had decided in the interests of safety, that it would be wiser to return and land at Prestwick so that repairs could be carried out. Passengers would be provided with hotel accommodation overnight, and it was hoped that the journey would be resumed the next morning. He deeply regretted the inconvenience that would inevitably be caused, but everyone would surely appreciate the reasons for the decision. Toronto airport had been informed.

There were a few seconds of silence before the full impact of his words registered and there was an outburst of exclamations, protests, lamentations—and even sobs. The air hostesses continued to serve lunch, serene smiles on their well-schooled faces, pausing only to reassure the panicky, and to placate the merely cross. It was just, they repeated from row to row, one of those things.

Jeffrey agreed wholeheartedly. Someone, somewhere, had to be playing games. A single throw of the dice had changed the whole picture. His number had come up. Best of all, the responsibility was not his—it was none of his doing. All he had to decide was how to make the most of it.

Sounds of distress on his right made him look round. His neighbour's pink cheeks were pink no longer, but a dirty grey. The little man was sweating, and breathed with difficulty, a hand clutching his throat.

Jeffrey signalled urgently to the air hostess, who took one look and brought a large brandy.

"Here, drink this."

The sufferer obeyed. Gradually his colour began to return, his breathing quietened, and he seemed to revive.

"You okay?" Jeffrey's voice was anxious. The man replied with a faint nod. There were lines of pain on the gentle face.

"Is there anything else we can do? Do you have some pills I can get out for you?"

A faint shake of the head was the only reply, and he looked worriedly at the air hostess.

"Perhaps you'd better appeal for a doctor."

"There's no need," the little man spoke with difficulty. "So very sorry. All right now. Spot of heart trouble. Silly of me . . ."

"Are you sure, sir?"

"Quite sure. Brandy does the trick. Clever of you. Such a shock. The Lord's will be done. God bless you."

Jeffrey looked at him doubtfully. The piety was unnerving. His parents, too, had accepted every reverse of fortune with the same docile phrases. They had never seemed to suspect, as he did, that some power somewhere spent a significant amount of time deriding the human race, quietly splitting its sides in cosmic amusement at its pleas for pity. "As flies to wanton boys, are we to the gods"—he had seen through it all, old, blind, Gloucester.

There seemed to be nothing more he could usefully do. The brandy had clearly saved the situation. The little man's breathing was even again. As he sat there with his eyes closed, Jeffrey thought he looked extremely like a dormouse. Presently he opened them and smiled, a gentle, apologetic smile which lit up the long-suffering face and the mild eyes. He was the sort of individual it would have been cruel to dislike, all his intentions were so obviously good.

Reassured, but privately resolving to watch over him, Jeffrey turned back to his meal. Verity touched his arm.

"Is he all right? Was it his heart? Are you sure we shouldn't ask for a doctor?" The air hostess was still hovering in the aisle behind her. Both looked worried.

"I guess he's okay. Says the brandy's done the trick. That announcement seemed to shake him up for some reason."

The air hostess moved off with an air of relief. Jeffrey picked up his knife and fork to attack his half-cold steak, but he remained preoccupied.

"Strange little guy," he murmured to himself. He had perceived a great tension beneath the outward serenity of the man—as though a desperate anxiety were being repressed only by gigantic effort of will. He felt oddly sorry for him—his parents had been like that, too. Anxiety had been inadmissible, a sign of weakness of faith.

Methodically, he dealt with the contents of the tray, and was just contemplating with satisfaction the large cream cake which did duty as dessert, preparatory to demolishing it, when he realized that all was not well on his left. He had hardly dared to look at Verity since the announcement that they were turning back, for fear of revealing his pleasure. He forgot that now in his concern.

She had gone very white, and was toying with her food. As Jeffrey turned to her, she laid down her knife and fork with shaking hands. Her eyes were full of tears.

"Do you think it's all going to be all right?" She spoke in a whisper, clenching her hands, grappling with her fear. The appeal woke all Jeffrey's protective instincts.

"Of course it is," he declared, with more assurance than he felt. "These guys know their job. That's why we're turning back—they know better than to run the slightest risk. They're aware of their responsibilities. You're letting that imagination of yours run away with you. I suggest you turn it in a different direction. How about regarding a night in Scotland as a bonus? Haggis as well as maple leaves. Have you ever been to Sauchiehall Street?"

"Never." He was succeeding. A smile was dawning in those spellbinding eyes.

"Allow a simple Canadian to inform you you've missed something. My mother came from Glasgow. Your whole life is about to be enriched. Flexibility, that's my philosophy. Stay on your toes. Pick up what comes and run. I always knew I should have been a company president. Pomposity comes naturally to me."

Now she laughed.

"I don't think you're pompous. I think you're right."

"You do? That makes you one special lady—it confirms my first impression of you. So we'll think positively. We'll look on Glasgow as a challenge—which it probably is, even for positive thinkers. But I've just remembered there's a difficulty."

"There is?"

"We haven't been introduced."

"Why—allow me to present Verity Wells."

19

Gravely, she held out her hand. He took it, and with matching gravity conveyed it to his lips.

"Jeffrey Wren at your service, ma'am. And now, that problem overcome, may I request the pleasure of your company for the evening?"

"I'd be delighted." Laughter had dispelled the panic, his clowning had routed the hobgoblins. The sudden threat that had so abruptly shifted all their perspectives was forgotten as the warmth of his hand, which still held hers, seemed to spread over her entire body.

"Then we'll hunt the haggis together, and the good people of Prestwick will one day tell their children of our bold, bad deeds."

"You're a fool, Jeffrey Wren."

"You're beautiful, Verity Wells." He kissed her hand again. "Let's have some more wine, and drink to bonny Scotland."

Lifting their glasses, with eyes only for each other, neither of them heard the whispered "Amen" from the figure by the window. He was watching the two young people, as if weighing them up, and his eyes were thoughtful. Every so often his fingers touched the bible in his lap, half hidden by the shelf on which lay his untouched meal, as if making sure it was still there—a gesture which would have amused Jeffrey, had he had the detachment to notice it. Detachment was, however, an asset he had just discarded. He was, after all, between books. He could hardly be expected to live always looking on, always intent on spinning intricate and dangerous situations, controlling the artistic occurrence of violence and horror. He was subject to the same laws as all around him, and, though he did not know it, he was merely obeying them. He had a part to play in the game.

Chapter 2

The hotel room was modern, impersonal and overheated. They had not been able to open the window.

Jeffrey lay on his back, staring at the ceiling. His arm had gone numb beneath Verity's weight, but he made no attempt to free it. She was asleep, her body warm and relaxed against his.

He should have foreseen how it would turn out, he thought wryly. There had been warning signs in plenty—the tensions between them on the plane, their self-conscious light-heartedness, and, in his case, the over-intensity of his desire for her. It had all gone wrong. He had failed her. His face burned at the recollection. She had been kind, and gentle, and understanding. He would almost have preferred it if she had screamed or sworn at him, or physically attacked him. It was what he deserved. But she had not uttered the slightest reproach.

None of the evening had gone as he had anticipated. There had been an atmosphere of hysterical gaiety in the coach that had brought them from the airport to the hotel in Glasgow. Even the veteran fliers had betrayed a certain relief when the aircraft had finally taxied safely to a standstill at Prestwick. The lightning had not struck this time and life was still for living. Even so, the conversation between himself and Verity had been stilted as they sat over dinner. The food was dull and pretentious, and even an inordinate amount of Spanish claret did nothing to loosen their tongues.

Afterwards, he had proposed a sightseeing trip round the town, and she had accepted. But they never did see Sauchiehall Street. They had been carried off by a noisy crowd of fellow travellers to the nearest pub, and it was there, fired by a dram of the most potent whisky he had ever swallowed in his life, that he had at last dared to pull her into a quiet corner and kiss her. After which there had seemed to be no option but to return at speed to the hotel.

They had been leaving the lift when they had bumped into the mousey little man from the plane. He seemed to have been waiting for them. He had clutched Jeffrey's arm, apologizing humbly, and in a feverish whisper had begged him for a few words in private. Irritated, his head singing from the whisky, Jeffrey had been about to shrug him off impatiently, when Verity intervened.

"You'd better humour him. We don't want another heart attack on our hands," she murmured in his ear. "I'll be waiting for you." She had slipped away before he could stop her, leaving him facing the meek-eyed intruder in a not very amiable state of mind.

"Well, mister—er—mister—what is it you want?"

"Not here. Could we go to your room, please. Forgive me—I'm so very sorry . . ."

Cursing not altogether under his breath, Jeffrey led the way to his own room. He was too frustrated to notice the other's nervous glances up and down the corridor as he was unlocking the door. He cut short the flow of apologies which began again the moment they were inside.

"Look here, mister—what the hell is your name?"

"Venables."

"Mister Venables. Your timing is terrible. Just tell me what you want and make it quick."

"It's this."

To Jeff's amazed anger the little man had thrust at him the bible he had been so intently studying on the plane. He was losing precious minutes of his gift from the gods being raved at by a religious fanatic. He restrained with difficulty an impulse to bundle him out of the door.

"I'm afraid you've got me sized up all wrong, mister Venables. I'm not interested."

"This is not what it seems, mister Wren." The earnestness of the gentle voice made him grit his teeth. He did not notice the use of his name.

"Aw, come on, don't give me that. It's what they all say. The next line is it will change my life. I'm sorry mister—you've picked the wrong guy this time. What's more, I'm late for an appointment."

He turned to open the door, but Venables again clutched his sleeve.

"Wait. Listen to me please. You don't understand. I'm not trying to convert you. I need your help."

"My help? You?"

"Just let me explain. I'll be as brief as possible. I am in danger —because of this delay."

Jeffrey eyed him wonderingly. He went on with the same feverish intensity.

"My work for my association takes me to all parts of the world, carrying the Word. Recently I was in Vienna. There I was taken to meet a group of Polish refugees, all of them wanted at home by their secret police for spreading religious propaganda and insurrection."

"A bit unwise, wasn't it, getting mixed up in politics?"

"Unwise, and against my principles, I quite agree. The reason I visited them was that they had brought out of Poland with them an icon, a small one, but of great rarity and power. The priests had used it to stir up the religious feelings of the people and to encourage them to unite against oppression. The police had made several raids to try to get hold of it and destroy it, but it was too carefully hidden. So then they murdered a priest."

"Surely I read something about that in the papers—it wasn't long ago . . ." Jeffrey was interested.

"No doubt. It created a political furore. As a result it was decided to send the icon out of the country, for its own safety, and that of those who guarded it. One of the priests had a brother who became a bishop of the Polish church in Toronto. They decided to entrust the icon to him. His church has a substantial congregation of emigrant Poles and their families. He would use the icon to rally support for the suffering and oppressed at home in Poland—support that is desperately needed. That way it could go on working its miracles without danger."

"You're not going to tell me they asked you to take it for them?" There was incredulity in Jeffrey's voice. The little man seemed a very fragile messenger to be entrusted with so important a task. And yet, the writer in him argued, his very unsuitability was in itself an effective disguise. Venables nodded apologetically.

"I'm afraid that's just what they did. And I have to confess that I

23

hesitated, Mr Wren. In the first place icons, or any other type of image, play no part in my own faith. In the second, I do not think it is good to break the law. For a simple man like me, these are strong objections. I prefer to spend my life carrying the Word into forgotten places. Political quarrels are not for me."

"So what made you agree to help them? I take it you did agree?"

Venables turned his large, mild, blue eyes on Jeffrey, and smiled.

"It was when they told me how much they had suffered for their beliefs. They told me about the murdered priest. He was, it seems, only a young man, but much loved by his people, and passionate in his sincerity. They say he knew he was going to die, but that did not stop him speaking out. Young and old flocked to his church to hear him. And when those tired, battered men spoke of him, the love and reverence in their voices spoke to me. Indeed, I believe the Lord himself spoke to me through them. I could not turn away from them, not when they were asking me for help. I took the icon for them. It is hidden in here."

Again, he held out the bible. This time Jeffrey took it.

It was a commonplace, modern edition, shabby with much use, as he had noticed on the plane. He riffled the pages curiously—and now he saw what he had not seen before: not all of it opened. A narrow block in the centre had been cunningly glued together. The bookmarks he had observed before were dummies. Carried by a man like Venables, the hiding place was perfect in its simplicity—an old trick cleverly given a new setting.

"Did you notice anything unusual about it? You were sitting beside me for several hours."

Jeffrey shook his head uneasily. An alarming suspicion of what was coming had formed at the back of his mind.

"I take it they showed you this icon?"

"Yes. I did not expect it to have any particular significance for me, but when I saw it I found it—strangely moving. It is what they call an Umilenie icon or an icon of Loving Kindness—in which Mary is portrayed carrying the Holy Child, her cheek laid tenderly against His head. Perhaps it was that very beautiful name that brought the tears to my eyes, Mr Wren—and I am not a man who weeps easily. It is very old, and in a beautiful state of preservation—probably of great commercial value, though that was not a consideration that influenced me."

"So why are you telling me all this? Aren't you taking a risk? I'm a complete stranger."

The question was already rhetorical. There was a prickling sensation at the back of his neck. He was about to find himself in an impossibly difficult situation.

"This unexpected delay has upset everything. When I reached London I was warned that we had been betrayed, and that the secret police were on my trail. If the plane had gone straight to Toronto the icon would have been in safe hands by now. As it is—Mr Wren, you saw what happened when they announced the delay. My heart will not stand this sort of pressure. I am very afraid that I will not reach Toronto. I watched you while we sat together. You are resourceful, intelligent—and kind. You are also, as you say, a complete stranger. So was the Good Samaritan. Mr Wren, I am asking you to take the icon to Toronto for me. You are my only hope."

Jeffrey stared at him like a hypnotized rabbit. He wished fervently that he had not drunk so much whisky. He tried to summon his wits, but none seemed to be available in working order. He almost laughed. The whole thing was absurd. He was far too old a hand to be taken in by such a mug's trick. He tried to calculate how much heroin or cocaine could be stashed inside the hidden compartment. How could anyone imagine he would be crazy enough to carry a sealed package through Customs for anyone else? It was ridiculous. But he said nothing.

"Will you help me, Mr Wren?"

"Why don't you hand it over to the police? Surely they would help. The British police are not like the Communists."

"You do not understand the strength of those who pursue me. They have the power of the State behind them. I would not be believed. Your police would check with the Poles—and then I would be arrested as a thief. East-West relations are in a precarious state of balance at the moment—no-one wants it upset by embarrassing incidents. Your police would have no choice but to hand me, and the icon over—and that would be the end of the story. No, I am alone in this, Mr Wren—and that is why I am now forced to appeal to you."

Jeffrey had stood there, awkward and silent, staring at the mild eyes which now seemed mild no longer, but painfully compelling. As his conviction increased that the little man was telling the truth he could feel a trap, the bars of which had been forged during his childhood, closing in on him. He thought he had broken free of it years ago when he had rejected his home and his upbringing, but now he knew he had never really been free. He was not free now. He could not simply shrug and turn away.

"May I see the icon?" His voice had sounded weak and uncertain. He hated the way his heart was thudding.

"You want to make sure I am not asking you to carry drugs, or diamonds, or microfilm? Of course you do. I understand. Anyone would. But I am afraid you must trust me, Mr Wren. It would be a simple matter to open up these sealed pages, but neither of us has the skill or the means to repair the damage. See—it has been expertly done."

After a minute inspection of the book, Jeffrey had been forced to agree. He was being driven back on his last defences by this gentle aggressor.

"But I must have *some* proof. You are asking me to break a traveller's cardinal rule. There is no reason on earth why I should trust you. You must think me a crazy fool."

Venables stared at him with burning eyes. He had gone very white, and he seemed to be having trouble getting his breath again.

"Sometimes, my friend, we are called upon to be just that—crazy fools. To trust a stranger in these cruel and violent days is one of the craziest things a man can do, especially when there is no reward in it for ourselves. Yet if we lose the ability to trust altogether, we lose one of the most precious gifts the Lord has bestowed on human kind —the gift of loving one another. Yes, I am indeed asking you to be a crazy fool and to trust me. I have no proof to offer you. I can show you my passport—it could be forged. Even the details of the icon's destination could be false. What proof is there? No, I am asking you to commit an act of faith, in the name of those unfortunate people who trusted me. You do not need to be a religious man to have faith. You only have to love, or to have loved. If you have ever done that, you will believe me, Mr Wren, and you will know it is possible to be crazy enough to undertake this task—just because we are your fellow human beings and we need your help."

He could think of no further argument. Others might have turned away with a laugh—he could not. For him it would have been like turning his back on a drowning child.

"What would happen if I was searched going through Customs, and they found the icon?"

"You would be obliged to explain. You would not be believed —and the icon would be lost."

"Couldn't the Canadian bishop help?"

"Possession, Mr Wren, is still nine-tenths of the law, even in our civilized countries. Once the icon is in his possession, and revealed to his people, he will be able to protect it. If it is impounded by Customs and its origins discovered, he would have little power. The politicians would surely intervene."

"So it's really all a matter of luck."

"I don't believe in luck, Mr Wren. If it is the Lord's will you will deliver it safely."

"And if I refuse to take it for you, that's the Lord's will too?"

Venables smiled for the first time.

"I believe whatever the Lord intends for the icon will duly come about. He is giving you a choice."

"Is he indeed?! I'm not so sure—but we won't tangle on that one, I've been there before, and it's very time-consuming. Okay. I'll take your icon for you, mister V. It won't be the first foolish thing I've done. Only please let me make this clear: in my eyes at least, and whatever you may think, this has nothing to do with God. I don't happen to believe in Him, see? I'm taking it for you because I have strong feelings about thuggery masquerading as legal government, and because I think people should be free to worship whatever they please—ancestors, standing stones, totem poles, *anything*—just so long as it doesn't harm anyone else. And now, having got that straight, could we please cut this short? Like I said, I have an appointment. Just tell me what you want me to do."

Venables scribbled a few words on a sheet torn from a diary.

"This is where you are to take the icon. Memorize it now, then I'll burn the paper."

Jeff's lips twitched.

"Do we have to be so melodramatic? You sound like one of my books."

"You don't understand yet, Mr Wren. We are not playing games. From the moment you take charge of the icon, you are in deadly danger. Do not underestimate our enemies. They know exactly what they want and they will use any means to get it. *Any* means. Please, do as I ask."

Moments later, the only evidence of his visit was a small heap of crumbled ash in the ashtray by the bed, the shabby bible on the table beside it, and the fading echoes of the stream of blessings with which he had taken his leave.

Doubts clutched at Jeffrey the moment he found himself alone. He stood there in the middle of the room blinking at the closed door. He felt as if he had just blundered on to a brightly lit stage where he was expected to act the leading role in a play of which he knew neither the plot nor his own lines—a situation he had occasionally experienced in nightmares.

Now he was free of the spell of those burning eyes, he was realizing the enormity of his own folly. What he had just agreed to do was not merely crazy—it was directly opposed to all the principles of the life he had so carefully constructed for himself since rejecting his family and his upbringing. The little man's plea had reached some deep-buried spring of feeling over which, it seemed, his rational mind had little or no control.

Gingerly, he picked up the bible. His fingers itched to prise open the sealed section in search of at least one fragment of tangible evidence, but he could see that this would be a mistake. Once he destroyed its present hiding place there was nowhere else he could conceal an icon amid his scanty hand luggage. He sighed. He was caught, well and truly caught. He had indeed just committed an act of faith.

His eye fell on the page in the Book of Revelation that the little man had been studying so intently on the plane. The words, "no more dying", had been underlined more heavily than the rest. He smiled bitterly. They were part of one of his father's favourite passages, one he always used at funerals. What a blind, desperate hope! What a failure to accept the reality of the world as it was, with its cycles of light and dark, birth and death! How necessary it was to face up to pain and loss, to learn to live with them, as Verity had said . . .

He closed the book abruptly, and put it down. It was time he went to her.

He had been about to open the door when he paused. Whilst the bible might have been perfectly camouflaged amongst Venables's belongings, it was hardly so amongst his. He could not leave it casually lying around. The hiding place would survive a fleeting glance, but not a thorough search.

Resignedly, he picked it up to take it with him, only to realize that it looked even more conspicuous—especially on his present errand. Finally, cursing with impatience, he disguised it inside the evening paper he had bought in the foyer of the hotel. Clutching it tight under his arm, he had finally knocked on his lady's door. He was grievously in need of human comfort.

Perhaps, Jeffrey mused, as he lay now wakeful and miserable, it was precisely because that need had been so overwhelming, that it had all gone wrong. He had longed to pour out all his troubles to her, to ask her advice, but he dared not—he was bound both by his promise to Venables and by his fear of involving her in any danger. Perhaps, in view of that, it was hardly surprising that his performance in bed had been less than heroic. She seemed so superior to himself, so wise, so vital, so beautiful in every way—and he had let her down. He had been unable to make love to her as she deserved. Slow, shamed, scalding tears forced their way between his lids as he recalled the humiliating details. She was so soft and fragile—he wanted to protect and cherish her, to shield her from all hurt—and he had thrown away the chance to prove himself. He was a clumsy fool. God, how beautiful she was! Gently, he kissed her hair, and the smooth skin of her cheek.

She opened her eyes—and smiled.

"Hello, Jeffrey."

"Hi, Verity."

She lay there quietly, still smiling, looking at him. She had been awake throughout the greater part of the night, while he slept, and now she wondered if it was in her power to help him. What should have been simple, and straightforward, and glad, had been furtive and guilt-ridden, and apologetic. She had been unable to soothe away his tension, and as a result had become tense and anxious herself. She had felt as if he was trying to push her up on to some sort of moral and physical pedestal from which he would not let her descend to be an ordinary, warm human being. She had reassured and encouraged him—but to no purpose. Now she was in need of reassurance herself. She felt heavy-eyed, and nervous.

Yet, as she looked, she became aware of a deep tenderness for him. There was something about him of a lost, unhappy child—a mixture of innocence and vulnerability that made her feel curiously maternal. She was determined to reassure him. She longed to tell him how little this initial failure mattered, how they only needed time, but she was afraid of hurting his bruised pride. Somehow she must bridge the frightening gap which had opened between them. In the end, she threw across it the lightest of strands.

"Did you know you talk in your sleep?"

"I do?"

"Yes, indeed. You were making quite a speech. You rambled on and on. I couldn't make most of it out, but there was something about not knowing your lines. Who's Julie, by the way? You kept calling out her name."

Surprised, she saw a painful flush spread gradually over his face and neck. The muscles of his jaw tightened, and he drew slightly back from her.

"Oh, I'm sorry," she was dismayed. "I'm not trying to pry. We don't have to talk about it."

She put out her hand to touch his face. He caught hold of it, and held it tightly against his cheek.

"It's okay. It's just that I've never talked about her to anyone. But you're different—I guess you'd understand. Julie was my sister. She was two years younger than me. She died suddenly when I was twelve. That was bad enough, but the truly awful part of it was that after her funeral my parents never spoke about her again. They threw out all her things. They seemed to be pretending she'd never lived. For me it was like killing her off a second time. I hated them, and I hated their hypocrisy. Thanks to them, I'd even begun to forget Julie myself. When you said yesterday that sudden death wasn't easy to live with, I thought of her for the first time in years. She was the only person I've ever really cared for—until now."

She leaned over and kissed him gently. It was as if he had just handed her a rose. The gap created in the night was closing.

"Perhaps that little matter of an electrical fault made everyone think harder than usual. There's nothing like being thirty thousand feet up in the air and being told there's an electrical fault among the controls for giving one intimations of mortality. I always think there's a kind of impertinence about flying."

"You feel that too? So do I. I call it my Daedalus complex."

They both laughed.

"Tell me about your parents. Why do you think they wouldn't talk about your sister—or couldn't, more likely?"

"I guess it's because they never allow themselves to show feelings. My father is the most rigid person I know. He's a clergyman. He substitutes doctrine for any form of personal thought. His life is governed by negatives. Julie was the only person who could unbend him a little. After she died, he became harder and stiffer than ever. My mother never opposed him, nor, to my knowledge, questioned him. She just did everything he told her—still does, I expect. I wouldn't know—I left home as soon as I finished high school. I worked my way through college. It took longer like that, but at least I could live among people who laughed sometimes."

"Don't you ever visit them?"

"Nope. I can't stand them. There's nothing I could say to them."

There was a pause. Verity could sense the anger that filled him.

"Are your parents alive still?"

"Yes. I don't see much of them, either. They divorced when I was eleven. They both remarried almost at once, and neither of the step-parents was very keen to have my sister and me to stay. We lived most of the time with an aunt. She was kind to us in her way, but she was a vague sort of creature who never seemed to be quite with us. She illustrated children's books. It was really Hope, my sister, who saw me through my teens. She's five years older than me, and I loved her more than I did my mother. It was a bad blow when she emigrated to Canada immediately after her marriage—I was seventeen then . . ."

"You must have felt you had no-one left."

"Like you."

It was the first time he had ever experienced the comfort of sharing that old, immense desolation with another human being. He pulled her to him and held her close.

"I hated my brother-in-law for taking her away. I still find it hard to accept him. She didn't want to go at all—she told me so, over and over, but he was dead set on it. Apparently he felt it was the only place he could build himself the career he wanted. He seems to have been right—he's been tremendously successful, according to Hope's letters. I gather they're extremely well off."

"So why haven't you been to visit them before this—you did say it was your first visit?"

She flushed.

"Somehow it's just never been possible. They didn't write much. I was worse still. I went to art college. They began to raise a family —they have triplet daughters. Our lives seemed to head down different roads, especially after I married James. After he was killed, Hope began to write more often. She kept on inviting me to stay, but I—well, I didn't want to. I didn't feel I could face living in a large, happy family. I'd lost the baby I was carrying as well, you see."

"It seems to me what you've been through would have finished most people off. You must be very strong."

"I had help. I don't think I'm stronger than anyone else." She had no wish to go into the details of that long battle to keep hold of life.

"And now you're ready to face them?"

"I think so. It's not that I've forgotten what's happened—I've just learned to accept it as part of my life. I've moved on. Now I'm looking forward to seeing my sister again. I'll even try and make my peace with Leo, my brother-in-law. I want to try to pull all the threads together again and make a whole."

"I envy you." His voice was bitter.

"Why? Don't you ever want to do that? Your mother at least must miss you badly. She's lost both her children and your father doesn't sound like a load of fun."

"If she'd only stand up to him sometimes I guess I'd be keener to visit her and try to help. He just walks all over her. He's turned her into his idea of the perfect wife—all meekness, humility and obedience. It makes me sick to see an adult human being behaving like a mouse. Venables reminded me of her—he's another . . ."

The name had slipped out before he could stop himself. He stiffened as recollection rushed back. Verity did not notice at once.

32

"Do you mean that funny little man on the plane? Is that his name? You know, you never did explain properly what he wanted last night. I suspect you're embarrassed. Was he out to convert you? Is he a Jehovah's Witness or something?"

He did not seem to hear her.

"You'll be telling me next he succeeded . . . Jeffrey, is something wrong?"

He looked at her longingly. He was strongly tempted to confide in her. He had already told her so much. She was wise. She was a survivor. But he was sworn to secrecy. Nor must he put her in any danger. He loved her. She had made his shortcomings seem unimportant. In a few hours she had come closer to him than any human being had come before. It was his duty to protect her. More than ever he cursed his own folly and weakness in listening to Venables. He must have been far more drunk than he had realized, and the little man had seized his advantage. He'd been mistaken in thinking he was like a dormouse—a stoat would have been a more apt comparison.

He'd better leave her—soon—at once. He must not risk being spotted coming out of her room. It was still very early. And then he must keep away from her. She must not be associated with him. He should not really have come at all.

How was he to explain to her? He was in danger of destroying this new confidence which had so miraculously formed between them. He did not want to lose her.

"Jeffrey?"

"Nothing serious," he answered reluctantly. "The man's a nutcase. I was just trying to think whether or not I remembered to lock my door after he went. All my valuables are in there. I'd better go take a look. Forgive me, honey."

He was halfway out of bed before she could speak.

"But you'll come back, won't you? It's only six . . ."

"Would you mind very much if I don't? I guess I'm feeling a shade rough—that whisky packed a helluva punch. I'll take a shower—and see you at breakfast."

"You could take a shower here. There's lots of time—and I asked them to give me an alarm call to make sure we wouldn't be late. Jeffrey—something's wrong, isn't it? Can't you tell me?"

33

She was hurt and bewildered. He had, as usual, made a hash of it. He hated himself.

"Verity, I swear there's nothing wrong. Please believe me."

Already he was dragging on his clothes. She watched him changing back into the stranger who had sat next to her on the plane. She was losing him. She sprang out of bed and rushed to block his way. In her haste she knocked the newspaper which he had brought with him, and left lying on a chair near the door, to the floor. Venables's bible slid treacherously into view.

In the surprised silence that followed Jeffrey did not trust himself to look at her. Trying to appear unconcerned, he stooped to pick it up, but she was there before him. She was looking at the name on the flyleaf.

"You mean I was right? He *was* trying to convert you?!"

He said nothing. Hypnotized, he saw her fingers turn the pages, —and stop when they came to the sealed block. She stood very still. Then she closed the book and handed it back to him.

"I take it this was what he wanted to see you about?"

He nodded miserably.

"What's in there, do you know?"

He nodded again.

"Do you want to tell me about it? You don't have to. Not if you'd rather not. I mean, if you and that man are involved in some racket, it might be better if you didn't. It's none of my business. It doesn't change the fact that I care about you. Think about it while I get some clothes on."

She realized, as she dressed, that what she had just said was not true—at least not altogether. She cared about him, but she could not go on caring if he could not be open with her. Dishonesty doomed all hope of a real relationship. If anything was to grow from this unexpected night together, he would have to trust her.

He had returned to sit on the bed, and had buried his aching head in his hands. Everything was awry. He no longer knew what to do. She stood watching him, sensing his struggles. Then she sat herself beside him, and put her hand on his arm. The contact finished him. He gave in. He could not bear to lose her.

"I promised him to keep it secret. I wish now I'd never set eyes on the guy."

34

He told her of the scene in his room.

"I know you're going to think me crazy. Right now I think I am myself."

She did not reply, but picked up the book again, and inspected it carefully.

"I don't see why we shouldn't open it . . . I think I could reseal it. Nail varnish would do the trick."

"Why do you want to open it?"

"To find out if he was telling the truth, of course," she said, surprised. "At least we could establish that it isn't drugs—or diamonds—or anything else that would fit into that space."

"But don't you see that there wouldn't be any sense in his passing on drugs or diamonds to a complete outsider like me? He wouldn't care enough about them to take such a risk. And if we open it up and find it's an icon like he said, it still wouldn't prove anything—it could still be part of an ordinary art robbery." Absurdly, he found himself using Venables's own argument. "And, to be frank, I don't think nail varnish *would* do the trick—not if you look how expertly the job's been done."

"Jeffrey, are you telling me you are still prepared to swallow this—this fairy tale?"

He looked her in the eye then.

"Yes," he said bravely. "It's hard to explain how I feel about it. Venables gave me a choice. I either trusted him or I didn't. He said that. He also said that if people can't ever trust each other any more, there's nothing left. As it happens, I agree with that. It's the only bit of my father's religion I *do* agree with. I can see that you differ."

Verity hesitated.

"I think there are different kinds of trust—at different levels," she answered slowly. "And the trouble with fanatical people like Venables is that they use the word loosely to manipulate others. I think he's manipulated you—and you can't see it. Do you realize what he's persuaded you to take on? Are you really ready to risk your life to help people you've never even met? Are you sure you really would be helping them? Life is precious, my dear—don't forget that. I've learned it the hard way. So have you. Why should you face pain and hardship for someone else's ideals? It isn't necessary. It doesn't make sense. Jeffrey, darling, please change your mind!"

35

"Change my mind?"

"You could find the number of his room and take his icon back to him. There's still time. You could tell him that now you've had a chance to think about it you've decided you don't want to be involved. It's only fair. He sprang it on you, after all. And it isn't as if you've signed a contract."

"I gave him my word. I promised of my own free will."

She sensed that he was wavering. She almost pitied him. She could feel the intensity of the struggle that was going on in him. But she pursued her advantage. He had to be protected from his own romanticism. She had to force him to be realistic.

"Everyone makes mistakes. He'd understand. You're a human being, not a plaster saint. Jeffrey, please, take it back. I simply couldn't bear it if anything happened to you."

He looked into her eyes, and was lost. He made his second choice.

"I love you, Verity. You win. I'll go ask his room number."

She kissed him then, a long, lingering kiss.

"Let me phone Reception. We don't want anyone to connect him with you if we can avoid it."

He admired her presence of mind as she picked up the phone. He admired the smooth roundness of her arm, and the grace of her body as she lay on the bed speaking to the receptionist. He adored her. All the same, at the back of his mind, there was a nagging thought that he would never quite forgive himself for what he had just done.

She put the receiver down, and turned to him. She had gone very pale.

"We're too late. They say that Mr Venables had a massive heart attack during the night, and was taken to hospital. He died a couple of hours ago."

36

Chapter 3

They sat there in a state of shock.

"I was talking to him only a few hours ago."

"Do you think he knew . . . ?"

"Sure he knew. It explains it all. Why he was so determined. He'd realized he wasn't going to make it to Toronto. He was telling the truth. And I didn't believe him . . ."

"What are we going to do now?" Verity's voice shook slightly.

He didn't answer.

"We'd better hand it over to the police. It's all we *can* do. It isn't our problem, after all."

Still he said nothing.

"Well what else can we do? Do say something, Jeffrey."

"He said last night that handing it in to the police would mean handing it back to the enemy."

"Enemy? What enemy? We aren't at war. You aren't going back on me are you? The fact that he's died doesn't make any difference. It still doesn't make sense."

But even as she spoke she was aware that it had made a difference. That lonely death had involved them as nothing else could.

He looked at her unhappily.

"His last act was to trust a stranger. His last wish was that I should carry his icon to Toronto for him. And I promised: The way I see it, the fact that he's dead makes that promise binding in a way it wasn't before. I'm sorry. I'm just like that. It's not something I can change. I've got to do it, Verity. I don't share his beliefs—it isn't that. It's just that he asked me for help, and I promised. I can't betray him now. Oh—*please* understand . . ."

She sat quiet for a moment, and then moved to sit close beside him.

He had touched her deeply. There was, she realized, something admirable about this young man, something she would be arrogant to criticize, or interfere with.

"I do understand, Jeffrey. At least I think I do. I—I'm only trying to dissuade you because I'm scared. I don't want this promise of yours to drive us apart. I feel it's threatening us. We've had so little time together."

"Don't be scared. I won't let it separate us, at least—only for a short time. I think you should keep away from me during the rest of the journey. But I'll be in touch with you the moment the job is done, and we'll meet up again. I want to show you Canada."

She thought about it.

"You said that Venables told you the Polish police were already on his trail, that you would be in danger the moment you took the icon?"

"That's right."

"So in fact they could be watching you right now? I mean, I take it they would know of his death if they're as close as all that? They may even have been responsible for it. We don't know what triggered the attack that killed him. It could have been another shock, or fright. There's no way we can find out. Jeffrey, did anyone see you come here last night, do you think?"

"I was extremely careful. I don't write detective stories for nothing. I'm almost certain no-one did." He smiled at her. "What are you driving at?"

"I've had an idea. A good one. Let me take the icon while you lead them off on a false trail."

His smile vanished.

"Are you crazy? I'm not letting you get mixed up in this. It's not a game. I don't want you in any danger. You wouldn't even have known about it if I hadn't left that stupid book too near the edge of the chair."

"Don't be blasphemous. The point is you *did* leave it there and I already *am* mixed up in it. You can't just shut me out now, Jeffrey."

"Honey, listen to me. Venables gave the thing to me, not to you. He wouldn't have wanted you to be in danger any more than I do. And now I'd better go." He stood up.

"Haven't you forgotten something?" She placed herself between him and the door. Her grey eyes were clear and determined.

"What do you mean?"

"My feelings. What I want. You seem to think of me as some kind of china doll, or delicate pet. I can't stand that. I've come to care for you a lot in a very short time, but I think I'd better spell this out: if you can't accept me on equal terms, as your partner, there's no future for us, Jeffrey. I'm not going to end up like your mother."

He flushed.

"That was below the belt. You're making it sound like an ultimatum."

"I'm aware of that. This is too important to mince words. The way I see it, if you can't let me share this with you, it means you don't trust me."

"That's not so! It just means I care for you too much to let you run the risk."

"You're wrong, you know. You're not looking at it objectively. You don't think I'm fit to share the risks and the danger with you. You want me to sit at home and spin while you go out and kill the dragon. Well I think spinning's boring, and two of us would stand a far better chance of killing the dragon than one. Oh, can't you see the sense of it? Listen—nobody saw you come here last night. If we keep well apart from now on, no-one can possibly connect me with Venables. I wasn't sitting next to him on the plane—you were. He went to your room last night—he never came near me. Don't you see . . . ? I'm not going to be under suspicion—you are."

"But listen . . ."

"No, you listen." She could feel him weakening, and swept on. "Why reject a perfectly good idea?—They're rare enough, you should know that as a writer. If I take the icon, you could create a diversion, attract the attention away from me. Act nervous at Immigration so that they decide you're suspicious and search you, make a fuss. I look far less suspicious than you do, and I'm going as a simple tourist, not a crime writer returning from what could be a highly suspect trip abroad. Surely it's more important actually to get the icon to the bishop than which one of us does it? What are you laughing at?"

"I haven't a hope, have I? You ought to be in politics. So tell me what we do once we're safely through Customs and all that."

"I suggest we lie low for a couple of days to throw them off the scent, then we meet up to deliver the icon together. You choose a place. I'd wait for you there. I'd give you, say, an hour, and then if something had gone wrong and you didn't turn up, I'd take it by myself. Once it's safe with the bishop the heat's off us anyway, and we could make contact openly."

"Don't you think we should try and deliver it immediately?"

"Not unless you fancy some sort of car chase through the streets of Toronto. That's what they'll expect us to do. That's what they'll be watching for. Whereas if I take it with me into an ordinary Canadian family and act as normal, I doubt if they'll find it."

"I guess you're right." He looked doubtful. "Have you thought that it might be putting your sister and her family in danger?"

"Now you're being melodramatic. Look, I'm an ordinary tourist going to stay in an ordinary family. Who on earth is going to suspect me or them?"

"I guess you have a point."

"Well, can you think of a better plan?"

He made up his mind.

"Okay, we'll play it your way. Here, you take it."

He handed her the bible.

He could not bring himself to tell her that he felt she had just deprived him of something important to him. Venables had given him a chance to perform an act that transcended all the trivial routines of daily life with its petty occupations, its superficial relationships—a chance to commit himself entirely, with his life itself at stake. Once he had brought himself to accept the chance, he had felt exhilarated, as if he had just acquired a value in his own eyes he knew he could never achieve in any other way. And even if he were to die, it would be with a sense of personal worth. He could not expect anyone else to understand that, not even Verity.

She had changed it all. She had bathed it all in the clear, hard light of common sense—and he had been forced to give in, faced with the threat of losing her. He had already failed her once. He would have to find a different way of winning his spurs. If he was not to be allowed to play Sir Galahad, perhaps at least he might make a reasonable job of Sir Lancelot, and protect his queen from all danger. It was not such an insignificant role. It could even prove a heroic one.

He felt a little better.

40

"Let's plan the details," he said, and kissed her.

High above the Atlantic cloud-fields once more, they sat carefully apart. Ingenuously, Jeffrey had asked the air hostess why the seat by the window was now empty, to be told that its occupant had been taken ill in Glasgow, and would not be making the rest of the journey. Whereupon he had shrugged, and moved across to sit in it himself.

He did not look at Verity, nor she at him. Her flight bag, with Venables's bible inside, lay on the floor at her feet. He took out a book. She sat with her eyes closed. The empty place between them was a constant reminder that this was no game that they were playing.

The other passengers, especially the younger ones, were in a party mood. Friendships had been struck up during the long delay. Many had spent the night together, making the most of their temporary freedom from normal restrictions. Now wisecracks were flying —mostly at the airline's expense, and the drink flowed freely.

Verity felt sadly out of tune, and isolated. She longed more than anything to move into the empty seat beside Jeffrey, and so close the artificial gap between them. The night had taken its toll. Her whole body ached with tiredness, but she was too nervous for sleep to be a possibility. It was as if Venables had thrown a dark shadow over both of them, blighting all the delicate buds of their relationship.

She ordered a drink, and, catching the eye of a middle-aged woman sitting by herself on the other side of the aisle, began a polite exchange of remarks with her.

The woman appeared perfectly ordinary. So did everyone else around. No-one was showing any special interest in her, or in Jeffrey, so far as she could see. Yesterday, she would have enjoyed the friendly atmosphere, the jokes and the laughter. Yesterday she would have been a random individual in a random crowd. Today the adjective seemed to have no meaning. Instead, everyone seemed to be caught up in a network of cause and effect too impossibly complex to be truly coincidental. It scared her to think about it. Yesterday she had looked around at her fellow passengers with casual, superficial curiosity. Today she watched them apprehensively. Somewhere in this cheerful, noisy crowd there could well be someone whose actions in the next few hours would affect the whole future course of her life.

41

There had been just such a person yesterday, and she had not guessed it. Who was significant? Who was not? How could she tell?

The intercom crackled, and the captain spoke once more. His voice this time was full of goodwill—the party spirit had clearly reached the flight deck.

"We've passed the halfway point," he told the listening passengers. "Today we're going to Canada, folks."

A cheer greeted his words, followed by a louder one as smiling air hostesses appeared with trays of champagne—the airline had clearly felt some concern for its reputation.

The blinds were lowered, and everyone finally settled down, a little muzzily, for the film show. Verity would have welcomed a soporific romance, or a comedy, however laboured. As it was, she found the contrived tensions of the newest James Bond episode anything but conducive to quiet nerves—each burst of gunfire made her start, and each separate act of villainy caused the sweat to break out on her forehead. She felt as if the icon must be glowing with a bright light inside its hiding place. Sooner or later, someone would notice. Sooner or later, someone would start asking questions. But for the time being all were intent on the film. She envied the hero his arsenal of ingenious gadgets—she had nothing but her wits to help her out of difficult situations.

It was a relief when it reached its foreseeable end. As they raised the blinds and let the bright daylight pour in, she envied the characters their tidy, moral ending, too—with all the villains satis-factorily disposed of, and the hero clutching his latest female acquisition to him with undisguised intent. She doubted if real life was ever so hygienic.

Word went round that they were flying over Canada. Instinctively, Verity leaned over to see if she could see anything from the window. The movement reduced for a few seconds the distance between herself and Jeffrey, and brought a momentary comfort. He was still reading steadily, but now he looked up, and, with the faintest flicker of an eyelid, acknowledged the bond between them. It was the first sign he had made since he had left her in her room early that morning. It was enough to hearten her. Through the window she caught a glimpse of land far beneath them. For the first time, the arrival in Toronto began to seem real. This hiatus in her normal life was drawing to a close. Then her foot touched the flight bag, and she wondered if life could ever, in fact, be normal again.

Jeffrey, realizing that he had read the same page several times without having the least idea of its contents, finally closed the book and, in his turn, stared down at the clumps of cumulus cloud far below. Verity's sudden move had disturbed him. He had sensed her need for comfort. He wished they could simply step off the plane together, and vanish into the landscape of forests and lakes that appeared and disappeared beneath the clouds. No-one would find them there. No-one would threaten them. They could work out their lives together in peace.

By now, of course, he was bitterly reproaching himself for letting her take the icon. He should have stood up to her, braved her anger, called her bluff. Even if she was right, and they stood a better chance of success this way, he knew he would never forgive himself if anything happened to hurt or frighten her.

He glanced furtively at the flight bag. He longed to make a grab for it, and to hand Venables's bible in to the air hostess, explaining that he had found it down the side of the seat. That would end any involvement in the matter for both of them. Unfortunately he suspected that it would also end any involvement between them. They had gone too far. Both would lose too much face. He could not do it.

He was virtually sure no-one had seen him leave her room. Back in his own quarters, however, his confidence had received a bad jolt.

He had barely had time, the previous evening, to unpack his overnight kit from his hand luggage. As a result the surfaces of the room were untidily strewn with a litter of small objects, making it almost impossibly difficult to tell whether anything had been moved. He, however, had found proof. Experience had taught him the necessity of placing the small, double-ended phial in which his contact lenses spent the night always in exactly the same position, with the right lens, the end with the blue cap, uppermost. He had schooled himself to regard this as an unbreakable rule, since it averted infuriating mistakes in the blind rush of early morning. So that, when he picked up the little phial with its white top—the left lens—uppermost, he had looked at it thoughtfully. It must have rolled off the table when someone opened the drawer beneath. They had replaced it carefully—but not quite carefully enough.

The realization was a shock. Somehow, for all the talk, until that moment Venables's story had been no more than that—a story. It was something that had happened to other people, somewhere else. Even the news of his death had not seemed real. Working out a plan of action with Verity had felt no different from plotting a book.

Now, for the first time, it had come home to him that he was dealing with realities. The violation of his room was like being brought up short by a bad smell while exploring a new and interesting landscape. Venables had spoken of deadly danger. He himself had used the word, tossing it into the discussion like any other. Standing there in the middle of his room, staring at the telltale phial, he was suddenly physically aware of its meaning. A chill crept slowly down his spine.

The hearty voice on the intercom told them they were beginning the descent over Toronto. He risked a glance at Verity, and saw that she was very pale. The laughter and chatter around them seemed to swell in volume as his anxiety grew. Everyone else was happy and relieved. Everyone else would resume their lives undisturbed by this brief hiccough. It seemed savagely unfair that he and she, two ordinary people, should have been singled out to face this problem —when both stood in such need of rest, and peace, and kindness.

Then, for some reason, he remembered what Venables had told him of the murdered Poles. Perhaps peace and loving kindness were what they had been searching for too. Perhaps their icon represented all they ever knew of it. They must have seen something more in it than its commercial or artistic value, since they had been willing to give up their lives in trying to save it. Perhaps it stood for a way of life they had lost, or an attitude, a set of values, and they were smuggling it out to Canada in a desperate bid to give it a new lease of life, to graft a shoot of the old, threatened plant on to sturdy new stock. The Old World was appealing to the New to assert their common humanity. He could not therefore isolate Verity and himself in the way he had just been doing. Like it or not, they were part of a greater whole, links in a chain. If they were to fail, the significance of that chain would be lost. Without realizing it, he sat up a little straighter. They

44

must not fail. For the first time since leaving Verity that morning, he felt he knew what he was trying to do.

He allowed himself one last look at her. He wanted to imprint every detail of that perfect face upon his memory. He wished they had been given more time. There had been no chance to make amends for his failure. Instead, he could only do his utmost to prevent harm coming to her. In that, at least, he would not fail.

Disembarking from the plane was like a sequence in slow motion. Verity was struggling from her seat to join the dense queue, when Jeffrey pushed his way past her, and elbowed himself nearer to the door, accompanied by angry protests. She lost sight of him, and for a while was too preoccupied with sorting out her passport and landing card whilst retaining her balance to worry about anyone but herself. It seemed hours before at last they all began to shuffle towards the group of stewards and air hostesses clustered at the door to wish them an enthusiastically smiling farewell.

By the time she reached the Immigration desks, long queues had again formed ahead of her. She hung back, and caught sight of Jeffrey already in line. Swiftly, she moved to the adjacent queue, and took her place behind an elderly couple fussing anxiously over their travel documents in broad Yorkshire accents.

With painful slowness, the line inched forward. By now her hands were clammy, and her throat dry. Sweat trickled down between her breasts. Venables's bible was burning a hole in her mind. She noticed that the official at the desk took plenty of time over each individual —there was no European casualness here. Each question he put was accompanied by an intent stare, with not a hint of a smile to relieve the tension he was deliberately creating. She wondered if he would hear her heart beating.

At last came the turn of the elderly couple in front of her. They doddered forward with maddening vagueness, only to drop all their papers in panic the moment they reached the desk. They turned out to be both very deaf, as the immigration official and everyone else soon realized: questions had to be put to them in a stentorian roar that carried all over the busy hall, and even then had to be frequently repeated. Verity found herself giggling hysterically, and could not stop even as the moment she had been dreading arrived, and she moved forward to stand before the desk.

Just then a fresh commotion broke out in the adjacent line. A red-faced Jeffrey was declaiming his rights as a Canadian citizen at the top of his voice, and gesticulating angrily to an impassive official. Everyone turned to watch, and Verity had just time to notice two more uniformed figures moving in as reinforcements, when a meaningful cough recalled her to her own ordeal.

The man at the desk was mopping his forehead in a way that suggested he felt it was being one of those days. She smiled at him sympathetically. For a moment he could not prevent his face from relaxing into a tired grin. His image changed at once. The Grand Inquisitor was gone, and a fellow human being appeared in his place. She found she could answer his questions calmly. He stamped her passport, raising his eyebrows appreciatively at the photo, and let her through.

They had done it.

Clutching the strap of the flight bag in a hand that felt as if she would never be able to unclench it again, she took a few paces forward, and stopped. Her legs were shaking.

It had been too easy. It could not possibly be as simple as this. Making a show of rearranging her papers, she glanced back. A whole group of uniformed figures appeared to have gathered around Jeffrey.

She knew that at all costs she must move on, or she would defeat his whole purpose—but it was one of the hardest acts she had ever been called upon to perform. She must make no sign. She must betray no special interest. She must turn and walk off with everyone else to the luggage hall, leaving him there, alone, surrounded by hostile faces. Suddenly she wondered if she would ever see him again.

The area where friends and relatives waited to greet arriving passengers was separated from the luggage hall by a large plate glass window. Verity, pausing before joining the throng gathered round the carousel, found herself searching desperately among the distant blur of faces. She needed her family. Then she recognized Leo's head of curls blazing like a beacon above the crowd, and her spirits lifted.

Leo Springer was a tall, solidly built man whose mass of brilliant ginger hair would preclude anonymity until the pigment yielded to old age. In the past, Verity had suspected that he regarded this

46

unusual gift of nature as some sort of personally-merited distinction. At all events he carried himself with an arrogant self-confidence which she saw as amply justifying the suspicion. Right now, there was something reassuring in the sight of that massive figure surmounted by its orange halo. He might have been St George.

Hope was standing just behind him. At least, she thought it was Hope, she could not be sure.

Waving to attract their attention, Verity realized how entirely the events of the journey had prevented her from giving any thought to the family situation in which she was about to find herself, and live for the next two weeks. As she hefted her heavy suitcase off the belt, she felt unexpectedly apprehensive. She had spoken confidently enough to Jeffrey of picking up the threads again, but now she wondered if this would, in fact, be possible. Eleven years of separation, spanned only by banal, uncommunicative letters, had created a great stretch of nomansland between them. So much had happened. She and Hope were now strangers. Leo had never been anything else. Their children were photographs.

Yet she and Hope had loved each other once. That gave them something to build on now. Leo was a different matter.

She had been sixteen when Hope had first introduced him to her. When she had learned that he was to marry her sister and carry her off to distant Canada, she had immediately hated him with a pure, deep, childish hate that would listen to no reason. He was the enemy, the destroyer of the only security she had known since the break up of their parents' marriage. It was time to view him now through adult eyes, to make a fresh start. Yet even as she turned, conscious of his gaze upon her, to join the last queue, and hand over the last document, she was conscious of a twinge of the old resentment.

He had, there was no denying it, destroyed something very precious. All the trauma of James's death and the loss of the baby would have been easier to bear if Hope had been near, if she had not felt so unutterably alone. She had longed for her sister then—wept for her—but Hope had been far away and busy with her own life. There had never been any question of her coming. And even when, two or three years back, she had started inviting her to visit them in Canada, there had been no word of support, no indication that she understood any of Verity's difficulties. She had written casually of

47

her children, as if unaware that meeting them for the first time represented a forbidding hurdle to someone who had lost a whole family.

As she finally reached the door, she saw her nieces waiting excitedly for her, and drew in a deep breath. It was impossible to mistake those three heads of red curls, so identical that everyone around turned and smiled. They were suddenly overcome with shyness as she walked towards them, and rushed to hide behind their parents.

It was Leo who reached her first. He gathered her up in an all but overpowering hug, the warmth of which surprised and touched her.

"Welcome to Canada, little sister-in-law. We've waited a long time for this."

Hope's embrace was less effervescent. Verity sensed a restraint that had never been there when they were young.

"I'm so sorry about the delay. Did it put you out very badly?"

"Luckily we phoned the airport before setting out yesterday, so there was no harm done—except Leo feeling he'd lost a whole day of the first real holiday he's taken in years. I dare say he'll make up for it now you're really here. You look well. I won't say you haven't changed, because you have. So've I, but perhaps not in the same way." There was bitterness in her smile.

The extent of the change in her sister staggered Verity. Hope had been pretty as a girl, but now the coarsened skin, the dyed blonde hair, the sagging lines of mouth and jaw had transformed her into a tired, middle-aged woman who wore her expensive clothes with a total lack of interest, and whom no amount of make-up could rejuvenate. Her eyes, as they examined Verity, belied her name. Hope, it seemed, at some point in the last years, had given up.

"I'd have known you anywhere."

"You always were a lousy liar. I certainly wouldn't have known you. The ugly duckling's done what the man said. Here, you'd better meet the family." She dragged the reluctant children forward. "What's the matter with you kids? Cat got your tongue? For the last week they talk of nothing but Verity's visit, and now, the moment they see you, they clam up. Typical! This one's Laura—I think. This is Claire, and this is Diana—at a rough guess. You won't be able to

48

tell them apart, so don't bother to try. I can't and I don't. They answer to each other's names."

The three little girls stared at her curiously, and Verity smiled back, trying to hide her shock at Hope's tone. She looked carefully at her nieces, trying to find some individual mark, some clue to future recognition of separate identities, but could see none. The resemblance between them was uncanny. They might have been clones. Yet they were not clones, she told herself angrily, they were three independent people, and needed to be treated as such, whatever Hope said. Yet try as she might, she could see no difference between them.

"Don't look so worried." Hope gave a little laugh, "I did warn you in my letters, but you probably didn't believe me. No-one does until they see them. Mass production makes better business sense, as Leo says, but it does have its drawbacks. It might even, on this occasion, have been one of his few mistakes."

Verity could not believe she was hearing correctly. Hope had seldom been unkind to her when they were young—how could she be so insensitive as to say such things in front of her own children? She opened her mouth—but shut it again unable to think of anything to soften the cutting edge of those casual words.

Leo came to the rescue.

"Say, you guys—aren't you forgetting something? Verity's come a long way to see you, and she's had one rough trip. How about a hug for her?"

The children responded instantly. As she embraced each in turn, tears came to Verity's eyes. These three little nieces were the family she had never had. Now, as they wound their soft arms round her neck, and planted their butterfly kisses on her cheek, she wondered why she had been so afraid of meeting them. She loved them already. She would learn to tell them apart, to get to know them. She only needed to spend some time with them.

Time—she suddenly remembered that it was one asset she did not have, not, at least, until she had delivered the icon. For the first time it occurred to her that it was going to be no simple matter to extract herself from the family without arousing suspicion in order to deal with it. She was no longer independent—a factor she had not previously taken into consideration, though perhaps Jeffrey had.

49

Jeffrey—she had been forgetting him too. She looked back anxiously into the still-crowded luggage hall, but could see no sign of him. There was no hint of disturbance, nothing to tell her what had happened.

"Is something wrong? Have you lost something?" Leo had noticed her anxiety.

"No. Nothing at all. It's all right. I was just looking for someone I met on the plane. She's probably gone by now—I was a long time waiting in Immigration."

"You must be deadbeat. Let's get you home. Laura, you and Claire take Verity's bag, I'll bring the case."

Verity just managed to bite back a protest. She hated allowing the flight bag out of her possession for even a few minutes, but she realized it was better to show no particular interest in it. Above all, she must behave normally. Once they reached Hope's house she would be able to think more clearly how best to hide and protect the icon.

It made her feel very vulnerable to walk out of the terminal building with her family. She was entering a new country, a new continent, and she was leaving her friend behind her to his fate. She comforted herself with the thought that at least there was nothing they could do to him—nothing they could prove. They could search him and his luggage for the rest of the day. He did not have the icon. She had been right to insist on taking it.

The heat, masked inside the building by the air conditioning, came as a shock as they moved outside. Verity looked around her with interest. There was not much to see. The airport buildings were depressingly similar to those at home. The appearance of the crowds was different, however—she noticed the general informality of dress and manner, and a startling predominance of baseball caps, so generally worn that she wondered if they represented some relic of tribal headgear. She was struck by the twanging accents around her, too, which made her own speech feel curiously foreign. She had been relieved to find that Hope had retained her gentle English intonation, though Leo appeared to have merged completely with his adopted background.

Looking back one last time as they waited to cross the road to enter the car park, she was suddenly aware of a large, potbellied man wearing a particularly unfortunate combination of flowered Bermuda shorts, pink check shirt, and orange baseball cap leaning against the wall near the door. He was eating an ice-cream and staring about him with an apparently total lack of concern. She had an unpleasant feeling that he had been watching her. She felt a prickle of fear, and, as they crossed the road, quickened her step to walk beside Leo.

He was clearly pleased at this show of preference for his company, and gave her a reassuring grin.

"It's great to have you here at last. She may not show it much, but Hope's over the moon. You mustn't worry about her—she's kind of tired and edgy these days. She doesn't mean half she says. Having you around will help her a lot. I just wish you could stay longer. I've worked out a schedule—but it's going to be kind of difficult to fit everything in. Are you sure you can't stay longer? I could easily change your flight."

Verity's heart sank. A carefully planned programme was the last thing she wanted.

"I'm afraid I could only take a fortnight's holiday. As it is there are one or two business appointments I must fit in. I promised I'd try and see some agents over here."

"Agents? Oh, sure, you run a gallery, don't you? Well, that's a real shame when it's such a short holiday, but I guess we'll manage to work it in. Hope should be interested—she's crazy about painting, these days—she's probably told you in her letters."

"No," Verity was surprised, "she's never mentioned it. I don't remember her ever showing any particular interest—she had a business training."

"I gathered it was very much regarded as your speciality. But she took it up a few years back—found herself a teacher and went overboard."

"You surprise me. I wonder why she's never said anything to me."

"I guess she's kind of shy about it—and she looks on you as the expert. She'll probably tell you when she's ready. I hope she will. Like I said, she needs you right now."

"The roles are reversed," Verity gave a laugh. "We've all changed, haven't we?"

"I guess so. You certainly have. You were a kid when I saw you last."

"And you've become a Canadian." She smiled up at him, remembering the cultured accent and immaculately cut suit of his younger days. She had detested his sophisticated manner and confident bearing. They seemed to have fallen away now, and in their place was an easy vigour, an indefinable air of prosperity which she found herself reluctantly admiring. Leo exuded enjoyment of living. She was glad of his tall, solid presence beside her. She glanced back at Hope almost guiltily, to see her smiling silently, as at some private joke.

"Guess which is our car!" she called out to Verity.

The sleek Mercedes outshone every vehicle in the vicinity. Leo stopped beside it with a naive pride that was somehow endearing.

"Don't you listen to Hope! She says I'm a materialist. So I am. We didn't have a car when I was a kid. I always vowed I'd have a Merc one day. Isn't she a honey?"

"It certainly is a fantastic car." Verity was sincere.

Happily, he unlocked the doors, and helped her into the front seat.

"We'll put the bags in the trunk."

For the second time she had to check a protest—she would have preferred to keep the flight bag beside her. Instead, she turned to Hope, who, with the little girls, had taken her place in the rear seat.

"You must admit it's an improvement on Auntie Hilda's old Escort!"

"It's only one of his cars. You haven't seen anything yet."

Disconcerted, Verity said no more. As Leo stepped in beside her she glanced at her watch.

For a moment she stared at it in disbelief, before remembering that she had adjusted it to Canadian time just before the plane landed. Its hands wiped out her hours of travel as if they had not existed. She felt unreal, disoriented, as if she had just been robbed of hours of consciousness. The events in Glasgow seemed to belong to a different existence.

A nudge from Leo's elbow brought her back to the new reality. He wanted her to admire the Merc's spectacular array of gadgets. She did so, with some amusement, and also, somewhat more genuinely, his expert handling of the wheel as he nosed the big car out of the

52

crowded car park and on to the road. The splendid piece of machinery purred its obedience to his commands as it glided out of the slip road and on to the highway. In the bright morning sun, Leo's ginger curls looked like a crown. She was quite willing, for the present at least, to pay him the homage he so clearly enjoyed. She needed his protection.

She had been too preoccupied with him and the Mercedes to notice, as they drove past the entrance to the terminal, the potbellied man still leaning there against the wall. He had finished his ice-cream, and appeared to be doing nothing in particular. He made no move when he saw the Mercedes pass, but merely scribbled something on a pad he took from his pocket. Unlike Leo, he was not the sort of man anyone remembered for long.

Chapter 4

Although Verity had gathered from Hope's brief and infrequent letters that Leo had been extraordinarily successful in the Canadian business world, she had not understood the full implications of his meteoric rise in fortune. Even the Mercedes had not completely enlightened her. The long, rather boring drive along straight, busy roads rendered somehow tatty by a profusion of overhead cables, followed by a quieter passage across open country merely dulled any feeling of expectancy. So that when the car finally turned off through a pair of elaborate wrought iron gates into a gravelled drive through landscaped grounds she could only stare in amazement. When the house itself came into sight she could not stifle an exclamation.

Leo glowed. Her reaction delighted him.

"I had it designed for me by a Norwegian architect. He made a good job of it don't you think?"

"He only made it ten times as big as we needed," Hope put in before she could reply.

"What the hell! I like plenty of space. You can't say we don't use it."

"True. Why you don't put a sign up and call it a hotel I can't imagine."

"Do you like it, Verity?" He sounded like a small boy showing her something he had made at school.

She could only nod, her eyes wide.

The house stood on rising ground, which had given the architect a chance to exploit the use of different levels so that the result was a complex interplay of geometrical shapes. Her first impression was that of the spaciousness of wide, gently sloping roofs, and of the openness of big windows that seemed to drink in the light.

It was built of a mixture of a peculiarly beautiful, subtly coloured stone, and wood—so much wood that it seemed almost to grow out of the tree-filled gardens that surrounded it on three sides. On the fourth, the slope had been levelled out to make a wide terrace with a low balustrade overlooking a big swimming pool. Everywhere hard lines had been softened with creepers and shrubs, and the many flowerbeds were brilliant with roses.

Verity could only gaze at it in admiration. It was big, it was opulent—but it was too outstanding a piece of architecture ever to be accused of vulgarity. It took her breath away.

"It is quite lovely," she said sincerely. "Why did you never send me a photo? I'd no idea it was anything like this. Why didn't you at least describe it to me?"

"It didn't occur to me. Besides, you never asked." Hope answered in the same flat tone which seemed now to characterize her speech.

Verity tightened her lips. It was true. She had not asked. She had not really wanted to know about her sister's life since it had moved outside the orbit of her own. Her curiosity had remained stifled by the old hurt and anger, and she had stayed aloof. She was beginning to realize now that it might well be no simple matter to break down the barrier that had grown between them, and join up the threads again. It might even, the thought slid into her mind, prove impossible.

She brushed it aside. She intended to try.

"I wish I had. It's so beautiful it might have cheered me up. I'm afraid depression tends to make people very selfish, if not totally egocentric. You must forgive me if I've seemed that way. I'm better now, and all ready to admire."

"Great. That'll please Leo. It's what he's been waiting for."

Somehow, it was not the answer she would have liked.

If anything, the interior was even more successful. Light poured through the great windows. Plants were everywhere, their vivid greens standing out sharply against pale, deep carpets and up-holstery. Random touches of colour gave depth, perfectly echoing the pools of brilliance formed by the abstract paintings on the walls. Wood, often strangely marked, had been left to its own warm tones.

Leo insisted on taking her off at once on a guided tour, overruling

55

Hope's mild objections. She was already beginning to find his naive pride slightly irritating, and to experience a desire to puncture it.

"Aren't you afraid the children will damage these lovely things?"

"Oh, we thought of that. The girls have their own quarters. They don't come in these rooms unless under strict supervision. I'll show you."

He led her to a separate level of the house, at the rear, and higher than the rest. Here, it seemed, the architect had let his hair down and enjoyed himself. The triplets had their own large sitting room with a wooden gallery at one end, from which opened their bedrooms, and, as Leo explained, a room for the nanny. Verity raised her eyebrows at this, but said nothing. Still beaming with pride, he showed her the rooms. Each was decorated with a separate style and colour scheme, with tough, bright fabrics, and well-sealed surfaces—everything had been contrived with children's needs in mind. She had genuinely admired the reception rooms, but now she felt that she preferred these, perhaps because they had been designed for people to live active lives in, rather than merely to impress visitors. Even the pictures seemed more approachable.

"We were lucky to find an excellent nanny," Leo had paused outside the door of the fourth room. "She's not only wonderful with the kids, she's also been giving lessons in oriental cookery to Mrs Matt, our housekeeper. I increased her wages when I found out —she's transformed our dinner table."

"Do you have any other staff?" Verity was beginning to have visions of a liveried retinue.

"Only Matt, the gardener and odd-job man—living in, that is. Cleaners and so on come in on a daily basis—we like to keep it simple." There was no trace of irony in his tone.

Verity wondered where precisely Hope fitted into the picture. She had been a good cook once, she remembered—full of imagination and enthusiasm. She seemed to have no role in this family, no place in this splendid house. Every moment that passed seemed to be dividing the sister of days gone by from the sister of the present more definitively. The Hope she had known seemed to have disappeared without trace.

It was a relief when Leo at last released her to be shown to her own room. She needed to be alone to try and make some sense of her impressions.

She liked her bedroom. Here, soft greens and midnight blues replaced the harsher contrasts downstairs. A thick carpet and woven wall-hangings muted all sound. She could rest in it.

Going to the window, she found herself looking down over what might well have been the park of a great English country house, except that most of the gracefully grouped trees were still immature, and in the far distance a dark line of fir and pine seemed to lurk, as if the forest had only temporarily drawn back, and was biding its time before it once more overran the tailored green lawns, and weedless flowerbeds.

Leo, she reflected, turning back to move around the room, feeling the textures, running her finger along the smooth surface of the wood, had clearly taken off into an altogether rarer atmosphere. She was ready to swear that no part of this house, no piece of furniture, however humble, no fabric, no tile even, had come off a conveyor belt. Every detail was the result of individual skill and care, bearing silent but irrefutable testimony to its owner's wealth and excellent taste.

It would have been hard to find a greater contrast with her cottage at home. There, the furniture had been acquired piece by piece after bloodthirsty hagglings in local salerooms, to be restored and polished to new life by her own hands. Nothing was new, and each piece had a history, of which its stay in her possession was only a chapter. In this house she found the recentness of everything disturbing. It was as if Leo, and Hope with him, had rejected their past. A new life in a new land—it was said to be the goal of emigrants everywhere. She suddenly felt very alien. She was only too well aware how much strength she had drawn, and still did draw, from the feeling of having deep roots.

She decided to take a shower, to rid herself of the atmosphere of the plane which still clung to her hair and clothes. Standing there, bending her neck so that the thin, hard jets of water beat a tattoo on the tense muscles at the top of her spine, some of her fatigue left her. Leo's ebullient energy, coming as it did on top of all the drama of the last twenty-four hours and an all but sleepless night, was exhausting. She found herself longing for the quiet, humorous company of

Jeffrey. If only she knew what had happened to him at the airport. They had definitely agreed not to contact each other until they met, or until the icon was safely delivered. Now she wished she could hear his voice once more. He was so different from Leo—so gentle, so unassuming—so safe. She wanted to be reassured that he was unharmed. She would not know for another thirty-six hours. It was too long.

She had been told to change into swimming gear, and to join the others on the terrace above the pool for lunch. She was about to leave the room when she paused. The icon was still in the bible, hidden in the flight bag. She realized she would have to find a new hiding place for it, but there was no time now to give it real thought. Quickly, she shoved the flight bag to the back of one of the big fitted cupboards. She would decide what to do with it later. Right now it was better to avoid incurring comment by being late.

Gathering up the presents she had brought, she went down to join her family.

Despite the heat, it was pleasant on the terrace. An exuberant Russian vine had been pruned into obedience over a trellis, so that it provided abundant shade for the lunch party.

Hope spoke very little during the meal, though Leo and the little girls maintained a constant stream of chatter. Verity noticed that he seemed to experience no difficulty in telling them apart, and was clearly enjoying their company. He seemed to have an altogether more intimate relationship with them than their mother. They hung on his words, and competed for his attention while she sat silent, smiling from time to time, picking at the food on her plate. She seemed to be under great strain, but her expression dared anyone to question her.

Verity was beginning to feel worried at the change in her. It was as if Hope had decided she no longer wanted to live in the world with everyone else, and had taken refuge in some inaccessible place deep within herself where she could be safe from intrusion, leaving a mere automaton to perform the role she had once played. Leo, for his part, seemed to be covering up for her. From time to time he referred some question from one of the children back to her, only to answer it himself when the silence became too noticeable. Occasionally Verity thought she heard a pleading note in his voice, but if so, it made no impact on Hope, who avoided his eyes.

It was a far cry from the family atmosphere she had anticipated. Some sort of struggle seemed to be playing itself out, but she could not begin to guess its nature.

They had seemed admirably suited, this pair, when they were younger, even to her angry, adolescent eyes—the quiet, self-effacing, pretty Hope, and the extrovert, ambitious, formidably intelligent Leo. She had appeared completely happy to play the supporting part of wife, mother, hostess and housekeeper, whilst he, from their earliest days, had treated her with an arrogant, if tender possessiveness which, far from annoying her as it had Verity, she had seemed to go out of her way to provoke. Nor would she listen to the slightest hint of criticism of her magnificent young man, or of her own submissive attitude to him.

The submissiveness was still there, but now it was expressed in a deference of manner so accentuated that it was insulting. It was a barbed weapon, and Leo seemed to have some difficulty protecting himself from it. He turned for support to his daughters, who gave it unstintingly. In their eyes, at least, his magnificence was untarnished.

Once, Verity felt she had made real contact with her sister. When she opened her present, Hope reddened suddenly, and her eyes filled with tears. It was a gentle Victorian watercolour, a landscape painting of the Sussex Downs near where they had lived as children, set in a delicate antique frame Verity had spent hours choosing. The conventional kiss of gratitude was accompanied by a jerky hug —which only rendered the silence which followed more baffling than ever.

The choice of gift for her nieces was less happy. Unfamiliar with their personalities, she had decided on books, going to much trouble to choose editions with good illustrations, and hunting down old favourites of her own she had felt sure could not fail to please. Too late she realized now that these were children of a different culture. Although their sitting room boasted a big colour television with attendant video, and they each had cassette players and decks of tapes, she had only noticed the most perfunctory of bookshelves.

"Why don't you three guys go take a swim?" Leo had observed the disappointment they were too young to hide, and was trying to spare her feelings. It was a relief when they obeyed him, with polite smiles of gratitude at their aunt.

At least there was no doubting his pleasure in the cashmere sweater she had bought for him. It lay on his lap, and every so often he would gently run his finger along it in a way that for some reason brought an inexplicable tingling sensation to the back of her neck.

The meal finished, they moved over to the comfortable loungers at the side of the pool. The housekeeper appeared with coffee, and Leo helped her to adjust the brightly coloured parasols to the correct angle. The triplets waved to them merrily as they frolicked in the pool, diving and jumping with an absence of fear that spoke of long familiarity with the water.

Verity watched them sleepily. The noise and vibration of the aeroplane had receded into a different era. The summer afternoon lay around them in a haze of heat. The air was heavy with the scent of roses. Her eyes kept closing. She was incapable of further effort.

"Did they explain to you why the plane turned back?" Leo's mind, it seemed, was never still.

"They said there was an electrical fault among the instruments."

"Incompetent bastards. They put you up in a hotel?"

"In Glasgow. It was pleasant enough—just rather a bore."

"I bet there were complaints."

"A few. Most of us were simply glad nothing worse had happened. They gave us free champagne this morning to cheer us up."

She wished he would stop talking. She longed to sleep. She did not want to answer his questions. She knew she could never confide in him, for all his power and wealth. The problem of the icon was between her and Jeffrey. Leo, the great moneymaker, would never ever be able to understand why they were trying to save it, and with it some message from the past. He had no time for the past.

"Huh! I thought you were all looking kind of relaxed, considering the length of the delay. They know their PR even if their planes are falling apart. Hey! Wake up there! You'll regret it if you fall asleep now. If you want to avoid jet lag it's best to try and adjust to our time as quickly as possible. Come and swim."

Despite her weariness she found herself rising to her feet. Leo's

60

friendly manner did not altogether conceal his natural authority, nor his own confidence in it.

"For heaven's sake let the poor girl rest if she wants to. She has had a ghastly flight." For once, Hope tried to intervene, but this time it was Leo who did not seem to hear. He held out his hand.

"I take it you do swim?"

She nodded. Suddenly, she did not want to take his hand. Shaking off the robe Hope had lent her, she walked past him and dived neatly into the pool.

The cool water refreshed her. She turned on to her back and floated lazily, staring up into the huge blue sky where she had so recently been travelling. Then there was a splash, and Leo swam up beneath her, knocking her off-balance, his arms brushing her bare skin.

"Race you to the far end."

Again, she found herself falling in with his wishes, and they raced, cheered on by the triplets.

Leo won easily. He caught her as she headed blindly for the edge with her splashy, breathless crawl. He seemed to be taking every possible chance of physical contact, and she did not like it. She tried to avoid him by joining the children, whereupon he suggested a game of tag. In the end, foreseeably, this meant that he was chasing, and catching her, pouncing on her as she dived behind one of the girls, and, for a few seconds, holding her against him. She was immediately, unnervingly aware of him, of his muscular body and extraordinary strength. Almost hysterically, she kicked out, and, catching him in the groin, succeeded in freeing herself. She heard a grunt of pain, but swam as fast as she could to the steps without looking round.

It was a relief to climb out and rejoin Hope, still sitting comfortably on her lounger, smiling. She had obviously not noticed anything.

"Aren't you going to swim?"

"Later, maybe, when the kids have finished. You may remember I never was any great shakes in the water."

She remembered then. A sadistic teacher had tried to teach Hope to swim by throwing her in the deep end, creating a fear of the water that had never been completely overcome. She had eventually

61

learned, but swimming had never been a pleasure for her—each painful length was a self-imposed ordeal. Verity eyed the big pool with all its expensive accessories. Leo could hardly have had his wife in mind when he planned them.

"It can't be much fun if you don't join in. Don't you get bored?"

"Of course I get bored. It goes with the job."

"Can't your nanny stay out here with the children and let you off the hook?"

"Not really. Nelly's a complete non-swimmer, even worse than me, so it wouldn't be very safe. The girls are learning life-saving this summer, which ought to help. Leo gets professionals in to teach them. In the meantime I'm on duty. There are worse fates."

"I suppose so, it depends what you really want to be doing." Hope's mouth tightened, and she looked away. Verity saw that Leo had climbed out of the pool and was approaching them.

"I hope I didn't hurt you," she said brightly. "I can't bear any-one catching hold of me like that."

"So I realize. I promise I'll be more careful another time." He smiled at her. She flushed.

He dried himself, taking his time about it as if to make sure she had a good view of his tanned shoulders and powerful torso. She tried not to look, but it made no difference to the unexpected and disturbing reactions of her own body. She began to feel a little frightened. This was not a situation she had been anticipating. Her feelings were, she had thought, completely taken up with Jeffrey. She was only begin-ning to know him, to appreciate the subtle colouring of his person-ality, his gentle, quirky humour, his old-fashioned idealism—and here she was suddenly experiencing attraction to someone else. It was not like her. She had never behaved like this before.

"I thought I'd take the girls to the Mall," he said to Hope. "We need some new fishing gear up at the cottage. Want to come, Verity?"

"No thanks. I'll stay and talk to Hope. I'll have more energy tomorrow."

"I hope so. You're going to need it. There's a lot waiting for you to see and do, and a short time for you to do it in."

A few minutes later, the two women heard the car heading down the drive. As the sound faded, a hush fell over the garden. The pool lay like blue glass. The air was heavier than ever. Verity saw Hope's face relax again.

"Hope, is anything wrong?"

"Wrong?"

"You don't seem very happy."

"Don't I? I must be very ungrateful, mustn't I, when I've got everything a woman could possibly want—a rich and successful husband, a fantastic home, healthy normal children, status . . . How could anything possibly be wrong?"

"Suppose you tell me."

"I wish I could. It isn't that simple, especially when you look at me like that with those big grey eyes of yours. I'd forgotten your eyes. They always seem to see right inside you, did you know that?"

Verity shook her head, smiling.

"They can't see very much right now. Too much time has gone by. But if there's any way I can help—"

"I think the fact that you've come at last may help more than anything else."

"I'm glad. I'd have come before if I could, you know that. I've missed you. I really needed you, Hope."

"You always did. Leo was the same. Then the girls came along and they needed me too. They say it's a great thing to be needed. I wouldn't know—I've never been anything else."

There was a pause. Verity did not quite know what to say. Presently she tried again.

"Leo told me you'd taken up painting. Do you enjoy it? At least that's a small corner you can call your own."

Hope looked at her with a strange expression, but said nothing.

"Why did you never mention it in your letters? I think it helps to have a hobby of that sort. It allows one to grow a little, if nothing else, and one learns to see. It's meant a lot to me even though I've never made the Summer Exhibition. I still get excited when I sell a painting. Won't you show me some of your work? You never know—you might find you could make some pin money—or perhaps you already have?"

"I'll show it you some time," said Hope, almost unwillingly, and still with that unfathomable expression.

"It might be fun to do some art galleries together, too. Would

—would Leo want to come, or could we just go together? Have you shown him your paintings?"

Hope laughed.

"Show Leo? It's nothing to do with him—that's the whole point!"

"I should have thought he'd be pleased to know you've found something that makes you happy."

"Maybe he is—I wouldn't know, we don't talk about it. Leo lives in a different world from me. He's a doer, and he's turned the girls into doers as well. They're all sports-crazy. Laura, Claire and Diana are only seven, yet all they think about is swimming, skiing, riding and baseball. Nothing else interests them. They're not like we were. They've no time for the quiet things."

"I don't remember Leo being like that."

"He wasn't. He changed when we came out here. Perhaps it was his way of adapting. He aimed to build a business empire, and he believed he had to stay physically fit to do it. There wasn't time for anything else. It's been a successful formula."

"Except that it didn't leave a space for you, p'raps?"

"Oh, I accepted that long ago. I just tag along. I come in useful for servicing the equipment. I quite like the cross-country skiing—the landscape is breathtaking—but they're not so keen to have me along for that, I slow them down too much. Nelly usually goes instead. I'm not a doer—not in their sense of the word—so where would I fit in?"

"Yet as I remember you were always very practical and efficient. Leo always used to say you were a superb secretary."

Hope laughed again, and this time there was no mistaking the bitterness.

"I dare say I was. I looked on work as an escape route. I didn't realize that it led straight into the trap."

"I'm afraid you've lost me."

"You wouldn't understand. Forget it. You know—I'd really like us to visit some art galleries together. You could improve my education. Tell you what—we'll go to Kleinburg. It isn't very far."

"What's that?"

"It's a place that's helped keep me sane. I bet you've never seen an art gallery like it before. You must have heard of the Group of Seven?"

"Heard of, yes. I've never seen any of their work."

"Great. I'll introduce you—always provided Leo allows us some time off."

"If it's what we both want is there any reason why he shouldn't?" Verity spoke with a touch of belligerence—she was not used to asking permission.

"Oh, it's just that he's been laying some pretty intricate plans. You don't know how honoured you are—he never takes a holiday as a rule. We're supposed to be spending a few days in Northern Ontario as well as seeing all the sights. I had to work on him to let you have this afternoon in peace."

Verity sighed. The last thing she wanted was to have the whole visit masterminded by Leo.

"I did explain to him at the airport that I had one or two business appointments," she said plaintively. "It saves the expense of sending someone over here specially. He seemed to understand. When is this trip to Northern Ontario?"

"At the weekend. Wednesday he wants to take you to Niagara."

"That's the day after tomorrow. And I'm very much afraid that that's the date of one of my appointments. I don't want to change it—it was difficult to arrange." Nothing and nobody on earth, she thought to herself, could induce her willingly to miss that appointment. Jeffrey had become her Pole Star, her only fixed point in an ever-shifting landscape where dangers gathered like banks of fog on a motorway, threatening catastrophe. She longed to hear his warm voice again, with its faint suggestion of a Scottish accent beneath the Canadian twang, to listen to his absurd jokes, to bury her face in his shoulder. She wondered for the hundredth time what he was doing and saying and thinking—if he was worrying about her.

"Oh well, then he'll just have to change his precious plans, won't he? He's supposed to be making them to please you, after all—not himself."

"The best way he can please me is by making sure I get plenty of time alone with you—you and the girls."

"I think that could be more than a little tricky to put across. Leo does care a good deal about you, you know."

Verity stared at her in surprise.

"He hardly knows me."

"You've hardly given him a chance. When you wrote to tell us about James he'd have flown over to try and help out if things hadn't been very difficult here just then."

"I'm glad he didn't. If I needed anyone just then, it was you. I'm afraid Leo's no substitute, Hope. I've missed you terribly."

"You mean you think you have. I couldn't have helped you, you know. Come to that, I don't think anyone can really help anyone else. We're all of us on our own. We have to find our own way through. That's what Leo doesn't understand. It makes him happy to think he can help you by giving you what he thinks is a good time. It would be cruel to disillusion him—especially now he realizes I'm a lost cause."

Verity was feeling far from sure she understood. She wondered if Hope knew exactly what she was saying. She could still feel the touch of his hand on her bare skin, and she was still shaken at the way her body had responded. Shaken and angry—with herself and with him.

The old dislike flared up, stronger now than ever. He had wanted her sister and had taken her away. Now, it seemed, he wanted her as well. No doubt he collected scalps. It was a complication she had never for a moment foreseen, and one she would gladly have done without.

She suddenly realized that the swim had brought her close to exhaustion. She was probably exaggerating everything as she was prone to do when overdrawing on nervous energy. There was only one remedy. She stood up.

"I can't seem to think straight any more," she told her sister. "If I don't get some sleep I won't make any sense at all by this evening. Give me a couple of hours, would you—and never mind what Leo says . . ."

Back in her room she heaved a sigh of relief to find herself alone. She had not thought that family life could be such a strain. She drew the curtains to shut out the huge, bright Canadian sky. The dim light and the afternoon quiet soothed and reassured her.

Within minutes, she was deeply asleep.

Chapter 5

A gentle tapping on the door woke her. Hope put her head round.

"It's five o'clock and Leo says that's long enough. I've brought you some tea. Are you feeling any better?"

For a moment Verity could not make out where she was. Sleeping at an unaccustomed time had completed her feeling of disorientation. Night and day seemed to have become interchangeable. She smiled drowsily at her sister.

"Do you remember how we used to take turns at making early morning tea for Auntie Hilda? It was the only way we could be sure she'd get up for breakfast."

"Frankly, I'd rather not. I loathed Auntie Hilda. I said, are you feeling better?" Hope's voice was dry.

"Am I—? Oh—yes, yes thanks. I'm sorry—I must have zonked right out—I can't remember a thing. I hadn't realized I was so tired."

"I expect it was scary when the plane turned back, wasn't it?"

"You're telling me. I was petrified. I couldn't imagine we'd ever land safely. I didn't sleep very well last night, either." She sipped her tea gratefully. Hope seemed to be thawing a little. "This really does remind me of old times. I didn't know you felt like that about poor old Auntie Hilda. She was good to us in her way. At least she stood by us and gave us a home."

"She was good to you. I never looked on it as a home. Perhaps you never noticed who did all the work. I prefer to leave it all where it belongs—in the past. Do you want to come down and face the zoo again or would you rather stay quiet a little longer?"

"Just give me a while to get myself together, then I'll join you. Was it really that bad, Hope?"

Hope's mouth twitched.

"Not for you, maybe. I'll see you later."

She was gone before Verity could say anything else. She felt rebuffed. Her view of their childhood did not seem to be the same as her sister's, and this was curiously disturbing, as if hitherto solid ground had just given off a faint tremor.

She lay for some time trying to summon the will to make a move. The big, shadowy room seemed impersonal, almost hostile in its size and affluence. Her bedroom at home was small, with a crazily sloping floor, and a tiny sliding window that looked out over rough fields to the sea. She liked the feeling that generations of people had lived there before herself—it made her feel safe.

Not like now. She felt anything but safe in this big, luxurious house. Not just because of the icon. There were too many unexpected tensions. It had been foolish and naive of her to imagine that this long-postponed visit to her sister could give her a restful holiday. Too many hobgoblins were being woken from their sleep, and she was by no means sure she had the strength to deal with them—not, at least, on top of the matter of the icon.

At the thought of it she sat up. She must at least decide the question of how best to hide it over the next thirty-six hours. She could not afford to be careless, however small the likelihood of being suspected. The bible was no longer suitable camouflage.

Retrieving it from the cupboard, she marvelled that she had had the audacity to carry it through Customs. Pored over by Venables it had appeared completely unremarkable, but amid all the frivolous bits and pieces that had overflowed from her suitcase it seemed to stand out like a clergyman in full robes on a Mediterranean beach.

Holding it, she could imagine herself once more in the Glasgow hotel room listening to Jeffrey's embarrassed explanations. She could feel again the maternal desire to help that had swept her into proposing that she take the icon rather than him. She could not regret that. It had been the right thing to do, she was sure of it. She still felt the same about him: he was simply too sensitive, too insecure a personality to be exposed to the brutality of physical danger. He had fine qualities, but he was no hero-figure. He was essentially a contemplative—an observer who saw far beneath the surface, who thought and felt deeply. He could not play James Bond—to ask him to try would be like deliberately sending a poet into the trenches of the Somme. At least in his present role as decoy, he ran less risk of permanent emotional hurt.

The thought comforted her. The book felt very solid in her hands. It was the proof that the events of the flight had really happened. It was also the tangible link between the Verity Wells who lived alone in a Welsh cottage and this Verity Wells of the present, on holiday here in this strange new continent, who was beginning to doubt that she knew herself quite as well as she had thought, and whose body seemed to be capable of living a very different life from her mind. Whatever it was that was hidden inside had fallen into her life out of the blue, almost as if it had been sent to test the extent of her recovery. She squared her shoulders. She knew how far she had come. She would do her best.

It was time to discover exactly what it was that was adding to her difficulties.

She hunted out a pair of nail scissors, and brought them over to the bed—only to hesitate. She felt exposed and vulnerable in the middle of the big room. Carrying the bible through to the bathroom, she set it down on the vanity unit. She felt safer away from windows.

Holding her breath, she began delicately to slice at the gummed pages with the open blade of the scissors. After a moment, she had to stop—her hands were shaking too much and she was afraid of damaging whatever lay inside. She took some slow, deep breaths to steady herself, and gave herself a feeble grin of encouragement in the mirror before continuing.

Gently, she lifted free the pages that had formed the lid of the inner box. In it, fitting snugly in a bed of cotton wool, was a flat, hard package encased in white satin, and sewn with stitches of gold thread.

Suddenly she was sure that Venables had been speaking the truth. Jeffrey was justified in his act of faith. So, too, was she. This was no con trick. With an odd feeling that she was intruding on something sacred, she lifted out the packet, and carefully snipped through the gold thread.

"An icon of Loving Kindness!"

She had seen many pictures of icons when she had studied art history at college, but she had never before set eyes on the real thing.

Now, gazing at the one in her hands, she felt unaccountably close to tears.

In the past she had always experienced a special feeling, almost a longing, when she looked at pictures of those icons which show the Mother of God with her head bent, and her cheek touching the head of her baby in an attitude of ineffable tenderness. Yet she had never felt it before with this force.

Somewhat unusually, the icon was set in a frame of intricate gold filigree, set with tiny gems, which partially covered it. It was obviously very old—the paint was crazed, the gold leaf dimmed, the colours faded—yet for all that the two figures stood out with amazing clarity. The slanting eyes of the Byzantine girl-mother looked away into the distance from beneath a calm, resigned brow, with a sadness that the passage of centuries had done nothing to diminish, while the baby reached up to touch her face in a gesture that expressed all the helpless need for love that is the lot of every human creature. She had always felt that icons of Loving Kindness spoke more directly to those who contemplated them than any others—perhaps this was why she responded so strongly to them, and why she was responding now.

She had never thought of herself as religious. Because of what had happened to James, however, she was still, even now, searching for a way of facing up to death. She wished that she could accept a system of belief that promised its defeat, but in all those she knew of this involved denying the value of life as well, and this she could, with her experience, no longer do. Perhaps the terrible randomness of his extinction had something to do with it, and the fact that she had not been there, so that in effect it had meant only a failure to return, a perpetual absence, and above all a permanent loss of the feeling that life had any meaning. She had recovered, and was once again leading a normal existence, but she was living it piecemeal, and this did not wholly satisfy her. It was a way of surviving, but all the time she knew that she was looking for something more.

This was also, perhaps, why she so much liked to visit cathedrals, and old churches. It was not so much because of the creed that had inspired them. Rather, she was drawn to the building itself, the result of so much human labour, and the presence of the dead lying in and around it, and not least the living continuity of the music that had echoed in it since its earliest days. People came together in these places in their common need, as others had throughout the generations before them, forming a line stretching back through the centuries.

The beautiful old icon spoke to her in the same way. Venables had told Jeffrey that it was reputed to have great powers, that it had performed miracles. The miracle, she thought as she looked at it, lay really in the strength of the feelings it kindled in the hearts of all those who had prayed to it for help, so that their separate lives seemed to fuse into one, great, urgent plea—so great that it could not be without meaning.

Tears filled her eyes. Venables too, however narrow his beliefs, had responded to its message. It had cost him his life, but in doing so he had taken his place in the line. She and Jeffrey were doing the same thing.

She suddenly felt the immensity of her responsibility. This was not simply an art treasure that she was holding. Its value had nothing to do with money. It was priceless in the true sense of the word. If she failed to hide it and to deliver it safely she would destroy some great living current that flowed from the past into the future, dim some of the light that was needed if ever a meaning was to be found. She was alone, and at this moment she was the icon's only chance.

It felt a frighteningly slight one. She had not realized to what extent she would lose her freedom of movement, nor had she foreseen the new complications in her relationship with Hope and Leo.

She felt threatened on all sides. She longed now to deliver the icon to its destination immediately, to rush out, highjack the Mercedes and drive straight to the bishop. Direct action. Immediate results. Only they were not likely to be the ones she desired.

Suddenly it now seemed hardly likely that she should escape suspicion. She had been sitting too close to Venables. She had been seen with Jeffrey. However successful he had been in creating a distraction sooner or later the enemy were going to wonder about her.

Her best hope, therefore, surely lay in acting as normally as possible, in taking advantage of every scrap of natural cover. She must play a calculated game of grandmother's footsteps. For the next

71

thirty-six hours she must watch every word and control every act. After that, she would be able to relax. She was an amateur, but she must think like a professional. And the first professional decision must be concerning the nature of the hiding place she chose for the icon.

Deep in thought, she walked back into the bedroom to look round—and stopped, cold with horror. One of the triplets was standing by the bed, watching her with deep interest.

"Mommy told me to ask you if you'd like to come down and have a drink before we eat, if you're ready. Aunt Verity, what *were* you doing to that book?"

She had lived so long alone that she took privacy for granted. It had simply not crossed her mind that anyone might come in. So much for professionalism. So much for control. She wondered just how much the child had seen. She had only to prattle to her sisters, or worse still to Leo, and all hope of secrecy would be gone. She tried to play it down.

"Which one are you?"

"I'm Claire. It's easy to tell me because I've lost a tooth. Look!"

"Thanks Claire, I'll remember that. Do you think you can keep a secret, just between you and me?"

"*Sure* I can."

"You see, when I travel by air I don't like to put my jewelry in my suitcase, because cases often go missing. So I make a special hiding place for it inside an old book, and put it in my hand luggage. No-one's likely to steal an old book, so it's safe like that. I was just unpacking it. Only I'd rather you didn't tell anyone about it because if you did it wouldn't be secret any more, would it?"

"That's one smart idea, Aunt Verity. Can I see? Will you show me your jewels? Are they very precious?"

"Not very—only to me. I *will* show you, but not right now." Firmly Verity stood where she was, blocking the child's view of the bathroom. The sharp seven-year-old eyes tried to peer round her, but without success.

"You run and tell your mother I'd love a drink and I'll be down in ten minutes. And Claire—"

The triplet looked at her hopefully.

"—another time would you please knock before you come into my room?"

"Okay. You won't forget, will you?"

"Not if you go now. I want to get changed." Smiling, she propelled the visitor to the door, locking it behind her with a strong feeling of futility. The damage was done.

She felt weak at the knees. She had just made her first mistake. While she felt reasonably certain that Claire had believed her, and that she had not spotted the icon, she knew she must waste no more time: she must decide immediately on a new hiding place.

Frowning, she thought hard. At last, hesitatingly, she picked up a large, flat straw handbag she had brought to wear with her summer dresses. If she wanted, like Venables, to keep the icon always with her, it seemed the only possible camouflage, obvious though it was—obviousness, after all, could be regarded as a form of subtlety. The alternative—to hide it somewhere in the house or grounds —appealed even less. She wished she could consult Jeffrey, he would probably have devised a far neater and subtler solution. Jeffrey—she tried to imagine him—he would doubtless be back in his own home by now. How long had he contrived to distract the authorities at the airport? He had probably made a wonderful nuisance of himself, setting all his professional skill to keep their interest concentrated on himself. She smiled at the thought. Just as long as he hadn't overdone it, and was at this moment languishing in some police cell, regretting the enthusiasm he had put into his part. He would certainly have played it to the hilt in his zeal to protect her. He was like that. Her strongest impression of him was of his trustworthiness, his chivalry.

Well, she must play her part to the hilt, too. She must not fail his trust in her.

She looked at the handbag dubiously . . .

She would have to think of some way of protecting the fragile treasure from the inevitable bumps and jostlings. She eyed her quilted linen make-up bag. It was new and unmarked. Tipping out the contents and tucking in some fresh cotton wool, she found that the icon in its thick satin cover fitted neatly inside. Zipping up the bag again, she looked at it with satisfaction. It would do. She smiled a little grimly—it seemed a strange, and curiously intimate hiding place for a sacred object.

Quickly now, she made the handbag ready for use. Slipping her purse into it, she smiled again as she reflected that she needed it rather as a decoy than for its own importance.

Time was running out. She changed into a fresh dress, and tidied her hair. She must face the family again.

She was about to leave the room when she realized that the mutilated remains of Venables's bible were still lying on the vanity unit. She could not leave them there. She could not think how to dispose of them. She stared round frantically. In the end there was nothing for it but to sweep them together and stuff them back into the flight bag. She had no sooner done so than she pulled them out again, tore off the flyleaf with its telltale inscription, and flushed it down the lavatory—not without a peculiar feeling that she was drowning all memory of the little man.

Hope and Leo were sitting in silence when at last, breathless, she reached the drawing room. Leo sprang to his feet when he saw her, and wagged a playful finger at her.

"Don't say I didn't warn you when you wake up in the small hours!"

"Want to bet on it?"

"I'm far too kind to bet on a certainty. I'm an old stager when it comes to flying, and I know the ways of jet lag. The longer you can stay awake this evening, the less you'll suffer from it. Don't worry —we'll do our best to help."

Verity could not help thinking it sounded like a threat.

"Where are the children?" she asked.

"They join us at table." Hope spoke for the first time. "I find that half an hour or so without them just before a meal is a great aid to the digestion."

"Not for me it isn't. I find them kind of soothing. They remind me of a Greek chorus." There was a trace of wistfulness in Leo's voice. Verity wondered which particular drama he had in mind.

"Even a Greek chorus spends some time off-stage. If you had your way they'd be underfoot the whole day long. You spend every minute of your precious free time with them as it is."

"Which isn't very much as I'm sure you'll agree. They need to know they have a father."

"If you're implying . . ."

"Honey, I'm not implying anything. I'm simply saying that they need my interest and support, and I don't get much time to give it to them."

Hope pressed her lips into a thin, straight line and said no more. Verity looked nervously from one to the other. She could feel the anger crackling between them, but could not make out its cause.

"Mrs Springer—would you mind coming a moment?" A head appeared round the door—it was a girl with the flat features, creamy skin, and almond eyes of some oriental race.

"Oh Nelly, not now! Surely you can deal with it?"

"I'll go," Leo rose to his feet but Hope put a hand on his arm.

"She asked me. You stay and entertain Verity while I sort it out. We promised her a drink, remember?"

"What'll it be?" Leo turned to her when Hope had gone. The atmosphere seemed suddenly lighter.

"I'll have a Martini, please."

Their hands touched as he gave her the drink. There was a long pause. He was looking at her with open admiration.

"You're very beautiful, Verity Wells," he said at last, softly.

"Thank you."

"I knew you would be one day. I wish you'd come to see us before."

"I'm afraid I couldn't," she said, stiffly.

"Will you really not be persuaded to stay longer? Couldn't you quit the job?"

"There's no reason why I should, I enjoy it."

"A woman like you is wasted in a fossilized, overcrowded dump like the UK. In Canada there's space and freedom. It's a growing country, it's young, it's got a future. You'd get a far better job over here. More money. I'd help you. You could build up a real life for yourself. And you'd be with us."

He put his hand on her arm. She shivered. She had never known anyone quite like him before. He had the ability to focus the beam of his intelligence, his charm and his sexual attractiveness on the woman he was speaking to so that she felt flatteringly singled out, exclusively understood. Rationally, she was aware that he was behaving according to a recognizable stereotype, and that every gesture and every inflection was predictable. But when he touched her and looked at her, her response was not rational. It scared her. Her body seemed to be trying to pay her out for the long abstinence she had imposed upon it, not to mention the disappointment it had suffered the previous night at Jeffrey's apologetic, inexpert hands.

She tried to defend herself by thinking of Jeffrey, and of the loyalty she felt she owed him, but her memory of him seemed to be fading more with every minute she spent in Leo's tingling, sparking presence. She tried to think of Hope, instead, Hope who was so plainly unhappy and lost, and who needed her support. She ought to be feeling revulsion at this man who had clearly failed his wife, and who thought nothing at making a pass at his sister-in-law under her nose. She could not possibly feel anything else for someone with values like his. Of course she felt revulsion. Yet she stood there without moving as his hand moved up her arm to caress her cheek, then down her neck to stroke gently along the collar bone, and down again until, as if inadvertently, it touched her breast.

The sound of angry voices and protesting wails outside the door broke the spell. She turned away abruptly, humiliated and furious with him and with herself. Hope entered, dragging a tearful child.

"This time Leo you can handle it. Just look what Nelly caught this—this young hooligan doing."

To Verity's discomfiture, she held out a large, calf-bound volume of the kind that sits permanently on display on a bookshelf and is never opened. This one, however, had not only been opened, but had sustained a determined attack with a pair of heavy-duty scissors, so that mangled strips of paper hung from its gilded edges, and, as Hope opened it, fluttered forlornly to the floor.

The expression on Leo's face was so comical she had to stifle a laugh.

"That's one of my college prizes. Claire, what the hell does this mean? What in Christ's name has gotten into you?"

"She was handing us some nonsense about making a jewel case like Verity's," said Hope, "a jewel case, I ask you!"

Claire looked at Verity with an expression of tragic appeal.

"Oh dear!" Verity spoke in a light, bright voice. "I had no idea I was going to cause any trouble. It's quite true—I use the inside of an old book as the hiding place for my jewelry when I'm travelling. I'm afraid Claire saw it when I was unpacking . . . I didn't realize it had made quite such an impression on her. I'm so sorry—I really think this was all my fault."

No-one, it seemed, knew quite what to say.

Leo put an end to the uncomfortable silence by turning the child about and marching her to the door.

"Your aunt is a grown-up, and what she does with her books is her own affair. You're a kid, and in this house no kid *ever* destroys books or any other personal property for *any* reason. Okay? Now just you scram and finish getting yourself ready for the meal."

The triplet took to her heels.

The three of them sat sipping their drinks trying not to look at the mutilated book lying on the coffee table. Verity was mortified. So much for grandmother's footsteps. She might as well have waved a flag. They must be thinking her at the very least eccentric.

"Leo, I truly am sorry. I hope it isn't too valuable a book. It honestly never crossed my mind she might try to copy me. You must think me very strange, but I'm a bit paranoid about theft. My trinkets aren't specially valuable, but as James gave me most of them there's no way I could replace them."

"I think it's a very clever hiding place," Hope was disarmed, at any rate.

Not so Leo. "Sounds to me as if you worry too much. You must learn to let things go. If they're stolen they're stolen. Just as long as they're insured."

"I'm afraid I don't see it quite like that."

"Then you must learn to open your eyes. The past is finished, over—it's the future that's important."

"Do you really think you can separate the two?"

"If I didn't I wouldn't be sitting here now in this house I've built, on my own land, with my own money. If you look at my family tree, you'll find my ancestors in the workhouse, on the dole, going bankrupt. I play the game differently. I look ahead—I—"

He was interrupted by the entrance of Mrs Matt, who announced that the meal was ready. As they were passing through the door, she whispered something to him.

"You girls go ahead. Start without me. Matt wants a word."

Verity followed Hope into the dining room, where three clean and subdued little girls were waiting for them. She looked at the table with its exquisite lace cloth, big bowl of white roses, and shining crystal—Hope obviously made no concession to her daughters' tender years when it came to entertaining. It made a charming scene.

The incident with the book had brought home to her the threat that her own presence represented. Now that she had seen the icon it was all too easy to believe that she was in danger—she could no longer doubt the gravity of the warnings Venables had given to Jeffrey. She could see, too, the justice of Jeffrey's own objection that she might be putting her sister and her family into jeopardy if she took the icon with her. She had swept it aside so lightly. Too late, as she looked at the faces gathered round the table, she realized that he had been right.

She tried to comfort herself with the thought that the danger was only temporary. It was already Monday evening. On Wednesday she and Jeffrey would meet up again, and the icon would pass out of their hands. Surely little could happen between now and then.

Her appetite seemed to have deserted her. She picked at the tempting morsels on her plate with a heavy heart. Glancing at her watch, she realized that at home in Wales it would be the small hours of the morning. Hope sat morose and withdrawn, making no attempt to quell the rising voices of the triplets, which seemed to be growing ever more shrill. Verity's head began to ache. She was not used to the company of children.

It was a relief when Leo joined them. The little girls quietened at once. He was frowning.

"Anything wrong?" Hope's tone was casual.

"Nothing to worry about. I'll tell you later. One at a time, you guys!"

It was only when they were in the drawing room, drinking their coffee, and the triplets had been dispatched to their own part of the house to watch television that he opened up.

"Matt saw someone snooping in the grounds. He wanted to know whether to call the police. I told him not to worry but to leave all the outside lights on and to let the dogs loose. The burglar alarm will be set as usual so I don't think there's any real cause for concern. Just check your windows are locked, that's all. It must be someone after your precious jewels, Verity."

The blood drained from her face. He saw it.

"Hey, I was joking. There's nothing to be scared of. It's happened before. It's the price you have to pay when you live in a place like this. I take good precautions—and it's not as if you're alone."

"No, I'm not, am I?" She was struggling to steady herself. She had never felt more alone in her life.

"You can trust me. I'd never let anything happen to you—or to any of us."

"I know you wouldn't." She managed a shaky smile. "I'm sorry. I'm being stupid."

"If you get scared, just give a shout. Hope takes knockout pills every night so she wouldn't hear you, but I'm a light sleeper. I'd be with you in seconds. Look—I'll phone the police if it'll make you feel any easier . . ."

"No—there's no need—I'm all right. It was just a shock. You must remember I live in a village where we don't even lock the doors, let alone the windows. I've obviously led too protected a life."

"You'd soon toughen up out here. Leo would see to that, wouldn't you honey? Look at me—he's done a good job on me, don't you think?"

Verity looked at Hope's discontented face and dyed blonde hair, and found it hard to relate this cynical, middle-aged woman to the star-struck girl who had once forbidden her to criticize her fiancé. They should have been happy these two, but it was all too plain that they were not. She wondered why.

She was too disheartened to puzzle over it. She was fagged out. The news that there was an intruder lurking in the grounds seemed to have sapped the last of her energy.

"I'm sorry," she said, standing up. "Despite that rest this afternoon I have reached the stage where I no longer know exactly what I'm doing or saying. Jet lag or no jet lag, I've got to get to bed. I'll see you in the morning. Goodnight, both of you."

"Goodnight."

Leo hurried to open the door for her. As she reached it, he spoke.

"Don't forget what I said—if anything scares you, just give a shout."

"I won't forget." Behind her smile, she knew she would rather die than utter a sound that might bring him to her room. She would prefer to face a hundred intruders than a single Leo.

Chapter 6

Once she half woke—just enough to realize with a surge of relief that though her cheeks were wet with real tears she had only been dreaming. She was alone and quiet in the big, soft bed. She fell asleep again—to plunge back, even deeper than before, into nightmare.

She had dreamed that James had come to her, and had lain down beside her. She had thrown her arms round him in delight, but he had not moved. She had kissed him, but he had made no sound. Then she had seen people standing round the bed, whispering and pointing. One of them was a priest carrying a cross sparkling with jewels. Another held flowers, a huge wreath of blood-red carnations slowly shedding their petals, which fell on to the bed in bright-red drops. Then she knew this was a funeral, and turned to James for reassurance and comfort. She saw he was dead. She bent over him chafing his cold hands, desperately trying to coax a spark of life back into the flaccid body, only to find it was not James lying there after all, but Jeffrey. Her efforts to rouse him became frenzied—she begged him to wake up, to live. The people crowding round the bed began to laugh at her. The priest advanced, raising the cross as if he would strike her with it. She hid her face and wept—and the hot tears had woken her.

When she slept again, it was worse. Her old terror dream, the one that had begun to prey on her after James was killed and which for a couple of years now had left her in peace, returned in all its original force.

She was trying to run from some horror. There were wings on her back, but they could not lift her high enough to carry her to safety. Half flying, half running, she rushed through a grey, empty landscape of fells, and crags, and dry-stone walls. She came upon the ruins of an old house, and slipped inside to cower down among the rubble, only to discover that the wall behind her was missing, and she could clearly be seen. She could hear the pursuit coming nearer and nearer. Putting out all her strength she ran outside and tried to beat the clumsy wings to fly away, but she could not move them at all. Terror seized her. Stones were clattering only yards away. She was running again, but her feet were heavy and her legs gave way. She fell, and began to roll, slowly, down and down. Cold hands clawed at her, and she screamed out in revulsion . . .

It was a real scream, and it woke her completely. She lay there sweating and shaking, and sobbing in a misery of fear so abject that no rational thought could find a foothold.

The bedroom door opened softly.

"Verity? You in trouble?"

She quietened, like a panicking horse at the sound of kindness in a human voice, but she could not reply—no more than she could control the trembling of her limbs, or the rasp of breath in her constricted throat.

Someone came over to the bed.

"Verity? Has something scared you? Are you okay?" A hand touched her wet cheek.

She could not help herself. She clung to that warm, questing hand as if she were drowning and it alone could save her. She needed its warmth and life. Its partner began to stroke her hair, gently, rhythmically, until her harsh breathing subsided into the whimpering of a child comforted by its mother. And when the owner of the hands slid into bed beside her, and the rhythmic stroking was transferred to her neck, and breasts, and flanks, she could only cling to him to keep him close to her, afraid that he would go and leave her alone again in the dark. All she could feel was an overwhelming gratitude for this proof that he and she were alive, as his warmth carried her up and away from the desolation of her dream, and his strength took her higher and higher until at last her body seemed to melt into his, and he stifled her cry with his hand, prolonging the shudders that ran through her until she lay limp and relaxed beneath him. Then he moved to lie beside her, still holding her in his arms. Since those initial questions he had not uttered another word, and neither had she.

She kept her eyes closed. She did not want to speak. The memory of the nightmare was still lurking at the back of her mind even as she absorbed the solid comfort of his presence. It was a long time since it had visited her with such ferocity. She had begun to hope that she was free of it for ever.

It had first come to her a few nights after the police had knocked on the door to break the news to her that James was dead. He had been blown up by a terrorist bomb as he walked past a Jewish restaurant during a business trip to Paris. Others had been badly injured, but no-one else was killed. Only James.

For days she had been unable to accept the facts they had gently unfolded to her. The obscenity of such an end could not possibly have befallen the quiet, gentle man who had been her husband, and the father of the child whose limbs had recently begun to flicker inside her. James the shy, James the lover of Mozart and Vivaldi, James who hated violence—had been reduced in seconds to a mere spatter of flesh and fragments of bone on a foreign pavement. In seconds. That was all it had taken. And those who had deprived him of his life had not even known him.

It was unbelievable, unacceptable. He could not have gone without saying goodbye. Not gone for ever. He had loved her. People who loved did not just disappear. Not for ever.

But James had not come back. And the dream had begun to visit her, fastening upon her sleep until she had been, like tonight, afraid to close her eyes. Then it had begun to spread into her days as well until the lines between dream and reality had begun to soften and blur. She had grown more and more haggard. She could not talk to anyone, for the simple reason that there was no-one to talk to. In her monthly visit to the ante-natal clinic, alone among a crowd of other women, no-one had noticed. She could not eat, she could not sleep—there was no comfort anywhere. Only when she miscarried, and was taken into hospital, and she finally broke down, did they at last see the distress they had been too busy to notice.

She had been lucky. For if the help had come too late to save the baby, it was at least in time to save her. In the long months that followed she had learned to acknowledge her pain, and discovered that it was possible to live with it. She could look the Gorgon in the face and not lose her humanity. Gradually she had inched back up the rocky slope to health of mind. The nightmare had continued to visit her from time to time, but with ever-decreasing effect. When she had moved to Wales it had ceased altogether.

But tonight its strength had been as great as in the days immediately after James's death. It was as if its force had merely been lying dormant, slowly accumulating.

She opened her eyes and stared out into the darkness. She was increasingly conscious of a great gratitude. Whatever she might feel the next day, the man beside her had rescued her from the nightmare, and for now that sufficed. Her body had been pleasured and comforted. While she lay in his arms the fear could not touch her.

Quite suddenly she fell asleep, a deep sleep this time, without dreams. When she opened her eyes again it was morning outside—a thin line of bright light was visible at the edges of the curtains. She was alone. For a moment, still half asleep, she lay smiling with pleasure at the thought that she was on holiday, and in her sister's house. Then she remembered the night, and the smile vanished, to be succeeded by a look of horror. What had she done?

She sat up, the better to consider.

It was certainly a situation that she had never, in her furthest flights of fancy, imagined could arise. If it had not been for the dream, she told herself fiercely, it would never have happened. On the other hand, she had learned in the past that there was almost always a reason for the dream's coming, even if she could not always discover what it was. Perhaps this time it was a warning that she was not really strong enough for what she was trying to do. The scream for help had been a deep, instinctive reaction—and Leo had merely responded to it as any man would.

She frowned. It would not do. Leo was not any man. He was a successful opportunist, and last night he had not hesitated to take what seemed to be on offer. It was her own reaction that appalled her now.

She had been right to distrust and dislike him all those years ago. She remembered him as he had been on the day of his wedding, standing tall and serious beside his glowing bride, gravely repeating his vows. She had hated him then. She had not wanted even to attend the wedding, much less to share Hope's limelight as the solitary bridesmaid, but she had not been able to refuse, and mar her sister's happiness. And when, after signing the register, he had tried to claim a kiss from her, she had drawn back, white-faced. They had laughed at her—but she had not let him kiss her.

Childish it might have seemed, but children often see very clearly. It was obvious now that Hope had been hurt, and hurt again during the eleven years of their marriage. She was probably far from being the only other woman to succumb to his extraordinary sexual magnetism—which did not excuse her in the least. Tears rose to her eyes—hurting Hope had been the last thing she had intended on accepting the invitation to Toronto.

All she could do was to make sure that it never happened again —and to make equally sure that her sister never found out. She would have to contrive to live through the next twenty-four hours without arousing suspicion. After that she would move in with Jeffrey. There was at least no guilt to clog her relationship with him, unless she counted the fact that now, albeit unconsciously, she had cheated on him. She could no longer think exclusively of him. She frowned unhappily. The last thing she wanted was to hurt him. It was beginning to seem as if whatever she did she was going to hurt somebody—the choice was only a matter of degree. Moving out would mean offending Hope and snubbing Leo—but perhaps not irrevocably, in time all might still be mended. Whereas if she stayed, all would be destroyed, and for ever. Surely it was better to cheat on Jeffrey—just a little. One day she might be able to explain. She could not imagine living a lie with him.

There was a tap on the door, and she hastily dragged the bed-clothes into some semblance of order. Hope appeared, carrying a tray.

"It's your own personal tea-lady again. I expect you've been awake for ages. This is to help you make it through to breakfast."

She set the tray on the bed, and perched beside it.

"Leo and the girls want to know if you're game to face a trip to Niagara today? Leo had intended to make it tomorrow, but you've got that business appointment. He's very keen to fit it in before we go off to the cottage at the weekend—says that if 'tis to be done 'twere best done quickly. Niagara's just another waterfall to the likes of Leo. I said I'd see how you felt. You may still be feeling too tired . . ."

She looked at her intently. Verity did her best to smile

84

reassuringly, but behind the smile she was squirming beneath that intent look.

"I'm fine. I'd love to go. I didn't sleep very well, I'm afraid—but that's only normal the first night."

"Yes, I expect it is."

There was an awkward silence. She tried to cover it.

"I was disturbed, too, at the thought of there being an intruder in the grounds. Did your man see any more of him?"

"Nope. It was probably just some old hobo lost his way. So I can tell them it's on, can I?"

Verity nodded.

"Is it far?"

"Not very. You'd better get up as soon as you've finished your tea—Leo wants to make a day of it and show you Niagara-on-the-Lake as well. It's the usual tourist run. We'll be taking a picnic lunch which should make you very popular with your nieces—picnics being Nelly's speciality. Breakfast's out on the terrace, by the way—we always eat out there when it's fine. See you later."

"I'll be right with you. Thanks for the tea, Hope."

She finished it thoughtfully. She had an uncomfortable feeling that she had just been subjected to a very thorough examination, and that Hope's eyes had missed no detail of the rumpled bed, and the torn strap on her nightdress. Leo had said that she took sleeping pills. There was surely no reason why she should suspect anything . . .

The proposed expedition came as a distinct relief. The day ahead would pass far more quickly, and with the triplets around it would surely be easier to keep her distance from Leo. She bit her lip as she thought of him. She wished she did not have to see him again. At this moment she felt she almost hated him. Yet she could not altogether forget the feeling of completeness she had known as she lay beside him. She pushed away the thought, and tried to conjure up the image of Jeffrey in its place, but the night in Glasgow now seemed even less substantial than the nightmare. Already her main memory of him was fading into a vague impression of kindly humour, and gentleness. Leo had been gentle, too, but in a different way . . .

A little later, when she joined the family at breakfast, she took great care to avoid his eye. He did not appear to notice, nor did he pay her

85

any special attention, to her relief. He was devoting all his to the triplets—fielding their incessant questions, supplying their needs, checking their excesses while Hope merely sat gazing aloofly out over the gardens. For the first time Verity felt a prickle of irritation, and could not help wondering if some, at least, of this studied detachment was not being assumed for her own benefit. It was difficult to imagine it continuing permanently. And if it was for her benefit, what did it mean? If she was trying to tell her something, what was it?

The morning sun had turned the surface of the pool into a sheet of light. The gardens were vivid in the clear atmosphere. The grouped trees seemed to be posing artistically against the acrylic green of the lawns, where sprinklers were already at work, and the roses in the adjacent flowerbeds appeared to be visibly unfurling their petals to catch the cool spray. It was a beautiful place. Hope, who had once had nothing, must surely derive some comfort from living in it. No-one could be wholly unhappy living in such surroundings. Whatever else he might have done, Leo had at least given her this.

She risked a glance at him.

He was wearing brightly patterned shorts, and a dark brown sports shirt that set off his powerful arms and neck. A white baseball cap was tilted on his mass of ginger curls. He was smiling as he listened to his daughters, and she noticed the firmness of his lips and chin. She could not help, albeit reluctantly, admiring him as a physical specimen—rather as one admires an animal built for speed. He had, it seemed, been designed for prompt decisions, for action—for survival. It was pointless to blame such a being for the destruction he left behind him. He obeyed his instincts. The best hope for weaker creatures who found themselves in his path was to hide.

Not all weaker creatures. She watched as one of the little girls climbed into his lap and laughingly pulled his face down to hers. The two red heads close together gave her a sudden, unexpected pang —she could not have said why.

He looked up and saw her eyes on him. To her surprise she saw him colour deeply, and turn away to speak to another of the girls who was pulling at his arm. It was not at all the reaction she would have expected.

She ate her breakfast in silence. She was beginning to feel as if she had lost all sense of direction. She seemed to be travelling under

86

completely unknown stars. In the end, longing for reassurance, she touched Hope on the arm.

"What time are you planning to leave?"

"Leave?"

"I thought you said we were going to Niagara."

"Did I? Oh—yes—sure. Forgive me, I'm a zombie at breakfast. It must be the sleeping pills. Ask Leo. He makes all the decisions round here—or hadn't you noticed?"

"I reckon we ought to hit the trail in about an hour. Nelly's doing the lunch right now—it's why she's not here. I need to put in a call to the office before we leave."

"Bankruptcy looms, does it?" Hope's lip curled.

"Big joke. I can't help wondering what you'd say if it did."

"It might surprise you."

"It's quite hard to surprise me. I'll be in the study. You'd better get the kids ready—Nelly can't do everything." He disappeared into the house.

Hope stayed where she was, making no attempt to restrain the triplets, who ran in noisy pursuit of him, ignoring her.

"I don't know about you, but I loathe breakfast," she said to Verity, pouring them both more coffee. "It's the time of day when I can least stand the family."

Verity understood that this was intended as some sort of apology. She shrugged.

"I rather like it myself."

She thought of her quiet early mornings at home in Pembroke-shire, and was suddenly flooded by a wave of longing for all she had left behind.

Her cottage stood on the outskirts of the village, a position which gave her as much privacy as she chose. She knew everyone in the tightly-knit community, and everyone knew her. Thanks to the fact that she owned an excellent singing voice, she had been accepted far more quickly than was usual, for her deep contralto had filled a much deplored gap in the local choir, and she attended rehearsals faith-fully. The villagers had soon grown used to seeing her sitting at her easel, absorbed in her painting. Some even bought her work, if only because their own homes figured in it. She belonged there now. She fitted in. It was where she had grown whole again.

She looked round at the swimming pool, the resplendent gardens, the gracious house. Here she was alien—alien and somehow threatened in her innermost self. It struck her then that perhaps this was what Hope felt too. After all, they came from the same background. Perhaps Hope, condemned by Leo to live in this country where everything seemed to be on a grander scale, also felt lost, and even defeated.

A black squirrel ran down from a tree a few yards away and sat on the paving stones, observing them. It was glossier and bigger than the thin grey creatures that visited her apple trees at home, as if it had grown up better able to fend for itself. Its eye was speculative as it waited to see what they might have to give. Absurdly, it made her feel more displaced than ever.

"It looks a very successful squirrel," she remarked to Hope.

But Hope, though she was looking at it, was smiling at some thought of her own, and did not appear to have heard.

A few hours later she was sitting beside Leo again in the front seat of the Mercedes. She had asked to be allowed to go in the back, with the children, but Hope would not hear of it, insisting that she sit where, she maintained, she would have the better view. Afraid of appearing to make an issue of it, she had weakly acquiesced.

There was, in fact, no view to speak of. The road was long, straight, and wearisomely congested with heavy traffic. There was a momentary interest as they drove skywards over the great, twisting flyover near Hamilton, but even there she could only see the parapets. At least the conditions had the virtue of requiring Leo's full attention, for which she was grateful.

He drove with a slight smile on his face, as if pleased at his own skill as he cut from lane to lane in a manner which would have earned him general opprobrium on a British motorway. She found herself hating that satisfied smile. She hated, too, the way her body was once again registering his nearness.

She touched the big straw handbag propped against her feet. The icon, concealed in the make-up bag, was inside it. She had not dared to leave it in the house during her absence. The feel of the rough straw steadied her. She had a job to do—the one she had hijacked from the unwilling Jeffrey, leaving him all the anxieties of the role of on-looker—a job which needed all her own skill and concentration. Even so, she wished that the drive, and the day with it, would soon come to an end. All she wanted was to put as much distance as possible between herself and Leo.

"Not far now. We'll see the river any moment." Hope was reassuring the bored triplets in the back of the car.

"There it is! There it is!" Their shout came in perfect unison a few minutes later.

The Mercedes had turned into a broad thoroughfare. With a sudden, childish thrill, Verity caught sight, through the distant trees, of a grey mass moving at implacable speed, its surface dashed with foam. For a moment, as the car halted in the traffic, she forgot both Leo and the icon, and could only gaze, struck by the contrast of the power of the moving water, and the fragility of the trees that grew beside it.

They cruised slowly along the boulevard towards the car parks. She was pleasantly surprised by the colourful flowerbeds, and broad lawns. She had been expecting something more like Cheddar Gorge, with its cheap-jack shops and tawdry souvenir stands blowing raspberries at the grandeur of the great cliffs above. She said as much. Leo grinned.

"Don't you worry, we can do it too," he said, "—we're just being careful not to show you that bit. We have our self-respect."

It was, Verity reflected as they moved slowly on, as if those responsible for building the solid stone ramparts, topped by stout but not ungraceful iron railings, for laying out the parks and planting the trees had been trying to demonstrate some dignity of their own in the face of the huge, threatening force they had tamed. They had mastered it, but they could not outlive it, though their stone walls might outlast the trees.

She was glad to get out of the car. The air was fresh, and she inhaled great lungfuls of it as they strolled over the grass toward the Falls. She took care to keep the triplets between herself and Leo, who was carrying the lunch box.

"Who are those?" She pointed to an outlandishly dressed knot of people leaning against the parapet some way ahead.

The men wore shabby black suits and what looked like floppy bowler hats. The women were in grey or blue cotton dresses which hung well below their knees to reveal, with anything but coquetry, thick black stockings and clumsy shoes. Their hair was hidden inside disfiguring close-fitting black bonnets, not unlike swimming caps. There were children with them—the girls in the same ugly bonnets —children with bare feet, their toes a bright, cold red on the pavements wet with spray.

"They're Mennonites," Leo answered her. "It's a religious sect that settled round here just before the French Revolution. They go in for the simple life—no cars, no TV sets, no empire-building. All horse-and-buggy-and-do-it-yourself. Everything else has the devil's hand in it."

"They look as if they're in mourning."

Verity's tone was disapproving. There was something chilling about the sombre clothes and austere faces here in this holiday, honeymoon place, with its crowds of casually dressed tourists with their cameras and their picnic baskets.

She wondered how they would react if she were to show them the icon. No doubt they would see it, with its gold paint, its exquisite frame and its jewels, as the handiwork of the devil, a piece of idolatry. They would not be the first to do so. They would be deaf to its message, blind to its beauty, and oblivious of its history. And now for the first time she wondered if the people in Poland had not been naive in believing that their treasure would be safe and honoured here. At first, perhaps—but for how long? Wherever extremes existed, it would never be entirely safe. All they would gain was a little time.

They reached the parapet at a spot just above the Falls. Looking down, she saw the great river rushing towards the cliff. Instinctively she took Hope's arm. She needed to feel someone close beside her. She had never before seen anything so overwhelming in the sheer vastness of its power. It made her aware more than ever of the puniness of all the people standing there watching it, of the fragility of their bones, and the brief flicker that was their minds.

One of the triplets pulled her sleeve.

"A mother dropped her baby over here last year."

"And what happened?"

The child made an expressive gesture.

"Splatt!"

Verity shivered. Were they all thinking the same thoughts as they watched the water slide towards the edge?

For once, Hope reacted.

"Let's move further along, beneath the Falls. Standing here makes me feel dizzy. One moment the river's there, the next it's not. It's like falling off the edge of the world."

Arms still linked, they strolled along the pavement behind the line of people leaning over the rail. The triplets danced in their wake, their identical appearance attracting an attention to which they were obviously accustomed, and which, Verity suspected, they very much enjoyed. Leo brought up the rear.

He called out to them to stop, explaining as they turned that they were now in the best position to gain an overall view.

Spray formed a dense cloud around them, settling on hair and clothes, cooling the air. Again Verity shivered. She had no head for heights, and she had to force herself to look down at the tiny pleasure steamers far below, impudently advancing almost to the foot of the great foaming wall of water before retreating to a safer distance. Their decks crawled with what looked like black-fly—the oilskins and sou'westers of sightseers intrepid enough to trust themselves to fallible human machinery.

"Want to ride in one?" Leo, seeing her fascination, spoke in her ear. "The kids tried it last time we came. It's quite something."

She shook her head. She was carrying too great a responsibility to play games. She opened her mouth to explain, but she never spoke the words.

Someone stumbled against her, so violently that she lost her balance and fell heavily against one of the Mennonite women leaning over the rail beside her, a small child in her arms. At the same time, her handbag was wrenched brutally from her grasp.

Frenziedly she caught at the strap, clinging to it, struggling to recover her balance. Someone behind her screamed. She herself gave a hoarse cry.

No-one seemed to notice her plight. All eyes were fixed on the spot where she had been standing. Still she hung on to the strap, until her assailant, with a vicious twist that all but pulled her arm from its socket, broke free and raced away.

She forgot fear now. Anger took its place. Furiously she set off in pursuit. The icon could not be taken from her so easily. She was a fast runner, but the thief was a young man, with longer legs. The distance between them was gradually increasing when absurdly, miraculously, he tripped over a tree root and went sprawling. Even so, he was on his feet and on his way again, before she could catch up, scooping up his booty as he ran. She was about to put on a desperate spurt when she noticed what he had not—something small and flat had fallen from the bag, something oblong and brightly-coloured —the make-up bag. She had pounced on it, and slipped it into her pocket as he glanced back to see how much ground he had lost, before racing on to be lost among the strolling groups of tourists. She thought she saw him leap into a moving car, but she was not sure.

She did not care. It was not important. Her heart was thudding so hard she could not breathe, and the blood sang in her ears. Afraid that she might faint, she stumbled over to the tree whose root had interceded so providentially on her behalf, patted its trunk gratefully, and leaned against it to recover. Reaction was setting in. Her knees were weak, and her whole body was shaking. It was like her nightmare—she had not been able to run fast enough then, either.

She looked round for Hope, Leo and the triplets. She needed their support. She could not think why none of them had followed to help her.

The crowd by the rail seemed to have swelled considerably, and now she saw a number of people running to join it. Even as she watched it parted to allow the passage of a number of men carrying a ladder taken from a nearby building. She caught a glimpse of them lowering it carefully over the parapet, and securing it with ropes.

Suddenly, she remembered the scream she had heard behind her as the thief dragged her along. It had not, then, been on her behalf. Sweat beaded her forehead as she tried to picture what had happened. She had fallen with all her weight against a woman—one of those down-trodden Mennonite women—and the woman had been holding a small child sitting on the rail in front of her. She clutched now at the tree for support. The triplet's words rang in her ears.

"Last year a mother dropped her baby over here."

Sick and faint, she stood there, unable to move, her eyes fixed on the silent, staring crowd. If the icon, however indirectly, had caused another death she knew she would not want to have anything more to do with it. And if she herself had harmed another child—she could not bear the thought.

She knew she must join the other onlookers, and face it, whatever it was—but still she leaned against the tree, as if trying to draw strength from it. This time, however, it could not help her. This time nothing and no-one could.

Even at this distance she could feel the tension of the crowd, though she could not see what was happening. Tears were sliding in a constant, unnoticed stream down her cheeks. There was a hard knot in her chest. She tried to will herself to walk across the bright green grass to get a better view, but she knew that if she let go of the tree she would fall. She could only lean there and wait as the nightmare continued.

A burst of cheering jerked her to her feet. A surge of hope galvanized her, and now she ran to push her way into the fringe of the crowd. People were exclaiming and hugging each other.

"That wonderful, wonderful guy!"

Squeezing, squirming, shoving and apologizing, she fought her way forwards towards the focus of attention—just in time to see Leo, a small, bonneted child in his arms, step over the rail to the safety of the promenade. Eager hands stretched out to seize him and help him down. Cheer after cheer saluted him. Women struggled to touch him. Men thumped him on the back. Streaked with dirt and sweat, his ginger curls in a glinting halo round his head like some medieval saint, he grinned modestly, and handed the baby back to its hysterical mother.

"Take it easy folks. I just happened to be on the spot. We were lucky, that's all."

The Mennonites did not believe in luck. Several of them sank to their knees, their lips moving in ardent prayer, leaving Leo standing looking uncomfortable.

The triplets rushed in to the rescue, bursting through the crowd to smother him with enthusiastic hugs and kisses that released a fresh salvo from a battery of cameras.

"You were *terrific!*"

"You're so *brave!*"

"Daddy, we're so glad you're *safe!*"

Squeezed and jostled, Verity watched it all. Tears were still

93

trickling down her cheeks, but she made no move to brush them away. For the second time in twenty-four hours, all she could feel towards Leo was gratitude, but this time it was a gratitude so profound that she knew she could never lightly pass judgement on him again.

Then the irony of it all struck her. The joke, she felt, would have appealed to Jeffrey, with his writer's relish for the incongruous and the absurd. He might even have enjoyed the fact that the joke was on him, too. Quietly, helplessly, she began to laugh. Her shoulders were shaking, and she was fighting for breath when an arm, gripping her round the shoulder, steadied her. It was Hope.

"Let's get out of this. Leo can handle it. I don't know about you, but I could use a drink. Come on—there's a bench over there, we'll open the picnic box."

"What about the children?"

"Wild horses couldn't drag them away from their father right now. They'll come when they're hungry and realize we've got the food. Good thing I picked up the box."

There was no trace of emotion in her voice. Verity looked at her curiously as they sat down. Whatever Hope's feelings had been when she saw her husband risking his life for another woman's child, they were not apparent. She was very pale, but her hands, as she opened the big Thermos lunch box, were perfectly steady. She drew out a bottle of wine, and rummaged for glasses and a corkscrew.

"I could have used a Scotch, but this'll have to do. Canadian, of course, grown by one of Leo's clients, naturally. The effect's the same."

She handed Verity a glassful, and poured another for herself.

"Cheers."

"To the hero."

"Crazy bastard!"

It was like a small explosion. The feelings were obvious enough now. Her eyes were glittering with anger. She drained her glass and poured herself another.

"Hope, what on earth do you mean? It was an incredibly brave thing to do. He saved that child's life."

"Brave my aunt Fanny! Like he said himself, he was lucky. He acted instinctively. I don't call that brave. He just wanted to shine. He always does."

"You can't be serious. You're just upset."

"What do you know about it? I wonder what you'd be saying now if he'd been killed trying to save that moronic female's brat."

"I know I'd still have said he was brave." Verity could not help her voice faltering a little.

"You see? You're not so sure. You're just blinded by his success. Everyone is—always. It's all that matters. No-one stops to question his values. Leo just backs his luck, anywhere and everywhere, and he always wins. Like back there. He was in the right place at the right time."

"What did happen exactly—I didn't see?"

"I didn't see everything myself—I was looking the other way. One moment you were there and everything was normal, the next everyone seemed to be falling over. You'd vanished and the Mennonite dame had dropped her kid over the rail. Didn't you hear her yell?"

"I didn't realize that was the reason."

"It only fell a little way—the cliff isn't quite sheer just there —before it hit a ridge and got hooked up in some bushes. And while everyone stood around with their mouths open trying to work out what to do, who should take it upon himself to be Tarzan and climb down in hot pursuit, without so much as a piece of string round his middle in case he fell, but my heroic husband. I don't know how he thought he was going to climb back up again with the kid in his arms—but of course it all worked out in the end. Just as he knew it would. You don't keep the Leos of this world down for long."

Verity felt it was wiser to say nothing.

"How come you didn't see it yourself? What happened to you?"

"I was busy being mugged. That's how I came to fall against that woman. Some kind soul grabbed my bag."

"We'd better report it to the police. Have you lost anything valuable? I meant to warn you—there's been an outbreak of pick-pocketing and mugging recently."

"Some money. My compact camera's the worst loss. Surely it's hardly worth reporting—I'm not likely to get anything back. The police would most likely shrug and tell me I should have been more careful."

The last thing she wanted was to have any contact with the police. The icon seemed to be weighing heavy in her pocket. All she wanted was anonymity.

"I daresay Leo will insist. He won't like the idea of anyone mugging his sister-in-law when she was with him—loss of face, you know. If he doesn't hurry we'll have drunk all the wine—he won't like that, either. Damn him!" She drank another glass.

"I don't understand why you're so angry."

"Of course you don't. You're free, aren't you? You can go where you like, do what you like. You've got no-one to worry about."

"No."

Hope paused.

"That was ham-fisted of me. I'm sorry. But it's true that you can't understand. You've no idea what it's like to be tied to someone for eleven years and feel yourself being slowly suffocated while they flourish . . . There's nothing more destructive. I feel as if the life is being gradually squeezed out of me . . ."

"Surely you're exaggerating. Surely it doesn't have to be like that. You've got so much. Those three beautiful children—they must mean something to you—"

Hope looked at her scornfully.

"I knew you wouldn't understand. There's no reason why you should."

"You're my sister, and I care about you. I'd like to help."

The memory of the previous night flashed across her mind, and she flushed darkly. Hope merely laughed.

"You already have helped—more than you know. You needn't worry—I'm learning to look after myself. I'm working on it. This little episode merely serves to turn up the heat . . ."

"Mommy! Mommy!"

It was a relief to Verity to see the triplets hurtling towards them. What insight she had gained in the last few minutes had not been reassuring.

"We've been looking for you *every*where!"

"We're *star*ving!"

"Where've you *been?*"

"We wanted you in the *pho*tos."

"They're going to be in all the *pap*ers."

"We're gonna be *fam*ous!"

"Can we please have something to eat?"

"Verity, did you catch that man?"

"Has he got your purse?"

Three pairs of eyes at least had missed nothing. They fired their questions in strict rotation, as if their minds worked in perfect synchronization. The effect was unnerving—it made Verity feel slightly dizzy. She began to understand how easy it would be to feel inadequate in the face of demands always couched in triplicate.

Hope merely cut them short unceremoniously.

"Do you want to eat here, or shall we go look for somewhere quieter?"

"Here! Here!"

"We're too hungry to wait."

"Just smell those rolls—Nelly makes the most heavenly fillings."

"Here comes Dad!"

"Wasn't he *won*derful!"

"He's a *hero*!"

They clustered round the picnic box, waiting impatiently for the distribution of its contents. Hope ignored them. She was watching the approach of Leo, smiling acknowledgement to waving groups of admirers.

"The kids want to eat here, but you may want to get away from all this," she said in greeting. Nothing more. No word of congratulation or endearment. Verity felt a rush of sympathy for him. He looked quizzically at his wife.

"I guess I could use some food—a drink too, if you've left me any. We'd better eat here—we've still got to report the theft of Verity's bag."

"You saw then?"

"Sure I did. I'd just turned to run after you when the kid fell. I take it the bastard got away?"

She nodded.

"Have you lost much?"

"Money and a camera," Hope replied for her, handing him a roll and pouring a glass of wine from a much depleted bottle. "Not a very good start to her holiday."

Verity passed the wine to Leo, and then on impulse lifted her own glass.

"To a brave deed."

Hope looked stonily in front of her. Verity took no notice, and quietly drank the toast. Leo gave her a quick smile that was almost shy.

She could have slapped Hope for her lack of simple generosity. Leo had dared to act where others had hesitated. To dispute his achievement was meanness of spirit. She was forced, however reluctantly, to admire the immediacy of his reaction. Whatever else he was, he was quick, and alive, like the flame of his hair. He could warm all those around him, or he could consume them, if Hope was to be believed.

Suddenly aware that she was ravenously hungry, she turned her attention to the lunch. Nelly had lived up to her reputation. The home-baked rolls, with their spicy, delicate fillings, the glazed chicken-legs, the small bowls of exotically dressed salad, and, to finish, the exquisite little concoctions of macaroon filled with a mixture of cream, and nuts, and liqueur made a feast worthy of a more sophisticated setting. Everyone's face wore a dreamy, introspective look by the time the last crumb was eaten.

Hope was the first to rouse herself. She eyed the knots of sightseers gazing at them from a distance with distaste.

"We should have found somewhere less public."

Leo wiped his mouth and belched contentedly.

"Nelly's lunches taste like manna wherever you eat them. I needed that. We'd better deal with the handbag right away. We should have done it before this."

"It can't make much difference. They never catch them. He's probably in Hamilton by now. Do you want coffee here—or later?"

"Later." Leo got to his feet.

"Do we really have to go to the police? I'd much rather not." Verity put in her own appeal.

"Look, both of you—a crime's been committed and it ought to be reported. The place'll get a bad name if pockets are picked and purses stolen and no-one does anything about it. I didn't see a single patrolman around when that kid fell. It's not good enough and I intend to tell them so. I've already said as much to the Press . . ."

"The *Press*?"

"Sure. You can trust *them* to be on the spot—it's how they stay in business. What are you looking so worried about?"

"I hate publicity, that's all." Everything seemed to be conspiring

98

to defeat her plan of lying low until the time came to meet Jeffrey. For the first time it occurred to her that she might be no better equipped to play the leading role in all this than he was, for all her experience and proven powers of survival. Certainly, he could hardly have made more mistakes.

Leo saw she was upset. His face softened.

"It's just a formality. I'll play it down all I can—there's no reason to be scared. Come on you guys, there's nothing left. Let's get it over with, then we'll take Verity for a drive to Niagara-on-the-Lake. There's a lot of Canada still to show her, so lead the way."

It had been painless enough, Verity reflected thankfully as, sitting in the passenger seat beside Leo once more, they drove smoothly along the pleasant road to Niagara-on-the-Lake. Huge fruit orchards stretched away into the distance, the trees heavy now with plums and peaches. She had had no idea that anything so delicate as a peach could be grown in so severe a climate, and had made the mistake of saying so to Leo, thereby incurring a long, and largely incomprehensible lecture on geography, which was probably at least partly responsible for her present somnolent state.

The police, as she had hoped, had been far more interested in Leo's exploit than in the loss of her bag, and the short interview had ended in a great deal of congratulation and back-slapping, to the delight of the triplets.

She herself was feeling more and more unsure about the mugging. Everyone else seemed to be accepting it as a normal, everyday occurrence—one of the hazards of visiting a tourist centre. It might well have been just that. The trouble was that she could not be certain. It was perfectly possible that it had been another move in an elaborate and deadly game of tag—in which case it was possible that Leo had unwittingly done her a great service by stepping into the limelight, and by letting it be known that she was under his protection. The enemy, she reminded herself, also preferred anonymity. The glamour and publicity now surrounding his name might well give them pause before attacking her again.

Suddenly she found herself longing to take him fully into her confidence. Surreptitiously, she observed his head profiled against the passing countryside, studying the strong lines of jaw and mouth.

He would take the weight of responsibility off her—her life could return to normal, she could enjoy her holiday.

He turned his head. Their eyes met. Every nerve in her seemed to quiver, and she looked quickly away.

She knew then that it was out of the question. In no way must she allow him a further foothold in her life. She could not undo what had already happened, but she must not allow it to be repeated. She loved her sister. She repeated the words firmly to herself. She and Leo might be having problems, but they must work them out together, without adding further complications. The faster she moved out of their house, the better.

"Hope tells me you want to go to Toronto tomorrow for your appointment. Would you like a ride? I need to call at the office so I have to go anyway. We could look round for a replacement for your camera."

He was not going to make it easy for her.

"That's very kind of you," she said stiffly. "It would be a great help—though I'm afraid I'll be too taken up for shopping. I'll make my own way back afterwards."

"You might find that tricky," Hope put her word in. "Better arrange to meet up somewhere."

Verity did not reply. She could not. It was almost as if they were conspiring against her. She felt unutterably lost. It was all too complicated, and she was so very tired. Nothing was straightforward any more.

She found she was gradually being submerged by a rising tide of sleep. Her eyes closed. She forced them open again, and struggled to take an intelligent interest in the scenery, but her head was growing heavier and heavier, and before long fell back against the headrest. She gave up then. It was, after all, the only real escape that was possible.

She had rarely felt such relief as when she finally found herself in the privacy of her room that night.

It had been one of the longest and most difficult evenings she had ever spent. Everyone had been out of sorts. She herself had had a headache after sleeping in the car. The children had bickered and whined until even Leo had lost patience and summoned Nelly to take them off to bed. If it had not been for the arrival of some friends dropping by for drinks, the tension and antagonism would, she felt, have become unbearable. After that it had been merely boring, for she could not concentrate on the conversation, most of which, being about baseball, went over her head anyway, and she was too weary and anxious about the meeting of the next day to make any effective contribution.

Now at last she was alone. The traumatic day was behind her. Whatever had gone wrong, the icon was still safely in her possession. Tomorrow, it would start on the last stage of its journey.

It occurred to her that she must find a better way of concealing it. She had no other suitable handbag, and she could not very well leave it in the patch pocket of her skirt where she had thrust it after the mugging—it would be far too vulnerable in a crowd. She thought hard, but for a long time could not think of an answer to the problem. In the end, she decided to make a pouch from the material of a denim skirt, that she could sling round her waist under whatever she was wearing. That way, they would have to strip-search her before finding it. A chill ran down her back at the thought. She hoped it would not come to that. She tried to comfort herself: no doubt once she was with Jeffrey again everything would fall into place once more—she would not feel so alone, and so frighteningly vulnerable. In only a few more hours they would be together again. They would plan it all out together as they had once before. He had the eye for detail that she lacked. He would know how to select the best path out of danger. Together they would protect each other. She did not feel threatened by him, nor experienced any fear that he might take her over, engulf her in his own personality. They would work as equal partners. But it was becoming curiously difficult to picture him as she had first seen him on the plane—or in the hotel room. She could remember the sandy hair, the high cheekbones, the shy smile—but all the colour seemed to have drained from her memory. The face seemed to grow fainter and fainter, and, like it or not, another would superimpose itself—Leo's.

Angrily she took out her sewing kit, and picked up the small scissors. Then she paused. She went to the door, hesitated for a few moments, and firmly locked it. There must be no more unexpected interruptions—not now, and not later.

Chapter 7

Jeffrey opened his eyes—only to shut them again quickly. The light from a bare electric bulb sliced through his eyeballs to meet the throbbing in his head in one searing burst of pain. Gingerly, he touched his scalp. His hair was matted and sticky.

Shading his eyes with his hand, he tried again.

This time he saw he was lying on a decrepit mattress on a rusty iron bedstead set against a wall. There was no other furniture in the room except a bucket. The room itself was little bigger than a cubbyhole. Dirt and debris littered the bare floor. The walls had once been whitewashed, but this had flaked away to reveal plaster fantastically patterned by mould. A tall, narrow window was secured by a wooden shutter with a padlocked bar. There was no way of telling where-abouts in the building it was located—any more than there was of knowing whether it was night or day, for his watch was gone. Time and space had no meaning here. Sun and moon had been replaced by that one ugly, relentless bulb.

He listened intently. He could hear no sound. The silence was unnerving. The slow beat of his heart seemed to be the only measure left.

With an immense effort, he raised himself on one elbow in an attempt to sit up. At once, the pain seemed to explode in his head, and a roaring filled his ears. He fell back unconscious.

When he came to again the electric bulb was still glaring. Nothing whatsoever had changed.

He had no idea how long he had been lying there. He ran his tongue over his cracked lips. His whole mouth felt swollen and dry, and there was a jagged stump in place of one of his side teeth. Every inch of his body was aching.

Something, he could not have said what, some shapeless, un-identifiable anxiety deep at the back of his mind urged him to try once more to sit up. Cautiously, doggedly, he levered himself until he could prop his back against the wall. Then he saw the jug of water on the floor near the bed.

It meant another struggle, but the drink revived him, and lit a match flame of hope. The water must have been left for a reason. He had not simply been left to die. Leaning his head against the cool plaster he tried to thread a way through the fog that filled his mind, searching for the path that led to the incomprehensible present. But the fog, far from thinning, grew thicker. He felt sick and dizzy. He would have abandoned the effort but for the insistence of the inner voice that would not let him rest, and finally spurred him into a foolhardy attempt to rise to his feet—which ended abruptly in another plunge into total blackness.

When he next opened his eyes he felt stronger. He drank more water, and, dipping his fingers into the jug, moistened his eyelids and forehead. He realized that he was desperately hungry, but whatever the reasoning that had led to leaving him the water had not extended to food.

The fog in his mind was breaking up. He had been in England. Scenes, faces appeared. There had been a party. They were pub-lishing *The Avocado Affair*, and were predicting large sales. They had made a big fuss of him. So was he still in London? No. He had boarded a plane. Something had been wrong with it. What had happened? Julie. Why should Julie's face come into his mind? And the words of that hymn they had sung at her funeral:

> "Time like an ever-rolling stream
> Bears all its sons away.
> They fly forgotten as a dream
> Flies at the opening day."

His mind seemed to be splintering. He had slammed a door in it shut, and someone had been trying to force it open. He had felt it giving way beneath the pressure. No. He did not want to remember. Better to forget. Leave it. Lie down, go to sleep again.

He shook his head in puzzlement, and regretted it as the pain sliced again. He was confused by this swirling fog. Better to give up, wait until he felt stronger. But the nagging anxiety within him would not let him be. It whipped up his heartbeat and forced open his heavy eyes. He must not give up. He must get out of this place. There was something he had to do—someone he had to warn. Whatever it was that had happened, why ever it was he had been hurt and abused, he must use the last of his strength to escape. He must not allow this evil to befall anyone else.

He listened again. The silence was thick and heavy with floating dust. There was something threatening in it, something that seemed as if it might suffocate him any moment. He broke out in a clammy sweat.

With a huge effort, he succeeded in getting to his feet. He staggered over to the bucket and urinated into it, grateful for the living hiss of the fluid as it hit the plastic. The silence was becoming unbearable.

He tried the door. It was locked, as he expected—and solid. He turned his attention to the shutter. There was nothing he could do about the padlock, as he saw at once—it was big, heavy, and obviously new. The same, however, was not true of the hinged bar it secured in place. He looked speculatively at the rusty screws, and the dry cracked wood into which they were driven. He picked at it with his nail, and a splinter fell out. It might be worth trying.

Again he listened. Surely they had set a guard, whoever had left him here? Since they had left him alive, instead of dumping him in some ditch or lake, it followed that they still had some use for him. If only he could remember what had happened . . . The fog swirled again. Nothing was making sense. He wrote books. Everything in his books made sense. Why was he so lost now? He was not in charge —he answered himself. All this was the contrivance of some alien mind. Alien. The word danced and flickered. No. Better leave it. Concentrate. First get out of here. There was something he had to do.

Those rusty screws and rotten wood were his only hope. He felt in his pockets for a tool, but they had been emptied. Not quite. His fingers closed on an English halfpenny piece he had picked up years ago on a trip to London, and kept for luck. It was stuck half in half out of a small hole in the lining. He guessed, as he brought it out, it was thin enough to fit the head of a screw.

He tried it out, and knew a moment of triumph as it fitted

perfectly. But it was short-lived—either the screw was too rusty, or he was too weak—he could not budge it. He turned his attention to the flaking wood around it. This was more successful. A few more splinters fell out, but not enough to make any real impact. He needed a better tool—the coin gave insufficient leverage. Despairingly he began to poke among the debris on the floor. Then he found it—buried beneath a fall of plaster in the corner of the room—a long, thin masonry nail.

Soon he was prising out long slivers of the soft, porous wood. Every now and then he stopped to listen, but the silence hung thick and dead as ever.

After a while, he was forced to rest. The pain in his head was growing worse, and other areas of pain throbbed and needled. He drank some more water. His whole body begged to be allowed to lie down and sleep, but he resisted with all his will. If he slept, he might wake up with less strength, not more, and he would lose precious time. Time. The word seemed to echo. He had to be in time.

With difficulty he focused again on the shutter. This was all he must think of. If he could break through it he would discover what to do next. He had control of nothing but this nail and this wood, but small as it was it constituted a first step. His mind might be trembling in panic, but it could still direct this.

Tenaciously, he scratched and dug with his blunt, inadequate tool. Little by little, the wood yielded. Sliver by sliver it parted beneath the tooth of this patient rodent. Slowly he cleared and freed the shafts of the screws, loosening them until at last, triumphantly he drew them out, still rusted fast in the bars. He could move the shutter.

Behind it he found an old-fashioned sash window of cracked and filthy frosted glass. He could see nothing through it. He leaned his forehead against it. The effort of moving the shutter had brought on a wave of sickness, so strong that he stumbled to the bucket and retched.

Clenching his teeth, he returned to the struggle. The window was stuck fast. Probably it had not been opened for years. He heaved upwards. It moved a fraction, tantalizingly, with all the frustrating stiffness of age. It was ominously heavy. He gathered himself for another effort. He was not sure he had sufficient strength. He tensed his muscles. He must have the strength. He could not afford to indulge in doubt. Fiercely, he heaved again, every nerve, every muscle, every tendon summoned into service. And the window reluctantly shuddered upwards in obedience, with a groan of dry pulleys, to leave a gap of some five or six inches. It was enough. He fell to his knees and shoved his shoulders in to prop it—if the desiccated rope snapped and the pane smashed down he would be finished.

Cool night air, pouring in, refreshed him. Night air. Which night? How long had he been here? He stuck his head out and tried to see where he was, but the darkness was almost as impenetrable as the silence. He stared round. As his eyes adjusted he made out the silhouette of a building against the sky, but there were no lights, no traffic noises, nothing at all to help him orientate himself.

Looking up, he saw the sky was bright with stars, but they did not give off enough light to penetrate the shadows below and around his window. He seemed to be in one of a group of buildings. The air smelt fresh—not like city air. He held his breath, the better to listen. He thought he could hear the faint hum of traffic a long way off, but it could have been the beat of his blood in his ears. The sky seemed to be lighter far off to the right—perhaps there was a road. A road meant people—ordinary people going about ordinary lives.

Wonderfully, he suddenly heard a definite sound: high, high above, the winking lights of a plane moved across the sky. Joyfully he gazed up at it. It was a proof of reality, of life itself. It was something else—a reminder of something luminous and fugitive that he had buried away behind that closed door in his mind. Something he had dreamed maybe—and forgotten. Something that had happened in a plane.

For several minutes after it had disappeared from sight he lay staring sightlessly out into the dark, weighed down by a feeling of immense loss, drained of all will. Then he roused himself once more. More effort was required of him. It was time to shift his focus. He had dealt with the first problem, now he must look ahead. The nail and the rotten wood were already part of the past. He must go on. He drew a deep, painful breath.

He looked down. Now he could just make out what appeared to be a flat roof some feet below, though it was difficult to gauge the distance. If there was a roof, there must be drains. Drains went to the ground. Spinning minds needed the simplest of logic. He could think no further.

He edged his stiff body painfully through the gap in the window and let himself down until he was hanging by his hands, praying that the pulley ropes would not choose this moment to snap. Then he dropped. The distance was greater than he had guessed, but his very weakness was an asset, and he landed safely. Success renewed his strength. He found he could now see the area of the roof, and crawled over to the edge. Sure enough, there was a gutter, and in the corner he could just see the dark head of a drainpipe.

He peered over. He could see the drop this time, and he judged it to be greater than the first. For a fit man it would have represented few problems. He had always taken pride in his physical condition, in the tone of his muscles, the power of his lungs, and the general harmony of his being. Perhaps it was the remnants of this pride which carried his battered body past its doubts and over the edge of that cliff-like wall.

The guttering was eaten away with rust. A section of it broke off as he eased himself past it, groping for a foothold on the drainpipe, and fell with a ghastly clatter to the ground. Jeffrey froze. He felt as if he had sounded the trumpets of the Apocalypse. Was all his effort to be wasted? Surely someone would have heard, and come to investigate.

Minutes passed. Still there was no sound—not even the bark of a dog. His arms were weakening. He had to go on—there was no choice.

The drainpipe was rusty, too, and far from stable. Its brackets creaked as it took his full weight, and fragments of mortar pattered down with each movement. He increased his speed—at least if it gave way there would be less distance to fall.

He was almost two-thirds of the way down when the pipe finally came away from the wall. He and it fell the remaining distance together. His head seemed to explode—and then the blessed darkness swallowed him up once more.

But he could not give up. Relentlessly the anxiety that drove him forced the message through to quivering nerve and punished muscle, and he opened his eyes—to realize that he was lying on the ground. He had escaped. The nightmare of the room was over.

He tried his limbs. Nothing seemed to be broken. He could still move. Shakily, he got to his feet. He could feel warm blood seeping down his neck from the re-opened wound in his scalp—but he could still move. All he had to do now was to get far away.

The window through which he had escaped shone out in the dark like a malevolent eye. Someone must see it. They would come after him again, or lie in wait for him as they had at the airport. The airport. The word lit up in his mind like a neon sign. That was where the pain had begun. In the taxi. They had wanted him to tell them something and he had refused. But what?

No. No. Better not to remember yet. First get away. Then, when he was safe, he would let himself remember. Dazedly, he looked around him. He was standing on some sort of dusty track between empty buildings. There was a smell of rotting straw and machine oil. He hesitated, not knowing which direction to take. He remembered the faint glow he had seen from the window, and what he'd thought was the distant hum of traffic. Better make for that. He must get back amongst people, friendly, normal people.

The pain hit him with his first step, so sharply he cried out. His ankle had joined with his head in a pincer movement as if to form a torturer's implement—like the cigarettes. No. Don't think of that. Just keep going.

I can't.

You must. Red hot, the message burned into his body. He found he was praying. Garbled phrases. Words worn thin by centuries of use. Words to drive back darkness and pain and death. Match flames of defiance.

Muttering, bleeding, half crazed, he began to drag himself along the track towards that far-off glow in the sky.

The watcher in the shadows saw him go, and smiled.

At this early hour there was not much traffic on the highway—not, that is, judging by daytime standards. Evie Thomson, during the months that she had been using the route regularly, had noticed that the unusual amount of freedom this afforded had a peculiarly adverse effect on the general quality of the driving. She swore fluently as, for the second time in a few minutes, a flashy car with US number plates suddenly cut in front of her, forcing her to brake abruptly. She was beginning to detest this drive home after night duty.

She had far preferred working in the old hospital buildings downtown, for all their antiquated design and general inconvenience. Not only were they situated close to the duplex where she lived, but, surrounded as they were by office blocks, and stores, and crowded streets, she had felt them part of the very heart of the busy city, at the nerve centre of all its vibrant energy. Now, everything had been split up, and many departments, including her own, had been transferred to a great new monolith of a building set far away on the outskirts, among vast parking lots, the advance guard of the army of new housing estates steadily marching outwards, swallowing up the rich green farmland. She had found herself faced each day with a long and tedious drive to and from work, which she accomplished with steadily increasing resentment.

In the past she had always known a certain enjoyment in night duty. There seemed to be a conspiracy between herself and her patients as the world gradually fell asleep around them, an intensification of their joint battle against sickness and pain. The light on her desk was a beacon which continued to shine as the lights in the city dimmed and went out, and it sank back into sleep.

That feeling was gone. The huge, stark new hospital offered no contrast with the great empty spaces outside. When she drove away from it in the early morning through the grid of new roads lined by half-finished estates of identically angular dwellings, each, doubtless, with its fridge-freezer, its giant electric cooker, its light fittings and its fitted carpets, her fatigue seemed far greater than it ever had before.

On a sudden, angry impulse, she turned off into one of these estates. Tired as she was, she wanted to take a closer look. For some weeks now she had been considering the idea that it might make sense to move house. It certainly made none at all to waste her energy on this daily journey if it was possible to cut it out. She had to admit that it probably was possible. If she were to sell her apartment she should raise enough for at least a down payment.

She drove slowly along the brand new road which had been thrown down over what had once been open country. It was not a reassuring sight. Only the end houses, the ones nearest the highway, were finished. The rest were in various stages of construction. The raw earth was littered with builders' debris. Machines stood around like forgotten toys. Most of the trees had been cut down. Those that remained stood self-conscious and mournful, as if they knew their role had changed. Stopping the car, she sat taking it all in.

The land, no doubt, had formerly been one of the many big farms now sold to developers. She could see a dirt track running between the houses and out across the open towards a cluster of buildings just visible in the distance—the farm itself, no doubt, probably derelict by now.

She wondered what had happened to the people who had lived and worked there, and what they had felt when they signed away their land. Whoever had first built the farm had probably been a pioneer, staking out his claim far from the safety of the city, clearing it, planting it, labouring in a primitive fight against the wild and the cold. His place was now being taken by commuters, fighting for survival against enemies just as deadly, a fight in which the wounds were the ulcers, the coronaries and the attempted suicides of those who daily found their way into her ward.

Money and power were the new enemies. It was they who had built that showcase hospital where no-one wanted it—where families were cut off from their sick by distance and expensive transport, where efficiency and capacity were valued above care and compassion, and humanity had been sacrificed to the new, intricate technology which mended bodies while it crushed the spirit that identified them. Back in the old hospital she had had time for her patients, time to listen to them, to speak the reassurance that calmed destructive anxieties—to nurse them in the full sense of the word. In the new, she was forced to lavish most of her energy on machines.

Looking now at the mass-produced hutches that stood gracelessly around her, thrown up at top speed with no thought for criteria other than profit, without a trace of individuality, or craftsmanship, she knew that her spirit, too, would be crushed if she came to live among them. She would simply have to continue to endure the drive—or even, if it came to it, to change her job.

She yawned mightily. She realized that she was exhausted. She must get home before she fell asleep at the wheel. She started the engine. A few days' leave lay ahead of her. She would think about it when she was rested. But she was glad she had taken these few minutes to look behind the billboards with their lavish promises and offers of bargains. It had helped her to understand that her apartment, on the first floor of a house in one of the older streets of the city, meant more to her than she had thought. It expressed something of her attitude in the struggle to preserve individuality. It would be harder to leave it than she had thought . . .

Deep in thought, she reversed the car into the farm track so as to retrace her route. She did not see the man until it was too late. One moment, she was ready to swear, there was no-one and nothing there apart from some machinery and piles of rubble—the next, she had backed straight into him. She heard the soft thump as the car hit his body.

Horrified, she grabbed her first aid kit and leapt out. Her fatigue was forgotten, as she knelt beside him.

After a brief examination, she straightened up, puzzled and shocked. He was certainly injured—quite badly so. On the other hand she was sure, apart from a small number of fresh contusions, that his injuries could not possibly have been inflicted by the car. It had barely hit him hard enough to knock him off-balance. The deep wound in his scalp, though still bleeding, was surrounded by blood long since congealed. The discoloured swellings on his face and jaw were hours, if not days old. He was bruised all over, and there were what appeared to be burn marks—red, circular blotches and blisters on his chest and neck. One ankle was swollen, but there were, so far as she could judge, no bones broken.

It was, in fact, the worst beating up she had ever seen. It was worse than a beating up. The burn marks could only mean one thing —something she had believed could never happen in her country.

She stared around, shivering slightly in the chill early morning air. She would have been glad of help. No-one was in sight. The builders and drivers of the mechanical diggers had not yet started their shift. A solitary white car was parked outside one of the completed houses at the end of the road, but there was no sign of its driver, and the house was obviously empty. She was not easily scared, but now she felt a stab of real fear. The malice that had been at work on this pathetic heap in the road was like a sudden manifestation of pure evil.

The man opened his eyes. She could see him struggling to focus on her and smiled her instinctive, carer's smile.

"You sure are lucky, mister. If you must walk under a car, you make sure it's a nurse's. You'll soon be fine. I'm going to get you to hospital—there's one quite near, it's where I work."

"No!" His whole body contracted with the effort to articulate his will. "No! Not hospital! Please—I'm okay." He tried to sit up.

"Hey, take it easy mister! I know what I'm doing. You need help—expert help. You may have internal injuries, and without a proper investigation I can't tell. You've taken a helluva beating— and most of it wasn't from my car."

"I tell you I'm fine. I can walk. I've *been* walking . . ."

"Well, it sure wasn't for your health, by the look of you. I'm sorry mister, I *must* take you to hospital. No-one's catching me on criminal negligence. You need proper care, believe me."

He grabbed her arm, gripping it so hard she cried out. His eyes, red-rimmed and bloodshot, glared at her. He was trembling with the effort to be coherent, to surmount his pain and exhaustion.

"Please. I'm begging you, *please* understand. I can't, mustn't go to hospital. There's something I have to do. Please help me. All I want—get away from here—into town. That's all—please—"

Doubt and hesitation showed in her face. He drew a shuddering breath.

"It's life and death. Must warn her. For God's sake help me. All my fault. Look—I can walk—I'm okay—I'll show you . . ."

Before she could prevent him he had staggered to his feet, and stood in front of her, swaying. He even grinned at her lopsidedly from his swollen mouth.

"I'm not dangerous. I just need help."

It was an appeal she could not refuse. Knowing that she was about to break every rule in the handbook for the survival of single women, she opened the back door of her car.

"Okay. You win. I'll compromise. I'll put my reputation on the line, not to mention my professional judgement. I'll take you down-town to my apartment. I'll check you over thoroughly and clean you up. But it's on one condition: if I then say hospital, to hospital you will go with no further argument. I don't want to find myself in court."

He was too exhausted to answer. With some difficulty, she helped him into the back seat of her car, and made him as comfortable as she could.

Her mind, as she drove off, was a whirl of conflicting arguments. Her common sense was screaming at her that she was behaving like a crazy fool, and could well be heading into bad trouble, but another voice, a deeper one, insisted that she was doing the right thing in listening to him—if she acted in opposition to the willpower that was sustaining him she would be risking its collapse. It was wiser to go along with him, at least for a time. She set her jaw. Her profession was caring, and he had asked her for help. Someone had deliberately hurt him and it was not her job to make matters worse. It was enough that he could still trust her enough to accept what she could offer. She had to build up that trust, not destroy it.

Glancing at him over her shoulder, she was rewarded by another lopsided grin. His courage was incredible. She grinned back, and turned to concentrate on the road. One accident was enough. She slowed as they came to the highway. If she turned right she would take him to the hospital she had left such a short time ago. She turned left.

She was too absorbed in her thoughts to notice that the white car which had been parked outside the end house had begun to move, and, following her out of the estate, had settled into position a short distance behind her.

Transferring the wounded man from the car to her apartment proved no simple matter. Expert though she was at utilizing her own strength, he had come to the very end of his. For once, as she struggled to hoist his limp body up the narrow stairs, she would have given her soul for an elevator.

"You need help, Miss Thomson?"

It was hardly Mephistopheles, but someone at least had come in answer to prayer. The quiet voice belonged to Mr Ho, the Chinese occupant of the ground floor apartment. She had once nursed him through a bad attack of bronchitis, and since then had counted him among her friends. He was the most reserved man she had ever met. His quiet dignity never left him, even when ill. He spoke excellent English, but seemed to prefer silence to speech. Although she had lived on the floor above him for some years, she felt she hardly knew him. He never spoke of his past, never mentioned a family. The only subject which tempted him into communication was herbal medicine, of which he was a practitioner, and occasionally, when she had time, Evie enjoyed drawing him into amicable arguments over its efficacy. His apparently total solitude moved her, and she liked to think that one day her cheerful teasing might find a crack in the iron walls of his self-discipline. She suspected that some tragedy had overtaken him to bring about so complete a withdrawal. Now she beamed at him.

"Mr Ho! You have never in your life been as welcome as you are right now! Could you help me get this poor guy upstairs? He's in a bad way. If you support him from behind I think we could manage. I'll explain it all once we get him to bed."

She was glad now of his inscrutability. He made no comment, raised no eyebrow, offered no advice—but as he took the sufferer's weight she knew his eyes were missing no detail of swellings, bruises and blood.

"I'm afraid he's badly concussed," she said breathlessly, as with a last united effort they got him on to her own freshly made-up bed. "He kept passing out in the car. I'll clean up that head wound first. For some reason he's terrified of going to hospital—that's why I've brought him here. I'm taking a crazy risk—he really ought to be X-rayed, but I'm almost certain nothing's broken. Take a look since you're here—then p'raps you won't think me so crazy. Are these, or are they not burn marks? Wait—I'll take his shirt off. Oh my God!"

There was a hissing intake of breath beside her as the Chinese helped her remove the torn and filthy shirt, and they both saw what had been hidden beneath. She shot a surprised look at her friend. He had gone very pale, and he was sweating profusely. She was careful to appear not to notice.

"What do you think?" she asked him gently.

"I think, Miss Thomson," he spoke very slowly and precisely, "that this man has been tortured. I have seen marks like this before." She could feel the rigidity of his control, but also, for the first time ever, she could hear the emotion it was holding back.

"So do I. That's why I brought him here. He needs special care. Do you think I'm right—or do you think he ought to go to hospital?"

"No!" The eyes in the battered, discoloured face on the pillow remained shut, but the negative snapped out in immediate response from the cracked lips. It was as if, even as he slipped into unconsciousness, he had left part of his mind on guard.

Mr Ho shook his head.

"I think he has just given you the answer. If we care, we must sometimes take risks. If you oppose his will, you may do more harm than you know. I say keep him here. If you will allow it, I will help you. While you bathe him, I will go and find salves for those burns. Miss Thomson, I never thought I would see such things in this friendly country which has given me a home."

It was the longest speech she had ever heard him make. He was clearly deeply shaken. Shaking his head, he went off in search of his remedies.

Despite her weariness, she set to work methodically to wash away the blood and dirt. Her patient lay very still and made no further sound while she completed her ministrations. When the Chinese came back she straightened up with a sigh of relief.

"I guess I'm going to be glad of some help, Mr Ho. There are burns just about everywhere—and I do mean everywhere. Whoever did this was an animal, not a human being. Some of the marks will be there for good. The head wound is what bugs me—it's been un-attended too long. I've done what I can but it may need a doctor, which could be a problem."

She was silent for a moment before continuing.

"You know, I'm not green when it comes to nursing—I've seen plenty of sights that would make Superman throw up—but I can't recall ever seeing anything quite as—as—vicious as this. I can't figure out how he ever found the strength to make it to where I found him. It was in the middle of nowhere . . ."

She told him of the encounter. The Chinese listened attentively.

"You say you saw no-one?"

"Not a soul. Do you suppose someone had dumped him there after getting whatever it was they wanted out of him?"

"It is possible. Or it could be that he was allowed to escape."

"What do you mean?"

"Perhaps he did not tell them everything they wanted to know. Miss Thomson, are you certain no-one followed you here?"

Evie stared at him in dismay.

"I never even thought to look. Are you telling me he could still be in danger? Surely no-one wants to hurt him any more?"

"It is possible they think he may still be of use—lead them to something, or someone . . . I have known it to happen. Those who do this sort of thing—" he gestured to the burn marks—"have no human feelings. They have been programmed to an idea. Individual life has no value for them. Pain and death are a means to an end, switches on a computer. It is not wise to try to fight them. Better to run, to run as fast and as far as you can. Believe me, I know."

"Are you suggesting we may be in danger too—just because I did my Good Samaritan act? This is Canada, Mr Ho, not Shanghai, or—or—Moscow!"

"Which is precisely what distresses me, Miss Thomson. It is not good to see something like this happen here. We must be vigilant. But do not be afraid. He is safe here—and so are we. Once, many years ago, I allowed myself to be taken by surprise. Since then I have learned to take care of what I value. I took my precautions soon after I came to live in this house. Now I go to make sure they work. There is much to do, for you as well as for me. I think you will find the salves efficacious, however ancient the recipe—" he allowed himself a faint smile—"I think also he needs a little nourishment. He is going to need all his strength to face his memories. If you need more help, please call me."

Evie looked thoughtfully after his retreating back. She wondered what it was that had happened to him before he came to Canada. It occurred to her with a pang that this hitherto almost silent friendship was another reason why she did not want to move from her apartment.

The threshold between sleeping and waking had become blurred. His wits had floated away out of reach somewhere. The comfortable bed, the soothing touch of a pair of gentle, competent hands had eased open the desperate grip he had struggled so long and so hard to keep on himself. He could no longer prevent it from relaxing. Relief seeped slowly through his exhausted body to its innermost recesses —to be brought up short at a watchful, terrified creature crouched in the very depths of his mind, desperately trying to hide something he could no longer recognize, a creature on whom no kindness would ever again have impact, no reassurance ever soothe. But he could no longer heed its commands. Better now to sleep. Better far to forget.

He found himself wandering through a shadowy house. He was looking for someone, someone he knew was not there. He wandered on, telling himself that he must go on searching, opening up room after room. It was a familiar house. There were pictures of his grandparents on the wall. He saw his mother sitting by the fire, reading, and the leaves of the book on her lap kept fluttering to the floor. It was a bible.

He turned, and found his father at his shoulder, frowning angrily. His father wanted him to do something, but he did not know what it was. They came to a locked door. The key was in the lock, and he tried to turn it, but it would not turn. He shook the handle, and shoved with all his strength, but the door would not open. Then he knew that Julie was on the other side. He called her name, but there was no reply. It was Julie he had been looking for. It was his fault she was locked away. In his distress he turned to his father only to see a face distorted by hatred, and a hand uplifted to strike him. He backed away, then ran, and as he ran he knew that he must leave the house, and find somewhere else to live.

He opened his eyes to find himself in a strange room bright with pictures and cheerful curtains. A pleasant-faced young woman with a snub nose and a wide, generous mouth had just nudged him awake. She was holding a bowl of soup, and now she was making it clear that she wanted him to swallow some. He took it obediently, parting his lips for more like a fledgling bird waiting to be fed by its parents, until at length he closed his eyes again to resume his wanderings in slowly increasing misery.

This happened several times. Each time the house seemed darker and his fear greater. The young woman's face, when next he saw it, wore a worried look. He wanted to reassure her, to explain about the locked door, but he had no voice. Another time the light seemed too bright—it hurt his head and eyes. He screwed them up and saw her asleep in an armchair by the bed. He wondered who she was. Tendrils of blonde hair had escaped from the severe knot on top of her head and curled over her forehead. She was not pretty, but her face was warm and strong. He would have liked to touch her cheek, but he could not move his arm. He turned away again, back to his house and his haunted, wanderings.

"Miss Thomson, there is something I think you should see."

Evie woke with a start of surprise. Mr Ho was standing at

the window. Now he beckoned her over, lifting the curtain slightly.

"That car."

A white car was parked a little further down the street, on the opposite side.

"What about it?"

"It had just arrived there when I first saw you this morning. It has been there ever since. Always with that man in it."

"So what? P'raps he's meeting someone."

"It is not a joke, Miss Thomson. Please think carefully. It is a Lada. Were there any cars like it around when you picked up this man?"

"There was one—and it was white, though I didn't stop to see the make. But it was empty—if there'd been anyone in it I'd've asked them for help." She could not help shivering at the thought.

"Did you go right up to it?"

"No. It was a little way off and I had my hands full."

"I see. They are not naive, these people. But then I am not naive, either. Not any more. And I have a long memory. I do not want this friendly country to become like the rest. That is why I—and my friends—took precautions. We make sure there is no place for bullies and torturers here. Now I shall go to complete my arrangements. All is ready. Excuse me, please."

"Don't you think we ought to go to the police?"

"Now it is you who are being naive, Miss Thomson. Please do not show yourself. He must not know you have seen him." Whereupon, he left her again.

From time to time, as the patient lay oblivious, she returned to the window, and, taking care to keep behind the curtain, looked out. The white car had not moved. Reluctantly, she admitted to herself that her Chinese friend had grounds for suspicion. The man on the bed had certainly been tortured. She remembered her feeling of some lurking menace as she had stared round the housing estate that morning. She shivered again. She wondered what sort of arrangements Mr Ho was making. The quiet apartment on the ground floor where he received his patients, Chinese for the most part, had clearly not been as peaceable as she had imagined.

She was standing in this way peering from behind the curtain when she noticed a couple of small Chinese boys sauntering down the street with somewhat self-conscious nonchalance. As they drew abreast of the white car, one of them took a large, sharp stone from his pocket and deliberately began to score a deep scratch along the wing. With an angry shout the driver jumped out and hurled himself at the culprit, only to be surrounded by a whole gang of older youths who materialized from nowhere. She distinctly saw the elegant knife hand which laid him in the road, after which he was picked up, unceremoniously bundled into the back of his own car, and driven off at speed.

The whole incident was over in seconds. Suddenly there was an empty space where the car had been. No-one had shouted out. No-one had raised the alarm. A blind man making his way along the sidewalk beneath her window continued his way unaware that anything had happened.

She felt a little sick. She felt as if she had just seen the symptoms of a pernicious, contagious disease: first the condition of the man on the bed, and now this silent, deadly violence in the street—her own street, where she had her home.

She had believed Mr Ho to be as dedicated to healing as she was herself, but she had overlooked the fact that he had come here as a refugee, and that he had therefore brought with him the pain of his past—a past that could never be completely forgotten and that bore its own bitter fruits in scenes such as the one she had just witnessed. How many other Mr Hos were there in the crowded streets of Toronto, or Ottawa, or Vancouver, or Montreal? A new country, they said, a friendly, peaceful country—but for how long?

"You saw, Miss Thomson?" The Chinese had come quietly back into the room.

She nodded.

"I think there will be no more trouble. Your patient should be safe enough now."

"And the man in the car?"

"He is in good hands, too. You need not worry any more."

She did not dare to question him. There was a long, uncomfortable silence. Mr Ho hesitated.

"Miss Thomson, I think I have frightened you a little. Am I right?"

"A little."

"I want you to know—I do not believe in violence any more than you do. I came to Canada to escape from it. Others risked their lives to help me. Here there are others who have suffered like me. We work together. We are grateful to this good country that gives us a home and allows us to be free. We make ourselves useful. We are not terrorists or guerrillas, but sometimes, very rarely, it is necessary for us to take steps to protect that freedom. You cannot understand, for you have not had our experience. We know it is necessary to deal with animals like the one in that car before they have too much power. Do not be sorry for him. He was an enemy of everything you value. Do you know what I mean?"

"I think so."

"I value your friendship. I do not want him to destroy it."

She held out her hand. There were tears in her eyes.

"Of course we are friends, Mr Ho. In any case, it was all my fault. I should not have brought him here. I did what I thought was best. I'm grateful to you for your help."

Gravely, he took the proffered hand, and conveyed it to his lips, a gesture so out of character that she was shocked. She realized that events had changed things between them. The wall of reserve had been breached, and now she had to deal with what had for so long lain hidden behind it. She looked at him nervously. She was not sure she could cope with a personality at once so complex and rooted in so alien and ancient a culture.

"I am happy to help someone like you, Miss Thomson."

He was looking at her strangely. Then he closed his eyes. When he opened them again his face wore its old inscrutable look. He moved over to the bed.

"How is the patient?"

"Fair. I'm afraid he is going to need a lot of care. Good job I've got some leave."

"The other day you told me you needed a rest. Would it perhaps be better if I tended him for you?"

"Mr Ho, I'm as strong as a horse," she said quickly. "I'm perfectly able to look after him. It's sure kind of you to offer, and I appreciate it, but I'll manage."

He smiled a little sadly.

"Of course you will. There is no better person to give him what he needs. He is a fortunate man, Miss Thomson."

"You could have fooled me! It's not the word I'd have chosen. But I'll do the best I can."

"That's what I meant. At least sometimes you will let me help—when you need to sleep, perhaps?"

"Sure I will—and thanks."

She watched his retreating back with troubled eyes. The last thing she wanted to do was hurt his feelings.

With a little shrug of perplexity, she turned back to the man on the bed. His colour was a little better, but the length and frequency of the periods of unconsciousness were beginning to bother her. It was obviously a bad concussion. She hoped it was no more than that. If infection set in the situation would be difficult.

She stood gazing at his sleeping face. There was something about it that moved her strangely. She put out her hand, and lightly stroked the fine hair just above the temples. Then she turned away abruptly.

She was behaving as much out of character as Mr Ho. In all her years of nursing, she had never allowed herself to become personally involved with patients, believing that to do so would affect her judgement and thereby her skill. She had taken her emotional needs elsewhere—when she had time, for she had never, except once, taken them very seriously.

Yet from the moment she had first set eyes on this man she seemed to have sailed clean off-course. She had immediately felt a sense of responsibility towards him—and not just as a nurse. She had, after all, added to his hurts. But it was more than that: there had been something inexpressibly poignant about his courage, something almost childlike about his appeal for help that had stirred some of her deepest feelings. She had never before felt so maternal and so possessive towards a patient as she did now towards this stranger lying in her bed. She did not want to share the task of nursing him back to health. She only wanted to protect him. Her profession was caring. It was only right that she should care.

He opened his eyes. He looked at her, frowning in the effort to focus on her face.

"Hi," she said softly, leaning towards him. "Feeling any better?"

He was looking at her, but she quickly realized that he was not seeing her. She felt his pulse. It had grown more rapid.

"So very kind. Gentle . . ." She could barely hear the words.

The frown puckering his forehead deepened.

"Julie?" he whispered.

"I'm Evie," she told him gently. "I'm taking care of you. You're gonna be okay."

But the weary, red-rimmed eyes had closed again, and she could not be certain that he had heard. It did not matter. She would still be there the next time he woke.

Chapter 8

A large grandfather clock ticked its portentous way through the seconds and the minutes, its moon face staring vacantly at the aspidistras and the bentwood coat stands. The room had been decorated to resemble a Dickensian coffee house. Despite considerable attention to detail, and lavish expenditure, the effect was not altogether successful, at least to British eyes.

Verity, slowly sipping her coffee, was passing the time till Jeffrey appeared trying to work out why. She remembered similar establishments in London—there had been quite a rash of them when she was last there—but they had not irritated her in the same way. Perhaps it was because they had been planted in their native soil, and so speedily took on the same colour as their surroundings, settling down to become inconspicuous continuations of a tradition.

No such blending could possibly take place in this young, strident, polyglot country where the trappings of British Victoriana meant little or nothing to the majority of the population. The teenage waitresses, with their spiky, rainbow hairdos, and confident assumption of intimate friendship seemed to emphasize the point. The place was a passing gimmick, nothing more. Its cleanliness would always be one hundred per cent hygienic, and its reproduction furniture would always be immediately replaced if ever it should be scarred. The fashions of the past held no real meaning here.

Gimmick or no, she had been glad that Jeffrey had selected such a snug corner for their reunion. Her first sight of the towering, shining facade of the Eaton Centre just round the block had been far from reassuring. She had experienced much the same reaction as at Niagara: she had felt she was in the presence of another uncontrollable force, and one that was equally threatening. It had been with considerable relief that she had finally located the small restaurant. At least the aspidistras and potted palms created a possibility of privacy, while the continuous small stir of movement as people came and went allowed a degree of anonymity that might have been impossible in a more formal setting.

She was feeling absurdly nervous. So much more had happened in the interval since they were last together than she had bargained for. Decisions taken in the Glasgow hotel room now seemed to have been made in a different world. A new, dynamic, far more complex reality had taken the place of the old one which, had it not been for the icon hidden in its home-made pocket beneath the loose folds of her dress, would have had little more substance than a dream.

This new reality, she was forced to admit it, was entirely dominated by the personality of Leo. He was affecting all her behaviour, all her decisions. Try as she might to preserve a safe distance between them everything seemed to be conspiring to throw them together. She was like someone lost in a maze—no matter which path she took, it always brought her back to that one central, focal point. The last thing she had wanted, for instance, was to find herself alone in the car with him, yet that was precisely what had happened this morning, for Hope, who was to have come with them into town, had suddenly elected to remain at home.

She had switched on the car radio, and turned the volume up loud, to preclude the possibility of conversation, and had stared forbiddingly out of the window at the sprawling estates of new houses on either side of the road. He, in any case, had been forced by the density of the traffic to concentrate on his driving, with the result that throughout the entire trip they had barely spoken. Yet it had made no difference. The absence of words had only served to intensify a different sort of language—a far more eloquent one—that they seemed to share whether she wanted it or not.

When he had finally set her down he had suggested that she meet him at his office at the end of the day for the ride home, and she had agreed—but this was one appointment she knew she would not keep.

It was her only certainty. Come what may, she had decided she must move out, however much this hurt Hope. She would hurt her far more if she stayed. If she continued to live under the same roof as Leo she could not answer for the consequences. She was too vulnerable, and her need for support too great.

With all her heart she wished that Hope had been different, better able to defend her territory. The years seemed somehow to have diminished her, sapping the colours of her personality and infusing it with a corrosive bitterness. She was no longer the older sister she had once looked up to and relied upon. And the process of self-destruction would certainly be aggravated and accelerated if ever she became aware of the currents flickering between her husband and her sister. Whatever happened, thought Verity, Hope must not be made to suffer any more—she was already unhappy enough.

She sighed. She was longing for someone to confide in, to offer advice. She looked at her watch. Five more minutes before the appointed time. Any moment now and Jeffrey would come through the door. She felt a prickle of apprehension. He was vulnerable, too. Perhaps it would not be wise to tell him everything that had happened. He was not strong—she had felt that when she had insisted on taking over the icon. Even she was tougher than he was—her powers of survival had been tested and proved long ago. Not that either of them would stand much chance against actual physical violence—but she could not believe it would ever come to that. Their plan, in any case, had been a good one. She wished he would come. Once she saw him again perhaps the old reality would reassert itself, and however impossible it seemed, everything would once more become simple.

The restaurant was growing increasingly busy. Everyone seemed to be meeting friends. Greetings sang through the air. The general loud, casual informality was beginning to get on her nerves. It was as if all quiet ceremony had been rejected as a social evil, to be replaced by an ideal of instant intimacy. Even the effusive friendliness of the waitress grated on her ears. She was used to village life where acceptance was slow in coming, but was accordingly prized.

The five minutes were up. Now he must come. It was almost impossible to maintain the pretence of being interested in anything or anyone other than the people entering through the door. Her heart was beating hard. She felt a little light headed. A man with sandy hair appeared, and she caught her breath, only to release it as he made his way smilingly past her table to join a noisy group in the corner. She clenched her hands.

He was late. She felt a prickle of resentment. She herself had taken good care to be punctual. It was succeeded by a wave of uneasiness. He was not the type to be casual about appointments.

She touched the flat bulk of the icon beneath her dress. Its presence was oddly reassuring. So long as she had it safe it did not really seem possible that anything could go seriously wrong with their plan. It was almost as if it were protecting her rather than the other way round. Here in this alien place it seemed to offer a confirmation of all her values. It did not seem possible, feasible that anyone could use violence to gain possession of it when it stood for the very opposite of everything that was hostile or destructive. Surely nothing could have happened to Jeffrey?

Slowly, painfully, the minutes crawled past. She was beginning to feel conspicuous sitting there alone. It was becoming glaringly obvious that she had not come into the restaurant merely in search of a quick cup of coffee. Resentment was increasing into anger, uneasiness into fear. She wondered if she could possibly have mistaken the time of the rendezvous, but decided that that was out of the question.

Twenty minutes late. Twenty-five. Half an hour. To give herself something to do she signed to her would-be-friendly waitress, and ordered lunch.

"Stood you up, has he? Slobs, the lot of 'em. Can't trust any of 'em."

Despite her anxiety she had to smile. There was a certain comfort in the show of female solidarity.

In due course a bowl of soup, a cube of processed cheese impenetrably wrapped in foil, some crackers and a dish of lettuce were placed in front of her, along with a fresh cup of steaming coffee. She looked at the coffee uncertainly—by the time she finished the soup it would be cold—then shrugged. This was not the moment for gastronomic fastidiousness. She did not actually want any of it—it was merely a reinforcement of her camouflage. She picked up her spoon, and made a pretence of starting on the bland, insipid soup.

She had not, she realized, for one moment allowed herself to consider the possibility that he might not keep the appointment at all. She could not imagine why he should fail to appear—apart from wholly unlikely extremes. It was not as if he were carrying the icon. His role was simply to have created a temporary diversion to enable her to pass through Immigration and Customs, nothing more. There was no way they could have detained him for long. If he was afraid of being followed and so leading their enemies to her surely he would have found some means of warning her? He was not without imagination.

Too late, she saw the mistake it had been to sever communications. This long, potentially dangerous wait was bringing home to her with cruel clarity what clumsy amateurs they both were. She sighed again. They had known that from the start. They had not been trained to foresee all eventualities, however many characters Jeffrey had killed off in his books. They could only guess at the best course of action, as intelligently as they could.

She made the light meal last as long as possible. The coffee, when she finally came to it, was tepid and a little sour, but she drank it notwithstanding. She was not really aware of either eating or drinking. Her whole consciousness was focused on the door. She was willing him to appear with all her strength.

The grandfather clock ticked on in senile repetition. Customers continued to arrive and depart, but Jeffrey was not among them. Little by little her concentration began to flag. She rested her aching head on her hand. There was a lump of self-pity swelling at the back of her throat.

"More coffee, honey?" The spiky-haired waitress, her eyes glazed with sympathy, was standing beside her again.

Verity nodded. She could not speak. A tidal wave of panic was threatening to sweep her away. It was dawning on her that it was up to her now—she must carry the icon on the last stage of its journey by herself. That was what they had agreed. There was no-one else to whom she could turn.

Despairingly she looked at her watch. She had been waiting for just over an hour. She knew now that he was not coming. Something had gone very wrong. She also knew that she must on no account try to discover what—not until the icon was safely delivered. If Jeffrey had laid his neck on the line to draw attention away from her, she must go on without him, and at once, or she would render all his efforts futile.

She squared her shoulders. Taking sole charge of the icon had been her own decision. Now she must prove it had been the right one. But she would give him five more minutes . . .

The lunch hour rush was almost over, and the number of customers had dwindled. A couple of middle-aged women at the next table were discussing a recent visit to an art gallery. It reminded her of her conversation with Hope. She listened a trifle wistfully.

Perhaps if she and Hope could have taken a holiday alone together their relationship might have stood a chance. They would have found common ground in the new interest in painting. She wondered what her sister's work was like. It was a relief that she had not been obliged to comment on it after all. It would not have been easy to choose words that would not wound someone as negative as Hope seemed to have become, and to encourage her talent, however slight.

She would never know now. She had no intention of returning to the Springers' house. She would deliver the icon, and then go at once in search of Jeffrey. She would phone Hope afterwards and explain. She would not, could not, go near Leo again.

Beckoning to the waitress, she began fumbling amongst the unfamiliar coins in her purse, not without a last, hopeful glance towards the door in case a panting, apologetic Jeffrey should even now appear. He did not, and she paid the bill, giving the girl a generous tip to reward her for her friendship. She was about to move, when she stopped and sat still.

She must be careful. Far more careful than she had been so far. If something had indeed happened to Jeffrey, it must surely mean that she herself would be the next in line.

Anxiously, she scanned the room. A man at a table in the corner, reading a newspaper, had come in just after herself, and was still showing no sign of making a move. He looked perfectly ordinary. Further off two men were facing each other, conversing in low voices, beyond them was a group of four. It was just as it had been on the plane. She had not the slightest idea how to distinguish friend from foe. There was simply no telling which was the office worker spinning out his lunch break, and which was the pursuer, there only because she was. A professional might have known. She did not.

There was, she told herself, nothing for it but to exercise a certain amount of female guile. It might be possible to force the enemy, if he was present, to reveal himself. Once he was visible, she could set about losing him. The perfect place for such a manoeuvre, what is more, lay close at hand.

As offhandedly as she could, and with a rueful smile at her waitress, she made for the door. She did not dare look back—it was important not to appear worried.

Outside, she paused for a moment to get her bearings, then hurried in the direction of the great entrance to the Eaton Centre. This time she did not pause to look up at its threatening height, but allowed herself to be carried in by the crowd of shoppers.

The sight inside took her breath away. She suddenly felt that she understood the point that the Mennonites were trying to make. For, with the high walls lined with windows, and the huge vaulted glass roof, the building resembled a cathedral rather than a shopping precinct—a cathedral dedicated to the god of commerce. Raising her eyes, she saw a flight of carved Canada geese suspended from the vault above her, their wings frozen in mid-beat. She fancied that they, like herself, were trying to escape from this trap in which they found themselves. The thought made her smile grimly—at least she stood a better chance than they did.

The cheerful, brightly dressed crowd was, she felt, her main hope. It thronged the escalators, the walkways, and the myriad shops. Without knowing, it would be her *corps de ballet*, around and through whom she could perform a whole series of intricate steps. If she was quick enough, and observant enough, she would soon know if she was followed or not—and be able to retreat in good order if she was.

Hastening past the trimly pruned trees in their spotless white tubs—trees which had never known rain, or wind, or snow—she joined the swirling stream of human bodies. She glided up escalators, along walkways, and pirouetted in and out of a score of shops and boutiques, flitting from display to display, from one group to another. Her confidence increased. She was almost beginning to enjoy herself, until, pausing to catch her breath, she looked carefully back along the level she had just quitted and caught sight of the man who had been reading a newspaper in the restaurant. He was looking round, frowning. For a moment she stood there hypnotized—and saw him looking intently at the crowd around her. She dodged hastily out of sight, her heart thudding. Now there was no more room for doubt. She must get away immediately.

For some reason, now she had actually seen him, she felt less frightened. He had become tangible, and she could deal with that —it was the unknown, the uncertain that terrified her. Weaving and twisting she gradually moved forward into the current of shoppers heading for the further doors, and making herself as small as possible, moved with it out once more into the street. She had found out what she wanted to know.

On the pavement, the heat came down over her like a hair dryer. It was now early afternoon, and there was an overpowering stench of petrol fumes and hot rubber that had accumulated throughout the morning. She pushed her way to the edge of the kerb and looked round urgently for a cab. She was too exposed and vulnerable to wait there long. Her luck held—a cab stopped. She was inside it in seconds, and gave the startled driver the address she had so carefully rehearsed with Jeffrey. They drove off at speed, and she was only just in time to catch a glimpse of the man from the restaurant emerging from the swing doors and glaring wildly about him.

It had not been difficult after all. There had been no sudden attack, no struggle. She felt a surge of elation. She had beaten them at their own game. She need not have been so scared. She was certain they were not being followed. Now all she had to do was hand over the icon. In a few minutes she would be free of it, and the world would seem a very different place.

The driver had left behind the skyscrapers, and the crowds, and they were already in a quieter, leafier part of the city. Somewhat to her surprise, they drew up outside a pleasant, but unpretentious modern house. In her mind, bishops lived in palaces among the pages of Trollope, close to their cathedral precincts, their dean and chapter, and preceded always by stately processions. She thought of the beautiful, dignified old building in Wells, with its lawns, its gatehouse, and its moat. She had assumed that such was the type of environment to which she would be taking the icon. Its place surely had to be in some exquisitely carved niche, guarded by statues, its beauty enhanced by music and illuminated by candles. It came from too ancient and majestic a tradition to be anything but out of place among the banal and the everyday.

For the second time she wondered if those who had chosen to send it to Canada had known entirely what they were doing. Here it was likely to become little more than a jewel torn from its setting—still intrinsically beautiful and valuable, but deprived of all its accumulated symbolic significance. In this vast melting pot of many cultures, soon only the very old would have the slightest, faded recollection of what that significance had once been—and when they were gone it could well be lost for ever.

She gave a little shrug. It was not, she told herself as she stepped out of the taxi, her problem. Her responsibility ceased the moment she placed his brother's gift in the bishop's hands.

Asking the driver to wait, she walked firmly up the path to the front door, and knocked. Her heart was beating hard again. This was the moment she had been waiting for throughout two long days.

The house seemed very quiet. The afternoon sun shone full on the doorstep, and little drops of sweat began to gather on her upper lip as she stood waiting. A fresh doubt had just germinated at the back of her mind.

She knocked again, and smiled back reassuringly at the taxi-driver as he sat nonchalantly waiting for her. It was herself she was trying to reassure.

At last she heard the sound of approaching feet. The door opened to reveal a plump, elderly woman with a frizzy mass of grey hair, rosy cheeks, and an expression of beaming kindliness.

"May I—is it possible for me to speak to His, er—to the bishop?" she stammered in answer to an enquiring look. "I'm afraid I don't have an appointment, but it's extremely important, and I don't mind waiting."

"I am sorry—this is not possible—" the woman spoke with a heavy, if unidentifiable accent "—the bishop is away from home right now at a conference."

"Oh *no!*" Verity felt sick. How idiotic they had been not to foresee such an eventuality! She tried again.

"Is the conference very far away? I mean, would it be possible to reach him? I'm only in Canada for a short time, and I have brought something for him from his brother in Poland—something valuable. It has to be given to him personally."

The woman looked dismayed.

131

"But the bishop is in Europe! He is in London, England. He left three days ago and will not be back till Wednesday of next week. He said nothing of this to me. My dear—" as Verity clutched the doorpost for support—"you are not well! Come in out of the heat. Come—sit down. I fetch you some water, yes? This is bad news, yes?"

Verity allowed herself to be drawn into a cool hall, and sat down thankfully while the woman hurried off to fetch her a glass of water.

Her mind was reeling with the absurdity of it all. The bishop, she realized, must have set off for London the evening of the very same day that she, Jeffrey and Venables had first boarded their plane at Heathrow. If it had not been for that chance electrical failure Venables would have arrived in time to catch him, and she and Jeffrey would never have become involved. The delay, she thought bitterly, could hardly have cost the airline as much as it had cost the three of them. One small electrical fault had radically affected two lives, and ended another . . .

As she drank the water, she eyed the woman's motherly face, almost beautiful in its kindliness. It would be simplest to hand the icon over to her, no matter what Venables had said about giving it personally to the bishop. It was just that she knew she could not bring herself to do it. It would be like passing her an unexploded bomb. She could hardly entrust her, or the bishop's deputies, with a priceless treasure as if it were an everyday gift of food or flowers. It could endanger them all. No, she must stick to the instructions— somehow.

"I am so very sorry. Do you want you should leave it with me? I keep safe for you and give to the bishop next week. I would like to help . . ."

Verity managed a smile and shook her head. No doubt battered strangers often knocked on this door in search of succour. Had she been hungry, or pregnant, or abused no doubt all she needed would have been immediately and gladly given, but the burden she carried could not be so lightly lifted from her, for it was heavy with given promises made sacred by a man's death.

"Thank you, you are very kind—but I can't do that. I have promised to give this—this present to the bishop himself. Next

Wednesday, you said? I'll just have to come again then, as soon as he's back."

"Can't one of the priests help? Father Smolenski's here—he came over to work in the garden. I call him if you like."

Verity hesitated, but only fractionally.

"No—I'm sorry. I don't think I can do that. Please don't worry— luckily I'll still be here next week. I'll just have to come again."

"I'm so very sorry."

Verity got to her feet. Her head swam and for a moment she thought she would faint.

"Are you sure you're okay? Sit a little longer."

"No—thanks—but I'm all right. I must go. My taxi's waiting. There's just one thing—please don't tell anyone except the bishop about this visit—anyone at all. I'll be able to explain when I come again. It's an important private matter between him and his brother, and they won't want anyone else to know about it. I'm sorry I've bothered you. I realize now I should have phoned first. Goodbye, and thank you."

Not, she reflected as she walked back down the path, that phoning would have made any real difference: it would have spared her the expenditure of nervous energy and the frustration of wasted effort, but she still would have faced the same basic problem. Somehow or other, she must protect the icon for eight more days—alone.

She stepped into the cab, lifting her hand in farewell to the woman still standing in the doorway, watching. The driver turned round expectantly for his instructions. Suddenly, she realized that she had not the least idea what to say. Yet again, the whole picture had changed. Against all expectation, the icon was still in her possession. Going in search of Jeffrey was, therefore, now out of the question. So what was she to do?

Her brain felt numb. The heat was greater than ever.

"Where to, lady?"

Frantically, she tried to order her thoughts. There was no real choice. Without Jeffrey, without a single friend to whom to turn, or sufficient money to maintain herself independently, there was nothing for it but to return to Hope and Leo—to re-enter the trap she had left so triumphantly that morning. If she was to attempt to survive for eight more days with the icon in her care she must have a minimum of help, and a degree of protection. Somehow she must find a way of dealing with Leo. If only she could find some place to which she could retreat, where she could be safe from both the threats that menaced her . . .

There was only one person left whom she could ask for help. She was also the very person who was least able to give it. There was, however, no alternative: she would have to appeal to Hope—poor, tired Hope . . .

"Lady? You still with us?"

She jumped. She looked at her watch. Never dreaming that she would actually keep the appointment, she had agreed to meet Leo in his office at four o'clock for the drive home. She could just make it. He would not know she had not intended to be there. He would be expecting her. Everything would appear perfectly normal.

She gave the driver the address.

"Verity!"

Heads turned as Leo emerged from the elevator into the lofty, luxuriously furnished reception area, and came to meet her, hands outstretched. The coolly-groomed receptionists looked on with interest, causing her to wonder if he often descended from his Olympian heights to welcome a visitor in person.

"You look tired. Come up to my office. I'll fix you a drink."

"I'd rather have a cup of tea."

"Then my secretary shall make you a cup of tea—though she may have to go out and buy some!"

He took her hand and tucked it under his arm. There was an extraordinary, almost frightening relief at walking at his side, under his protection. She could feel the respect, amounting almost to reverence, with which he was regarded by all around.

This was a Leo she had not yet seen. Here he was in his hunting territory and the other beasts acknowledged his sway. This was where he had battled his way to domination, where, perhaps, he was most intensely alive. His vitality seemed to kindle everyone around him. She longed to be honest with him, to turn to him and pour out her troubles and ask for the help he could so easily give, but she knew she must not. His strength was not for her. She must try to depend on her own.

All the same she was grateful for the respite as she sat in his soap opera office, and sipped the weak tea brought in by a deferential secretary. No-one could hurt her while she was here. She was safe for a little while at least—except from herself.

"Have you had a good day?"

"So-so."

"Gotten through the business?"

"Some of it."

"Hmm. I must say you don't look like a girl who's just clinched the deal of a lifetime. Tell you what—why don't I cheer you up by taking you out for a meal? I'll phone Hope and explain—she wouldn't mind. You could rest up for a time, then I'd show you the town, ending up at a place I know with French cuisine and an incredible view. What do you say?"

She ached to accept. Every fibre of her longed to let go, for one short evening, and let him spoil and cosset her. But she knew it would not end there. However hard it was, she had to refuse him.

"Leo, it's sweet of you, and it's a lovely idea. Another time I would love to do it, but right now I'm just feeling too exhausted. I've not been well all day. I think I'm still suffering from the effects of the flight. I'd rather go home if you don't mind."

He looked at her intently.

"Of course. We'll do whatever you want. I'm sorry—I should have realized you'd be very tired. Would you like to go now?"

She nodded miserably. She did not want to go at all.

"There's nothing wrong, is there Verity? I mean between you and me. Are you angry with me about the other night? Because if you are—I can only say I never intended it to happen. I went into your room because you screamed out—I honestly thought you were in trouble. After that—I guess I got carried away. Any man would have been. If I've hurt you in any way I'm sorry. I never meant to—hurting you's the last thing I want to do."

"I'm not angry."

She went to the window and stood looking out at the magnificent view over the city. She did not want to face him.

"There's nothing to be angry about. I got carried away too. But that's all there is to it, Leo—all there's ever going to be. You're married to my sister. To take it any further would create an impossible situation, you must see that. I happen to love Hope."

"And me? What do you feel about me?"

She stayed silent, her back to him, staring down at the patchwork of green trees and buildings far, far below.

"You're my brother-in-law," she answered at length in a low voice.

Suddenly, she heard him behind her. His hands grasped her shoulders and turned her round so that her face was close to his.

"That's no answer, is it Verity?"

She sensed that he was about to kiss her. She knew that if he did, her treacherous body would betray her. With all her strength she twisted free, and in seconds had put the big oak desk between them.

"There *is* no answer. Not for us. You know it as well as I do."

"I don't know anything any more. Only that I love you, Verity."

"For God's sake, Leo—don't *say* that! Listen. Since you and Hope left England I've learned a few things. I've learned about loss, and grief, and despair. I've learned how long it takes to build up a life again. I've done it, but it's not been an experience I'd wish on anyone. And I'm not going to be the cause of it happening to Hope. I'm not sure she *could* survive."

"Hope is stronger than you think," he said strangely.

"I very much doubt it. I do know she's unhappy, even if I'm not sure why. And I know there's no way I'm going to add to that unhappiness if I can avoid it. Nor am I forgetting the children. Do you really want to risk breaking up their whole world? Think, Leo!"

"I have done. It doesn't help. Look, all I'm asking is this one evening. At least give me that. Afterwards I promise I won't ask for anything more. I'll do whatever you want. Please."

She hesitated, but not for long.

"We've already made one mistake," she told him gently. "Let's not compound it. I told you—I love Hope."

"And me? Do you love me? You still haven't told me . . ."

She looked him in the eyes then. She did not know how to reply honestly. There was no word to describe the chaos of feelings he awoke in her. As she searched for a reply she could feel the tension between them growing.

"Take me back to the house Leo." Her voice was little more than a desperate whisper. "Please take me back now. You say you love me, so please do what I ask. I want you to stay away from me as much as possible until it's time for me to go back to England. It isn't going to happen, Leo. I won't let it."

He glared back at her. He looked almost crazy. His mouth was working, and a pulse was beating in his neck. The struggle he was having with himself was all too visible. He took a few steps round the desk towards her. Instinctively, she recoiled. The movement stopped him.

There was a long, long silence.

When he spoke again, she saw he was in complete control.

"Okay. I'll do as you say. We'll play it your way. But something tells me it isn't what you really want. And that means it isn't finished yet. It can't be. You can't just break off something like this, not without leaving us both—mutilated."

Still she said nothing. There was nothing to say. She stood and looked at him, and her eyes were full of tears.

"Come. I'll drive you home."

She turned, and, as if she were walking in her sleep, took a few steps towards the door.

"Oh, I nearly forgot," his voice halted her. "I bought you this. The insurance people take for ever and it seems a pity you should be without one for your holiday."

He picked up a package lying on the desk, and handed it to her. She tore off the wrappings to discover a neat, and clearly very expensive, compact camera in a soft leather case.

"I hope this is allowed, at least."

"It's a far better one than the one that was stolen. You're very kind. Thank you, Leo." She turned the camera this way and that in her hands. "Leo—I'm sorry." She was blinded by tears.

He touched her lightly on the cheek.

"Don't cry. I want you to be happy. God knows—it's time you were. I've told you—we'll play it your way. Just don't expect the game to be perfect. I'll kick off by driving you home."

The swimming pool glittered invitingly. After the heat, the humidity and the emotions of the day Verity was strongly tempted to join Leo and the little girls in the water. Instead, she went to take a shower before joining Hope on the terrace. She did not feel she could cope just then with any more accidental collisions in the pool.

Now she lay comfortably sipping a tall glass of iced lemon, watching the tree shadows lengthening over the lawns. She was in no mood to talk, and for once she was grateful for Hope's silence. She needed to come to terms with all that had happened. She had been forced to play the last few hours entirely by ear, and only now was it possible to assess the decisions she had taken. She knew she had done what had seemed best at the time, but already the doubts were beginning to raise their heads, and she was conscious of a deep, gnawing anxiety.

If only she could discover what had happened to prevent Jeffrey from keeping their appointment. Surely if something had gone badly wrong he would have found some means of warning her, despite their agreement. He would never have let her sit all that time alone and exposed, waiting for him. She tried to imagine what might have happened, but gave up, almost, she realized, as if she were afraid to find out. She toyed with the idea of phoning him, or going to the address he had given her, but she knew she would not dare, for fear of making matters worse. There was nothing she could do—but the realization made it no easier to bear the thought of her gentle friend alone and in trouble. He had not the resilience of a Leo.

Leo. She had hurt him—but she had had no choice. He would soon get over it. He was no sensitive plant. If he was really bent on destroying his marriage he would soon no doubt find someone else to help him, someone with fewer scruples. All the same, there was a bitter irony in the knowledge that the one person who was in a position to help her and who would have fallen over himself to do so should be the one person she could not ask.

Involuntarily, she glanced down at the pool where the triplets were poised on the edge, beside their father, about to dive in. The evening sun gilded the four bright heads. They made a pleasing, almost beautiful picture. She knew as she looked that this decision at least had been the right one—she could not be responsible for breaking up their world.

Which meant that there was nothing for it, as she had realized earlier in the taxi, but to confide in Hope. What is more, she must lose no more time. It was essential, from all points of view, that she remove herself as quickly and as quietly as possible from the twin threats of Leo and the men who were trying to get hold of the icon. If only Hope had been less of a broken reed . . .

"I said, how was business?"

At least for once she was initiating the conversation. Perhaps it was a good omen.

"Sorry—I was miles away. Not very good, actually—but it had to be done."

"Were you looking at paintings for your gallery?"

"Not exactly."

"I suppose you often get called on to judge them?"

"I wouldn't say that. It happens from time to time."

Verity suddenly saw that her sister was in a state of considerable nervous excitement. Something was clearly on her mind. It was hardly the best of moments for asking for help—yet this fragile oasis of calm here on the terrace might well prove to be her only chance to speak to Hope alone—she was fast learning the rarity of privacy in family life.

"Hope—"

"Verity—"

They both laughed. They had spoken simultaneously—a trick they had often had as children. It broke the ice.

"You go first, you're the elder." That was the old formula, too.

"Don't remind me—it's no longer an advantage. Okay then—I want to ask you a favour."

"Go ahead."

"There's something I'd like to show you. I need your honest opinion and your advice. Do you mind?"

Verity smiled. It was a day for irony, it seemed.

"Of course I don't mind if I can be of any help. What is it?"

"A bunch of my paintings."

"You mean you want to show me now?"

"Uh-huh. I'd been hoping we might get a few moments together some time today. I'd say they're good for at least another twenty minutes," she gestured towards the bathers. "To tell you the truth I've been kind of screwing myself up to it ever since you arrived; I can't wait any longer or I'll go crazy. You're sure you're not too tired?"

"I'm fine. I'd love to see your work. I'm really glad you've taken it up."

"Wait here then, I've got a selection all ready."

She disappeared into the house with a speed of movement which had nothing depressive about it, to return carrying a large portfolio.

Verity's heart sank. This was the last thing she wanted at the end of a difficult day. She had strong feelings about art teaching, and always went to considerable pains over any criticism she was called upon to deliver, to make it both constructive and detailed. She knew now, however, that complete sincerity would be out of the question—Hope's state of mind, her circumstances, the pressures on her—all had to be taken into account. She would need to choose her words with a care requiring the sort of effort she was not sure she still had the strength to make.

With an inward sigh she took the portfolio, noticing that the hands that were passing it to her were shaking.

Hope gave a strained laugh.

"I've been too chicken to show them to anyone else—so that I'm at what you might call a standstill. I need to know what I'm doing and where I'm going. I wouldn't have bothered you with it otherwise."

Verity's apprehension increased. She had not bargained for so much responsibility. She knew from experience the amount of relief from mental distress that is to be found in the act of painting. Whatever she felt, it was vital that she fan this faint creative glow that was the only sign of emotional health she had perceived in her sister since their reunion. However great her fatigue she must now find exactly the right phrases of encouragement, and speak them from the heart.

Urgently summoning all her failing powers of concentration, she opened the portfolio.

It was as if she had opened the shutters of a darkened room to find herself suddenly in a new, luminous world. She gave a little gasp. The fatigue, the trials of the day fell away. The apprehensiveness was forgotten. Instead of the absence of technique, the clumsiness of composition, the inadequate understanding of colour harmonies that are the hallmark of the amateur, a rare and accomplished reality lay before her startled eyes.

She was looking at a series of brilliant little scenes in gouache, beautifully drawn, and revealing an exquisite feeling for colour and tone. Hope had taken her subjects from the countryside around her and created them sometimes with humour, sometimes with poignancy, but always with extraordinary freshness of vision. The medium suited her style, allowing her to express a sensitive perception of detail, as well as the freedom to convey atmosphere and mood.

Slowly, attentively, she considered each in turn. Several she laid on one side. One she placed by itself—a picture of a group of horses in a snowy field fringed by woods, their heads patiently bent before the bitter wind that swayed the trees.

When she came to the end, she sat silent. Hope watched her.

"You say this is only a selection?"

"There's a load of oils up in the studio, and a few watercolours. I picked these because they're my own favourites. Do you want to see the others?"

"Very definitely—but not right now. These tell me enough. Tell me—what tuition have you had?"

"I took lessons for a while from an old French-Canadian artist who used to live near here. She died a couple of years back. Since then I've gone on by myself. Hélène got me going, taught me to see, showed me how to find a way for myself. She was a great teacher. I guess she also saved my sanity."

"However have you found time—I mean with all this?" Verity waved her arm to include the house, the grounds, the people in the pool. She felt she was just beginning to understand what had been puzzling her in her sister.

"I make time." There was something close to quiet ferocity in Hope's voice. "You might call it a matter of life and death. This—" she picked up the picture of the horses in the field "—is life." There was no trace of flatness in her tone now.

"What does Leo say about them? I take it he's seen them?"

"You still don't understand, do you? Do you honestly think that I'd show them to him? This is *my* world. The only one I've got. Do you think I'd let him take it over, the way he takes everything else? He'd probably turn me into another of his business concerns—start paying me a salary. If I didn't have this I'd've ceased to exist as a person by now. This is the only part of my life that still seems to have

141

any meaning. And if it isn't going to die off like the rest of me, it's got to grow. That's why I'm taking a risk now, and letting you see it. Like I said, I need your advice, maybe your help. And you still haven't said what you think of it."

Verity felt a hysterical desire to laugh. The shutters had indeed been thrown open. Now at last she was talking to the real, living, passionate being that was her sister—a being she had stupendously, insultingly misjudged.

"I think it's absolutely incredible—"

"What is?"

"Let me speak. I think it's absolutely incredible that our Mr Super-Businessman hasn't scented something."

"Meaning?"

"It's not like Leo to miss out on the discovery of a lifetime. It warms my heart. To realize that I should be the one to make it. This is the perfect end to a ghastly day!"

"You're talking in riddles, and it isn't funny. It means a lot to me, Verity."

"Hope, dear Hope—I'm absolutely serious, and you know you understand me perfectly. You can't kid me that you don't know how good these are. The real artist always knows, deep inside. You know more than that—you know they're not just good, they're brilliant."

She looked steadily at her as she spoke, and saw, moved, a tide of red suffuse Hope's shoulders, and neck, and face. The tired eyes brimmed with tears.

"Do you really mean that?"

"Do you think for one moment that I would say it if I didn't? You must let me look at the oils, then we must think about an exhibition. I know one or two dealers over here—I'll give you their names, and you must get in touch with them. Once I'm back in England I'll be in a better position to help, though I suspect by then you won't need me. Once they see these they won't hang back. I prophesy you're going to be the discovery of the decade."

"It's no good—I simply can't believe it. You're just trying to cheer me up."

"If you think I'm that stupid why did you ask me? You'd better believe it, Hope."

"You're a serious artist yourself. You've been to college, had

142

all the training. You surely can't compare these—the work of a nobody—with your own painting? They can't be in the same class."

Verity smiled a little grimly.

"Sadly for me, you're right. You can't and they're not. They're in a different category altogether. Yes, I've had the academic training, and the discipline, and the result of that is that I paint pleasantly acceptable pictures that people occasionally like to buy. I just make a living. I'm happy enough because I'm doing what I enjoy doing, and I'm not particularly ambitious for more. There are lots like me."

"So?"

"There is one somewhat galling fact that I and those like me have to face, and that is that there are some artists, a very few, who go straight there, you might say—without the grind. I suppose they have what could be called the divine flame. You are one of them. Your old teacher must have seen it, and was wise enough to give you just enough to free you without trying to push you into a mould. I wish I'd known her. She did a great job."

"And you really think my work will sell?"

"I predict they'll be queuing up to buy it."

All the tension had now left Hope's face. She sat staring out over the garden with shining eyes. At last she turned to Verity.

"I guess I needed to hear that more than anything else in my entire life. You're right, of course—deep down I knew, but I just had no confidence. Ever since Hélène died I've been totally isolated. It's been like trying to hide away some great secret passion, and in the end it seems to start eating you up. I've been so unhappy. It's terribly hard to keep going on alone."

"I know."

"Yes. You do, don't you? But you're strong. You always were. You must be or you wouldn't have survived."

"I think perhaps you're even stronger, Hope." She recalled Leo's words that afternoon in his office.

Already she was beginning to look at her sister with different eyes. This was no broken reed. The irritable withdrawal from the trivia of the domestic world no longer seemed a sign of weakness, not in a woman who possessed so great a talent and knew that it needed nourishment. It was extraordinary that she had found the strength to carry on in such spiritual isolation, and in the face of so many pressures.

Hope, her sister, was indeed light years from being the worn-out defeated woman she had taken her for. She possessed an inner force that matched Leo's. Now that she had at last received some of the reassurance that she craved, the confirmation that she truly was what she had secretly believed herself to be, Verity foresaw that her strength would be hidden no longer, and she would take her rightful place in the world.

She felt little envy. She had accepted long ago the mediocrity of her own gift. It had the virtue of allowing space in her life for other pursuits, other enjoyments—other emotions. It would never consume her. Hope, on the other hand, was probably going to face problems even greater than those she had known so far—problems and choices. Though to judge from her air of barely suppressed exultation as she slipped the precious paintings back into the portfolio, they would not hold her up for long. Hope had just fixed her bearings.

Suddenly she felt as if it were she herself who was the weary and all-but-defeated one, struggling vainly in turbulent waters, way out of her depth. But at least she could turn now to her sister in the way she had always done when she was little.

"It's my turn now. I need your help too."

"Fire away—only you'd better be quick about it—the family's about to descend on us. No more intense conversations today."

A glance at the bathers showed that she spoke truly. Fortunately at that moment one of the little girls dropped some trinket in the pool, and the others turned back to help her look for it. Verity seized her chance.

"I can't possibly tell you quickly—it's too important, and too complicated. Can you fix it so that we have a few hours alone together, away from the house and the family? Tonight would be best, but if that's out of the question tomorrow would do. It's urgent Hope. There's something I've got to ask you—I just can't handle it alone any more."

Her voice broke on the last words. It had been a crushing day.

Hope gave her a quick look, then there was a pause while she thought.

"I know. We'll go to Kleinburg. I mentioned it, if you remember. We'll tell Leo we want to do some painting at the cottage, and you want to see some work by Canadian artists before you go. I might persuade him to take the girls out for the day—he's been promising them that for a long time. That way everyone would be happy. We'd have time to ourselves, and as well as dealing with whatever's bugging you I could show you the marvellous collection of paintings by Canadian artists they've got there. One of the very best of them was completely self-taught, too."

Verity had to smile. Hope was very transparent.

"That sounds perfect. I'm in a real mess, or I wouldn't ask."

"I'm glad you did. We'll set off in the morning, and have lunch there. I don't see how Leo could object . . ."

"Surely it's only normal I should want some time alone with you after all these years apart. I'll ask him if you like. He can hardly refuse then."

"That's true. Not if it comes from you." The words fell with a small, dead weight, like little stones. Hope was looking at the children, and Verity could not see her expression.

"I only meant . . ."

"It's okay. I know what you meant. I understand. Ask him now if you like while I go and have a word with Mrs Matt about dinner. You're quite right—it's far better if I leave Leo to you."

With her portfolio under her arm, she hurried off into the house. Verity stared thoughtfully after her. Despite all the recent revelations, and the consequent shift of perspective, she was by no means sure that she had, even now, got the true measure of her sister.

Chapter 9

As soon as she set eyes on Kleinburg the next day, with its wide, low-pitched roof and great triangular doorway set rock-like in a landscape of tree-covered hills and sunny expanses of grass, Verity guessed that Hope had some special purpose in bringing her there.

With the exception of the Springers' own house, it was the only piece of architecture that she had spontaneously admired since her arrival. It stood at the opposite pole to the Eaton Centre. For one thing its main function was not to promote the making of money, and for another it seemed to have been built not so much to dominate its surroundings as to be an integral part of them. Its designer seemed to have been trying to express some feeling about them.

Hope watched her, smiling, as she walked slowly round the sculpture of a polar bear standing with one paw protectively round her cub. It had been placed just outside the entrance, and Verity, as she looked at it, felt a flicker of excitement. Despite the urgency of her plight, she did not want to turn a deaf ear to what Hope was trying to tell her. She smiled at her. Hope took her arm.

"I knew you'd like it. It's just how an art gallery should look—in harmony with its setting as well as with all that's inside. Come in and see."

They joined the small queue waiting to buy tickets. During the short car journey they had spoken very little. Verity had slept badly, and felt depressed and lethargic, and disinclined to hurry the moment of revelation. Since the conversation on the terrace the previous evening she had felt even more disorientated than before. It was as if her whole relationship with her sister had been built on false premises. Her whole image of Hope had been false, and it was going to be no simple matter to reconstruct it—it was as if she had suddenly

146

changed role in mid-play. It did not make for ease of communication to discover that someone whom she had believed to be crushed by the circumstances of her life almost to the point of breakdown should possess to such a degree a talent which, of all artistic gifts, was perhaps the one which she admired most. Hope seemed to have grown in stature overnight.

Now, as they stood waiting their turn, she felt her spirits beginning to lift. They were, after all, on common ground—ground it was going to be possible to share far more fully than she had ever dreamed. It had been a stroke of genius on Hope's part to bring her here for their talk—as if she had felt that in these surroundings Verity could ask for her help knowing her true rank. The goosegirl had turned into the princess, and perhaps, as a result, had the power to defeat those who sought to harm her.

She shivered a little. She must not put off telling her story too long. Every nerve ending told her danger was near. Yet she longed to enjoy for just a little while the sensation of being at last in full communication with the sister she had lost so many years before. She glanced round apprehensively. Nothing had happened to trigger this feeling that something was about to happen—there had been no more talk of intruders in the grounds, and the drive to the gallery had been along virtually empty roads—but she could not suppress it. Instinctively, she moved a little closer to Hope.

Just as in the restaurant the previous day, everything seemed perfectly normal. People were standing in twos or threes conversing quietly, or studying catalogues. After all the hectic emotions of the last twenty-four hours everything seemed to have subsided into calm and order.

Venables, Jeffrey, the bishop—they were like so many painted manikins on the turntable of an ancient clock, figures that disappeared back into the belfry once they had played their part. Only the slight weight of the icon, hanging in its concealed pocket beneath her dress, reminded her that the clock was still ticking, and that she did not know what sort of figure would emerge next.

For a moment she wondered if, despite the obvious advantages, it had been foolhardy to venture away from the house with only Hope for protection, but she reassured herself with the thought that the gallery was a public place, and her enemies were anxious to avoid publicity. They were more likely to wait till she was alone, and no help was near. Such moments lay ahead. She shivered again.

Hope squeezed her arm.

"Are you feeling okay? You're very pale. Didn't you sleep?"

"Not much, to be truthful. There's too much on my mind. You, on the other hand, look blooming."

It was quite true. The change was remarkable. Hope had shed her depressive droop overnight. She was still a middle-aged woman with lines on her face and straggly dyed yellow hair, but there was a light in her eye, and a firmness about the muscles of her jaw that had not been there before. At breakfast she had taken part in the conversation with a vivacity that had visibly startled Leo, and had taken charge of the organization of the arrangements for the day with a quiet authority which had caused even the well-trained Nelly to lift an eyebrow. Leo had, of course, made no objection to Verity's request, and this morning had meekly accepted the role allotted to him—accompanying the triplets to the fun park followed by lunch out and a movie, a proposal that was greeted by screams of joy—with no more than a rueful look. Verity felt almost sorry for him. He, she foresaw, was going to be far more discomfited than she was by the transformation in his wife.

Hope squeezed her arm again as, having purchased their tickets, they moved across the spacious entrance hall with its geometric waterfall towards the door that led to the gallery.

"I'm leaving the timing to you," she said gently. "We could look at the pictures and then talk—or if you prefer we could talk first, and look for the answers in the pictures."

"Let's see the pictures first." Verity could not help it.

"I was hoping you'd say that. They'll give you heart, whatever it is that's wrong. You're about to see the real spirit of Canada—the spirit I often think everybody is doing their best to destroy."

Intrigued, Verity followed her into a dim corridor lit only by lamps carefully trained on the paintings.

Over coffee the previous evening Hope had told her about the Group of Seven, the band of Canadian artists who, earlier in the century, had broken away from the European tradition to found one that interpreted their feelings about their own country. They had travelled all over it, visiting the far north, absorbing its life, even, in some cases, losing their own in the process, painting as they went. Much of their work was displayed in this specially opened and extended gallery, along with that of later artists, including Indians, and Eskimos, whose aims were the same. Verity had been fascinated, for she had heard of none of them, and had not seen so much as a reproduction of their work during her stays in London.

Now, as she moved slowly down the corridor behind Hope, she felt that at last she was beginning to understand something of her own confused reactions to this extraordinary country. For the first time she felt she was seeing it as those who had first come to it had seen it, in all its purity, and for the first time she felt that she, too, would come to love it.

For here, all around her, was a celebration of the magnificence and cruelty of natural grandeur—landscape taken to its extremes. Brilliant colours, vibrant forms radiated untamed life and energy. The hard, icy greys of lakes and skies, the reds and golds of autumnal forests seemed almost to explode into the shadowy rooms, so intense was their vitality. This was the force of life made visible.

Verity drew a deep breath. She had never seen anything like it before. Even in the chilly marble gloom of a British town hall such paintings would have made their effect, but here, in a setting specially designed for them, she found them overwhelming.

"I come here whenever I can get away. It restores my faith. You could say it's the only place where I feel at home." Hope was speaking partly to herself.

Verity thought of the portfolio of work she had seen the previous evening, and nodded. It was hardly surprising that Hope, isolated as she was, should feel drawn here to where others had tried to express a similar vision. There had to be some nourishment for this lone flame, all but extinguished by the asphyxiating trivia of domestic life.

On a sudden, urgent impulse, she searched in her handbag, and brought out a printed card, which she handed to her sister.

"I want to give you this now, just in case there isn't another chance. It's the name of a very reputable dealer in Montreal—a friend of my partner's—I was supposed to be trying to contact him while I'm here. Take a selection of your work to him and say that I sent you. He'll look after you. I would have preferred to go with you myself, but the way things are shaping it—it may not be possible."

149

"Why, that's great. Thanks a lot. I'll go as soon as ever I can." Hope took the card and put it carefully in her wallet. She did not seem to have heard the last sentence. She turned to stare thoughtfully out of the window at the trees which seemed to be crowding down the grassy slope outside towards the window as if to check what sort of pictures the artists had made of them. When she turned round again Verity saw her face was glowing.

"You've been very kind, little sister. I'll never forget it."

Something inside Verity seemed to break.

"Hope—please help me. It won't wait any longer. I need to talk to you now."

The words burst out. She could think of no rational introduction. Hope, startled, gave her a quick look and drew her across to the seat in the middle of the room.

"Suppose you tell me what's wrong?"

"It's a long story."

"Then begin at the beginning."

The practical, maternal tone was an immediate comfort. She obeyed—to find an immediate, sweet relief in at last pouring it all out. Hope listened incredulously.

"Why ever didn't you tell me before?"

"You seemed so tired, and I—I didn't want to worry you—you were already under so much pressure. I wouldn't be telling you now, but I just don't think I can manage on my own. If I stay any longer in your house you are all going to be in danger. I've thought and thought, and I've come to the conclusion that the best thing I can do is to find somewhere to hide—as far away as possible—and lie low there until the bishop gets back. The trouble is that I've hardly any money, and I don't know where to go. That's where I need your help."

There was a pause as Hope struggled to take it in.

"Are you saying that you've had this icon in your possession all the time you've been with us?"

Verity nodded.

"Is that why you were mugged at Niagara?"

"Possibly. I can't be sure."

"And the guy Matt saw lurking in the grounds?"

"Again, possibly."

"My God! And all without saying a word to anyone! And now you're saying you're stuck with it for another week. Haven't you any idea why this Jeffrey guy didn't show up?"

"None. We agreed it would be safer not to contact each other."

"Didn't that worry you? I mean, you only met him on the plane? It would have made me very suspicious. Weren't you being—well—naive, to put it mildly?"

"It wasn't like that. I—I got to know him quite well. He didn't want me to take the icon at all. I was the one who insisted."

"I bet you didn't have to insist very hard."

"But he wasn't even going to tell me about it. It happened quite by accident that I found out . . ."

"And accidents do happen, don't they? It couldn't possibly have been contrived? It sure was amazingly convenient for this Jeffrey . . ."

"Hope, you're wrong—quite wrong." Verity was stung by the sarcastic tone. "He isn't like that, I'm absolutely sure of it. He just isn't the type."

"I don't believe there's a man on the face of the earth who doesn't have it in him to be the type if it suits his purpose." It was a flash of the old bitterness. "It's my belief you've walked right into a cleverly prepared trap—a real gullible little tourist, that's you. Your Jeffrey is probably hitting the town right now, taking out his girl and rubbing his hands at having got you to do his dirty work for him."

"No. You've got it wrong. I know you have. He isn't like that. I trust him. There'll be some good reason why he didn't turn up yesterday, I'm sure of it. And even if you were right it wouldn't really change anything. I'd still want to protect the icon, and take it to the right person."

"The right person as I see it is a policeman. It isn't your problem."

"I've already told you why I can't do that. Oh Hope, please try and understand."

"I *am* trying. I just can't see why you're so determined to be involved."

Verity looked at her hopelessly, unable to see how to convince her. She tried a different tack.

"P'raps you've never really seen an icon, or understood its importance. First and foremost it's a religious symbol, of course—but it's also a work of art in its own right—and this one is a particularly beautiful one."

Hope shrugged.

"I never could get worked up about religious paintings. All those po-faced madonnas and fat babies. This—" she gestured at the landscapes on the walls around them "—is what speaks to me."

"When you see it you may find you change your mind. Believe me, it's no ordinary painting. It's a small masterpiece."

"It's still not your problem."

Verity lost her patience, and stood up abruptly.

"If that's how you're going to react, I'm sorry I told you. I don't happen to think that way. I believe that the fate of something so rare and so beautiful, so full of history, *is* my problem, and yours, and that of every caring person. But you seem determined not to understand. Forget I spoke. I'll manage by myself. I don't yet know how, but I'll find a way."

Hope caught her arm and pulled her down again.

"Take it easy. I said I didn't think it was your problem. I didn't say I wouldn't help. I guess I owe you. Look, if you won't hand it over to the police—and I think I can understand why you don't want to do that—could I suggest an alternative?"

"What?"

"Ask Leo to help you. He's got far more influence than I have. He'd know how to protect your icon and see you out of trouble. He'd be only too glad to do something for you. You must realize you'd never make it all on your own."

"Why not? I have done for years." The words came out in a snap.

"I know you have, honey." Hope's tone was placating. "You've been incredibly brave. But here you're in a strange country—*this* country—" again she gestured at the paintings. "It's a very different thing. It would crush you. Or they'd find you."

"Not if I went far enough away—somewhere out in the wild. They can't search the whole of Canada."

"But why not let Leo help? He'd take the whole thing off your shoulders."

"Hope, dear—just think what you are saying—" Verity did her best to keep her voice neutral. She had expected this reaction. "If you, who are an artist, can't or won't sympathize with what I'm

trying to do, what do you suppose Leo will say? You said yourself—he doesn't have the same values. If you could advise me to hand
it over to the police, he'd insist. He wouldn't even begin to
understand."

"You don't like him much, do you?"

"Is that so surprising? He doesn't seem to have made you very
happy." Verity had flushed.

"You mustn't judge him too quickly. If I've been unhappy it could
be that it wasn't altogether his fault. He's done what he could.
He's tried hard to give me what I needed—security, status, comfort—everything you and I both lost when our parents split up. But
there was one thing he couldn't give me, something he couldn't even
understand I needed—and which I now think is essential to
happiness . . ."

"What's that?"

"A sense of my own identity. When I got married I didn't know
who or what I was. I'd always done what was expected of me,
accepted other people's image of me. I didn't have one of myself. I
was a docile, self-abasing, anxious *child*. And all the time, deep inside
me, something was waiting to be released, something I had to find,
and work to free. It's a painful path to tread, that one, and it has to be
trodden alone. You can't really blame Leo if he didn't help, didn't
even know what was wrong—especially when you take into account
he's never known that problem—his self-confidence is a spontaneous
growth. He could hardly help taking me over."

"And yet now you're advising me to let him do the same thing to
me . . ."

"It isn't the same thing at all." Hope stared.

"Yes, it is. Perhaps I haven't made it clear enough how much this
matter of the icon means to me—how much, having taken on the
responsibility, I want to see it through. I didn't even realize it myself
at first, not completely, but I'm realizing it now."

"But why?"

"I suppose because my story is basically the same as yours. I
always leaned on other people—first parents, then you, then James,
then the professionals. Perhaps if I hadn't lost the baby I might have
grown up—but I did lose it. And when they'd finished stitching me
together again I crept off to my little Welsh village to lick my wounds

153

and keep away from trouble. I took care to live a very safe, gentle life. And for years I've been telling myself that was all I wanted. Only just like you, something must have been waiting all along to find the light of day and bring me back to life—because quite suddenly I began to realize that what I had wasn't enough . . ."

"—so you wrote to me."

"I wrote to you. I wrote several times—and tore up the letters. It was the hardest step I'd taken in years. And if I could have seen where it was going to take me I'd never have dared to take it. I'd have gone on hiding away . . ."

"But why is the icon so important?"

"I think—" Verity spoke slowly, gazing at a big, harsh Lauren Harris painting of a frozen lake surrounded by fir trees that hung opposite them—"I think that persuading Jeffrey to let me take the icon instead of him was one of the first truly adult things I've ever done."

"Adult?"

"Yes. I'd discovered, in the short time I knew him, that he was even more childlike than I was myself—childlike, vulnerable and idealistic."

"You must have made a fine pair."

"I'm serious, Hope. I couldn't let him run the risk of getting hurt. He's one of the most sensitive people I've ever met."

"And you think you *would* get over it? Have you really faced it Verity? What experience of violence have you—I mean violence to your own person? I don't think you've been any more adult than this Jeffrey of yours. And now you're refusing to ask for help from the one person who could effectively give it to you. Is that adult? Which do you put first—your own sense of personal fulfilment, or the actual safety of the icon?"

"Hope, that isn't fair!" Verity's cheeks burned. There was no way she could explain how deeply unfair it was.

"It's realistic. So is asking Leo. You know perfectly well that if you make it clear to him that the last thing you want is for the icon to be handed over to the police he won't go against you. He'd find some other way of seeing it's delivered safely to His Reverence. We may not approve of his values, but the guy sure knows how to get things done."

"That's not what you said at Niagara!"

Hope laughed, and stood up.

"As I recall, I behaved rather badly at Niagara. I was under great strain trying to decide whether I had the nerve to show you my work—and what I'd do if you said it was no good."

"You *must* have known I couldn't possibly say that!"

"Sometimes I did, sometimes I didn't. Either way, Leo didn't pick on a very good moment for his Siegfried act."

"You called it Tarzan at the time."

"Did I indeed? Quelle bitch! I expect I was drunk. Look—I suggest we carry on with this over lunch. I'm a great believer in taking care of the inner woman before trying to make important decisions."

"We weren't all completely wrong about you. You *are* practical!"

Hope grinned.

"I've never denied it. Only now you know I'm something else as well."

In the restaurant a table had been reserved for them by the window. On the terrace just outside people were eating their lunch under gaily coloured umbrellas.

"I thought you'd probably prefer to stay in the cool. It can get uncomfortably hot out there."

"You did right. I like the room."

The pale wood panelling on the walls, with small carvings of animals in low relief, was soothingly neutral after the vivid colours in the gallery. Verity remembered the aspidistras and bentwood coat stands of the previous day, and smiled.

"What's the joke?"

"This time yesterday I was still waiting for Jeffrey to turn up. I was thinking how different everything seems now."

"Different, and a whole lot more dangerous, I should think."

The waitress came to take their order, this time without the would-be-friendly overtures, to Verity's relief. When she had gone Hope leaned forward.

"Surely you can see that it's too big for you, Verity. You're playing around with something way beyond your capacities, and you could get hurt. I sympathize with your feelings but when I tell you to hand it over to Leo I'm giving you sound adult advice."

"And if I don't take it?"

"If you don't take it you're behaving like a romantic fool."

"According to you I'm that already, so it won't make any difference, will it? What I want to know is will *you* help me, Hope? Because there's nothing that you can say that will make me change my mind. I'm not going to hand the icon over to Leo, and I don't want his kind of help. I'm afraid that's final."

Hope's face darkened, and she compressed her lips. She did not reply. The silence grew more and more strained as they waited for their food to be brought. By the time it came Verity would have welcomed a contribution to the dialogue even from the waitress, but none was forthcoming. It did not help that she knew that Hope, had the circumstances been different, would have been absolutely right, and that the course of action she was recommending was the very one she herself longed to follow.

She picked at the dish she had ordered without enthusiasm. It was delicious, but she had lost all appetite. She saw that Hope was doing the same. Their eyes met. The older woman's face suddenly softened. She put down her knife and held out her hand.

"I seem to be putting on the big sister act. It's your decision, isn't it?"

"You'll help me?" Verity gripped the proffered hand.

"I guess I'd better try. Someone's got to be practical around here. Like deciding on where you're going to go and how you're going to get there. Don't you think it would be better to try and hide out downtown somewhere. It'd be a whole lot easier to fix."

"Quite honestly, I don't think I could stand it. I'd go off my head in the city. I'm used to country life, remember."

"Do you think you're being followed?" Hope glanced nervously at the other diners.

"I thought I was yesterday, but if so I must have thrown them off the trail. I'm certain no-one was behind us this morning."

"I wonder why they haven't just grabbed you."

"I've wondered that myself. I came to the conclusion that it must be because I'm staying with you and Leo. The last thing they want is

156

to hit the headlines—they're not to know I haven't brought you both into my confidence."

"So why not just stay on with us as planned?"

"Hope, these people stop at nothing. They must be getting desperate. You've got the girls to think about. I can't risk it."

"Mmm. I see that. Do you think they know where you're planning to deliver it?"

"I don't know. The most frightening thing about all this is that I don't know anything. I don't know who they are, what they look like, where they may be waiting, how much they know. It makes me feel like a mouse that's being played with by a large, invisible cat. That's why I want to get as far away as I can—out of their reach. And I must go soon, Hope. I just know it. I have a feeling that it will all come to a head before very much longer."

"So where could you go? Who do I know who'd help? I need to think . . ." For a few minutes she continued thoughtfully with her meal. Suddenly she pushed her plate away.

"Got it!"

"You know somewhere?"

"Just the place—if it's free. I'll call the owners. I'll do it right away, as soon as I've paid the bill—there's a better chance of catching them home at lunch time."

She signalled to the waitress. Verity pushed away her food.

"Where is it?"

"It's in Northern Ontario, much further north than our cottage. It'll mean a long drive, I'm afraid, but it has the advantage of being in a much wilder location. It's a fishing cabin by a lake which belongs to some friends of mine—at least the wife is a friend of mine. Mary-Lou's husband Bill is what you might describe as a lapsed Mennonite. He left the horse-and-buggy-and-plough-your-own-furrow brotherhood to carve himself out an empire in the food industry. He's done very well indeed. I've always suspected that his beloved fishing cabin is a sop to the old Mennonite conscience. They don't even use a plane to get up there for all their pots of money. Everything's done the hard way. Mary-Lou backs him because she's crazy about conservation. They bought the cabin off some trappers, and they've kept it exactly as it was. You'll find it primitive, to say the least—but as a hide-out it's perfect."

157

"How would I get there?"

"You drive, don't you?"

"Yes, but—"

"Then the only problem is finding you a car. If Leo had been in the secret you could have had one of ours and there'd be no problem—as it is I'll have to work on it. Money's straightforward enough—there's plenty in my account. You won't need much in any case—you'll be taking all your food with you. Where's that girl gone?"

"It sounds just the thing."

"Just as long as you think you can face the isolation. I've been there a couple of times with Leo, and I'm not sure I could. There's no phone, and no neighbours for miles. As long as we can get you away unnoticed, they'd never find you there."

"I'm used to living on my own in the country. It won't worry me. I'll borrow some painting gear off you if I may, and some books. I'd feel far safer than in the town. But won't your friends be using it themselves—this is the holiday season?"

"I was speaking to Mary-Lou only the other day, and I'm almost certain she said something about visiting their daughter in the States some time soon. We'll soon know." She was rapping her fingers impatiently on the table.

"But how will I get away without Leo knowing?" Verity was beginning to see pitfalls on every side.

"That, my sweet, is the real problem, and I need to think about it. If Leo gets wind of it you're sunk. He'd never let you go off on your own."

"He can hardly stop me if it's what I want."

"Don't you believe it. He'd stop you all right."

"What about Mary-Lou and Bill—won't they try and stop me too?"

"We're not going to tell them you're alone," Hope replied grimly. "There's no reason why we should."

"But Leo—"

"Verity, give me a break, will you? Like I said, I need to think."

She finally succeeded in attracting the waitress's attention, and settled the bill. They stood up to go.

"I suggest you have another stroll round the pictures while I go look for a phone. Tell yourself you may very well soon be seeing the real thing—it could give you fresh insight!"

Verity did as she was told. She found that she was, indeed, looking at the landscapes with different eyes. She could be about to see and experience for herself some of the scenes that had inspired the artists. For herself and by herself. And as she looked it occurred to her that she did not really have the faintest idea what was meant by living alone. Living just outside a village in tiny, human-scale Wales could not be compared with being a single, infinitesimal dot amongst these huge, wild expanses.

Suddenly the whole plan seemed totally foolhardy. They had overlooked too many factors. Above all they had forgotten that she was a foreigner and ignorant of this land. She could identify neither animal nor plant. It was madness to imagine that she could survive removed from all human contact.

She took a few irresolute steps after Hope, to call her back and prevent the phone call that committed them—only to stop. The alternative, hiding away in the depths of the city, was somehow more frightening still. If hide she must, she preferred to do so in the freedom of the wild. If the next seven days were to be a struggle for survival, it was more fitting that this should take place in a setting where such a struggle was general, where her own ordeal would merge into the general pattern. In the city she would finish up cowering in a locked room, lost and terrified. And if by any chance she were to die, she did not want to die like that.

Hope was taking a long time over her phone call. Wandering on, she went into a room they had not visited before lunch. It was full of Eskimo sculptures. Walking slowly round it, she stopped before the figure of a wounded bear in some sort of greenish, black-veined stone she did not recognize. The sculptor had captured the very essence of pain in the tense humping of the shoulder muscles. He had captured something else, too, something that spoke poignantly to her: the immense, patient dignity of the suffering beast as it faced its death. It seemed to be telling her that fear was out of place. Acceptance was the only answer—learning to be at peace with inner and outer pain.

Thoughtfully she turned away. She felt as if she were being given a choice—and that it might be one of the most important of her life.

"I'm sorry I've been so long!" Hope came hurrying back as she

159

was leaving the room. "There was a line up for the phone, and when it was finally my turn the number was busy. But all's well—she's agreed! We'd better get going right away. We've got to drive to their place to pick up the key, then go on to the bank. I'm afraid it'll make us later home than I agreed—I won't be very popular."

"Whatever did you tell your friend?" said Verity as they made their way back to the car park. "Isn't she very trusting to lend her house to a complete stranger?"

"Nuts. We're good friends, and you're my sister. Besides, you'd hardly call it a house. There's not much damage you could do—when I said it was primitive, I wasn't exaggerating. She often lends it. She's perfectly happy about it just as long as everyone goes along with all her conservationist do's and don'ts. I told her you have a wonderful new boyfriend, and are dying to spend a few days out in the wild with him. She's incurably romantic—she drank it up. There's nothing Mary-Lou likes better than to give young love a helping hand. You'd better try to look suitably dewy-eyed when you meet her. You'll like her—she's a good sort."

Mary-Lou turned out, somewhat unexpectedly, to be a tall woman with frizzy, platinum-blonde hair, enormous false eyelashes and flowing, vaporous clothes which almost, but not quite, disguised her generous build. When she smiled she was beautiful. Verity, encountering this smile across the polished expanse of her sitting room, was won immediately.

She left Hope to do the talking and concentrated on appearing full of happy anticipation—succeeding almost too well in that most of the exchange that followed went completely over her head.

At last, armed with key, map, and a list of instructions that rendered most of the preceding conversation superfluous, they took their leave. Mary-Lou, standing at the top of elaborate marble steps which were an eloquent clue to what lay inside the front door, enveloped Verity in a warm, moist, maternal hug.

"You have a good time, honey, and make the most of it. You're only young once. Be sure and come and tell me about it when you get back. Oh—and one last thing—don't either of you try diving off the bluff. It looks safe—but there are rocks just below the surface."

"Don't worry, Mary-Lou!" Hope called back as they climbed into the car. "They know how to take care of themselves. Have a good time in the States! You must come over for a meal when you get back. I'll call you."

Verity, waving out of the window, could not help feeling guilty. There was something base about lying to a smile like that.

Glancing at the map she had been given, her former doubts returned in force.

"I'll never find this place," she said despairingly to Hope as they drove back to the highway.

"Oh yes you will. I'll go over that and the other maps with you, don't worry. It's perfectly straightforward—just rather a long way. If you can manage Welsh mountain lanes, you'll find Canadian roads a walkover. You can even understand the signposts. I'll also give you a quick briefing about the pitfalls of country life out here—though you'll find most of it in Mary-Lou's instructions—I don't know why she doesn't publish a book and have done with it. For instance —don't go thinking she's neurotic about garbage disposal. She has good reason to worry, and you don't know the ways of racoons. She'll kill me if she and Bill have to spend their next vacation up there digging out the guests invited in by my sentimental English sister. You'd never believe the amount of damage they can do. I take it you read about skunks at school?"

Verity nodded, laughing.

"Just as well. And we must make sure you can identify poison ivy, too. I'll see if we've got a book with a picture of it. Wow—there's a heap of things to think of! We'd better put our minds to it now—there won't be much chance once we're back with the family."

The words were prophetic, as it happened.

When Hope, with a turn of speed that seemed wholly out of character, finally screeched into the long drive to the house, it was to find the broad gravel sweep before it crowded with police cars, the front door open, and the whole scene bearing a close resemblance to a newly disturbed ants' nest.

"What the hell took you so long?" Leo was white-faced with anger.

"What's happened? Are the girls okay?"

"Of course they're okay—they were out with me. It's Nelly you should be worrying about. We've been burgled, that's what's happened. Turned right over. It wouldn't have happened if you'd come back when you said you would. I gave Matt and Mary the afternoon off on the assumption you'd keep your word—which left Nelly here by herself. She's sure had a rough time."

"Is she hurt?" Verity's voice was thin and strained.

"A bump on the head. She'll be all right. It's been a bad shock and she's still very upset. They tied her up while they went through the house. The alarm system, of course, wasn't even set."

"Have they taken much?" asked Hope.

"That's the strange thing about it—I can't find anything missing at all. You'd better go check your belongings."

As he turned away to speak to a policeman, she and Verity exchanged a look. Verity shook her head warningly. They did not speak until they had reached the top of the stairs, when Hope gripped her arm.

"Are you thinking what I'm thinking?"

"I would imagine so."

"Where had you hidden the icon?"

"I had it with me."

"Thank heaven for that! I suppose it could be an ordinary burglary . . ."

"No. This time I'm sure. I told you—I felt it coming."

"Well, we'd better check, just in case . . ."

Verity stopped in the doorway of her room as if she had been struck. It was hard to believe in the reality of what lay before her eyes.

The room had been subjected to thorough, systematic violence. Chairs lay on their sides. The sheets had been ripped off the bed. Pillows and mattresses had been slit open. The contents of the open drawers lay in heaps on the floor, and even the lining paper hung in shreds. Pictures had been peeled from their frames and lay, covered with feathers, on the carpet, which itself had been yanked from its moorings. Nothing whatsoever had been left untouched.

Her heart gave a sudden, frantic skitter. In all the emotion of the last twenty-four hours she had completely forgotten to get rid of the remains of Venables's bible. She had left it where she had so hastily hidden it on her first day—in the flight bag at the back of the cupboard. For the second time she had been unforgivably careless.

She picked her way across the room and peered inside the cupboard. The flight bag was still there, beneath a tangled pile of clothes. Her hands shaking, she pulled it out. The bible was gone.

Frantic now, she began to search through the debris of the once beautiful room, but could find no trace of it. She went through her jewelry. None of it was missing, not even the pretty, valuable antique ring that had been James's engagement present. The enemy had not bothered to disguise the fact that he was looking for something more important.

Her knees were giving way under her. She sat down on the ravaged bed and buried her head in her hands. There could be no more ducking it, no more doubt. The proof lay all around her. This violation of her room and of her personal belongings was a foretaste of what lay ahead if she made any more mistakes, as was what they had done to Nelly. In forgetting the bible she had given them the final proof they needed—if they needed one—that it was she who carried the icon. It was almost as if she had wanted them to know . . .

"Good grief, I thought our room was a mess, but they've had one hell of a ball in here! Have they taken much?" Hope was standing in the door, shaking her head in disbelief.

Verity looked up.

"Only one thing. You might say it's enough. You see I never got round to destroying the remains of the bible the icon was hidden in for its journey over here. I meant to ask Nelly, but—well—I was rather self-conscious about it—it would have seemed such a peculiar thing to ask, especially after that scene with Claire. Anyway, they've got it now. Which means they can be absolutely sure I've got the icon, even if they weren't before."

"If you'd only told me about it sooner I could have got rid of it without the slightest trouble. I'd forgotten all about your episode with Claire. It's a wonder Leo hasn't suspected something. Right now he's a puzzled guy. It seems they cracked the safe and then left everything that was in it—even my diamonds. It's my suspicion he's feeling almost insulted—like he's been passed over for promotion. You and I had better watch our tongues."

"They can hardly help reaching the conclusion that whoever did it was looking for something. Oh Hope—I wish I could get away now—tonight . . ."

"I'm sure you do—but you must see it isn't possible. It *has* to be carefully planned. Of course, it would be different if you'd only change your mind about telling Leo—"

"I thought we'd settled that."

Hope shrugged.

"I know we did—but I can't help wishing you'd see sense, especially now you can see what sort of people you're up against. Okay—don't look like that, I'll say no more. Besides, I do have the glimmerings of a plan for getting you away. It's complicated, but it's the best I can think of to get you off to a good start. I'll come and tell you about it later. We'd better go join the others or they'll begin to wonder . . . I'll send Mrs Matt up here to make it more habitable for you."

Stepping over one of the damaged paintings to follow Hope back downstairs, Verity was suddenly struck by a stomach-churning thought.

"Hope—your work—they haven't damaged it, have they?"

Hope smiled.

"I wouldn't be here talking to you like this if they had. I'd've been out after them—with a gun! No—they threw them around a bit, but there's no real damage."

"Thank heaven for that."

"P'raps when we talk later you'll show me this famous icon. I don't take kindly to having my paintings passed over like that—I want to size up the competition. You realize that if they'd been damaged it would have earned itself another enemy—and even you might not have been able to save it then!"

Verity wondered, as they rejoined the general commotion downstairs, if the words had not been intended as a sort of warning. Hope, it seemed, had not only found her bearings, she had set her course. From now on nothing would be allowed to deflect her from it.

For the second day in succession, the evening meal was a strained affair. The food was a disaster—Nelly had been prostrated by shock, and Mrs Matt had been too busy looking after her and setting as much to rights as was possible to devote much attention to culinary refinements.

The triplets, too worn out even to quarrel by the world-shattering nature of an event in which their father's authority and importance appeared to have been completely flouted, sat unhappily picking at their food until one after another, as if at a pre-arranged signal, their heads drooped and they began to yawn helplessly. It was Hope, this time, who took them off to bed.

When she returned, it was to be greeted by Leo with all the reproaches he had, it seemed, been waiting to deliver. He obviously blamed the whole catastrophe on the lateness of her return. Verity would have thought him grossly unfair, had she not perceived how deeply he was shaken. She looked anxiously at Hope, afraid that she might be goaded into explanation. Hope, however, merely tightened her lips.

"I take it you've arranged for us to have a police guard tonight," she said coolly to her husband, ignoring his complaints. "If they didn't find whatever it was they were looking for they may come back. Are you involved in some secret takeover, or are you planning to overthrow the government?"

Verity held her breath. Leo, however, merely gave his wife a murderous look, and went obediently to the phone.

"I haven't, but I'll fix it if it'll make you feel any easier in your mind. I doubt if they'd come back now everyone's here—they'd never have come in the first place if . . ."

"You've already said all that, and I've said I'm sorry. I couldn't foresee what was going to happen. It was a mistake, and I won't make another. Now, if you don't mind, there's a programme I'd like to watch . . ."

Verity was tempted to laugh at the expression on Leo's face, but restrained herself. Once again, she almost felt sorry for him.

It was a relief, all the same, when she could at last return to her room. Mrs Matt had done her best, but the walls, bare of their pictures, seemed to stare at her reproachfully. She would be glad, next morning, to leave it all behind.

Mechanically, she began to sort out the clothes she would need. Having Hope as her ally eased all sorts of practical difficulties, she realized. She was glad now that she had let her into the secret. She was beginning to wonder how she could ever have been taken in by her first impressions of her sister—she had never suspected that so much strength could lie hidden beneath that tired exterior.

A soft knock on the door preceded her entry. With a stab of guilt Verity noticed how pale she was, and how dark the circles under her eyes.

"I mustn't stay long. I think Leo is beginning to wonder if we're plotting something. He didn't get to his present position through sticking his head in the sand. I'll tell you now what I think we should do, though there are one or two details I need to sleep on."

She outlined her plan.

"It sounds as if it could work," said Verity when she had finished.

"You sound doubtful."

"It's just that I think Leo may find it hard to swallow."

"Leave Leo to me. I'll convince him all right. No, as I see it, the only awkward part is phoning my friend Micaela so early in the day to ask her to have the kids. On the other hand it's an emergency—and she owes me. I'm nearly sure it'll be okay. I'll make the most of the burglary."

"Oh Hope, I seem to have put you to so much trouble! How can I ever thank you enough? It was meant to be an ordinary holiday."

"No need for thanks. You've helped me more than you'll ever know. And as for the trouble—how about giving me a quick peep at this icon everyone seems to be going crazy about? I sure am curious to see a painting that produces such an effect on people. You could almost say I'm jealous."

Verity brought out the white satin bag, and handed it to her.

"When you look at it carefully, I think you'll understand."

Hope slipped it from its coverings.

"Oh." Then, after a long pause. "Tell me about it."

So Verity told her all she knew.

"You see why it's called an icon of Loving Kindness, or Tenderness as some say—it's the pose. Other portrayals show the mother and child sitting stiffly apart, blessing the world, but in this it's the contact, the actual loving touching between the human and the divine that's important. You could say it symbolizes all the love in the world and in heaven, all expressed in maternity."

"It looks pretty old."

"I'm no expert so I can't date it, but it's certainly been around a long time. It's become a symbol in itself. It has a reputation for working miracles. That's why they're so desperate to save it, and why others are determined to destroy it. It's hard to imagine anyone wanting to destroy a thing like this, isn't it? But you only have to look at the state of your house to see they're in earnest. Why Hope, what's the matter?"

She had suddenly seen that Hope's eyes were brimming with tears.

"It's just that—maternity's never meant that for me. This is all about a feeling I've missed out on."

"What do you mean? You've got three beautiful—"

"You're the first person I've ever told. I had wanted to start a family as soon as we moved out here, but it didn't happen. As time went by, I grew desperate. We underwent batteries of humiliating, ghastly tests. I gave up hope. Then Leo persuaded me to try a course of one of the new fertility drugs—and it worked. When they told us I was expecting quads, he was over the moon."

"Quads?"

"One baby died—the boy. We never speak of that. The trouble was—I didn't seem able to feel anything at all. I'd wanted a baby, sure, but I wanted one Leo and I had made together—not the result of a chemical compound that had changed me into a rabbit."

"Didn't you tell anyone how you felt?"

"I couldn't. In any case they were all so delighted the thing had worked they wouldn't have taken any notice. For Leo and the doctors the birth was a triumph of technical success. As it was a caesarean you could say that in a sense I wasn't even there. They told me afterwards it had been a very complicated one and that I'd nearly died. I was so ill and weak afterwards, I wished I had."

"Oh Hope! If only I'd known! If only I could have helped!"

Hope smiled bitterly.

"I guess at that time you were just about the last person to be able to help. Nobody seemed to worry that I couldn't feel anything, anything at all, for my three daughters. They called my depression the normal aftermath of a difficult birth. They never looked further than that. It lasted till I met Hélène, and began to paint. Can you understand it? Can you understand that I've never been able to feel love for my children—to experience the—the radiance that's at the heart of this painting? It's simply never existed for me . . ." The last words came out in a little cry. The tears were running down her cheeks.

Verity put her arm round the bowed shoulders. This time there was no flinching away.

"I think it has," she said gently. "I think you've experienced it, but in a different form. You found your way to it through your work. It's what makes it so powerful."

"Even if that were so, it doesn't help the girls, does it? You can't say I haven't failed them . . ."

"I don't think you're the one that failed them. Other people failed you. But in any case you can't call them deprived. They've got an adoring father, a wonderful home, all the possessions they could want, and they're well cared for. You've done your best. Most people would have been completely defeated. You weren't—you've found your way to becoming a superlative painter. You can't call that failure. I wouldn't feel I'd failed if I could paint like you."

She knew she was not speaking the truth, and wondered if it showed. There was, she thought sadly, no substitute for the tenderness that was symbolized so poignantly by the icon. It meant too much—for it was at the same time both real and mystical, immediate and reaching out to the furthermost limits of life itself—beyond even, into death. The painters of icons such as this one had used all their skill to communicate a knowledge that in their day few had explored, a skill that now, several hundred years later, was speaking so painfully to her sister.

Through no fault of her own Hope had been barred from that knowledge, with the result that she had looked for it elsewhere—and the result was to be discerned in her paintings. And because of what she had found her work would live on, perhaps beyond her own life span, and that of her children. That, in itself, was wonderful indeed, but it was not, and never could be, the same as the real thing.

She was still staring at the icon.

"I understand now what you've been trying to tell me," she murmured. "I didn't before. I thought you'd been taken in by fairy tales. But this is—bigger than itself, if you know what I mean."

Verity nodded.

"All icons are supposed to be that," she said. "They were meant to be aids—a kind of doorway if you like—to the mystical experience. I'd read about it, but like you I only really understood it when I saw this one. It had the same sort of effect on me. I'm glad you understand. Perhaps you'll forgive me now for all the trouble I seem to have brought with me?"

Hope handed back the little picture.

"Forgiving hardly comes into it, does it? I guess I'm privileged to be given the chance to help you save it. I'd give you an armed escort if I could, but I'll have to make do with trying to get you away safely . . . I'd better go. I'll knock on your door first thing in the morning, and you can pass me your bags—you won't need much. Goodnight honey. Try and get some sleep."

She kissed her lightly on the cheek, and was gone.

Verity found she had a lump in her throat. For a short space she had been allowed to come close to this sister whom, she realized, she had never known. And now she was about to be separated from her again. She wondered if they would ever be able to be so close again. She doubted it. Leo would always be there to prevent it.

Angrily, she began to make a pile of the clothes she would need. She did not want to think about Leo.

Chapter 10

Jeffrey's wanderings had become more and more disturbed. He wanted to make a change, to move out of this dark house of his, but he was too afraid. He knew the door was guarded. In the end, fighting back his fear, he opened the old-fashioned sash window and climbed out. He fell—to find himself lying on soft grass, staring up at the night sky. All was blackness—universe upon universe unlit by sun or moon.

He jumped to his feet in sudden terror and ran towards the safety of the house. It had disappeared. It was as if it had never existed. Panic flooded him. He could not survive in this night without a house. He had been a fool to think of escaping from it when it was all the shelter there was. He stumbled in frantic circles searching for it, but all he found was a deeper emptiness, and deeper and still deeper darkness. Exhausted he gave up, and lay down to rest. He was too weak to search any more. It was better to rest, to allow the darkness to close over him as the failing swimmer finally allows the water to close over his head. The panic was subsiding. In its place spread a soft, sweet relief as he felt himself becoming part of the night. He no longer wanted his house. This peace was what he had always wanted, even if he had always feared it. He need not have been so afraid. This slow sense of release was kinder than anything he had ever known.

A light was approaching. He turned his head away. It hurt his eyes, penetrating his eyelids and dancing and flickering in his head. Again he turned from it. He only wanted the darkness now. He deserved it. He had earned it. But the light would not let him be. Insistently, maddeningly, it searched him out as the mosquito seeks its sleeping victim, stabbing again and again until the blackness hung in tatters and he saw he was back once more in the familiar shabby house—the house that was never sufficiently clean or orderly. Sadly he looked round it, filled with an aching sense of loss. He did not want the light. He only wanted peace. Yet it summoned him with an authority he could not disobey, as a candle flame summons a moth. Reluctantly he opened his eyes.

"My God! So you *are* in there! I was beginning to wonder . . ."

The voice was bantering, but the face he saw close to his, a face he seemed to have met somewhere during his wanderings, was wet with tears.

"Hi!" He could only manage a whisper. He tried to make out her features. It was not Verity. Yet he seemed to know that wide, generous mouth and slightly turned up nose. He also seemed to know the room where he lay, though he had no idea where he was. It was hard to focus. His head and body felt oddly light. He blinked. Now he saw he was looking into a pair of steady blue eyes.

"Hi. Have you come back to stay this time, or will I have to go looking for you all over again? You sure seem to have trouble making up your mind. Have we time for introductions?"

Her hand was holding his wrist. She seemed satisfied with what she found there, for presently she nodded.

"That's better. I'd say we have. I'm Evie Thomson. Your very own personal nurse."

"Jeffrey Wren. I'm a writer." There seemed to be something wrong with his voice—there was no strength in it.

The wide mouth curved in a delighted grin.

"Better and better. Welcome aboard Mr Wren. I was beginning to think you weren't going to make it."

"How long have I been here?"

"Three days."

"You can't mean that! I can't have been here three days!"

Anguish gripped him, and the blood began to pound in his ears. He tried to sit up, but now his body, instead of light, suddenly felt absurdly heavy, as if it did not belong to him. In his frustration he whimpered aloud, like a child.

She held his hand between her own, and stroked it.

"Take it easy, mister—" the voice, he had heard that voice, too, during his wanderings—"you've been travelling a long way. You very nearly went clean off the map. It's been a hard trip, and if I weren't a very stubborn dame with a built-in dislike for losing my patients, you'd never have made it back."

He opened his mouth to reply, but she laid a finger on his lips.

"Let's get one thing clear. Whatever it is that's bugging you, there's nothing you can do about it right now. Later, when you're stronger, we'll talk. Will you trust me?"

He closed his eyes, and the corners of his mouth twitched in a faint smile of acquiescence, though she could see a nervous quiver in the muscles of his throat that wrung her heart. She realized that she must not wait too long—he needed to be eased of the burden he was carrying before he could begin any real recovery.

It had been a hard trip for her as well. His temperature, as she had been afraid it might, had flared that first evening. At first she had not been too alarmed, but when it had continued to rise she had appealed to one of her old boyfriends, a doctor at her previous hospital, to come round and take a look. Powerful antibiotics had driven out the infection, but the patient had almost gone with it. The doctor had tried to persuade her to move him to hospital, but she had resisted, convinced that to do so would destroy what little remained of his will to live. She had a gut feeling about this patient. She was certain his condition was not just the result of concussion, and pain and shock, but of something deeper—as if he had fought and lost some vital moral battle. Something inside had broken. Whatever star it was he had been following had led him into regions where such as he stood little chance of survival.

She had observed him during these last days and nights, and her first impressions had solidified into the conviction that this was no average beer-swilling, sports-addicted member of the male sex. She noticed the nervously drawn nostrils, the broad forehead, and the sensitive lines of the mouth, and recognized in him one of those individuals who feel more deeply than most. What his reactions had been when he found himself at the wrong end of a lighted cigarette she could not begin to conjecture.

It was a case outside all her previous experience, and she knew no rules for its treatment. She could only rely on her instincts and her beliefs. In three days, she had only left his side to snatch brief periods of sleep, leaving Mr Ho to watch in her place. She had completely forgotten her original intention of using these days of leave to take a badly needed rest. She had forgotten the entire structure of her everyday life. All she knew was an overwhelming compulsion to persuade this man back to life.

For this was what it amounted to. As she had bathed, and bandaged and cared for him that first morning, she had sensed his gradual withdrawal. He had survived the horror of what had been perpetrated on him only to be undone by kindness. The awareness of being gently, lovingly treated seemed to have completed his defeat. He had put himself into her hands only to give up. The unfairness of this had only increased her determination.

He would, she was sure, have died in hospital. No overworked junior would have had the time to give him the attention she had lavished upon him these last days, no machine could have monitored the urgency of the real threat to his life, which was no longer physical.

"Tough cookie, aren't you?" her doctor friend had teased her, critically eyeing the purple shadows under her eyes, and her white face. "If you go on like this I shall be mistaking you for the patient. Sure you won't let me get you some help?"

She had refused. She wanted no stranger upsetting the balance of the complicated game she was playing, this prolonged wooing of a mind trembling on the edge of darkness. This man had put himself in her hands, and now her whole pride was committed to saving him.

It would have helped if she had known a single detail about him to use as a thread with which to attach him, but she knew nothing. Instead she used touch. Mr Ho showed her how to massage acupuncture points, and took turns with her in lightly scratching the soles of the feet, and the palms of his hands. In between she had talked to him quietly—telling him jokes, reciting nonsense verse, poems— anything she could think of that he and she might have in common. Hour after hour she had gone on, and refused to give up.

And now, this afternoon, it had all been justified. She had been right. He had come back. He had spoken his own name, and looked at her with lucid eyes. She had won the first stage of the battle.

She brought him food, and insisted that he eat a little. He fell asleep before he had finished, but this time she let him be. He would wake again. She had a meal herself, cleared it up, and lay back in the big armchair she had pulled up to the bed, watching him with triumphant eyes. She must have fallen asleep, for when she opened her eyes he was awake again, and his hands were plucking nervously at the sheets.

"What day is it?"

"Monday."

"Did you say I'd been here three days, or was I dreaming?"

"No, you weren't dreaming. I found you, and brought you here, very early Friday morning when I was coming home from work. Luckily for you I was on night duty last week."

"Oh God!"

She moved to sit beside him and take his hand in hers. Whatever it was, he must tell it now.

"Dear God, what have I done?"

Tears were sliding down his face. They welled up slowly and spilled down his cheeks in two shining tracks until they dripped on to the sheet. In his weakness he made no move to wipe them away, but lay there against the pillows in his misery, like the helpless child he had become. With infinite tenderness, she took a tissue and dried them away.

"Can you tell me about it? I may be able to help. I'm on your side—all the way."

"No-one can help. I've betrayed her. God knows what's happened. I've failed her, utterly."

She put her arm round his shoulders.

"Tell me," she coaxed. "You can trust me, Jeff—you mind if I call you Jeff? You must know by now that you can trust me."

For a long time he wavered between his fear and his need. She waited quietly.

At last, haltingly, in a voice so low she had to bend her head to catch the words, he began. She could feel him trembling with the effort, and she held him close, murmuring encouragement. The flight from London, the little bible-seller Venables with his mild eyes and impassioned plea for help, the unseen icon, the girl he had met on the plane—had it not been for his injuries she might have taken it all for the broken fragments of a dream, phantoms projected by sickness and delirium, but they bore powerful, if silent witness to the truth of what he was saying. His voice broke when he tried to describe the girl, Verity.

174

"Try again."

After a pause, he did so, but grew increasingly agitated as he told how she had discovered his secret.

"I didn't want her to know about it. I hated her taking it . . . it was my responsibility . . . I tried to insist but she wouldn't listen . . . She persuaded me there was a better chance of success if she took it . . . I was crazy to let her . . . crazy, blind and weak . . . Neither of us knew what we were doing . . . We were children, playing games . . ."

His voice died away. Then he broke out in a choking sob.

"If she's in the hands of those devils . . . If they do to her what they did to me . . . it'll be my fault . . . My job was to create a diversion, attract their attention away from her . . . it seemed easy enough . . . Only I didn't know, I didn't know . . . Oh God!"

"Didn't know what?" Very, very gently, she prompted him. She had to make him say it.

"What a coward I am!" The words came out in a shuddering groan.

He closed his eyes, and his head drooped against her shoulder. She laid her cheek against it, rocking him a little, feeling for herself the depths of his misery and self-loathing. She was thinking hard. Somehow, amidst this devastation, she had to find him a path that he might follow, that would take him back to a greener landscape. Otherwise he would wither. Delicately, she felt her way.

"Y'know, Jeff—that's one word I never use."

"Its meaning's clear enough."

"That's the point—it isn't. I think it's a word people throw around to hurt each other—or themselves. Hardly anyone stops to have a look at it."

"I'm a writer. I know what it means."

"And I'm a nurse. I deal in reality. I've been a nurse for a long time—which means I've seen a helluva lot of people trying to face up to pain, and tried to help them deal with it. I've watched their faces, felt it in their muscles, heard it in their voices. Long ago I made up my mind that it has to be one of the most destructive forces around in the world. It turns a kind and loving woman into a shrew, a gentle man into a brute, and a child into a wild thing. I'd never call anyone a

175

coward who's afraid of it. They're damn right to be. Pain is terrible and terrifying. I never, ever underestimate it."

She could see he was listening to her, but he said nothing. Presently, she went on.

"Tell me, Jeff, can you remember which day they picked you up?"

He hesitated, searching.

"The flight finally made it to Toronto on the Tuesday morning. I wasn't careful enough. Once the Immigration guys let me go, I dropped my guard—I didn't look hard enough at the cab I got into. That was where it began . . . I can't remember exactly what happened . . . I guess they took me away somewhere, and—and—" he swallowed convulsively.

"They not only beat hell out of you, they tortured you, didn't they? What was it—cigarettes, electrodes—?"

He could only nod. One of his hands crept up and gripped hers.

"And I didn't find you till Friday morning. That means you must have held out for close on three days?"

"I'm not sure. I kept blacking out. I don't know when I told them. But I *did* tell them. When I came to and found they weren't there any more, I knew I had to get out and warn Verity. I got out of the window—and fell. I remember the racket I made. Then I walked. I was half out of my mind. I kept falling and blacking out some more. Now I'm here—and it's too late—I've failed . . ."

"Hey, wait a minute—did you hear what I said? I said you held out for close on three days. You held out against a degree of pain you'd never have to bear in hospital without an anaesthetic, or at least drugs. Do you realize what I'm saying?"

He lay very still.

"I'm saying I don't know how you did it. It would have reduced me to a screaming wreck."

"I screamed," he whispered.

"It helps, doesn't it?" she said, matter of factly, "like swearing. You probably held out that much longer. Y'know—if it had been me I'd have told them what they wanted to know at the first slap in the teeth."

"Not if you were trying to protect one of your patients, or anyone weaker than yourself."

She pounced.

176

"So that's how you see this girl—Verity—weaker than yourself?"

"If you knew her, you'd understand. She's already suffered a lot . . ."

"I guess most of us have done that. Everyone gets a share, Jeff. You said just now that you were like two children playing games, but I sure get the feeling you see yourself as the adult and her as the child."

"That's not so," he protested. "It's just that—well—I would never have agreed to her taking the icon if I hadn't felt I could protect her—keep all harm away from her. It was a—a—promise I made to myself . . ."

It brought her up short. His voice had changed. He loved the girl. It was this that had given him the strength to hold out—a man of a type she had always regarded as being the least able to tolerate pain. Suddenly, unexpectedly, she felt a twinge of jealousy so strong it almost took her breath away. She had to bite her lip and steady herself before continuing, in the same calm, maternal tone.

"I guess it's time you moved into the twentieth century, you know. Girls today don't take too kindly to all that talk of protection. They like to make their own choices, go their own way."

"But by rights she should never have known about the icon." His voice rose. "Venables asked me for help, not her. It was my responsibility, I've already told you. She only found out about it by accident . . ."

"How does that change anything? So she found out about it. So it was an accident. What the hell—once she knew, it made you equals! She sure doesn't sound like a child to me. She'd never have taken your icon if she'd been scared of a little action. She sounds quite a spunky dame to me—in no way in need of care and protection."

He was silent. She realized it was going to be difficult to dislodge him from his self-appointed role, and therefore from his sense of failure. She was dealing with an idealist. She changed tack.

"What day were you supposed to meet up with her?"

"Thursday."

"And if you'd made it, you were going to go together to the bishop, and hand over the icon?"

"We agreed that if for some reason I failed to turn up, she'd go on her own."

"So in fact she could have done just that? It's possible that she'd handed it over before you—you cracked?"

"I suppose so." She heard the quiver of hope in his voice. "I just don't know. I lost all sense of time in that place. If only I could find out. We agreed we wouldn't try to make contact until after it was safe. Do you think she might have been trying to reach me?"

She winced at the eagerness in his voice.

"How can I say? I just wouldn't know."

"Maybe I ought to try and contact her?"

She thought quickly.

"I'm not sure that's a good idea. There's something I haven't told you—you see—you were followed here."

His whole body stiffened.

"It's okay, it's okay," she soothed him. "It's been taken care of."

"What do you mean?"

"My Chinese neighbour has been helping me look after you. When he saw you'd been tortured he got kind of excited—he seemed to see it as some sort of personal threat. Anyway, he and his friends got rid of the guy who followed you. I haven't asked what they did to him, and I don't intend to. All I know is they said he won't bother us again."

"Are you telling me—" he said slowly "—that I was *meant* to escape?"

"No I'm not—because I don't know. I doubt it. You were badly hurt. P'raps the guy had gone back to finish you off—or to get rid of your body—or just to check no-one else had appeared on the scene. There's no saying. But I guess it does mean we must move very cautiously. We ought to try and find out what, if anything, has happened before you try to make contact."

"But I must know! I must! Can't you understand—?" He tried to sit up, only to slump against her with a groan. She eyed his flushed cheeks and brilliant eyes with concern—she realized she must act quickly to allay this anxiety.

"Take it easy! I can't think if you pressure me like that. There must be a way. We do hold one trump: nobody knows about me—thanks to Mr Ho. So if I do a little snooping, I can't be connected with you. Do you want me to try?"

"You're an angel!"

"Okay then. You'll have to tell me where I can reach her. I guess I could even call the folks she's staying with—I could pretend to be a friend . . ."

He said nothing, but turned his head away sharply. She suddenly realized what she'd asked.

"Jeff—surely you believe me—I'm your friend. You don't have to tell me, not if it's too difficult, but I can't find out anything unless you do. I'd never do anything to hurt her—or you. You must have realized that by now."

Still he said nothing. She put her hand to his cheek and gently turned it so that he was looking at her again.

"Can't you trust me yet, Jeff?"

Her heart ached as she saw the look in his eyes, and began to understand the magnitude of the hurt he had suffered. She had used a word that had been erased from his vocabulary, perhaps for ever. She saw too that he was nearing exhaustion. She changed the subject.

"Tell me something else. Who's Julie? You kept calling out her name while you were running a temperature. She doesn't seem to come into the story. She one of your girlfriends?"

He shut his eyes. It was the second time in a week someone had asked him that question. The memory of Julie, undisturbed for years, seemed to have been playing games with him ever since he boarded the plane in London.

"She was my sister. She died."

That was enough. He did not want to say any more. He had had his fill of cruelty, without adding that of a ghost. Abruptly, as if he were deliberately pulling down a blind, he fell asleep.

Evie felt him relax with relief. They'd gone too fast and too far. She needed to exercise the greatest care. She would do no good if she pushed him beyond his strength.

The trouble was, she reflected as she looked down on his sleeping face, that she was finding it all but impossible to be completely objective. She could not ignore that twinge of jealousy she had felt when he talked about the girl. She knew now what it meant. She knew too why it was she had decided to care for him herself instead of taking him to hospital, and that it had not been her professional judgement she had been obeying. She had fallen in love with this guy, and from now on it was a fact she had better take into account.

She suddenly realized that she was herself exhausted. It was no use trying to decide what to do until she had had some rest.

With infinite tenderness she laid the sleeping man back on the pillow, and smoothed the bed around him. Wearily, she took herself off to the divan in the other room, and lay down. But she could not sleep. Worn out though she was, her mind was racing. She had not dreamed that anything like this could happen to her again.

Once, years before, she had fallen violently in love with a friend of her brother's—a young law student. She had been an idealist herself then, and had worshipped him, making him the centre of her entire existence. She had breathed warmth and depth into his stilted phrases of affection, and drawn infinite significance from his perfunctory lovemaking. She had endowed him with every virtue, with all the blind, silly generosity of youth, and had never allowed herself the slightest glimpse of the reality of him. He was in fact a clever, charming, promising young man, popular with his colleagues, successful in work and sport—but with the emotional capacity of a four-year-old child. She had continued in her blindness for a euphoric eighteen months before it became impossible to hide any longer from the fact that, far from reciprocating her feelings, he was gradually withdrawing before their intensity. His increasing coolness of manner wounded and confused her, the more so as he offered no explanations. Finally, a friend, finding her in tears one day, was brave enough to put her out of her misery: he had been two-timing her for months with another student.

She had been devastated. It had changed the course of her whole life. When, after many months, she had begun to recover from the humiliation and shame of rejection, it had been to channel all her energy, all her gifts, into her work. She had always been a good nurse, now she became an excellent one—tireless, efficient, resourceful. Little by little she had regained her balance. Promotion had restored some of her sense of her own worth. One day she found she could look back on her mistake, and laugh. She took other lovers, more in fun than in earnest, because she needed to be reassured that she was still attractive as a woman. But she never again let anyone near her deepest feelings, her real needs. She had learned the rules of survival, and adhered to them.

Until, that is, the moment when she looked down at the man, now sleeping so peacefully in her bed, lying bleeding in the road. Then she had not only sailed off-course—she had fallen clean out of the boat. Not only had she broken her most sacred taboo, but she had allowed her professional judgement to be affected. She was lucky he hadn't died on her. For the second time in her life she had been totally blind—only this time it was not to the reality of someone else's feelings, it was to that of her own. And now, as a result, it looked very much as if the whole painstakingly-built structure she had raised to defend herself had been undermined, and she was vulnerable again —and all because of a guy who imagined himself in love with a girl he had sat next to on a plane.

She turned and turned again on the lumpy divan. For the first time ever, she wished the apartment was air-conditioned. The windows were wide open, but she felt she could not breathe. Outside the sky was overcast, and there was a faint rumble of thunder.

In the end she got up, and went to the bathroom to take a shower and wash her hair. She made herself some coffee, and sat at the kitchen table, drinking it. She might as well accept, she felt, that there would be no sleep for her until she had worked through the whole impossible situation and made some attempt at deciding what to do. This time she did not want to make any more blind mistakes, or play around with dreams. So far her instincts had guided her. What she must do now was use her head.

Carefully, she reviewed the story he had told her. She had already accepted its truth—so far as it went. The difficulty was that it was already out of date. She realized that she could, in fact, plan nothing until she had found out if anything had happened to the girl—the whole of his real recovery hung on that. If the news was bad his guilt feelings would be increased to such a point that she would never be able to replace them by anything more positive—on the other hand if the girl was unhurt, there was nothing to prevent him from making contact with her again, and she, Evie, would be forgotten. She did not see how she could win.

She took her coffee to the window, and gazed thoughtfully down into the street. It was the end of the afternoon and people were returning from work, tired and sweaty after the humid heat of the day. The thunder was still growling softly. The only way she could

181

win, she decided, was if she took matters into her own hands. She was no longer a moonstruck girl. She was a woman more than capable now of giving fate a nudge in the right direction. It should not be too difficult. She would have to make sure that no information reached him that had not previously been edited by herself, and, more important still, that he and the girl did not meet again. It was not, after all, as if he had known her for very long. He would gradually forget her, always provided that he could be reassured that she had not come to any harm. Her holiday would be at an end long before he was strong enough to move out, and she had no idea where he was. No, the game was by no means hopeless.

Yet she felt unaccountably sad, as she stood there at the window sipping her coffee—sad, and a little apprehensive. Perhaps she had not really wanted something like this to happen. From time to time during the past few years she had wondered if she would ever know again what it was to be in love. She had hoped that she would, but now that it had come about she was less sure. She had been happy in her job and her independence. Even if it had been a hard-won, self-built happiness, she valued it and did not want to jeopardize it. She was very afraid of being hurt again.

She sighed. It was already too late. She was already deeply committed—but at least this time her eyes were open, which meant that she stood a chance.

"Evie!"

The faint call came from the other room. Her heart gave a leap. It was the first time he had used her name.

She hurried to his side. The short sleep had obviously done him good. His colour was better, and his eyes clearer.

"How d'you feel?"

"A little stronger."

"Like some coffee?"

"That would be great."

She brought him the drink, and helped him to sit up.

"You're very good to me. I'm afraid I've put you to a lot of trouble."

"You were in a bad way. I could hardly have left you lying in the road."

"You could have dumped me in hospital."

"You wouldn't let me, in case you don't remember. Besides, I'm a trained nurse. I felt you needed special care."

"You've sure given it to me. I take it I'm in your bed?"

She nodded, smiling.

"And didn't you say I'd been here three days?"

"Uh-huh."

"What about your job?"

"I had some leave due. I fixed that." She spoke shortly. She did not want gratitude.

"Some leave! I'm sorry."

"Sorry?"

"For involving you in my problems. This sure must have messed you up."

"Do you always blame yourself for everything that goes wrong?"

"What do you mean?"

"Just now you were blaming yourself because your friend—what was her name, Verity—took the icon you were telling me about. Now you seem to think it was all your fault I brought you here, whereas as far as I remember it was entirely my decision. You're very egocentric."

He grinned faintly.

"Is it egocentric to be grateful?"

"It's not the same thing at all, as I'm sure you very well know. Here I am pleased as hell with myself for pulling you through, and all you can do is say you're sorry. Don't you see it hurts my feelings?"

"Sorry."

They both laughed. Then he was serious again.

"I guess I'm apologetic because I still need your help."

"I know you do," she said gently. "That's where we'd got to when you fell asleep, you may remember. You were just going to tell me how I could contact your friend."

She heard his harsh intake of breath, and she saw the hand that was lying on the sheet begin to tremble. She covered it with her own.

"Jeff, honey, take it easy. Try to trust me. If you want me to help it's the only way. Would it be easier to write it down?"

He nodded speechlessly. His face was chalk white. She brought him a pad and pencil, and with a shaking hand, he managed to scrawl a number. At once she tore off the sheet and slipped it in her pocket, out of his sight.

"You see? It's okay. It won't hurt her. All I'm going to do is try to call her. Nobody can possibly connect me with you. I'll say I'm someone she met on the plane."

"And—and if everything's okay, will you tell her where I am and ask her to come?"

"Sure I will. Jeff, I do know how hard that was—but it's good you trusted me, believe me it is. Try and relax now while I go call the number. I feel sure it's going to turn out okay."

She disappeared into the other room. Jeffrey shut his eyes. Neither she nor anyone else would ever know what it had cost him to give her that number. Both times she had asked he had seemed to smell once more the sickening smell of his own burning flesh. It had been clever of her to suggest that he write it down. But then she was clever, this young woman with the blonde hair and steady blue eyes. She had saved his life. She had also cared for him in a way no-one had ever cared before. Unasked, unpaid, she had bound up his hurts, bathed his filthy body, and laid him in her own bed. She was surely the archetypal Good Samaritan. At this very moment she was still helping him, supporting him through the recollection of nightmare, urging him to move on into the rest of his life. He was filled with a warm glow of gratitude.

He looked up expectantly as she came back into the room, but his face fell when he saw her expression.

"I'm afraid the line's busy. I've tried several times. Suppose I get us both something to eat, then I'll try again. At least we know someone's home, so we've learned something."

"Evie, come and sit beside me a moment."

She obeyed, smiling.

"I've never met anyone quite like you before."

"That's not surprising. I'm unique."

"Seriously. I don't know how to thank you." He took her hand. She shivered slightly. "Are you cold?"

"No, I'm not cold."

He looked at the hand that lay in his—a square, strong hand, not beautiful but capable of infinite gentleness. It had dressed his wounds, and soothed his fever. Impulsively, he carried it to his lips.

"You're so very good to me. I can't think why."

She just looked at him, still smiling. To his surprise, he saw that her eyes were full of tears.

"Evie, I—"

"I'll go and get us a meal," she said, and hastily snatching her hand away, was gone before he could stop her.

When they had eaten and she had cleared up, she tried to call the number he had given her again. This time she got through. He could hear her speaking from where he lay in the bedroom, and his pulses began to race. He suddenly felt deeply apprehensive. He was not sure he could bear to know what had happened. He wanted to stay quietly here, away from it all, safe and cared for. He did not want to face any more pain.

"I'm afraid that hasn't got us very far."

Evie stood in the doorway.

"What do you mean? What's happened?"

"Your guess is as good as mine. Some sort of domestic answered the phone—you didn't tell me your friend moved in those sort of circles—and she sure wasn't talking. All she'd say was that the family was away and would I like to leave a message."

"And did you?"

"I didn't think it would be very wise. I asked when they'd be back and she said she wasn't sure—so I said I'd call again at the end of the week. I couldn't think what else to do."

"Now I think of it Verity did say something about a possible trip to Northern Ontario, to some cottage or other. P'raps they've gone there."

"In which case there can hardly have been a crisis. I'm willing to bet she's already delivered the icon—or else handed it over to the police."

"Just as long as the person you spoke to on the phone was telling the truth."

She looked at him quizzically.

"Optimism sure isn't your strong suit, is it Jeff? Look, if the woman on the phone wasn't telling the truth I don't see what we can do about it. I mean, I could go round to the house—but I'm sure all that would happen is that I'd get the brush-off on the doorstep instead of on the phone. It wouldn't help. But I'll go if you want me to . . ."

"No—Evie, look, I'm sorry—"

"There you go again. All I'm trying to do is work it all out. I want to know what's happened as much as you do, so just stop apologizing and concentrate, will you?"

She came and sat beside him again, and patted his hand. He took hold of hers. He felt he needed her strength.

"Do you think—" he began diffidently, after a pause, "—do you think it might be worth checking the papers—just in case? I'm almost sure they'd hush up anything to do with the icon, but if something had happened to Verity they'd be bound to mention it, don't you think?"

Evie thought quickly.

"That's not a bad idea. The only snag is I haven't bought a paper in weeks. I'll tell you what—if you don't mind being left for a while, I'll go have a word with Mr Ho. I know he buys the *Star* and he may well have some back copies. Shall I try him? Would it ease your mind?"

"Oh Evie, how—?"

"Not a word. I'll go now. You try and relax. I'll be as quick as I can."

Jeffrey's eyes followed her wistfully as once more she hurried from the room. He almost called her back, only he did not know how to tell her how afraid he was of learning the truth. It was a fact he could no longer hide from himself. The inner voice which had spurred him into making his bid for escape, into picking himself up each time he fell during that nightmare walk in the dark, was silent now. He had done his best, more than his best, and he had failed. He did not really want to know what had happened as a result of that failure.

He had made the promise to Venables without real understanding of what he was about. Sure he had been told that other men and women had risked or lost their lives in order to save the icon, but he had heard the words as if they had been part of some story or legend—they had never applied to his own self. They did now. Now he understood what they meant. Now, after what had been done to him, he found he could not really care any more—about the icon or about those other lives. His own had been violated. Something deep inside him had been maimed. No human treasure, no ideal, he knew with utter certitude, was worth that loss. And if Verity had suffered it too his own agony could only become the greater. No, he did not want to know.

His head was aching. Evie was taking a long time. The apartment seemed empty, almost hostile without her. Evie, she had been his good angel in all this, the one ray of light in all the terrifying darkness. Without her, there was no safety anywhere.

Outside, it was growing dark. There were spots of rain on the window. Shadows were gathering in the corners of the room. He had a sudden vision of that other room, the one he had escaped from, with its single electric bulb, the symbol of pitilessness. He began to tremble. He stared at the door, willing her to come through it, longing to feel her cool hand soothing away his fears. She had been gone too long. What would he do if she did not return, if anything had happened to her . . . Suppose someone else had followed him and had been lying in wait for her . . . Suppose he was to be left here alone . . .

As she entered, carrying a copy of the *Toronto Star*, Evie saw his haggard face light up with relief. She stood by the bed, looking down at him. A lump in her throat prevented her from speaking. He had, then, been waiting for her, anxious about her . . .

"Sorry I've been so long," she said at last, "but we've been doing a thorough check. Mr Ho had all the back copies, as it happened. I've brought you in today's, so's you can see for yourself—but there's nothing in any of them. Is something wrong?"

He took the paper she was holding out to him and laid it on the bed. Then he caught her hand, and pulled her till she was sitting once more at his side.

"Not now," he answered, stroking her cheek with his hand. "There's nothing wrong when you're around—only when you go away."

She kissed him then—first, gently, on all the hurt places on his face and neck, as if she could heal them with her touch, and then, finally, on the lips.

"I'm here," she whispered. "I won't go away. I'll always be here when you need me, Jeff."

And as he kissed her back he felt that perhaps all, despite everything, was not lost. His encounter with human malignance, with

187

evil in one of its purest forms had left him feeling that all his former values were worthless. He had always believed in the fundamental goodness of men and women. It had been his substitute for the bleak religion of his parents, the base on which he had built his whole outlook, and it had crumbled before the impersonal cruelty of strangers. They had proved him wrong, those men with the glowing cigarettes.

Yet even now, in defeat, someone else was insisting that he had been right all along. These warm lips pressed on his seemed to be telling him that the forces of destruction and cruelty could be driven back—that they were only part of a larger whole. And now he turned, and, regardless of his hurts, he clasped her to him, absorbing her warmth and vitality, drinking from her as if she were the very fountain of life. She was making it possible to hope again.

Evie lay beside him, returning his caresses, listening to his murmured endearments and words of gratitude. She closed her eyes. She must not allow this rush of happiness to carry her away, or blind her to the nature of the feeling he was experiencing for her. He was simply trying to go on living. She must not, on any account, imagine it was anything more. If there was ever to be more it lay somewhere in the future, and would have to be carefully nurtured by her own efforts. For the present she could at least permit a little of her love to show, she could cradle him in her arms and teach him to believe again in kindness, and generosity. But as timidly, tentatively, he stroked her breast, a tear slid unnoticed down her cheek.

The *Toronto Star* lay unheeded on the bed. After a while it slipped to the floor, where it lay undisturbed for some considerable time.

Chapter 11

"I guess you can come up now," said Hope, twitching away the corner of the rug that covered Verity as she crouched on the floor of the station wagon.

"Was all that really necessary?" Verity thankfully stretched her cramped limbs.

"Yes, it was." Hope's voice was grim. "We were followed all the way to Micaela's house. I'm ninety-nine per cent sure we're not being followed now. Which means they think you've stayed there with the kids, as I intended them to. Phase one has gone entirely according to plan."

Hope, thought Verity, with an apprehensive glance at the empty road behind them, for all her artistic bent had displayed powers of organization and quick decision this morning which would have done credit to a front line general. She was a woman transformed. All the flatness and bitterness that had struck her so forcibly both at the airport and at home with the family had fallen away. She had taken command of the disaster area that was her home with an assurance that had surprised Leo into unprotesting acquiescence, setting the shell-shocked staff to work repairing and cleaning and generally clearing up the mess, cajoling her friend Micaela into agreeing to have the triplets for the day, ensuring that Leo made a start on insurance formalities—and all the time evolving the plan that was to permit Verity to make her departure unnoticed for as long as possible.

"You said that Leo had fixed for us to have a police guard overnight. Couldn't it have been them tailing us?"

"Our police don't drive Russian cars," Hope replied succinctly. "Anyway, we seem to have lost them, so we'd better turn our minds to the matter of shopping. Got the list I gave you?"

"Yes." Verity produced it.

"I'd like you to read it out as we go along. If you can think of anything I've missed, say so, and we'll add it now. There won't be any shops where you're going, so you'd better think hard."

Verity obeyed.

"You certainly don't intend me to starve," she remarked as she came to the end.

"You're going to feel lonesome all on your own with no-one to talk to—if you're anything like me you'll want the odd nibble. I've put a radio in with your case—I can't remember whether there's one there, and I don't know what the reception will be like, but it's worth a try. I've put a whole load of books in, just in case—and some sketching materials."

"You sound as though I'm off to a desert island. I hope there's a complete Shakespeare among the books."

"You may laugh—but I'm ready to bet that by the end of the week you'll be learning passages by heart to pass the time! Now, be serious—do you think you can handle all that shopping? It'll save a whole lot of time if you see to it while I get on with hiring the car. I called the firm before we left home, but that's no guarantee they won't keep me waiting. I want you on your way as quickly as possible."

"Of course I'll manage it. Checking the change is the only part that baffles me. But Hope, tell me, however do you plan to explain it all to Leo? Won't he be furious? It seems so unpardonably rude on my part just to go off without a word."

"I can't see that it matters to you how furious he is. Our main aim is to ensure that he doesn't know you've gone until the last possible moment. So—once you're safely on your way I shall proceed with my own shopping at a leisurely pace. Round lunch time I'll call him to say we've been held up and are having a bite to eat at one of the places in the Mall. He won't like it, specially after yesterday, but he won't be able to do anything about it."

Verity was silent. Necessary though it undoubtedly was to deceive Leo, there was something distasteful about it all.

"That would give me until well into the afternoon," Hope continued, not noticing her preoccupation. "I could tell him that we'd agreed to go our separate ways for a while, but that you hadn't come back to the car. I found a note from you on the windscreen explaining that you'd met up with your boyfriend—Jeffrey, is it?—and were going off to spend a few days with him. Or some such, it still needs a bit of polish. Then by the time I'd picked up the girls and got back to the house you'd be several hundred miles away."

"Would he swallow it?" Verity asked doubtfully.

"I'll see that he swallows it."

"You won't mention the icon?"

Hope smiled sardonically.

"No, I won't mention the icon. Don't look so gloomy. It's what you wanted, isn't it?"

"It's—it's just that it seems such a childish and ungrateful thing to do. Leo's been quite kind in his way. I hate going off knowing that he thinks me capable of behaving like that."

"Look, honey, you can't have it both ways. You either trust him or you don't. You've made it very clear to me that you don't, so what the hell does it matter what he thinks of you so long as you and your icon are safe? Are you changing your mind at the last minute? Because if you are, say so right now before we go any further."

"No! No, I'm not changing my mind. I'm sorry. I realize I'm being stupid. I—I—just hate hurting people."

"Don't we all? But sometimes we have to if we're to survive. Now, please, think practical. Leave Leo to me and concentrate on the matter in hand, will you?—like trying to think if there's anything vital we've forgotten. Where are the maps, for God's sake?"

"It's all right—they're in here." Verity tapped the glove compartment. "What do I say if I get stopped by the police for some reason? The car's papers will all be in your name."

"The truth, of course: I lent you the car. They'd be sure to check your story which would lead to trouble, but I think it's less of a risk than hiring the thing in your name and leaving a trail anyone could pick up. Just make sure you don't get stopped, that's all."

"How will we communicate? I take it there's no phone at the cabin?"

"You have to be joking. The only concessions to civilization Bill allows are a Primus stove and a chemical john. No, if there's an emergency you'll have to drive several miles to the nearest village, and phone from there. I'm not sure you realize how isolated you are

191

going to be. Are you sure you can stick it? There's still time to change your mind, like I just said."

"Of course I can stick it. I've lived alone for years. And it's only for a few days."

Verity spoke stoutly, but her misgivings were growing by the minute. The fantasy was about to become reality, and she knew better than Hope how ill-equipped she was to face it. Without losing face she could not confess to the fears that already were besetting her. Hope's new found assurance and authority only heightened her sense of inadequacy—they seemed suddenly to have returned to the relationship of their childhood.

As a small girl, she had always felt inferior to her pretty older sister. Hope had everywhere been regarded as the sensible and mature one, and she herself as "artistic"—a label, she had quickly realized, used to cover up all her social deficiencies. It had inclined her more than ever to lean on her sister, and to turn to her for comfort and protection during the empty periods between Aunt Hilda's spasmodic and self-absorbed bouts of affection. She had always regarded Hope as stronger than herself.

So that whilst the shock of finding her apparently worn out and defeated by the events of her life had been considerable, it also had in it something faintly gratifying. She, the weak and artistic one, seemed after all to have made a better job of survival. The very fact of her arrival in Canada proclaimed her recovery and her independence, her renewed determination to enjoy life and surmount all difficulties.

But once again Hope had proved herself the stronger. The moment she saw her paintings, Verity knew that she had come up with the ultimate answer. She had cut free from all the defeats, the doubts, the self-questionings in one superb gesture. She might not envy her the possession of so powerful a talent, but there was no doubt she coveted this new self-possession she was already drawing from it now it had been recognized.

Looking at Hope's profile as she handled the steering wheel with an easy competence that resembled Leo's, Verity realized that she was dreading the separation that lay ahead. Somewhere in this affair of the icon, she had lost all her hard-won sense of her own worth. She had become again the frightened adolescent who had hated Leo for carrying off her sister. The life she had led in Wales, with her job, her painting and her cottage had become as faded and insubstantial as a fairy story.

"Hey—wake up!" Hope was nudging her to bring her out of her reverie. "We're nearly there. I was asking you which day you plan to come back and how you intend to play it."

"Good grief—I haven't thought that far ahead! I was told the bishop returns a week today. I guess I'd best take the icon straight to him, and then try to locate Jeffrey. There won't be much time before my flight home."

"He got out of it all nicely, didn't he?"

"You're just a cynic. You know I can't agree. We'd better say I'll phone you once I'm back in Toronto—unless I run into trouble, of course."

"Let's hope that won't happen. Take care, won't you? I shall be thinking about you all the time."

"I'll be fine. And Hope—thanks for everything. You've been a pillar of strength. I'd never have managed without you."

"Yes you would. You've managed for years without me. It's time you stopped underrating your own strength, Verity."

"You're a fine one to say that—after everything you told me last night!"

They both laughed, to become serious again as Hope pulled into the vast parking lot outside a garishly decorated shopping mall. There was much to be done, and no more time for talk, or laughter, or second thoughts. They, thought Verity as she finally made her way into the arcade with her list of instructions, would simply have to be left behind.

Her spirits rose a little as she pushed her trolley round a brilliantly lit supermarket, decorated as for a children's party with paper chains and baubles. She went from display to display, feeling like a teenager preparing for her first camping trip, locating the various articles she needed, adding others that caught her fancy as Hope had told her to do, taking pleasure in the unusual freedom from financial constraint, trying to foresee her every need in the unreal days that lay ahead.

This time, as she wheeled her heavily laden trolley to the busy check-out, where families were queuing with their weekly shopping, she was grateful for the effusive friendliness of the assistants, who, far from leaving her to struggle alone with her pile of purchases as would have been the case at home, not only stowed them for her in a profusion of free plastic carriers, but told her to have a nice day with such enthusiasm it was impossible to believe they did not mean it. By the time she reached the numbered section of the parking lot where she had arranged to meet Hope she was feeling almost cheerful.

Then she caught sight of her at the wheel of a smart blue Honda station wagon, and her heart began to thump. This was the first taste of reality. She hated driving strange cars.

"For heaven's sake watch the speed limit," said Hope unnecessarily as she stepped out. "They're a lot lower than in the UK. And keep an eye on the gas—petrol to you—so's you don't run out. I've filled the tank so you should be all right. If you do get more, remember to ask for unleaded. Okay?"

Verity nodded mutely. Together they transferred the luggage from the one car to the other, and added the shopping.

"Have you ever driven one of these?"

She shook her head. Her hands were wet.

"Then you'd better spend a few minutes with the handbook. It's all perfectly straightforward. Look, I'll put the maps on the seat beside you—and I've listed the highway numbers you take to get out of town. See, I'll stick the list on the dashboard in front of you."

Verity took her place in the driving seat. She felt numb with misery. She longed to grab Hope and beg her to come too, but she knew it could not be. A great sense of desolation swept over her. She did not want to find herself alone.

Hope saw her distress. She leaned through the window and planted a light kiss on her cheek.

"Don't look so glum. We've already done the most difficult part. You're all set now. The route isn't a bit complicated. Just don't try to navigate the last lap in the dark, that's all. Better to stay the night in a motel than try that. You'll find Mary-Lou's sketch map very good —I've used it myself and I found the way with no trouble at all—and I'm no orienteer. Come on, cheer up. Or have you left it till now finally to change your mind?"

With an immense effort, Verity pulled herself together.

"No, of course not. This is the only way that gives me the faintest chance of success. I was just wishing you were coming too. I feel I've only just found you again. At this moment I'm wishing I'd never set eyes on the bloody icon."

"You don't mean that. Ever since you showed it to me last night I've felt it has some special significance, for both of us. I feel I'm seeing things clearly for the first time."

"It's had the opposite effect on me. I thought I did. Now I'm not so sure. I only know I feel more alone than I've ever felt in my whole life. I can cope with it. I just wish I didn't feel it so acutely."

"We're all of us that. The trick is learning to live with it. P'raps this trip will help you. Saying which, you'd better hit the trail or you'll lose all the advantage we've gained. You know which way to go from here?"

Verity nodded, squared her shoulders, and switched on the ignition.

"You'll be fine." Hope lifted a hand in valediction.

She let in the clutch with a nervous jerk, and nosed the car across the parking lot and out to join the stream of traffic with a kangaroo leap each time she changed gear, causing the drivers behind her abruptly to switch lane.

The next hour was one of unremitting tension. The sweat trickled between her shoulder blades, and her knuckles gleamed white on the wheel as she fought to reverse her reflexes, locate and comprehend road signs, keep her eye on Hope's instructions and adjust to a different style of driving. She was hooted at as she hesitated at road junctions, hooted at whenever she slowed to verify the identity of a road, and hooted at even more as cars overtook to the right and left only to cut in viciously in front, impatient at her careful speed. Teeth clenched, tears of humiliation in her eyes, she drove on.

At last, just as she was beginning to despair of ever escaping from the sprawling suburbs of the city, the scenery began to open out, and the traffic to thin, and she found herself moving smoothly along a road far more similar to those she was accustomed to at home. She began to relax.

The sun came out from the dense cloud that had persisted throughout the earlier part of the morning, and once again her spirits rose. She could not help feeling elated. She had broken through the barrier of her own fears, and now she was free. The road stretched ahead, straight and inviting. By now she had the measure of the

Honda, and even the unfamiliar position of the steering wheel was beginning to feel less strange. She increased her speed—only to slow again as she remembered the lower limits.

She was driving through flat, wooded countryside spattered yellow with goldenrod. She had never seen the plant in such profusion before. Even when the dark coniferous woods advanced to the very edge of the road it seemed to take advantage of every patch of light to display its brilliant flowers glowing like rockets against the sombre green needles. Here, too, were bogs and pools, and the grotesque, contorted shapes of fallen trees that made her long to stop and take out her sketch book, but she pressed on.

To help keep herself alert, she kept a sharp lookout for the wildlife which she guessed must abound in a region so dense with trees, but the only sign she saw of it was the dead bodies of animals which lay at disconcertingly regular intervals along the shoulder of the road. Skunks appeared to be the principal victims—once she drove over one that had been recently killed, to judge from the stench which suddenly filled the car. She was forced to acknowledge that no description she had ever read of it had been in the least exaggerated. There were other, larger corpses, too. It seemed a macabre way to make the acquaintance of the fauna of a foreign land.

For a time she exulted in the contrast between the golden flowers and the varied greens of the leaves and needles, but after a couple of hours or so it began to pall, along with the straightness of the road. Accustomed to the complex changes of scenery at home, where a drive of this length would have taken her from the lush greens of Somerset to the Cornish moors, or from the Welsh mountains to the river valleys of Wiltshire, she found this absence of stimulus some-what mesmerizing—and slightly depressing. She decided to take the next opportunity to stop for a cup of coffee and a break—Hope had provided her with a Thermos and sandwiches in the interest of saving time.

Before long she was able to pull off the road on to a picnic area—a lawn of smooth grass set with tables and benches, and shaded by copses of deciduous trees, their leaves already touched with red and yellow, promising a carnival of colour for the fall that lay ahead. Sipping her coffee, she studied the map—to be amazed to see what a tiny fraction of the total distance she had covered. She must not stop for long. She looked at her watch. All too soon Hope would be on her way to collect the triplets. After that would come the scene of explanation with Leo.

She wondered how he would react to Hope's story. She bitterly regretted the necessity of it. It was as if they were deliberately trying to make a fool of him, and a man like Leo deserved better than that. Despite all her new-found respect for Hope, she was not sure she could trust her to handle it well. She did not want Leo to be wounded unnecessarily, and she had an intuition that this was exactly what would happen. Hope was not the woman to forgo an advantage in the long drawn out battle she was fighting. Verity sighed. However hard she tried to avoid it, it seemed she could not escape being implicated in it.

Carefully, she looked up and down the road before setting off again. There was not the slightest sign of pursuit. At first she had checked her mirror every few minutes, but as time went by and it became clear she was not being followed she had gradually eased off. Now it seemed that she could relax completely. Hope's makeshift plan had worked.

The road went on and on. Sleepiness was becoming a hazard. She sang songs and recited poems to ward it off. She switched on the radio, but the reception was so poor she switched it off again, wondering if that was an omen of things to come.

By now the anxieties and fears of the morning were beginning to seem remote and even neurotic. She was on a ship sailing out to sea—the anchor was weighed, and there was no more time for doubts. She was, she realized with a faint smile, actually enjoying herself. Even the Honda had become a friend.

At last there were signs of change in the landscape. Hills appeared. Once or twice she glimpsed the waters of a lake through the trees. A rocky crag would suddenly loom up beside the road. Yet there were still plenty of indications of human presence—painted signs beckoned her to camp sites and picnic areas, and, as the road ran beside a broad lake fringed with birch trees, she caught sight of bathers sunning themselves on sandy beaches, and tents, and someone water-skiing. She was conscious of disappointment. She was looking for something else—something she had seen at Kleinburg.

Flat fields, from which bare rocks jutted like bones, succeeded the hills as she drove on. Already this was the longest drive she had ever done. Hope's advice, that she should spend the night at a motel and not attempt to go further once the light began to fail, was beginning to seem eminently sensible. She was in fact beginning to doubt her ability to continue even that long, but she set her jaw grimly. She had to justify all the trouble that had been taken.

It must have been an hour or so later that the car suddenly swerved violently. She only just managed to keep it on the road. If anything had been coming in the opposite direction there would certainly have been a collision. She realized she had fallen asleep at the wheel. There was nothing for it now but to acknowledge her personal limitations. If she had been injured or killed it would all have been for nothing. Soberly, she drove on until, after a few more miles, she came to a straggle of houses and, to her relief, a stridently coloured sign announcing the imminent comforts of a motel.

She secured a room for the night without difficulty. The owner and his wife came from Cardigan, and seemed to be suffering from intense homesickness. When, a little later, she took her seat in the cheerful dining room, with plastic daffodils bright on every table, the wife came to take her order, and talked long and nostalgically of childhood visits to Newport Sands.

There were no other customers. She tried to imagine the slow succession of empty days that comprised life here, waiting for the road to wash up the occasional tired motorist to relieve the solitude and recall the existence of a different world. As the woman's voice, with the last telltale remnants of a Welsh lilt, droned on, her mind began to wander, and she found herself, inevitably it seemed, once more thinking of Leo. By now Hope would have told her story, suitably garnished. How had he reacted?

She gave herself a mental shake. It did not matter how he had reacted. She would not be seeing him again. However things worked out it would be better if they did not meet. She was sure of it. She repeated it to herself several times, only to feel more and more depressed. She badly wanted, before she left for London, to explain to him why she had behaved as she had. She did not want to leave him thinking ill of her. He was a threat—but not an enemy.

She perceived that the woman was looking at her expectantly, and realized she had been asked a question.

"I'm sorry?"

"I said, where you heading?"

"I'm on my way to join some friends on a camping trip," she replied, evading it and hoping there would be no further request for information. She was in luck—her hostess was not really interested, and immediately plunged into the next episode in her family sagas, which continued even while Verity fought her way manfully through a huge portion of steak and a greasy pile of french fries. At last, when she could eat no more, she seized the first pause for breath to excuse herself, and headed determinedly for her room. Solitary and vulnerable though she felt, she knew it would be worse if she remained any longer listening to the compulsive flow of words, and she was too weary to attempt to staunch it. It was strange, she reflected as she unlocked the door of her room, how much lonelier another's loneliness could make one feel when it found this way to express itself.

She settled in the easy chair to read. She had tried to switch on the television set but it seemed to be broken, and she did not want to risk exposing herself to a fresh verbal assault by appealing to the office.

It was impossible to concentrate, however. The evening ahead seemed empty and interminable. Try as she might, she could not prevent her thoughts from returning to Toronto. Now it was Jeffrey who occupied them. Hope's words at Kleinburg had not been entirely without effect. If he had kept their appointment she would not be here alone in this strange place. Whatever plan they had decided upon, they would have embarked on it together. She would not feel so utterly without support. Anger stirred in her. She could not help wondering if he had in fact ever intended to meet her, if he had not parted with the icon a shade too easily. The clumsiness of their arrangements struck her afresh. Perhaps he was, after all, no more than a stranger she had met on the plane, as Hope had suggested, a stranger she had liked, and spent the night with—to be conned for her pains. She would not be the first to make such a mistake. It was not a cheering thought.

The motel was oppressively quiet. No other cars had pulled in. The occasional truck rumbled past on the road outside. The room smelt slightly musty, as if no-one had disturbed it for months. She was glad she only had to spend the one night in it. It reminded her of a waiting room—somewhere where no-one could be bothered to care about anyone. It was still early, but she decided to turn in. She needed to make an early start the next morning, and unless she wanted to go for a walk in the dark there was little alternative. She wondered if the evenings in the cabin that lay ahead were going to seem as long as this, and shivered. It was a relief to hide away in the bed.

But she could not sleep. For hours she lay listening out for the trucks, or for the rare car—particularly the car. Confident though she now was that she had not been followed, she could not dismiss the feeling that she was a mouse being played with by a cat. Evil was abroad—what had happened in Hope's house was proof enough —evil in the shape of deliberate, cold-blooded destructiveness, and she was now unquestionably its object. As she lay in this limbo, this unfamiliar musty room far from anyone she knew or cared about, she felt an overpowering need for protection. It was terrifying to be alone.

Her hand slipped beneath the pillow to touch the satin case which contained the icon. Curiously, the feel of the smooth, rich fabric, the knowledge of what it concealed seemed to soothe and comfort her—though she could not have explained why. She wondered fleetingly if she would ever fully understand why she was doing what she was. Then still touching it, she fell asleep.

It was early the following afternoon that she spotted the first of the landmarks depicted in tiny thumbnail sketches on Mary-Lou's map. As Hope had promised, it proved easy to recognize—an oddly-shaped outcrop of rock on a low hill near the edge of the road. There were many hills after this, increasing in size, and thick woods that crowded down to the road as if they would take it over. One by one she counted off the remaining signs until at last she slowed as she caught sight of the cairn of stones that marked the entrance to a narrow trail.

She turned into it as triumphantly as any explorer coming upon a long-hidden city. Once again, she told herself, she had proved that she could surmount her fears. Then she hit the first pothole, and from then on had to concentrate with all her might on the steering as the Honda, in a cloud of choking, blinding dust, lurched along what in the event turned out to be little more than the roughest of tracks. Woods, dense with undergrowth, blotted out the view on either side, as well as the light from above. Half suffocated, she could only drive on, up and down hills, on and yet on until she had lost all sense of direction.

By the time it finally emerged from the trees, several miles, and several thousand potholes later, the smart blue Honda was unrecognizable beneath a layer of dust that coated every centimetre of its surface. Verity, peering with difficulty through the windscreen, brought it to a sudden, astonished halt, and scrambled out to gaze with wide eyes at the scene that lay before her.

She found herself standing on a broad, grassy plateau starred with wild flowers which, after some thirty yards or so gave way to the flat surface of a huge rock. Below it lapped the wrinkled waters of a great lake, larger than any she had ever seen at home. Grey and cold beneath the cloudy sky it stretched away into the distance to meet a dark line of hills, almost purple now in the unfriendly light.

On either side of the plateau, below her, she could see nothing but trees and yet more trees descending to the lakeside. Only a very few braved the exposure of the height where she stood: a little to her left, not far from the door of the plain log cabin set a few yards from the edge of the wood, was a clump of silver birch. She could not help an exclamation of delight at the sight of them as a sudden ray of sunlight transformed their trunks, far whiter than those of their British cousins, into ribbons of light. Nearer the lake, at the point where turf gave way to rock, a solitary spruce had contrived to root itself with sufficient strength to face the elements in weather-beaten defiance.

Her heart beat fast. She had never seen anything like it before. Here, at last, was the wild, untamed and unspoiled. Here were no water-skiers, no tents, no bathers, no hot-dog stands. The log cabin looked as weather-beaten as the spruce—it had possibly stood there even longer. Nothing detracted from the grandeur of the scene, from the atmosphere of sleeping power. Until today she had only been allowed brief, fragmented glimpses of it—in the imprisoned waters of Niagara, or in the carved geese trapped forever in the Toronto shopping centre, or re-created in the work of the artists at Kleinburg, who alone revered it—but now she was seeing it real, and alive, and whole, and knew that she was close to the source of the life of this great country.

She walked over to the spruce, and felt the texture of its bark, as if to reassure herself of its solidity. She felt lightheaded, intoxicated by the very vividness of her impressions. She felt that whatever lay ahead, she would never forget this first sight of the lake, the rock, and the far-off hills—it had given her one of those rare, prized moments of existence when the outer and the inner worlds seem to join in harmony and everything comes together into a perfect whole.

Moving to the edge of the crag, she looked down. She smiled as she remembered Mary-Lou's warning—even without it she would never have attempted such a dive, she had too poor a head for heights. She noticed that the rock face was scored with cracks and ledges, tempting to the adventurous climber, so that no doubt that warning had been found from experience to be necessary. Certainly she could not see the submerged rocks.

The idea of a bathe in the cool water was very appealing, notwithstanding, hot and dusty as she was after the hours cooped up in the car. She decided to defer the task of moving in while she looked for a safe place to swim. Scanning the plateau, she noticed a faint path leading across the grass from the cabin door and disappearing into the tangled undergrowth that covered the steep sides. Cautiously, she followed it, to find herself keeping her footing with difficulty as it zig-zagged sharply down between big clumps of bilberry and skinny, half strangled tree-stems until she came at last to an area of level ground, strewn with boulders, beyond which lay the lake. There, at its side, she found a small cove, with a gently sloping, sandy beach—the perfect place for bathing.

Gladly, she peeled off her clothes and ran to the water's edge only to leap back with a cry of disgust as thousands of tiny black flies immediately covered her feet and legs. Frantically she slapped and brushed them away, retreating to the spot under the trees where she had left her things. They seemed only to infest the sand near the water's edge for they did not return once she had rid herself of them, nor did they sting. The same did not go for the mosquitoes, however, which immediately took their place. Too late she remembered the cans of insect repellent heavily underlined on the shopping list, and which at this moment were still packed away in the depths of the

Honda. Now she could see why Hope had insisted on them. The wild, it seemed, had its humble, but potent defences against romantic human intruders, and, to judge from the angry red blotches already swelling on her ankles, she had better learn quickly to treat them with respect.

Hurriedly she dressed again. Her desire for a swim had vanished —she only wanted to get away from the mosquitoes. Once back on the plateau they disappeared, as if satisfied they had taught their victim a lesson. Ruefully, she realized that there were even more enemies to be on her guard against than she had foreseen, and that it would have been more prudent first to have established her territory.

When she finally succeeded in turning the big, old-fashioned key in the stiff lock, pushed open the protesting door, and looked round inside the cabin, it was to find that Hope had in no way exaggerated when she had called it primitive.

She had stepped into a single big room. An iron stove stood in the centre—a curiosity in itself with its prominent chimney that rose straight for four feet or so before turning at right angles to run the entire length of the building before disappearing through the wall, thus, she guessed, conserving the precious heat inside for as long as possible. A wooden partition divided one half into two sleeping cubicles, one with a double bed, the other with bunks, with the end nearest the heat left open. On the other side of the stove, at the back, was a table separated from the far wall by a bench, above which hung a hurricane lamp. A shelf on the wall over it held a few simple ornaments.

To the right of the door stood a cupboard with a zinc bowl on it beside which, she was heartily relieved to see, was a pump—at least she was not going to be obliged to heave buckets of water up from the lake. The top of the cupboard also obviously served as a working surface, for it proudly boasted a tin tray, on which stood a Primus stove. She couldn't help smiling as she looked at it—she wondered how an estate agent would have described so sumptuous a kitchen. A huge old closet stood against the adjacent walls. On opening it she found capacious shelves filled with blankets and linen, scented with bunches of aromatic herbs, and, higher up, neat rows of canisters containing dried foods. A ladder in the further corner led up to a roomy loft, where she discovered several extra mattresses, while a door beneath it opened on to a long, closed verandah—a recent addition to judge from the newer look of the wood. Here were racks of fishing rods, shelves of methodically stowed tackle, and, hanging from hooks just inside the door, a couple of ancient jackets with bulging pouched pockets, complete with frayed straw hats. Two shabby wicker chairs and a low table completed the furnishing.

Remembering the enormous house near Toronto she had visited with Hope, she shook her head in wonder. It could be no simple matter, she supposed, to be a wealthy, self-made man and live in conventional business circles when your entire childhood had been shaped by the Mennonite belief in simplicity, and austerity, and closeness to nature. This place had to be, as Hope had suggested, Bill's compromise with his conscience—his return to the womb. She admired him for it. He could so easily, with the unlimited finances at his disposal, have turned the old cabin into a comfortable holiday home with several bathrooms and a patio with crazy paving and a smartly painted fence. But he had left it to remain what it had always been—a humble extension of the woods, itself part of the wild. She felt she would have liked to know him better.

It was only as she began to transfer her belongings from the car that she noticed the gun hanging on the wall just inside the door. She stopped dead when she caught sight of it. It was not old, or simply there for show, but modern, and well-oiled, and ominous. She stared at it, trying to understand why, when all the comfort-giving appurtenances of modern civilization had been so rigorously excluded from the place, this ugly, deadly object should have been allowed to stay. She could not accept the obvious explanation—that her hosts enjoyed hunting as well as fishing, and the woods no doubt abounded with game—it was too out of keeping with the general atmosphere. There must be, she knew, another reason for its presence, and she did not want to dwell on it. Abruptly, she turned away, and busied herself with arranging her affairs to her liking.

She unrolled the sleeping bag Hope had lent her on one of the bunks—she would feel safer there than in the wide and lonely double bed. Her clothes she stowed in the big wooden chest that crowded alongside, while the books and sketching materials she arranged on the shelf on the wall. Then, after reading carefully the long list of printed instructions, for the most part duplicating those Mary-Lou had already given her, she set about locating the various necessities of life, such as the privy, the trash pit, and the carefully-sited incinerator. By the time she was through, she had conceived a wholehearted admiration for the thoroughness of her conservationist friends, who went to enormous pains to keep all traces of their visits to the cabin to the barest possible minimum. Apart from the lean-to which housed the privy and the fuel supply, and a primitive contraption of bricks and wire grating nearby, used, to judge from the smoke-blackened bricks, for grilling, the cabin itself was the only indication of human presence on the plateau.

Except for the Honda. Verity looked at its dusty blue paint and smeared glass with sudden dislike. It was absurdly out of place. It belonged to the world of skyscrapers and neon lights. She looked round for some means of concealing it, but could find none. Remembering a clearing she had noticed in the woods shortly before reaching the end of the trail, she made up her mind: she wanted this place to be perfect. With some difficulty she reversed the car back over the potholes, and manoeuvred it into the clearing. Stepping out, she saw there were tyre marks on the ground, and realized she had discovered Mary-Lou and Bill's private garage. She did not linger to admire their resourcefulness, however, for the moment she left the shelter of the Honda the mosquitoes descended upon her in swarms. Here, where the trees grew thick, she was in their kingdom, and they sang in to the attack. She was fighting back panic as she ran the short distance back to the plateau and the safety of the cabin.

Perhaps it was the panic that brought home to her the fact that she was both very tired, and very hungry. Not only had she slept badly the previous night, but she had had no food since breakfast, and it was now mid-afternoon. Hastily, she picked a tin at random from the mouth-watering selection brought from the supermarket, and made herself some lunch, taking it out, along with some cushions and a book, to eat under the lonely spruce. She did not want to lose a moment of the view.

In the event, she lost several hours for she finished her meal and read a few pages of extremely turgid nineteenth-century prose only to fall fast asleep, lulled by the quiet and the warmth of the sunshine which had finally escaped from the clouds.

When she awoke the sky had cleared altogether, and the sun was sinking towards the hills. Only a few, delicate wisps of cloud remained to vary the vast, salmon-coloured expanse above her. The ripples on the lake were glistening. The silence seemed more profound than ever. Everything—rocks, trees, hills and water seemed to be waiting expectant for some tremendous event. Breathlessly she watched as second by second the light changed. The salmon sky became orange and yellow, and poured fire upon the water. The sun hung above the hills as if reluctant to leave the splendour it had created, but the earth moved on in obedience to its laws, and slowly it sank from sight.

She found herself longing for someone to share it all with. Tears started unexpectedly to her eyes. Angrily, she brushed them away. She must not allow herself to descend any further down this dangerous slope, with a slough of self-pity waiting to receive her at the bottom. She must go on as she always had. She must keep her head high. Tomorrow she would do some sketching—however far the result fell short of the vision that inspired it. She would do her best. She had to leave something behind her to show that she had passed this way.

The daylight was disappearing fast now the sun had gone, and soon the lake lay in shadow. She was glad enough to go into the cabin and slide the bolts on the door. Inside its stout log walls she could create an illusion of safety. Others had sheltered here before her from conditions far more terrible than the summer night outside. The thought heartened her. She could imagine long winter evenings gathered round the stove while the wind howled over the lake. It was a snug and friendly place, this cabin.

Earlier, when she had been disposing her belongings, she had taken the icon from its now unnecessary hiding place and put it, in its satin case, on the chest near the bunk where she was to sleep. There was no point in hiding it any more. Whereas the musty room in the motel the previous night had seemed like a waiting room, some sort of limbo, here in the cabin she had come to the journey's end. She could not flee beyond this point. If her enemies should find her here there was nothing more she could do. She could not resist physical force, and by herself she would not stand a chance making a run for it in this rough country. All she could do was wait.

With a feeling that she was performing a time-honoured rite, she lit the hurricane lamp, and was just turning away to begin preparations for the evening meal, when she stopped. The scene was somehow incomplete. Looking round, puzzled, to see what was missing she suddenly knew what it was: going to the chest, she took the Umilenie icon from its wrappings, and set it on the shelf above the table so that it was illumined by the rays of the lamp.

For several minutes she stood and looked at it. She could not understand why she should suddenly feel so happy. It was as if, acting out of pure instinct, she had brought it to its rightful home. She had been mistaken in believing its place to be in cathedrals, among elaborate statuary and sophisticated music. Here, in this isolated cabin on the other side of the world from the land where it had been painted she had raised it up and set it against the elemental forces that ranged in the darkness outside and now at last she could feel the full power of its symbolism. As the gentle lamplight played on it, she was piercingly aware of the tenderness that bound the mother and child. The two saintly heads, touching each other, seemed to be reassuring each other as well as her that however deep and far-flung the darkness there would always, even in the furthermost outposts of the world, be a possibility of light, and a hope of warmth.

She moved about the room, preparing her meal, but her eyes continually returned to the icon, and did so for the rest of the evening. Before going to bed, she stood in front of it again, thinking. In the darkness she thought of her parents, who had failed her, and of James, who had disappeared, and of the baby she had lost. She thought of Jeffrey, who had betrayed her, and of Hope whom she loved, and of the little nieces she had not been given time to know, and she thought of Leo, whom she had hurt. All the tangled ends, all the painful unfinished business of her life seemed to be gathered there in the room about her in one great question—and the glowing, painted faces seemed to look back at her, calm and resigned, and to promise her an answer.

Chapter 12

Her sleep that night was fitful. The mosquito bites itched and burned, and she turned again and again in the narrow bunk in a vain attempt to find coolness. Her whole body was irritable and tense, alert for any sound that might spell danger. Dreams crowded into the brief periods of unconsciousness, fragmentary, incomprehensible yet disturbing dreams which vanished the moment she woke in an elusive, tantalizing rustle of memory.

Once she started up as a strange drumming broke out on the roof above her, followed by a series of scutterings and grunts. She lay on her elbow, listening, her heart thumping, long after everything was silent again and her animal visitors had concluded their ceremonies. By now she was beginning to be afraid of her own fear. Once before in her life it had broken free of the restraints of reason and common sense, with agonizing results. It occurred to her that perhaps after all she could detect a motive behind this self-imposed ordeal by solitude: there was something she wanted to prove to herself, something she needed to know before she could go on with her life.

She woke from a sleep more prolonged than the rest to find that she could dimly make out the shapes of the furniture in the cabin. Unable to bear the confinement of the sleeping bag any longer, she got up, and went to light the Primus and make herself a drink.

A mug of hot tea comforted her, restoring a little confidence in her powers of survival. Opening the door, she found it was nearly daylight. The darkness was in full retreat—the hobgoblins were routed. Suddenly she could laugh at her fears.

Slipping an anorak over her pyjamas, she went outside to finish her tea sitting in her favourite place under the spruce. A squirrel-like creature with a stripe along its side whisked across her path and she gave a little cry of pleasure at recognizing a chipmunk.

The lake lay almost hidden by a blanket of thick mist, so that the hills in the distance seemed to be floating on cloud. Once again, everything seemed to be waiting expectantly—it was the ritual of the previous evening in reverse. She was beginning to perceive the rhythms that were created by the coming and going of the light and now, as she sat waiting for the reappearance of the sun her sense of being in tune with all other living creatures returned, and she felt stronger.

As the light steadily grew she wondered if her earlier fears were not simply the instinctive reactions of a mind long out of touch with these natural rhythms, with these beatings of a simpler, grander pulse. Maybe this, too, was why she had felt the icon belonged here. In the days when it was painted the awareness of being part of a greater whole had not yet been lost. It was a sense which enabled people to face up to the dark—but not by denying its existence. Perhaps it was this that she needed so profoundly to regain, not merely in snatches, but as a sure, deep foundation for all her being.

The sun rose clear of the trees, and the last shadows fled. She decided to brave the insect life, and go down to the cove for a swim, and she had just risen, a trifle stiffly, to her feet when she froze, the hair on the nape of her neck prickling.

A sound had come from the lake. It was similar to the long drawn out hoot of an owl, but there was a difference. It was curiously artificial, almost mocking, sinister. She stared down at the layer of mist, but it was too thick to see anything. The call came again, much nearer. Her knees buckled, and she sat down again quickly, hardly able to breathe, straining to catch the faintest clue that would give a shape to her fear, but all was quiet. Nothing happened. There was no splash of paddles, no murmur of voices, nor scrape of a boat against the rocks. Minutes passed and still she sat there, hardly breathing, waiting, listening, unable to move.

At last she found the strength to creep to the edge of the bluff and peer cautiously down over its weatherworn face, only to find that she still could not see the water, though the mist was undoubtedly thinning. Trying in vain to penetrate its soft grey skeins, she felt again her vulnerability of the night, but, as the minutes passed, and she continued to crouch there, and nothing happened, she fought it back. The sun's rays, warming her shoulders, reassured her: whatever it was that had given that unearthly cry, it was neither man nor ghost. She gave a defiant little shrug—it was not going to stop her from having her swim.

She set off down the path between the bilberries. She knew better now than to linger under the trees, and, pausing only to drop her anorak and pyjamas at the edge of the grass, ran swiftly across the sand and into the water before anything with legs or wings could settle on her.

The lake lay flat and still around her. It was cold, but not as icy as she had feared, and she rejoiced at its silken touch on her naked body as she swam and dived and floated on her back, while the mist dissolved above her, pretending the world had just been born.

Suddenly the weird, echoing call rang out again, close at hand this time. She snapped into the vertical position and stared about her in terror. Soft wisps of mist were curling past. Then she saw them: swimming towards her over the glassy surface was a family of waterfowl—two parent birds and five or six little ones. They were of a kind she had never seen before—black, with precisely tailored bars of black and white, in size between a duck and a goose. As they approached one of the parents, summoning the young, uttered the very cry that had frightened her so much.

She gave an involuntary groan of relief, then laughed aloud—a laugh which suddenly, unexpectedly, turned to tears. By the time she reached the shore again, and was hurrying up the path to the plateau, she was weeping uncontrollably. She dried herself, and dressed, but the sobs only increased in violence. Throwing herself on the bunk she let them come—deep, racking sobs of humiliation, and inadequacy and an unutterable sense of loss. It was years since she had wept with such abandon. The absurd, trivial incident seemed to have touched some secret spring, and now everything she had ever mourned came pouring out in a paroxysm of grief that lasted until she eventually fell into a deep, exhausted sleep.

It was several hours later when she awoke. The sunlight was streaming through the open door, and the tiny jewels in the frame of the Umilenie icon winked and flashed. She stared at it sleepily. She felt immensely peaceful, as if the storm of emotion had washed away all the lurking shadows that had been haunting her not just since she left Toronto, but since she left Wales.

She made herself some breakfast, then went outside once more.

It was a golden day. The last strands of mist had vanished, and the lake lay blue and shining beneath a vast, empty sky. The hills had become little more than a grey smudge. The heat was increasing. She could see the family of waterfowl swimming peacefully near the bluff. It seemed inconceivable that so domestic a sight should have caused her so great a panic. Now she could smile.

Remembering the sketching materials Hope had lent her, she decided to fetch them out, and before long was settling down under the spruce to work. She felt her confidence return still more as she drew—here at least she was on familiar territory which held no surprises. This was her safety zone.

She worked on happily enough throughout the morning, with only a short break for lunch and another swim. To judge by the sun, it was well into the afternoon by the time she finally stopped. She had completed a fair number of sketches. Looking through them, how-ever, she felt sourly that all she had achieved was to pass the time. Never before had she felt so dissatisfied with her own ability. After the brilliance of Hope's work, all they had to boast was a certain pale charm. They were anaemic, academic. They bore no more relation to the scene before her eyes than the output of some well-tutored Victorian spinster. She might have been pleased enough with them once, but she suspected that now she never would be again. All her retreat into her safety zone had accomplished today was to heighten still further her feeling of inadequacy.

Her head was aching. She had caught the sun during her swim, and her shoulders and arms were smarting to an extent that boded ill for the tranquillity of the night to come. Crossly, she carried everything back into the cabin. She was tempted to tear the sketches up, but something held her back. There was, after all, a faint possibility that she might be able to improve a little on them the next day, and, at the very least, they would form a sort of diary.

A light breeze had sprung up by the time she returned to her seat under the tree, and she was grateful for its cool touch on her forehead after the heat of the afternoon. She was trying not to think of the long hours of darkness that lay ahead. The radio Hope had given her yielded only crackles, which left books as her sole resource against awareness of her solitude. She gazed out over the lake—wrinkling already to a darker blue as the breeze strengthened.

Suddenly she froze. For the second time that day the hair on the nape of her neck stood on end. There was nothing eerie now, however, about the sound that had just reached her ears. It was the unmistakable beat of a car engine, and it was coming up the trail through the trees.

Her stomach turned to water. All previous fears were but pale reflections of the panic that seized her now. Desperately she looked round for somewhere to hide. There was no time to run for the cover of the woods or the bilberry clumps—the car might emerge at any second—yet here by the spruce she was completely exposed.

There was just one possibility. She remembered the cracks and ledges she had noticed on the face of the bluff. It might be possible for her to climb down.

She ran to the brink and, shuddering, looked over. If she could only overcome the giddiness that heights always gave her it was not, in fact, too difficult. There was no choice. She did not wait to think about it. Carefully, she lowered herself over the edge, keeping her eyes fixed on the rock face, clinging like a fly to every hold until she reached a ledge several feet below. Here she found she could shuffle sideways until she found she was virtually hidden from above by a slight overhang. She could hardly, in fact, have found a better hiding place—she was invisible to all except a fellow climber or someone approaching in a boat.

The sun, lower in the sky now, was shining full on her, and the rock face was warm with the accumulated heat of the day. As she stood flattening herself against it, she could feel the sweat trickling down her body. She held her breath, listening.

She had left the cabin door wide open. The icon was still standing on the shelf where she had placed it the night before. Perhaps whoever it was would see it there, and simply take it and go. It was, after all, what they had come for—it had to be. She herself was of no importance.

The car engine cut off, and a door slammed. Then silence. She tried to imagine what was happening, but the silence defeated her. Then it occurred to her that the visitor might be Mary-Lou, or Hope.

But Mary-Lou believed she was here with a lover, and would hardly be likely to intrude, while Hope—Hope would surely not risk drawing attention to her hiding place unless there were some urgent message to communicate, or some emergency—and she or her messenger would surely call out . . .

Minutes passed. She was growing unbearably hot, and her hands were slippery with sweat. Still she could hear nothing—no voices, no footsteps, no sounds from the cabin. She began to wonder if she dare risk a look—anything was better than staying pinned here in total ignorance, with aching arms and a heart that was threatening to burst out of her ribs.

Ever so gently, she began to edge back the way she had come. Then she stopped, and stood utterly still—her ear had caught the soft grate of a shoe on the rock. Someone had come to stand near the edge only a few feet above her head. Instinctively, like a child seeking shelter against an aged grandparent, she pressed herself even harder against the pitted face of the cliff—and a fragment of the ledge beneath her feet gave way.

The world spun as she scrabbled wildly with her toes to find a new hold amid the patter and splash of falling debris. Her fingers had a strong grip in a deep crack, but she knew they could not take her weight for long. One foot encountered a slight ridge which took the strain off her arms sufficiently to enable her to look down in an attempt to locate a better foothold, but the move proved fatal. All she could see was the waters of the lake lapping far below, where the hidden rocks waited below the surface. The sight paralysed her. Her head swam. She could breathe only in short, dragging gasps, knowing that soon, any moment, she must fall.

"Verity!"

She would not have believed she could ever be so profoundly and entirely glad to hear Leo's voice. It broke the spell of those dark waters. She looked up. He was peering over the edge of the bluff, his ginger curls glinting brilliant against the blue sky—St George in person.

"I can't move." She could only just articulate the words.

"Hold on. I'm coming down. Keep looking up."

And then he was beside her and his arm was round her waist. He showed her where to place her feet, and guided her hands into new holds, all the time encouraging her in a voice of such confident authority that her fear melted away and the ascent became easy—so easy a child could have done it. Yet when at last she hoisted herself back over the edge to lie once more in safety on the flat surface of the rock, she could not stop shaking.

"You need a drink. I'll go see what I can find."

He disappeared into the cabin, and came back with a mug of wine.

She sipped it gratefully.

"Rescuing people off cliffs seems to be your speciality," she said lightly, as soon as she could speak.

Disconcertingly, he did not answer. She had been avoiding his eyes, but as the silence lengthened, she had to look at him. He was very pale, and there was a stubble of ginger beard on his cheeks and chin.

"I take it Hope told you I was here?"

He nodded.

"She broke her promise then. I wanted to handle this by myself and I told her so. It's my problem, no-one else's. I don't need help and I don't want anybody interfering. She knew that. I'm perfectly okay here. I'd never have tried that climb if you hadn't scared me."

He just looked at her. He did not appear to have heard. His silence and his gaze angered her. Suddenly she was furious with him. His arrival had not only terrified her—it had reduced her to abject humiliation.

"Why did you come, Leo? We've said all there is to say."

She had scrambled to her feet, and now stood glaring at him. The last thing she wanted was to be beholden to this man. Already he had destroyed all her pride in her adventure. He had intruded on a delicate process of adaptation as she strove to discover her own place in this different world. She did not want him here. She hated him for not respecting her expressed wishes, for his easy authority, and for his physical strength so far superior to her own. She hated him for the Mercedes, gleaming dully beneath the dust, that destroyed the beauty of the plateau, flaunting the wealth and power that threatened everything she held sacred. And above all she hated him for whatever it was that was now vibrating in the air between them.

"Tell me why you came!" She all but spat the words at him.

He did not heed them. He stood there looking at her with half-closed eyes. A pulse was beating in his throat as it had that day in his office in Toronto.

Then he grabbed her by the wrist, so hard she cried out, and fairly yanked her to him. With his arms hard about her so that she could not move, he kissed her, his tongue taking possession of her mouth like the advance guard of an invading army.

For a few seconds she tried to resist, but no longer. At the contact with his body some unsuspected, long-banked fire inside her blazed up into a conflagration of physical desire such as she had never known before, carrying with it all the hatred, all the fear, and all the frustration of the day, as if everything had been tending toward this moment, and this alone.

In Toronto he had taken her like a thief in the night. She had been conscious only of relief from nightmare, of human comfort—she had barely been aware of him as an individual.

This was different. He had travelled hundreds of miles to find her. Hope had sent him. She herself had done all in her power to avoid this happening, to keep faith with her sister. Now she could fight no longer. Here in this place they were no longer living under the same laws. Social conventions were meaningless. In his arms, locked against him, she could no longer feel him an intruder, nor a threat, but part of herself, just as together they were a part of everything around them. She clung now to him as she had clung to the rock, and now, truly, she was falling, falling with him into a sea of melting, unbearable sweetness.

He carried her over to the grass and gently set her down. Slowly, deliberately, he took off her shirt and jeans, clothing her instead with lingering kisses, stroking her until she moaned aloud. Then he took her, not once, but again and again, and again and again she came until it seemed that nothing could ever divide them. Never before had she experienced a pleasure so deep and so continuous that it was like a chemical process—a long, slow fusion of two substances so complete that separating them again became inconceivable. Even when they were exhausted, they did not draw apart, but continued to lie there in each other's arms. There was no need for speech, and it was a long time before either could find words. It was Leo who spoke first.

"Now you know why I came."

"Yes."

"This has been going to happen ever since I first set eyes on you."

"I hated you then."

"You thought you did. You were too young to recognize the feeling."

She considered it.

"You could be right. I suppose I *was* afraid—of you and of—this. I had no mother, and there was a lot I didn't understand. There was Hope—but you were taking her away from me. Yes. You're right. I was very, very afraid of you."

He kissed her.

"And now?"

"I love you."

The words seemed to speak themselves—she had not intended, nor even formulated them. Her body had taken over and was voicing its own long-delayed response, and there was no other verb to express what it felt.

The word seemed to hang in the air above them. It was a common word, threadbare with long and rough usage, but as it hung there it seemed to give off a great light that transformed everything—the rock, the spruce, the lake, the hills and even the huge arch of sky above, as if it were as powerful as the sun itself. And indeed it was, for it meant that she was no longer alone. Yet even as she rejoiced at the thought, she felt the stab of a new fear: she was afraid that he might go away and leave her, and she knew that she could not bear it if he did.

"I love you," she said again, as if in defiance, and hid her face against him, just as a cloud floated over the sun.

They had made up the big bed, and heated up food, poured wine and lit the lamp, and now sat side by side on the bench at the table, having, as it were, set up their house together. Outside the light was fading as great clouds rolled up over the lake.

They had spoken very little. Physical contact had replaced words. A magnetic force seemed to be at play between them—she could only marvel at it.

But the fear, the new fear, kept returning, and would not be driven away. She knew she must, sooner or later, face the problem of linking this fairy tale to real life. There were questions that must be put. Above all she needed to know just what Hope had told him—yet she was desperately afraid of the answer. She nerved herself.

"How did you react when Hope came back from town without me?"

It was his turn to avoid her eyes.

"We had a fight," he said curtly.

"Did you believe her story?"

"At first I did. Then the more I thought about it, the more unlike you it seemed. That's what led to the showdown."

She laid her hand on his arm.

"I'm sorry. I'm truly sorry. It's what I was trying to avoid. I didn't want to be the cause of trouble between the two of you. I didn't think you'd understand how I felt about it all. All I wanted was to find somewhere safe where I could hide until it was safe to return."

He was not listening. His eyes were fixed on her hand.

"She told me you had come here to get away from me."

Verity flushed. The words were true, but Hope had given them a cruel twist.

"I came after you because I didn't believe it. I couldn't. You would never have gone like that without a word to me. You knew how I feel about you. You're not callous, nor malicious. If there had really been someone else you would have told me yourself that day in my office. You wouldn't tell me then what you felt about me, but I knew. Even before that night when you screamed out and I came to you and found you were a part of my own self I knew. I've known ever since you played the reluctant bridesmaid at your sister's wedding."

"I thought you despised me because I was young and gauche, and had puppy fat." She laughed at the memory.

"I could see what you were going to become. So could Hope."

"Hope? Oh no—you're wrong there. Hope had no eyes at all for me. I was just the little sister, and a terrible nuisance. She couldn't see anyone except you. I used to be furious with her for being such an adoring slave."

"Perhaps you were jealous." He kissed her, running his finger lightly down her throat, so that she shivered.

"Jealous?"

"And Hope knew it."

"That's nonsense. Of course she didn't. Why, I didn't know it myself. Besides, I told you—she only had eyes for you."

"Don't be too sure. Never underestimate adoring slaves—they are seldom as weak as they seem. Hope was taking no chances. Why else do you suppose she badgered me into taking a job out here in Canada? She couldn't wait to get me away to safety."

"But that's not what she's always told me!" Verity was incredulous. "She's told me again and again she couldn't bear to leave me behind, and that she didn't want to emigrate. I've always thought it was all your doing."

Leo merely smiled.

"Are you really saying that it was Hope all along?"

"That's right."

"But—but if that's the case why did she invite me out to stay? She's invited me several times in the last few years—it was I who refused. Surely she wouldn't have done it if she looked on me as some kind of threat?"

Her voice faltered. She felt as if the only solid ground she had known in her life had just shifted violently under her feet.

She was remembering the years at art college when there had hardly been any communication from her sister, and how the letters started to arrive more regularly once she was married. Yet even during the years of semi-silence it had never occurred to her to question their relationship. Hope had always detested writing letters. She had always taken it for granted that their feelings for each other were reciprocal. It had only been natural to blame Leo for their separation.

"Some would say," Leo spoke slowly, "that the adoring slave had been liberated. Hope changed when the girls were born—she may have told you about it, she had a very bad time, and we lost our son. For some reason she felt it was all my fault. She withdrew—from me and from the children—a quiet but definite withdrawal, on every front. She began to stake out new territory of her own, and nailed a big keep-out sign on the fence."

"I suppose we all need to keep some areas of our life private. Hope's painting has been her own personal voyage of discovery."

"You don't understand—I can't be making myself clear. All I've wanted these past few years has been to find something we still could share. I wasn't trying to take her over."

Verity stood up and went to the window. The white trunks of the silver birch were luminous in the grey light. Now that Leo was here there was nothing ominous about the approach of evening. Everything had changed. A giant hand had just shaken the kaleidoscope and the familiar pieces had fallen into new patterns and relationships. She turned and smiled at him. His hair seemed to have turned into spun gold in the rays of the lamp. He loved her. He had always loved her. There was no way the world could remain the same.

"I was afraid you'd take me over, too," she told him. "I always thought you were only interested in power, and money, and success. I didn't think our values meant anything to you. You must admit the evidence is against you—the house, the cars, the pool, and the servants—I didn't look any further than them." She went and put her arms round him, and rested her head against his. He pulled her down beside him.

"So you were judging me, were you? I wonder why. I admit I like success. I'm good at business, and I enjoy being better at it than the next guy. I get a kick out of using my brain, and I sure as hell enjoy the rewards. I'm not an artist like you and Hope, but does that have to write me off? I love being alive just as much as the two of you. I love beautiful things. I love my kids. I love you. There's nothing wrong with those feelings. You like to sit, and look, and paint—" he gestured to the pile of sketches they had been looking at earlier—"I like to move fast, to feel the wind in my face, to drive my body to its furthermost limits. Does that make us incompatible?—it wasn't my impression."

She laughed.

"No, I don't think it does."

"I know what it's like to be poor. My mother brought me up on her own. I can remember the snoopers checking on her to make sure no lover was paying our bills. And how she had to account for every penny she spent, to justify every treat, every new pair of shoes. I can remember how she cried with humiliation when she had to ask rich relatives to help with my education. It killed her in the end. I vowed I'd climb clear of it all, and I did just that. Can you imagine what it meant to me to build that house for my family to live in? You know—it's kind of hard to find I've been judged for it . . ."

"Leo, Leo darling, forgive me! I didn't understand. How could I when I didn't know you? I'm beginning to feel as if I've never understood anyone, least of all myself. Right now it seems to me there's only one thing that's clear and straightforward."

"What's that?"

"This." She kissed him then—kissed him with a freedom, a total abandon that was gloriously new to her. In her kiss were all her recently awakened feelings for him, all her sense of newly discovered oneness.

It was a long time before they finally drew apart, and when they did it was only to sit looking at each other, marvelling. It was Verity who broke the spell. In a sudden urge to be practical, she began to clear the table, and stack the dishes. She put a saucepan of water on the Primus to heat. She did not speak.

"What are you thinking?" His eyes were following her movements.

"I was thinking how unhappy you and Hope must have been—and for so long."

"You're wondering why we didn't get a divorce?"

"Mightn't it have been better?"

There was a pause.

"You may find it kind of hard to believe after what's just happened between you and me," he said heavily, "but in point of fact I'm one of those square, old-fashioned guys who believe in the old values of marriage and the family. They say you always want what you didn't have as a child, don't they? I guess I've always hoped that things would get better. I've never cheated on Hope till now. I haven't been able to accept that she wanted out."

"But if she wanted out, why didn't she just go?"

"It's not that simple. Hope's got her bad memories too. I guess she remembers what it was like for the two of you when your parents split up. I've not made it any easier for her by not giving her a reason that would justify her in her own eyes for walking out. So she tried a long shot."

"A long shot?" Verity stared at him. "You don't mean—inviting me?"

"I mean just that. She was gambling on that gut reaction she'd had when she first introduced you to me—and she got it right. You, honey, are my weak spot. She had it all worked out. You never caused Hope any trouble. You were a godsend to her. The world will now have its say—and we've both done exactly what she wanted."

Verity looked at him wide-eyed. It was impossible to believe what she had just heard, yet somewhere deep inside her a voice told her that it was the truth. He would not lie to her.

She turned away abruptly. She did not want him to see the tears that had sprung to her eyes. She was struggling to bring herself to face this new image of Hope, to accept that all along her sister's feelings for her contained malignant elements of jealousy and resentment that had slowly poisoned them. She could not bear the idea that Hope had deliberately used her. It was not possible. But, as she thought back, she saw that it was. She had taken too much for granted. She had been wrong.

Leo had come to stand behind her. He put his hands on her shoulders. She shrugged herself free in an upsurge of grief and rage.

"You've told me about yourself and you've told me about Hope —but what about me? Did either of you ever stop to consider my feelings, or were they entirely predictable? Did it ever occur to you that I might get hurt in your messy affairs, and that I've been hurt already enough for one lifetime?"

He tried to turn her round to face him, but she broke free from him, dealt him a swinging slap on the face, and ran to fling herself on the bed. He followed her, and sat beside her patiently stroking her hair as if she were a fretful child.

"Verity, darling, listen to me. Hope may have thought she knew how you'd react, and it so happened she was right. Okay, she used you. But *I* didn't know, and I haven't used you. I've already told you—I came into your bedroom that first night because you yelled for help, and into your bed because I'm made of flesh and blood. It wasn't premeditated. It was only then that I discovered exactly what you meant to me. And when you came to my office I could see it was the same for you, though you wouldn't admit it. I knew then for sure that it could not end there, whatever you said. I was certain. So that when Hope came home and spun me that

221

tale, I went berserk. Then I thought about it. I thought long and hard. And I knew it couldn't be true. I realized I had to take a chance. *The* chance, in fact: Hope spelled it out—if I came after you she'd file for divorce. She must have got a terrific kick out of saying it. Verity, my darling, I'm playing for high stakes. I've gambled everything I've ever cared about on the chance you'd say what you said out there on the grass. Will you say it again now?"

There was a long silence before at last she made a sudden move towards him.

"I do love you Leo. It's just that I—feel so lost."

"And I love you. Nothing else matters, does it? Whatever it was that Hope thought and did that led to this moment is just not relevant. We can forget it."

Only then did she realize.

"Leo—wait a minute—are you saying that Hope didn't tell you anything else?"

"What do you mean?"

"She didn't tell you about the icon?"

"I told you—she said you'd taken off to get away from me. What icon?"

She went and fetched it from the shelf above the table, and laid it in his lap.

"This is the real reason why I came up here. Hope knew that. I suppose she felt if she told you about it she wouldn't be justified in making an ultimatum."

Leo whistled softly as he examined it.

"It's very beautiful. It looks old—and valuable. The story seems to be taking on a new dimension. Hadn't you better explain?"

So she told him. When she had finished he whistled again.

"I must say that clears up a whole lot of things that were puzzling me. An icon of Loving Kindness, eh—and people kill each other to get possession of it. I'd call that a paradox, I don't know about you. But I still don't understand why you yourself are prepared to run such risks for it. Why haven't you just handed it over to the authorities?"

"We were told that if we did, it would have been given back to the Polish police. Besides, I feel responsible for it. It's hard to explain —it's to do with the fact that Venables died after he'd entrusted it to

Jeffrey. It's more than that, though. It's all bound up with what I believe in."

"You mean—religion?"

"Not really. For me the icon represents a—a tremendous statement from the past—about how people looked on life, and death. They found some sort of sanctuary in it, some comfort. In a way I've found it too while I've been here on my own—that's why I put it on the shelf. I believe it has a value that has nothing to do with politics, or commerce—a value I feel I need to try to protect."

"But is it really your problem?"

"That's exactly what I said to Jeffrey," she answered soberly. "And then, when that funny little man died, I understood that it was. Since I came here, I'm sure of it. We all need icons. There has to be something to hold on to, and the occasional miracle. Do you know what I mean?"

"I guess so. I guess too that you're one brave lady. Haven't you been scared here all on your own?"

She told him about the sounds on the roof the night before, and he laughed.

"That wasn't the only fright I had. Some waterfowl down on the lake nearly gave me a heart attack. They must have one of the spookiest calls I've ever heard." She described the birds.

"They sound like loons. What did you think they were—hostile Indians?"

"You may laugh. I wasn't to know, was I? Hope didn't have time to give me much of a briefing."

"You know, I guess I still don't understand why Hope didn't tell me about it."

"Don't you see? If she'd told you I was in danger it would have been perfectly proper for you to come flying after me to the rescue, wouldn't it? It would have completely spoilt her ultimatum. She wasn't putting me at risk because she must have guessed you'd come. She knew what she was doing. She was determined to offer you a free choice—and you took it. Oh Leo, I do love you!"

He took her in his arms.

Later, as they on the bed, Verity found herself thinking about all that had been said. She wondered if she could ever bear to speak to Hope again. Their whole relationship had fallen apart. Its future, if it had one, was unforeseeable. The only aspect of it that was now certain was that she was no longer the one who was alone. Leo loved her. Her eye fell on the icon standing on the shelf by the bed where Leo had placed it. She smiled at it. It had performed its miracle. But even as she smiled, the fear stabbed again. A thought had struck her.

"Darling—when you left the house to drive up here—you did make sure you weren't followed, didn't you?"

"Followed? Who the hell would follow me?" His voice was sleepy.

"The Poles. They were watching your house when I left. They'd have followed me if it hadn't been for Hope's fooling them."

"I didn't see anyone. They must have given up. In any case I drove so fast they'd have needed a plane to stay on my tail. I guess I committed every traffic offence in the province. But it was you they were interested in, not me."

He spoke confidently, reassuringly, but a small crease had appeared in his forehead, and his muscles tensed.

"I hope you're right."

"You worry too much. You're not on your own now. I'm here to take care of you."

"You won't ever leave me, will you?"

"I won't ever leave you."

"Promise on the icon."

He raised himself on one elbow, leaned over, and touched it, smiling.

"I promise. And you?"

"What about me?"

"Swear that you'll always love me."

"I swear it."

"Tell me something."

"What?"

"This guy Jeffrey—the one who didn't show up—do you care about him?"

She smiled in her turn.

"Yes, I do. He's a very gentle person. I should hate anything to have happened to him."

"Did you sleep with him that night in Glasgow?"

"Yes. Do you mind?"

"I'm not sure. Yes and no."

She stroked his cheek.

"I care about him, but I love you. I was a different person when I got on that plane at Heathrow. Now I've found you, nothing will ever be the same again. Do you understand?"

"I guess so. I just wish it had happened sooner. We've lost so much time . . ."

"You mustn't say that. You once told me we mustn't dwell on the past. You said the future was what mattered."

"You must have thought me a complete prick!"

She chuckled.

"Too right, I did! But you weren't far wrong—not where we're concerned. From now on we're going to make every day count, just to make up. So what shall we do tomorrow?"

His reply was prompt.

"Make love."

"And the day after that?"

"Do you have any better ideas?"

"Not that I can think of."

"It sounds a wonderful programme to me. And we've got your icon here to watch over us. Loving kindness—there's little enough of it around, but some of it seems to have come our way at last. God knows I've looked for it long enough."

"Same here. In fact I was beginning to believe it was something I'd never know again."

"Well, you were wrong, weren't you? Because I'm going to make sure you know nothing else for the rest of your days . . ."

She lay quietly listening to him as he murmured to her, soothing away the memories and the fears. She relaxed in his warmth, and grew drowsy, and presently fell into a deep, peaceful sleep.

She was woken with terrifying suddenness by a violent blow on the side of the face. Her mouth filling with blood, she stared dazedly about her, unable to understand what was happening. The only fact that was clear was that Leo was gone from beside her. As she tried to take in the significance of that, a second blow smashed into her other cheek, jerking her head round. Then she saw them—the incarnation of all the fears and anxieties of the last week, no longer shadows nor remembered characters out of a discarded thriller, but real, and human, and evil.

There were three of them. The strangest thing about them was their ordinariness. She would have passed them in the street without a second glance. They were men whom in other circumstances she would have smiled at and wished good day to. As she looked at them, her hand touching her bruised lips, she saw something else: no communication was possible with them. Their eyes were cold. Tears, smiles, looks or words would make no more impression on them than on programmed robots. Physically, they were fellow human beings. Emotionally, they had rejected humanity.

She lay as if hypnotized. She could not move. One of them had struck her, and no-one had ever done that before. She was living the terror dream. In a moment she would start running, and they would follow her. She lay and looked. She had never believed that people could act this way—even when James was killed. She had not witnessed that. She had known them get angry, say hurtful things, make mistakes, panic—but there had always been, as a counter-weight, a desire to please, to apologize—a need for affection. Here there was nothing. Three pairs of cold eyes denied life. They were not seeing her as a human being. She did not exist. She was a piece of matter clogging their machine.

The figure nearest her drew back his arm to strike again. Now she knew everything was over. Leo had gone. Without him she had no more courage, no more desire to struggle. She could only submit.

"Please!" she begged, "please don't! Take the icon. See—there it is. It's what you want, isn't it? Take it, please—and go!"

She snatched the icon from the shelf, and held it out. The man took it, but still he kept his eyes on her. He passed it to one of his companions, and said something to him which she did not under-stand. They laughed, and turned to go, but he came nearer and seized her arm, twisting it so that she was forced closer to him. Her flesh shrank as he tore open her shirt, and put his hand on her breast. But even as he clumsily began to fumble with her jeans, shots rang out on the plateau outside. Then it was that she saw that the rifle was missing from its place on the wall by the door.

For several seconds the three men stood motionless, listening.

226

Then, after a whispered consultation, two of them made silently for the open door, drawing guns as they went, and slid outside, swift and poisonous as snakes. Two more shots were heard, precise, staccato, then nothing. Silence fell.

The man who was holding her was standing so still she could feel his heart beating. As the minutes passed and nothing happened, she could feel his tension increasing. It was clear he was uncertain what to do. Finally, he shoved her roughly down on the bed and crept over to the door, soundless as a cat. Keeping well in its shelter he peered out. She heard him suck in his breath. Whatever it was he had seen resolved his doubts, for in a couple of strides he was back beside the bed, grabbing her once more. She struggled frantically, but he dragged her up to stand close against him. Then, winding his hand in her hair, he jerked her face close to his.

"You stay so, near me. Or I kill you. We move so, my gun in your back. See—feel it. If they try to save you, I kill. We go to car. You tell them. You tell them no shoot."

She had no choice. One of his hands was agonizingly twisting her hair, the other was jabbing the barrel of a gun between her shoulder blades. Sheltering behind her he pushed her to the door and out on to the grass.

"You say. You say I kill if they try get you." His breath was hot in her ear.

"Leo! Leo! Don't shoot! Please! He says he'll kill me if you try." She called brokenly.

There was no sound. There was still enough light to enable her to make out the shapes of the trees, and the mass of the rock. There was no sign of anyone—except, beside a second car that stood near the Mercedes, two shadows darker than the rest lying on the ground. She heard the breath of the man behind her whistle through his teeth as slowly they moved towards them. The hand gripping her hair was transferred to her throat, half choking her, so that she was forced even closer against his body, shielding it. The gun was now at her head.

She knew there was no way Leo could save her. Her thoughts whirled crazily as they approached the second car. It was a good place to die, a good time of day, even, as the light gave way to dark. The first stars were coming out, as they would the next day and the day

227

after that, for all this was no concern of theirs. She wished she could have been given more time—time to do or say something that might be remembered, time to build on this great love she had so incredibly found—but it was not to be. She could only be thankful that she had known it, however briefly. For a few short hours she had been admitted to what had felt like the very innermost heart of life, and that, she knew, was a rare privilege. But she could not help wishing that she could have known it for longer. She thought of the icon, and suddenly she found herself praying—praying that there might be a miracle, and that Leo might be with her when she died, so that she would not have to face that alone.

The explosion behind her head knocked her off-balance. She fell forwards into the grass and lay there stunned, her eyes shut. She could feel no pain other than that of her bruised and lacerated mouth. If this was dying, it was wonderfully simple. Then she felt herself lifted into someone's arms, and a familiar voice spoke her name, and a mouth gently kissed her hurt face. She opened her eyes to find she was looking at Leo.

"Verity! Verity darling! Are you okay? I'm sorry. I had to try. It was the only thing I could think of. Tell me you're all right!"

She smiled, despite the pain. Everything had been given back to her. The miracle had happened. They were both alive.

"I'm all right. I'm not badly hurt. It's just my face where he hit me. Oh Leo! I love you so. How did you do it?"

She had caught sight of the body of the gunman lying on the ground, his neck at an odd angle. His gun was beside him.

"Karate," Leo said briefly. "It was the only way I could get rid of the gun and him at the same time. I wasn't sure I could bring it off—I'm a mite out of practice, and I was terrified he'd shoot. I had to try. I couldn't think of anything else. But when you fell I thought I'd mistimed it. Oh honey—tell me again you're okay."

"I'm fine." Wonderingly, as if she couldn't believe he was real, she touched his cheek.

"Can you stand? This was all my fault. The bastards must have trailed me here. If I'd known . . . Dear God, I love you so . . . !"

He helped her to her feet, and folded her in his arms. She leaned her aching head against him in a great rush of gratitude. This, this above all was what she had been so sad to lose—this sense of being at last a part of a perfect whole, and themselves part of a still greater, grander one. Together, they were not intruders in this place.

Cupping her face in his hands, he covered it with kisses, light, and infinitely gentle. She closed her eyes, marvelling. There would be no more fear, no more pursuit, no more aloneness. He had saved her. She did not see one of the dark shadows on the ground behind them moving slowly, and painfully, and taking aim.

The bullet hit Leo at the base of the skull. Lost in happiness, she heard the report as the gun went off, but did not understand. She felt him start, and, looking into his eyes, saw them widen suddenly. Then he sagged in her arms, pulling her with him to the ground.

"Leo?"

He did not reply. He lay very quiet. She lifted his head. Blood from the wound in his neck slowly seeped over her but she did not notice it. She could not take in what had happened. She looked round wildly but there was no movement anywhere. The dark shadows on the ground were still now.

"Leo?"

He opened his eyes, looked into hers, and tried to speak, but she could only hear an indistinct sound, that might have been her name. And then she saw that he was not seeing her any more.

"Oh no! NO!"

She hurled the negatives at the darkening world around her. It was not possible. It could not happen like this. To be one moment alive and warm and happy and full of love, and the next a bundle of flesh and bones growing slowly colder and colder, never to be warm again—it did not make sense. Leo was here, in her arms—how could he have gone? Desperately she clutched him to her, trying to infuse him with her own living warmth. Now it was her turn to kiss him gently, to heal him, to urge him to return with all the strength of her love—but she could not heal him, and she knew he would never come back again. Despite all the promises, all the prayers, all the cruel miracles. Leo, here in her arms, had left her just as surely and irrevocably as James had done all those years ago.

It was not possible. It could not have happened.

"Leo?"

For a long, long time she sat there on the grass with his head in her lap. Around her nothing had changed. The old spruce still stood defiantly, black against the evening sky. The lake still lapped beneath the bluff. Nothing seemed to be aware of what had happened. The cycle of life was continuing without acknowledgement of death.

"Leo—please don't leave me. Please don't go." But the fact that he *had* gone, *had* left her was slowly forcing its way into her reluctant brain. This man whom she had so blindly misjudged, whose worth and whose love she had only admitted a few short hours ago, this complex, brilliant man whose powers she had feared and despised only to love at last with her whole being, was dead. Leo would never be there again to cherish her. The loving kindness was gone for ever.

Loving kindness. Where was the icon? The slant-eyed Byzantine madonna had been laughing at her. Her promises, her comfort, her miracles were mere sadistic tricks. She had caused this obscenity to happen. She inspired acts in direct contradiction to the beliefs she was supposed to symbolize. Loving kindness, eternal peace—where were they? What were they? Here in her arms, and sprawled on the grass around her lay four broken human puppets with the sawdust trickling from them. It was enough to make any god roar with laughter.

Rage rose in her. Gently setting Leo on the ground, she bent over the two bodies of the men he had shot first. The icon lay on the grass near one of them, the pearls that outlined the headdress of the madonna gleaming dully. She picked it up, and gazed with hatred at the dark, stylized face with the impenetrable eyes that looked away from hers. No-one, no other desperate human soul should turn to it again, only to be mocked.

Holding it stiffly in front of her she walked slowly to the edge of the bluff. For several moments she stood there, not in hesitation, but as if she were a priestess pausing in her solemn ritual. Then she threw the icon as hard and as far as she could, so that it flew through the air in a wide arc before dropping into the water far below. Somehow it seemed a fitting end for it.

She stood there for a long time, staring out into the growing darkness. Then she turned and stood in doubt. She did not know what to do. There was no more meaning anywhere. Only one thing was certain: she must get away from this place. She had held out against everything—her isolation, her ignorance, her fears—but she could not be alone in the presence of death. She must look for help. She must phone Hope, tell others, share this meaninglessness with people who would not understand, and all the time she would be the only one to know exactly what it was she had lost.

With the angular movements of an automaton, she fetched blankets and carefully covered the bodies. She found her purse, and keys, and a torch, and meticulously shut and locked the cabin door. Without a glance she walked past the four mounds on the grass, past the two cars, only to halt at the mouth of the trail. Suddenly she turned and ran back to look one last time beneath the covering that separated her from Leo—just in case. He had promised he would never leave her, but he had not kept his word. Now she must leave him.

Stooping, she kissed his forehead. Then, her face set and grim, she turned, and set off once more to make her stumbling way through the mosquito-ridden darkness along the trail to find her car.

Chapter 13

The last limousines were moving off down the drive. The specially-hired waiters were beginning to gather up the debris of the buffet lunch, their movements graceful as ballet dancers.

Verity stood at the window, watching the departing line of cars. She had dreaded the funeral, but now it was over she found she was dreading the remaining two days of her stay even more.

Breaking the news of Leo's death over the phone had taken the last of her courage. All through the long, blind drive in the dark that had preceded it she had been too deep in shock to feel fear or fatigue. For mile after mile she had driven at little more than walking pace, peering dry-eyed at the tangled tentacles of trees and undergrowth that seemed to threaten at any moment to swallow up the car and herself for ever. All she could think of was the ordeal that lay ahead.

When she had finally reached a village and found a phone, the line was so bad that she had had to repeat her words many times. It increased the atmosphere of nightmare. It did not make the story feel more real. When she had finally come to the end, all she could hear was the cracklings of the instrument. She tried to visualize her sister's face. She remembered the day they had told her of James's death, and her refusal to believe in it. The silence went on and on.

"Hope, are you there?"

Still no answer. Then at last Hope's voice, hard and sharp as splinters of glass.

"Have you told the police?"

"Not yet."

"What happened to the icon?"

"I threw it in the lake."

"What did you say?"

"I threw it in the lake. It had done enough harm."

Silence again, longer still this time.

"Hope, what shall I say to the police?"

At last the metallic voice spoke again, decisive, practical, without the slightest trace of emotion.

"We'd better simplify. Tell them you went to the cabin to paint. I'll square Mary-Lou: Don't mention the icon. Leo went after you because we'd received a kidnap threat. We've had more than one in the past few years, so they'll believe that. Did you actually do any painting?"

"Some."

"Good. It'll help the media swallow it as well as the police. You'd better realize right now we're in for a rough ride—it's the kind of story they dream of. I'd prefer to avoid a mud bath."

"Hope?"

"What is it?"

"I—I just wanted to say—I'm sorry."

Hope did not reply.

"Hope—can you hear me?"

"I can hear you. You say you're not hurt?"

"A few cuts and bruises. I'm all right."

"You'd better get straight on to the police then. You went there to paint—just stick to that."

"Hope—I—"

But Hope had hung up.

The forecast had proved accurate: they did indeed give her a rough ride. For what seemed like hours on end she had patiently answered their questions, grimly sticking to her story. Everything was checked and double checked. Even when they took her back to the cabin she did not break down, but continued to give them the information they wanted in the same mechanical manner. The more she had repeated it, the less real it had become. It had all happened to someone else. She felt nothing. She had become disconnected—she was no longer a part of anything.

All the evidence, of course, had supported her. Bullets fitted guns, finger prints matched the requisite fingers, while Hope gave a precise account of the kidnap threat which had sent Leo speeding off to protect his sister-in-law. The pile of anaemic sketches she had completed before his arrival duly supported the truth of her story. The icon, which might have contributed a deeper voice, lay lost in the ancient mud at the bottom of the lake.

In the end they had allowed her to return to Toronto, and Hope. Every fibre of her body had shrunk from the prospect of encountering her sister, but she had no choice if her story was to be believed, and in the event it had proved less of a trauma than she had feared. It had been no more real than anything else. No tears. Few words. They seemed to eye each other from different sides of a thick glass partition.

The triplets, too, were quiet and withdrawn, with a tendency to hang around their mother as if they were afraid that she, too, might suddenly disappear. Verity, acutely aware of the ambiguity of her position, had tried to talk to them, only to find herself confronted by three pairs of cold, hostile eyes. Her words had shrivelled and fallen away like dead leaves, and she had turned from them in discouragement.

She had offered then to try and obtain an earlier flight back to London, or to move out to a hotel, but Hope had promptly vetoed the idea.

"You must be crazy. What the hell do you suppose the Press would make of that? Besides, I need you here."

She was not to be allowed to escape then. Hope was exacting both blood and flesh, making sure she was present throughout all the complex, prosaic procedure which surrounds an individual's loss of living status. Leo's death was duly certificated, and stamped with official approval. His presence among the human race became his absence, on paper as well as in fact, and his departure made public with all the careful rituals that confirm its reality.

The three other deaths were quickly shuffled out of sight. The moment their identity was established, diplomacy had intervened. Such small fish could not be allowed to trouble the heavily oiled waters of international affairs at such a delicate moment.

The day before the funeral she and Hope had driven downtown to pay the necessary visit to the family lawyer over the matter of Leo's will. It turned out to have been meticulously drawn up, and contained few surprises. Hope was now a very rich widow. Large sums had been left in trust for the triplets, and there were many generous bequests to staff and charities. There was also, the old lawyer informed them in his paper-dry voice, something for Verity: a small Renoir which was at present hanging in Mr Springer's study. Hope's lips had twitched at the announcement, but she had made no comment.

Verity had listened in total detachment. None of all this, none of the detailed arrangements made by the living Leo, signed by his hand, seemed to have anything to do with him or with them. The gift of a work of art, however wonderful, meant nothing now. She felt no interest, and the lawyer had glanced in some surprise at her unmoved face. She had been, if anything, more concerned with her plans for the afternoon.

She had decided to take the opportunity, while they were in the city, of paying a visit to Jeffrey. She had tried to phone him several times since her return, but always there had been no reply. She wanted to draw a line under their encounter, and turn the page, but it was not possible to do this until there had been at least an attempt at an explanation. She had even spoken of it to Hope—there was no-one else to consult.

"Write him a letter."

"But he might never get it, not if he's ill or hurt somewhere."

"Then you can't do anything about it, can you?"

"I feel I ought to make one last real attempt to contact him."

"Suit yourself. Write a letter and take it to his apartment. Or leave it with a neighbour. Not that I think there's any point. I'm sure you'll find your friend's taken very good care of himself."

So, after leaving the lawyer, she had taken a taxi to the once so-carefully memorized address. It turned out to be in an apartment block set near a small, tree-filled park. An elaborate fountain splashed in the forecourt, and flowerbeds and ornamental shrubs proclaimed its social status. Jeffrey's thrillers obviously brought in a comfortable income.

There had been no reply when she rang the doorbell. She had lifted her hand to try once more when, with a thrill of apprehension, she heard the lock turn. The door opened a few inches on the chain. A girl's face peered out at her—a pleasant, broad-boned face with blue eyes set wide apart, and fair hair caught back in a ponytail. For several seconds she simply stared, trying to collect her wits.

"Excuse me—I thought—does Jeffrey Wren live here?"

"He does—but right now he's moved in with me. I've just come over to pick up his mail and a few of his clothes. Do you want to give me a message for him?" She unhooked the chain and opened the door wider, smiling at Verity with watchful eyes.

"Perhaps you'd be so kind as to give him this letter?" she held out the envelope. "Tell him—tell him Verity Wells called, and was—was sorry to miss him." She was on the verge of moving away when she suddenly turned back.

"Has he been staying with you long? Forgive my asking, but it's—well—it's important."

"A week or so, I guess."

"Is he all right? I mean, he isn't ill or anything?"

The blue eyes widened in surprise.

"Who, Jeff? Why no—he's just fine."

"I see. Well—thanks. I'm sorry to have disturbed you."

"You're welcome. Have a nice day."

The door had shut gently in her face. Staring at its dark, polished surface she had stood for a moment unable to move. So Hope had been right all along. He had simply used her.

As if in a dream, she had walked back along the deeply carpeted corridor to the elevator. She had been so sure that she could trust him, but she had been mistaken. The whole of their short relationship had been based on falsehood, on a delusion. They had never really spoken to each other, never made any sort of true contact. Had anyone or anything ever been real?

Suddenly she was afraid. She was back in nightmare country. The old panic crouched in the shadows, waiting. Once she could no longer distinguish the real from the unreal it would pounce—and this time she might not be able to escape.

Back in the taxi, in the sunlight once more, she took several deep breaths. She had known then that she must fight. Even if there was nothing left that was worth living for she wanted to avoid the humiliation of that particular defeat. She owed it to Leo. Facts. She must force herself to sort out what had really happened from what had not. She must place the facts in order, and then face

236

and accept them. Then indeed she might be able to turn the page.

They had been attracted to each other—not in any way that could be compared with what had happened between herself and Leo, but gently, even childishly. She had liked his boyish looks and what she had taken for his candour, and she had appreciated his sensitivity. She had believed him compassionate. When the plane had turned back and she had been afraid, she had been glad of his humour and his apparent solidity. Beside all this she had not thought his failings in bed of any earth-shaking importance. Perhaps that was where she had been wrong. Perhaps they were what gave the lie to all the rest. It seemed like it now. His feelings for her had proved as shallow and as short-lived as his lovemaking.

It was hard to believe, and even harder to accept, but she had just been given irrefutable evidence that it was so. She had made an error of judgement.

But that was all it was—an error. It had borne terrible results, but that did not change it into anything else. It was real. It had happened and she could regret it. It was not, however, something to be afraid of.

By the time she had rejoined Hope, she was calm again. She had done exactly what she had set out to do. Jeffrey no longer mattered. He could not make any difference to the emptiness of the world around her, nor to the numbness inside her. Nothing could ever again do that.

Now, today, throughout all the interminable ceremonies, the numbness and the emptiness had been all she was aware of. The absurd rites, the mellifluous clerics, the technicolour flowers tortured into shapes that denied their real function—none of these had anything to do with the Leo she had so briefly and ecstatically known. That glinting ginger hair could never become dust and ashes. He could never have lain still so long in that ridiculous box.

It was not possible that any of all this could be real. Leo was not here. Any moment now he would appear and rescue her from it just as he had once before appeared to pluck her off the cliff face, and carry her off with him to the cabin by the lake, and they would laugh together at the antics of all these solemn-faced people. She simply had to hold on for long enough and he would come.

Even now, when they were all going, she was still waiting for him.

No-one realized. She had not wept. Heavy-eyed, the bruises still livid in her white face, she had played out her role of supporting her sister. It was essential to the credibility of their story that there should not be the slightest sign of hostility between them. The only clue to her state of mind was the way her eyes continually strayed towards the door through which he would come.

Hope had not wept, either. Wearing a simple black dress, her streaky yellow hair strained severely back from her face in which the lines seemed to be etched more deeply than ever, her eyes glittering, she had moved among her guests like an intricately programmed robot, accepting the formal words of condolence that flowed around her in smooth streams, and ignoring the speculative stares that followed her everywhere. The newspapers had thrown no mud, but imaginations had been fired.

The triplets had been present throughout. Verity had dared to query the wisdom of this, but Hope had insisted they should be there—their presence, she maintained, was absolutely necessary. They had shed no more tears than their mother or aunt. It was as if the faculty of weeping had been taken from all five of them. The tiny metal object which had buried itself in Leo's body seemed to have had an endless malignant power, draining them, as well as him, of all warmth and feeling. They had followed their mother round in a silent group, and it occurred to Verity that for them, too, it could not seem real.

Released at last from the incessant pressures of the occasion, she stood at the window, and pressed her hot forehead against the cold glass. Once again she was realizing that she had to face the facts: the guests had all gone, and Leo had not come. She was alone, more alone than she had ever been before.

But the truth was wider and deeper than that, and she fought now to follow it and to take it into herself so that she might learn whether or not this time it was possible to live with it. She did not want ever again to take refuge in dreams.

Leo would not come back ever again. He would not ever rescue her again. He was dead. Like James. All that was left was his absence.

But for some reason it did not seem the same as it had with James. There was a crucial difference. She forced herself to think back to the events of the fateful evening by the lake.

James had simply vanished, and it was this that had made his death so unbelievable and unacceptable. She had been left with nothing, an everlasting negative. Leo, on the other hand, had died in her arms. Now, for the first time, she began to see that this was a kind of privilege. His last taste of warmth had been from her lips. She had gone with him to the very boundary of life. He had not started out on his journey alone. They had been allowed to love each other to the uttermost edge. It was indeed a memory she could hold on to, and cherish, a royal gift to sustain her until she herself died, and perhaps, in itself, a reason for holding on, not in fruitless, deluded expectation but in the desire to preserve as long as possible something very precious.

She stared out at the garden, empty now. More and more red and yellow flecks were appearing amid the green leaves. She would have liked to see it in the fall—she recalled Hope saying that Leo had laid it out with that in mind. How censorious she had been then —condemning him out of hand for what she had perceived as an ostentatious display of wealth.

Today she felt very differently. It was no small thing to leave behind one a house built to be a home for the people one cared for, and a garden created out of bare fields. It was in its way just as much a gesture as Hope's painting. The trees would go on changing from green to gold, and the house sheltering other human lives long after they were all forgotten. They were the mark Leo had made on the face of the earth to show that he had passed that way.

There was a touch on her shoulder. She turned to find Hope standing behind her.

"I think this might be a good time for you to see the picture Leo left you."

"If you like." She had forgotten all about it. "Are you sure you aren't too tired? You look exhausted."

"I'm okay. I want to get it over with."

Verity followed her out of the room apprehensively wondering if some new ordeal had been planned for her. Both the timing, and the choice of words were odd.

Hope led the way to a small room she had not seen before, opening off the main bedroom. It was obviously Leo's study. The furniture in it was very different from that in the rest of the house. It was old, and

239

shabby. Decrepit books lined the shelves—a motley, battle-scarred collection of schoolboy favourites for the most part. Looking closely, she made out *The Thirty-nine Steps*, and *Twenty Thousand Leagues Under the Sea*—Leo had had a penchant for action, it seemed, from his earliest youth.

"He never would allow me to refurnish in here. That monstrosity, believe it or not, was his father's." She pointed to a huge, ugly Victorian desk set against the wall. "He was supposed to have committed suicide after going bankrupt, but he'd left them before that and his mother never really knew the truth. He left the drawers full of bills. Anyway, there's your picture."

The small Renoir was hanging on the wall just above the desk. It was probably, Verity thought as she leaned to examine it, a study for a larger work, for not only was it slightly unfinished, but it had about it the exuberant vitality of the first impressions of a great artist—a vitality which tends to dwindle slightly as these grow into a major set piece.

It was a picture of a baigneuse tying up her hair. She gazed at it, and went on gazing, unable to speak—but as she looked she could feel the numbness inside her giving way to a hot, throbbing ache of pain. For the model, painted though she must have been a good half century before her own birth, bore an extraordinary, a startling resemblance to herself. The artist, what is more, had painted her with a kind of passionate joy: sunlight caressed the soft, rounded limbs and smooth breasts, and danced on the red lips, and the dark, mischievous eyes—the whole work was a celebration of light, and life, and warm, sensuous beauty. And she knew, as, no doubt, did Hope, exactly why he had bought it, why he had hung it in this place, and why he had willed it to her. What she was looking at was a silent declaration of Leo's love.

Now at last the pain swept through her in a great tide of grief. More eloquently than words the picture spoke to her of the strength and durability of that love, illuminating the magnitude of her loss, and the pitifulness of the few hours they had had together.

Scalding tears rolled down her cheeks and splashed on to the faded leather of the desk. She covered her face with her hands, as if trying to hide them from Hope.

"I'm sorry, Hope. I'm so very sorry."

Hope made no reply, nor did she move. She stood, white-faced and rigid, just inside the door, watching. She waited until Verity had quietened a little before she spoke.

"It wasn't your fault. Or mine. Or Leo's. There's no point in apologizing to each other. Of course you're sorry. So am I. So, I daresay, is Leo, wherever it is he's gone. It won't bring him back."

"It might help the rest of us go on."

"I don't think I need any help."

"P'raps not. But the girls do—and so do I. It would be better for them if you and I could bring ourselves to forgive each other—or at least to understand each other."

"If you mean by understanding accepting the fact that we never will forgive each other, I'm all for it. We could go on from there. We both know that neither of us intended it to happen—but we both know too that if we hadn't been playing games, Leo would still be alive."

"It wasn't a game."

Hope gave a short laugh.

"Of course it was. It's all games. I realized that long ago when they told me I was expecting four babies instead of one. You could say that's when I grew up."

Verity thought to herself that, on the contrary, that was when something precious and infinitely vulnerable in Hope had finally died. But she did not try to argue. There was nothing any more that she could do about it—only grieve that it was so and try, perhaps, to help the girls.

"From then on I stopped trying to kid myself that anything else mattered other than winning or losing. I'd always lost out—to our parents, to you, to Leo, to the doctors. I made up my mind then that in future I was going to play to win. And I have, haven't I?"

"You mean—your painting?"

"Sure, what else?"

"Is that a game, too?"

"The most hilarious one of all. I didn't expect to find myself with a whole fistful of trumps. I owe you, you know. If it hadn't been for you I might have taken a whole lot longer to realize I had a winning hand. I wish you'd stay and help me fix that exhibition. Won't you change your mind?"

Verity shook her head. She felt slightly sick. In some ways this reality was more painful than any other. Hope had closed and barricaded all the doors.

"I'm sorry. It just isn't possible. By the way—could I possibly have one of those old books, if you're not keeping them for the children, that is?"

Hope looked at her in surprise.

"Of course. Take as many as you like. I can't think why he kept them. The girls won't care for them."

"I just want one."

She looked carefully along the shelves, and picked out a copy of *Mr Standfast*.

"This'll do."

"I guess I'll never understand you, Verity. Leo leaves you a painting worth a small fortune—it'll take some time to get it across to you, I'm afraid, by the way—and you ask for a battered old book."

"When did he buy the painting?"

"Oh, years and years ago—when he began to make his first real money. I thought he'd gone mad—till I saw it."

There was a silence. Then she continued.

"I'm glad he willed it to you. It wouldn't have looked right in my new place."

"Your new place? You mean you're selling this one?"

"You bet. I never did like this house. It was Leo's choice, not mine. I'm thinking of moving into Quebec. Are you sure I can't persuade you to stay—or better still, to move out here permanently? It would make a lot of sense. You could be my agent."

Verity had to smile. She suddenly realized that Hope had not the slightest idea what she was asking.

"That's a big question—it'll take time to answer it. The important thing meanwhile is to make sure we don't get out of touch again. You and the triplets might consider coming over to visit me. They'd love the cliffs and the sea. Where are they, by the way? Perhaps we shouldn't leave them alone too much just now. Why don't we go and discuss it with them—it might help them to have something positive to think about?"

"Oh—they're okay. They were helping with the clearing up —which in real terms means finishing up the canapés."

242

"Let's go and look for them."

At the door Verity stopped and looked back. The little room had once been Leo's private place. Traces of his presence still seemed to cling about it—it was as if for a short time she had just been close to him again. But he was in a more private one still now. It was time to accept that, and turn away, and go out among the living. Silently, she said goodbye.

They found the triplets hunched in a disconsolate group by the pool. Everything seemed unnaturally quiet. The hired staff had all departed, and there was no sign of Nelly, Matt or Mrs Matt.

Leo's absence seemed almost tangible. The pool and the surrounding garden had so often rung with his shouts, and laughter. She could almost see him diving into the water, followed as always by his children, all displaying the same athletic grace, the same love of motion. They had known, the little girls, where to find the warmth, the effervescent affection they needed in order to grow.

Verity gave a little sob as she looked at them. Then, impulsively she ran to join them, longing to comfort and be comforted—only to meet once again the cold gaze of three pairs of hostile eyes.

It was as if they had struck her. Miserably she stood beside them, trying to think of something to say that would soften this implacable judgement they had passed on her without giving her a hearing.

Laura, Claire, and Diana had been helpless bystanders in the drama that had played itself out in their home. She had no idea what they had seen, how much they had heard, how much they had guessed—she could only be sure that they had no reason to love her, and every possible one to hate her. She might have resigned herself to that had it not been for the fact that she knew that in loving their father, she had hurt them. For his sake, she had to try to reach them, to help them fight their way clear of the cold and the emptiness, before she left them to Hope.

She sat herself down on the flagstones beside them, and was careful not to look at them as she spoke.

"Your father saved my life, you know," she told them, touching the bruises on her face. "I don't know how much you've been told, and how much you've guessed, but if I give you the real story now, will you promise me on your honour to keep it secret? Really secret this time. Because if you tell anyone we could all be in bad trouble."

They stared at her wide-eyed, then, one after the other, they nodded. Hope, who had joined them, shook her head warningly, but she took no notice. The only way to win back their trust was to trust them with at least the greater part of the truth. It was a risk, for they were very young, but if she did not take it now she might never be given another chance—and they would be lost.

She began her story, and before long saw the hostility fading from their eyes, to be replaced by excitement. Soon they were hanging onto her words. When she came to the moment when Claire had so nearly caught her with the mutilated bible, they interrupted.

"So *that*'s what you were doing!"

"You told us it was your *jewel* case!"

"You said that to *Daddy*!"

"I had to. I didn't want anyone to know about the icon, not even him. I was afraid of putting you all in danger. You very nearly found me out, Claire. If you had, it might all have ended very differently . . ."

Her eyes filled again. It was true—it had all turned on so little. For a moment she could not go on. Then she saw there were tears in the children's eyes too, and she knew she must. This time, as she described what had happened by the lake, she did not feel that it was nothing to do with herself. This time there was no numbness inside her any more, and the tears fell without restraint. The triplets wept with her. Now at last when she held out her arms they crowded into them. Hope looked on, her face expressionless.

"I am so very sorry," she said, when she came to the end. It had to be said, just as it had had to be said to their mother. "I never believed anyone would actually be killed. It should have been me, not your father. He was a very, very brave man. I've needed to say that to you so badly."

"Poor Aunt Verity!"

She did not know which of the three said it, but it was the first word of true sympathy, spoken from the heart, that she had had. It renewed her tears, but for the first time, she felt a little less alone. Perhaps there was a small ray of hope for them all yet.

Gradually, they became calmer. The barriers were down now. She wondered if they would stay so once she had left them. If only they could have longer together. For a moment she was tempted to change her mind and stay on, but some voice deep inside her told her that was not the way. She needed time, and peace, and she had learned the hard way that she must sometimes listen to her needs. She had an idea.

"You know, you three, tomorrow is my last full day in Canada. I'm flying home the day after. Couldn't we do something special together, the five of us? Your father wouldn't have wanted us to sit around and mope, would he? He liked doing things, going places. Let me give you a treat. Is there somewhere you'd like to go that we'd all enjoy? I'd like to have one happy memory to take back home with me."

Their three faces brightened simultaneously, and silenced the protest that was on Hope's lips. It was a good idea. They were not callous, she knew. They were children intent on survival, and the offer of a treat was like a lifebelt thrown into the sea of their grief. They turned to her now like plants turning towards the sun, and it reminded her with a pang of the way they had clustered round Leo. They knew better than to turn to Hope, and she wondered with a sudden chill how, in fact, her sister would deal with them. Perhaps history would repeat itself, and the close bond between them was what would see them through. If it was real. She had still not completely digested the truth about Hope's feelings towards herself. Perhaps she never would.

"We could go to the Ex!"

"You'd love the horses!"

"There's the adventure park!"

She smiled at them, and they smiled back.

"You agree, Hope?"

Hope shrugged, half amused, half resigned.

"We might as well. We could have lunch at Ontario Place and make a day of it. I guess the house isn't in such danger of being burgled now. I can't guarantee the Ex will be exactly your scene, Verity, but—"

"Will somebody please tell me what is the Ex?"

"The Canadian National Exhibition. A kind of huge arts and crafts and everything-under-the-sun display and funfair all combined—held down on the lakeside. Take your camera—it's very colourful and *very* noisy."

"Can we go on the water-slide?"

"Can we see the 3-D again?"

"Can we take a boat trip?"

"We'll see the town," Verity promised them, and stopped abruptly. Leo had wanted to do that with her, and she had refused. If she had known then how little time they had left, would her answer have been different, she wondered.

"Aunt Verity," for once it was a single voice that spoke, "do you *have* to go home so soon? Couldn't you stay with us longer?"

She flushed as they all looked at her beseechingly. She knew that they, at least, were not playing games. It was not easy to disappoint them. One day, perhaps, when she had finally come to terms with all that had happened, it might be possible to come back and try again, if it was not too late, but now she needed above all to be somewhere where she could feel she belonged.

"I'm afraid I must go," she said gently. "Your mother's already asked me. I told her—I've used up all my holiday. I have a job, you see."

"Mommy could find you a job out here."

"She is going to be busy enough looking after you, and with her own work, without having to worry about me as well. Besides, I love my job at home. Maybe you could come and visit me instead. I think you'd like Wales. Don't look so sad—we're going to meet up lots of times."

"It would be easier if you came out here to live with us."

"For you, maybe—not for me. It isn't easy to pull up one's roots."

If Leo had lived there would have been choices to make, too—choices that would have been far from simple. Only they would have made them together, and there would have been none of this need to run for cover, to flee from the vast emptiness of this alien land where such terrible things had happened. But Leo was dead, and she must look for healing in the place where she had found it once before—in a quiet corner of a small, old, familiar country.

"I'll tell you what," she said to the dejected triplets, "—I won't say anything definitely now. I promise you I'll give it all a lot of thought. Will that do?"

It was the best she could offer—and at least she knew for certain that she would keep her word.

Late that night, when children and staff had long since gone to bed, she sat up with Hope. Both were exhausted, but neither possessed the energy to make a move towards turning in.

The house was very silent—almost as if its heart, too, had stopped beating. The air was chill, and the embers of a log fire glowed in the hearth.

"Are you absolutely definite about moving?" Verity broke the silence.

"Absolutely. I couldn't bear to stay here. I want something more casual. It isn't going to be easy looking after the girls on my own and getting on with my work at the same time, especially in the next few weeks when I really want to throw myself into it. That was partly why I hoped you'd stay. Did you really mean what you said about having them to stay in Wales?"

Verity smiled inwardly—she could see which way the wind was blowing.

"Yes, of course I did. It would be good enough for them to find out how the other half lives."

"I'd rather like them to have an English education. We might bear that in mind. You could make a few enquiries once you're home."

"They're a bit young to think of that yet. They're going to need you badly for some time to come."

"The story of my life. There's always been somebody needing me. Only I think you're wrong in their case. They need me far less than ordinary children—they have each other."

"For heaven's sake, Hope—they're only seven! Of course they need you! I take it Nelly will be staying on?"

"God, I hope so. If she were to leave I truly could not manage. I've *got* to have time for my work. I'd have to think about boarding school."

"Let's hope it doesn't come to that—I don't think it's a very good idea." Verity stood up abruptly, afraid that if she stayed any longer she might say something she regretted. "I'm going to bed. I need some sleep if I'm going to do justice to tomorrow."

"Tell me one thing before you go," Hope had remained in her seat.

247

"What's that?"

"I've thought and thought about it, and I still don't get why you threw the icon in the lake. To me that was an act of vandalism."

Verity looked at her wearily. She knew that there was not the faintest chance that she would understand.

"I threw it in the lake because it wasn't worth the life of a man like Leo," she replied.

"But by doing that surely you were making his death futile?"

"It already was futile. So were all the others. The icon was defeating its own purpose. They used to dispose of useless icons by setting them on water, and letting them float away. I did the next best thing."

"It was so very beautiful—it gave me quite a *frisson*. I don't think I can ever really accept that it was useless. It seems such a pity . . ."

"Indeed it does," said Verity. And as she bent to kiss her sister on the cheek the thought crossed her mind that this was the nearest Hope had come to expressing emotion all day.

It was near the water-slides that Jeffrey caught sight of them.

Evie had decided that he was strong enough for, and would benefit from an expedition in the open air. Her apartment was stuffy in hot weather, and both were suffering from the long confinement. He had petitioned for an afternoon stroll round the pleasure gardens near the lake, and she had agreed as there were plenty of benches around should he need to rest. She was still making all the decisions and he was content to have it so.

He was to move back to his own place the following weekend —and she was moving with him. It had been his suggestion. He felt he could not live without her. He suffered recurring nightmares, and he needed the protective presence of her smooth, plump, essentially maternal body, and the safety of those capable arms. He would bury his face in her generous breasts, and at the touch of her skin the dream—the glowing, red-hot tips of cigarettes circling like fireflies about his shivering flesh—would fade. He never dreamed of anything else these days. The smiling little ghost of Julie had deserted him. It did not matter. Nothing mattered just so long as he was never called on to face pain like that again.

Now he was growing stronger he thought less often of Verity.

There had been no word from her. She no longer seemed real. Perhaps he was afraid to think of her—she was too intimately bound up with the nightmares. She was also at the root of his sense of failure, which no amount of reasoning on the part of Evie would ever wholly dislodge. He had done what no honourable man is supposed to do: he had betrayed someone he cared for because he had been unable to endure pain.

It was better by far to turn away from it all, to put it behind him, to accept Evie's help and to try to go on living an ordinary life among ordinary people in an ordinary world. The heights were not for such as he. Thanks to Evie he had survived the consequences of his one great romantic gesture. He would never make the same mistake again. He wanted to live. With her beside him it was still possible.

She glanced at him as, arm in arm, they walked slowly through the park. It was a sunny day, and the brightly coloured flags were flapping cheerfully on the flagstaffs. He was looking much better. The breeze had brought some colour to his cheeks, though his eyes were still red-rimmed and wary. He was still liable to attacks of giddiness. She had managed, with a certain amount of firm-voiced lying, to get an extension of her leave on compassionate grounds. By the time she was forced to return to work, she judged, he would be virtually recovered—physically, at least.

Emotionally, she was less sure. The nightmares were not a good sign. She had been successful in keeping him in ignorance of the violent outcome of his brush with fanaticism—luckily a particularly bad train crash on the West Coast had quickly displaced "The Shootings by the Lake", as the papers called them, from the front pages—but she was aware that it might not be wise to leave him for too long to worry about all his unanswered questions.

She had not given him Verity's letter. She told herself that he was not strong enough to face it yet. He never mentioned her now—it was surely better that the contact should not be renewed. She had read the newspaper reports avidly, supplying the gaps in the stories from her own knowledge. After what had happened, the girl was unlikely to want to return to Canada. She, too, had clearly turned to someone else for support and it was he, poor bastard, who had paid the price of the whole foolish episode. She had wondered briefly why no mention was made of the icon, but decided that it had all probably been hushed up. She almost felt sorry for the girl. She would be bound, like Jeff, to be scarred by the experience. Certainly she would be in no sort of shape to help him.

No, Evie straightened her back as Jeff paused for breath and leaned on her—no, it was definitely wiser to keep quiet about the letter, for a time at least. Perhaps one day, when she felt the right moment had come, and everything was safely far in the past, she would show it to him and finally lay all the ghosts to rest.

From time to time they sat down on a bench, enjoying the sunshine, the brilliant colours, and the sound of a jazz band lazily playing blues in the distance. She could see the pleasure in his eyes as he watched the light-hearted crowds. Occasionally he chuckled aloud at the antics of excited children.

Suddenly she heard him catch his breath. She was instantly solicitous.

"What is it honey? Is your head hurting?"

He paid no attention to her. He rose unsteadily to his feet and stood swaying slightly, staring intently at the knots of people gathered near the water-slides. She tried to follow his eyes, puzzled and apprehensive. Surely there could be no more threats, not now.

Then she too saw them, some way off: three identical, red-haired little girls eating large ice-creams, and two women, one with her face half hidden by huge sunglasses, the other instantly recognizable since she had pushed hers up into her hair while she attended to the fastening of a child's dress.

"Verity!"

The name burst from Jeffrey in an anguished croak. People nearby turned to look at him. The colour had drained once more from his cheeks, leaving them chalk-white.

She was too far away to hear, and too taken up with her task to notice. After a moment she stood up, and readjusted her glasses against the glare. The little group moved off, away from them, soon to be lost in the swirling crowd.

"Verity!"

There was no strength in his voice—not enough to carry it above the bustle and roar of the nearby fairground. His breath coming in great rasps, he plunged after her, weaving drunkenly, barging into people, bent only on reaching her, on explaining . . .

"Jeff! Jeff! Come back! Wait for me!" Evie hurried after him. The crowd seemed to be growing thicker, and she was terrified of losing him.

"Verity!"

She could not possibly have heard above the noise, but, at the entrance to one of the big exhibition halls, she stopped suddenly and looked back, as if her attention had been caught by the very intensity of his appeal. He was struggling to breast his way through the crush of bodies towards her when she caught sight of him—just in time to see Evie finally catch up with him and put her arm round him to steady him.

Jeffrey saw her give a great start as she recognized him. Then she smiled at him—a sad, strained smile—raised her hand in salute, and turned to vanish into the dim interior of the building in the wake of her family. Frantic now, he tried to claw his way forward, but people resisted angrily. By the time he reached the entrance, she was lost to view. All at once he was certain he would not see her again.

"Verity!"

A buzzing filled his ears. The world fell in upon him, and he crashed to the ground in a dead faint.

When he opened his eyes, it was to see Evie bending over him, bathing his forehead with water from a plastic bowl someone had brought.

"It's okay, I'm a nurse," she reassured the ring of anxious faces around them. "He's only fainted. He's gonna be fine if you people will just stand back and give him some air."

She made him drink some water. Then, as his colour returned, and his breathing became easier, she helped him across to a bench under a nearby tree. They sat down together. Neither spoke.

He was the first to break the silence.

"I'm sorry. You must have thought I'd gone crazy. It was just that—I saw her."

"Who?" She asked it without a flicker.

"Verity. The girl who took the icon. She saw me, too."

"So where is she?"

"She—she just waved—and went. She didn't stop to speak to me. You don't think I was hallucinating, do you?"

"I saw someone wave at you—a dark girl wearing sunglasses. Was that her?" She was quick to see the advantage of this brief vision which had been so unexpectedly vouchsafed. Everything, it seemed, had finally played into her hands. "Well, at least you don't need to worry any more in case something awful has happened to her. It obviously hasn't. She looked in pretty good shape to me."

"But why didn't she wait, and speak to me?"

"Jeff, how can I tell you that? I guess it was probably her way of saying it was great knowing you, and now goodbye. They're difficult words to speak—she just chickened out. Forget it, honey. Let's concentrate instead on the problem of getting you home. That was all too much excitement for your first trip out. You need to rest."

For a moment he made no attempt to move, but sat looking at her sadly.

She was on his side, this Evie with her wide-set blue eyes, her firm chin, and sturdy shoulders. She was ready to fight all his battles for him, to help him carry his burdens, to cherish and love him. But it was just beginning to dawn on him that all this was not without its price.

She was stronger than he was, more firmly rooted, more in contact with the stuff of everyday existence. Living with her, he would have to accept that he must fly closer to the earth—he would never know again the lark rise, those heady breaths of a rarer atmosphere that he had experienced with Verity during those few brief hours they had spent together. Evie would not even recognize, let alone understand, the poet in him. Few did. It was a side of his nature that had always existed in solitude.

Accept it he must. He could not survive on his own. He had been too damaged, not just by what had recently befallen him, but earlier in his life as well. He simply did not have the strength now to throw off his dependency on her—perhaps he never would.

He glanced once more hopefully, wistfully, at the doorway where he had seen Verity turn and recognize him. The crowd was thinner now, but she was nowhere to be seen.

Then he looked again at Evie, and tried to smile.

"Sure. If you give me your arm I'll be okay. You're right—you always are. I need to get home."

Chapter 14

The old castle had been built on a steep hillside so that it looked protectively down over the village and out to the Irish Sea beyond. It was reached by a narrow lane which broadened temporarily before the stout gates of the main entrance before struggling on up the hill to peter out a few miles further on in the yard of a mountain farm.

In front of it, just below the low wall which bounded its sloping gardens, was a broad, flat space covered with fine, springy turf. Here a bench had been placed, doubtless to enable any who visited on foot to recover their breath before completing their climb, and to refresh their spirits with the splendid view.

It was a pleasant spot. Fuchsia bushes grew along the boundary walls, and ancient hawthorn trees, twisted and sculpted by the west wind, offered a possibility of rarely-needed shade. At night it was a favourite haunt of lovers—many a long-since respectably wed couple in the village had exchanged their first breathless kisses there.

Verity, ever since she first came to live in the village, had adopted it as one of her special places. Often, when she was free, she would make her way up to it to sit and sketch, or read, or simply to think, staring out at the ever-changing sea and the sky above it, watching the stately armadas of cumulus clouds sailing in towards the hills. For some reason she felt at peace there. The walls of the castle behind her were reassuring in their solidity, still standing firm despite centuries of storms, and the rumblings and bloodshed of countless wars.

She had gone there as usual on this fine afternoon in early September, and was sitting enjoying the sunshine. The light on the twin headlands, lying like whales basking in a still sea, was soft and golden. Red and white sails hovered over the water like tiny, distant butterflies. She had begun a sketch, but the pad lay neglected on her lap, and she seemed to have forgotten the oil pastels beside her on the bench, along with the letter she had brought to read, addressed in bold black script and bearing Canadian stamps—a letter which had arrived in the morning post.

It was just over a year since the plane had taken off from Toronto to bring her home. There had been no dramatic incidents on that flight, no delays, no attempts to engage her in conversation. A battery of babies had howled furiously throughout the night, depriving not only their haggard parents, but everyone else as well of the slightest possibility of sleep. Nothing could have been more prosaic.

It was when they had landed at Heathrow—perhaps because of the light-headedness that comes after a sleepless night—that she had suffered a return of the dreaded sense of unreality, the feeling that everything that had happened had been a dream, or even a dream within a dream. This time there had been no-one to hold on to, no-one to reassure her or answer her questions, and the feeling had persisted throughout the long journey to Fishguard and the taxi-ride to the village. It was only when she opened her front door and saw her own possessions waiting for her, and the bowl of fresh flowers set on the table to welcome her back that it disappeared. Everything here was real, and loved. She was safely home.

During those first days she had found other comforts. It had been a joy to hear again the soft lilt of Welsh voices, and to find herself greeted wherever she went. She had slipped back with ease to her old place in the community and it pleased her to find herself taken for granted.

It was a gentle place this village where she had chosen to make her home, inhabited by gentle people. The fine Atlantic rain that drifted so often over the slate roofs and stone walls seemed to have worn away all roughness. No doubt in their beliefs and ideas they were as narrow and prejudiced as any other small, isolated community, but they were saved from harshness by an immense, basic kindliness which showed itself particularly in the way they spoke to children. She had observed over the years that in summer many families brought their handicapped members to spend a holiday there, as if sensing they would not be rejected. Nor were they.

But as time passed, grateful though she had been to have the old routines close over her, for the small reassurances of familiar things, and places, and people, and for the longed-for chance to rest, she became more and more aware that the fear had not gone. It was lodged, shapeless, shadowy—an area of darkness somewhere in the centre of her mind. She was losing her way again—slowly drifting once more towards the edge of the abyss where she had fallen once before. She left the rolls of film she had taken in Canada undeveloped. She wrote no diary. One or two friends had inquired about her holiday, and she had answered vaguely, and they had forgotten to ask any more. She could not bear to make any move that might conceivably start the pain up again, even though the alternative was this grey helplessness, this growing apathy to the knowledge that she was slowly giving up control. It was as if she was waiting for something, some sign, some star that she might steer by to take herself back to some kind of meaningful existence.

Just when she had almost lost hope, it had come. She felt then that she should have known it would all along. She had in fact paid little heed to the fact that her period was late, assuming that the delicate mechanism of menstruation had been disturbed by the hours of flight, and for a while had even managed to explain away the bouts of nausea that had begun to affect her in the mornings, but in the end reality had solidly affirmed itself in the words of the village doctor as she sat facing him across the desk in his cluttered surgery.

"No doubt you'll be wanting to think about it." He was an elderly man with few illusions left, and he had eyed her dubiously over his spectacles.

"Think about it?"

"That's right. Think carefully. It is not easy for a young woman on her own to bring up a child. You do have options, you know. You must not be afraid to discuss them."

She had almost laughed aloud. He seemed to be completely unaware of the wonder that had happened. And when he had insisted that she take a few days to think about it, she had left his house with her head lifted and her eyes shining. She knew, if he did not. She had been given a second chance. She was carrying within her body a way forward, into the future. There were no options for such as her—not if she wanted to go on living.

And when she went to see him again, and told him, the doctor had smiled, and nodded as if the answer had been what he expected.

"Well then, we must take good care of you, mustn't we? And you must take good care of yourself. I've told you—it won't be easy for you, but it won't be the first time it's happened in the village, and you'll find you won't be left without help. The child is due in—May, isn't it? That is what I call good timing—we want you back in circulation for the Eisteddfod, don't we now?"

There had been no question of not taking care, not this time. She wanted this baby with a passion that was almost frightening in its intensity. She had obeyed all instructions to the letter, attended clinics and classes, controlled her diet—nothing was left undone that could help the pregnancy along to its proper conclusion. She had been given another royal gift, and there could be no question of neglecting or abusing it.

Something, some superstition, perhaps, had held her back from writing to Hope about it. It was as if she was afraid of her sister's reaction, anxious in case her anger, her wholly justifiable anger, should in some way blight the slow, invisible development that was taking place in her womb. Day after day, week after week she had put off the act of breaking the news. She had written—but the letters were little more than facile notes intended mainly for the amusement of the triplets, full of anecdotes of village life and detailed commentaries on the weather. Hope had replied in a similar vein. The children had not replied at all. She had the impression that they were all marking time.

The village, apart from a few significant glances at her rounding belly, had made no comment. No questions were asked but, as the pregnancy advanced, small gifts began to appear on her doorstep—a jar of home-made jam, new-laid eggs, a tin of cakes. At the gallery her friends watched that she did not stand for too long, or found some plausible reason for sending her home early. No-one said anything, but she was aware, as never before, of an unseen network of support that eased her loneliness. And when she had wept, as she did more frequently in the later months, they were not tears of despair.

Her son was delivered in the local cottage hospital by the same elderly doctor who had looked after her during her pregnancy. There had been no complications, and the baby she finally pushed into the world had yelled aggrievedly the moment his head was free. It was then, when, naked and slippery, he was placed in her arms, that she had once again experienced the miraculous feeling of everything having come together, of being an integral part of a great, living pattern—the same feeling she had known by the Canadian lake, and she was swept by a surge of love and gratitude so powerful that she could only cry, and laugh at herself for crying.

For hours afterwards she had lain gazing at the tiny, crumpled face. She was dimly aware that she had come to the end of a long search. He was not like anyone, her son. He was himself, and she loved him as she had never before loved anyone or anything, with a total, fierce protectiveness.

When he was some six weeks old, and they had both settled into a comfortable, symbiotic existence in the cottage on the outskirts of the village, she had at last brought herself to write the crucial, long-delayed letter to Hope. It was time. The shock of black hair with which he had been born had fallen off, and the small skull was covered with a fine down of rich auburn. Leo had established his paternity as efficiently as if he had signed a deed. She found herself constantly marvelling at this wonderful colour that had remained hidden throughout the long, lightless months in the womb to appear now as if summoned into bloom by the June sunlight. Leo had indeed lit a fire in her—one that was likely to warm her for the rest of her days.

Hope had not replied at once. At first this had not worried her, but as the weeks passed and no letter came she had begun to be uneasy. Damaged and unsatisfying their relationship might be, but it was still necessary to her. They had, after all, shared their childhood. She had wondered if she ought to phone, but picking up the receiver had seemed too much like an actual confrontation, and her courage had failed her. She knew she was not yet ready to face any real demands —all her remaining strength was devoted now to following the golden thread her lover had left her to lead her out of the labyrinth and into the daylight once more. She still needed quietness, and gentleness, and kindness. On the other hand if the news of the baby's birth had proved some sort of final straw, and touched off some shattering emotional trauma in her sister—if she was ill and needed caring for—she could hardly stand by and refuse what help she might give, knowing what her own part in it all had been. With increasing apprehension she waited for the reaction.

Today, at last, the reply had come. The postman had handed her the letter as she was leaving the cottage to put in a few hours at the gallery, taking the baby with her to sleep in his carrycot. Financially, this was no longer strictly necessary for as soon as he was safely born she had decided to sell the Renoir—the soft features of the baby were a far more eloquent reminder of his father than the mischievous smile of the baigneuse, and the proceeds of the sale would give them both the independence they needed and that Leo would have wanted for them.

All morning she had left it unopened, and had brought it back to the cottage at lunch time still unread. Even then she had continued to put off the dreaded moment until they had both had their lunch. Then, when it came to the time when she usually took the baby for his afternoon walk, she had suddenly known what to do. She glanced at him now as he lay in his pram beside her, blowing bubbles, and waving small admiring fists at the seagulls gliding overhead. With him beside her, and the castle walls behind her, she felt she had the support she needed.

With hands that shook slightly, she tore open the letter. A second envelope, addressed to herself in a hand she did not recognize, fell out. She put it on one side. Whatever it was, she must face Hope first. Tensely, she began to read.

My dear Verity,

Forgive the long delay in replying to your letter. Life's been crowding me lately—but I guess that wasn't the real reason for putting off writing.

I still don't know how to react to your news—or how you expect me to react. Congratulations would sound kind of phoney, coming from me, don't you think? All I can say, when it comes to it, is that if this is what you wanted—and I suppose it must be or it wouldn't have happened—then I'm happy for you. Truly I am. No need to worry about other feelings. There aren't any. What Leo said and did stopped getting to me a long time ago. I'm sorry he had to die, of course I am—but that's something we all have to face sooner or later, isn't it? So you needn't worry about me—I haven't fallen apart.

There hasn't been time, in fact. You'd never believe how busy

I've been. Thanks to your help I've taken off this summer in a big way. I went to see the agent you recommended, and guess what!—he really flipped! The result is that I'm to have a big exhibition in Montreal next month. I can still hardly believe it even though I've been slugging away all summer to make sure there's enough stuff. I guess I've flipped too! I've been experimenting with a new kind of acrylic paint, and it's as if someone had pressed a switch—the work's fairly pouring out of me. I guess all I needed was encouragement and a helping hand, and I'll always be grateful to you for setting the ball rolling. I feel now that nothing can stop me—I'm on my way!

I sent the kids off to summer camp to give myself more time. They seem to have enjoyed themselves. Long term I've decided that boarding school is definitely the best answer. I can't cope with them on my own, and I have my work to think of. I've found a real nice one not far from Montreal, and they're starting there after Christmas. They're very excited about it.

I've found my new house! Removal next month so make a note of the new address. It's up in the Laurentians—marvellous painting country. There's a whole community of artists round there—it's all much more my style. I never did care for the Toronto area, but then it wasn't my choice.

You must forgive the kids for not answering your letters. I don't have the time to stand over them with a whip, which is the only way to make sure they do it, and Nelly's too taken up with the packing. They love hearing from you though, so don't stop writing. They're very curious about the baby, so how about a photo? They approve your choice of name—David has a Welsh ring to it—to my ears at least—next thing you'll be writing that you're learning the language!

There's a parcel of baby things on the way. Nelly chose them—she's better at it than I am. Hope they're the right size. Let me know if you need any other help.

Your affectionate sister,

Hope

PS The enclosed arrived a couple of days ago.
PPS Any hope of you making it out here for the exhibition?

Coming to the end, Verity continued to sit and stare at the large, scrawling handwriting in a daze of relief. All the anxiety and dread had been for nothing. There had been no cataclysm. Hope's armour was, after all, impenetrable. Nonetheless, it was difficult to believe this airy dismissal of events which had so completely changed her own life, this casual waving away of her deepest feelings.

Uneasily, she read through it again, trying to see beyond its bland surface for some trace of ordinary emotion, but could find none—the only words which came to life were those that spoke of work. All the rest were like notices posted on closed doors.

Still, she reflected, at least this one was open, and perhaps she must continue to content herself with that. She was even invited to enter it. It was not the sort of invitation she longed for, but it would be foolish to despise it. In issuing it, Hope was offering her a place in her life—a place with precisely delineated boundaries beyond which she would not be permitted to go—and that was better than no place at all.

The little girls, on the other hand, had been shut right out, for they were a threat—sent away first to summer camp, then to boarding school. It was as she had foreseen—the loss of their father meant for them a total loss of adult love, unless she herself could in some small degree answer their need.

Of course she would continue to write to them, however rare the replies. She might also, tentatively, begin to explore the possibility of finding them a school in Wales—Hope had, after all, herself suggested it. It was not a decision to be made now, or with the slightest haste, but it was an idea that should be borne in mind. They would have, one day, to know that David was their half-brother as well as their cousin, and everything would hang on whether or not they could accept that knowledge. That was something that could not be foreseen.

As if he sensed his importance, the baby began to gurgle. She knew it would not be long before he grew hungry again, and turned quickly to the second letter while there was still time for reflection. She looked, puzzled, to see who it was from, and her heart missed a beat. The writer was Jeffrey.

She hesitated. She was not sure she wanted to read it. The memory of the moment of recognition at the Exhibition last year was still painfully vivid. She could still see the girl's possessive arm round him, and the dismay in his face. The shock, despite all Hope's wise words, despite finding the girl at his apartment, had been considerable. She had been only too thankful to slip away into the crowd—the last thing she'd wanted was embarrassed explanations. If he had kept faith, not only would Leo still be alive, but the whole crazy adventure of the icon would seem less misconceived—it only made any kind of sense if it had been undertaken wholeheartedly and in good faith.

Yet if he had not behaved as he had, a voice inside her argued, she might never have discovered Leo's love, nor he hers—and there would be no David.

She fixed her eyes on the faint edge where pale blue sea met paler blue sky, unconsciously shaking her head. There were, it seemed, no hard lines, no firm rules anywhere. Good grew out of evil, and evil out of good—all, it seemed, at random. Choices were less important than she had imagined. Then she shrugged, and turned once more to the letter, curious to know what he could possibly have to say.

Dear Verity,

I am writing to you at the only address I have in the hope that your sister will forward this to you.

It's hard to know where to begin.

Perhaps first I should explain that I never received the letter you left for me last summer. I came across it by chance the other day when I was clearing some drawers. When I asked Evie about it (she's the girl I've been living with all this last year), she told me that as I was still very sick at the time you gave it to her she had been afraid to risk upsetting me with it. She had, apparently, put it away to give me when I was stronger, only to forget all about it. You can imagine I didn't feel too happy about the explanation, but there wasn't much I could say.

You see, I owe Evie my life. It was she who found me after I'd been beaten up. She took me back to her place and nursed me intensively for several days till I was over the worst, then stayed on with me till I'd begun to recover psychologically. I don't think I would have survived without her—I went completely to pieces.

The Poles got me after I'd been released by Immigration. They

261

took me off somewhere—I never did know where exactly—and very professionally started extracting information from me. I won't go into details. Let's just say that I discovered then that I'm not much good when it comes to resisting physical pain. I'm afraid I told them what they wanted to know. I guess we underestimated them, and overestimated ourselves—at least, I did! You've known the results for some time—I've only just learned them.

That day at the Ex was my first venture back into the everyday world. And there you were. I always did say the gods played games. When you saw me with Evie you must have thought me a complete shit—no wonder you vanished so quickly! At least the sight of you relieved my worst anxiety—I'd been doing my nut in case, thanks to me, they'd given you the same treatment they'd handed out to me. I betrayed you, and I still can't forgive myself. When you turned your back on me, I felt you were passing an irrevocable judgement.

When I read your letter I realized at once what you must have thought when I didn't reply. I realized too that you aren't the sort of person who makes irrevocable judgements. I felt I must make an attempt to clarify matters—if only for the sake of peace of mind—and, at the very least, to tell you how desperately sorry I am for letting you down. I was a fool ever to agree to take on the icon in the first place—it was far too big a job for a thin-skinned, idealistic pen-pusher like me. You said it yourself that night in Glasgow. And I made it all worse by allowing you to become involved. It was one of the worst mistakes I ever made. I can't help wishing that you and I could begin again at the beginning—that I could be on that plane, and you could happen along to sit beside me so that we could take it from there in an ordinary way. We might have given each other a little happiness, who knows? As it was, we never really stood a chance, did we?

Now that I'm writing again, life has more or less gone back to normal. You may smile when I tell you that the plot of this new book is based on two people meeting on a plane—well, I have to do something with my fantasies, and my nightmares! Evie moved out a month or two back. I guess she found the reality of living with a writer a little hard to take. She's a person who needs to be needed, and hadn't realized that a novel can take the place of nurse, doctor and psychiatrist all at the same time. We're still very good friends. She seems to have taken up with some Chinese guy now, some sort of doctor who helped her look after me, ironically enough.

There's a chance I may be coming to the UK again early next year. I'm wondering how you would react if I were to ask if we could meet? There's so much more I need to tell you, and I would rather tell it to your face. I suppose what I am really hoping is that there might be a chance that you can forgive me.

I nearly forgot the icon. I can understand why you threw it in the lake. I guess I would have done the same. The guy who painted it surely never meant it to bring pain and death to people, even if his eyes were fixed on a better world. The way I see it, he most likely meant it to help them come to terms with this one. If he'd been around to see what happened he might have felt kind of hopeless. He'd have been justified—there doesn't seem to be much left to hold on to, does there?

It would make me feel more cheerful perhaps if you could bring yourself to write a reply to this.

Yours in hope,

Jeffrey.

So Hope had been wrong—it was Verity's first thought when she had finished reading—wrong all along. She had judged him with her own warped and bitter vision, and at the time it had been all too easy to be infected by it.

She should have trusted her own instincts. She should have given him a chance to speak to her that day at the Exhibition instead of running away—but she had been too full of grief and anger to give anyone a chance, much less believe them.

Only now did she fully realize how much his apparent treachery had hurt her, and gone on hurting. The knowledge that he had cynically used her had poisoned all her memories of the icon, and added layers of guilt to the pain of Leo's death. Learning that he, too, had suffered, that she had not been mistaken in him, transformed everything.

Now at last she could see the whole affair for what it was—a foolish, misguided piece of idealism. But foolish, and rash, and costly though it had been, it had one great redeeming feature: they had undertaken it because they cared—about each other, and about those who asked their help. They had at least tried to give it. They had done their best, however great the failure. For the first time since her return, she felt that it might be possible now to live with the memories, all of them, instead of wincing away each time they threatened to surface.

Carefully, she read through the letter again. She was conscious of a deep, quiet happiness. There was still, after all, one person in the world who understood, to whom it might be possible to talk freely.

Already she was planning her reply. Of course she would be glad to see him again. She could not take the baby to London, but she could ask him to come to her in Wales. She would take pleasure in showing him the countryside she had once described to him so enthusiastically, and introducing him to the village—and to David. She felt he might understand, too, about David. It would help them both to talk about what had happened, and, if nothing else, to comfort each other a little.

The baby's gurgles were beginning to assume a certain belligerence and his arm-wavings were no longer gestures of peace. Soon she must take him home and minister to his needs. She bent over him, and he smiled up at her, pleased to have a change from seagulls. Her heart contracted. It was hard to believe that when she had boarded the plane to Toronto he had not existed. His arrival had altered the whole shape and significance of her life—nothing, nothing at all was as it had been.

On impulse, as if to prolong this golden afternoon together, she lifted him from the pram, and held him so that he might see the view. Her cheek against his silky ginger curls, she stared out over the sea as if she could see all the way across to Canada. He seemed to sense what she was feeling, for he lifted up his hand, and gently stroked her cheek.

And perhaps if the man who had painted the Umilenie icon had been able to pass by at that moment and see them he would not, as Jeffrey had thought, have felt hopeless at all—he would merely have returned as quickly as possible to his workshop and, with reverence in his heart, taken up his tools to begin again.